SHADOW OF HOPE

SHADOW KNIGHTS
BOOK 6

MICHAEL WEBB

ALSO BY MICHAEL WEBB

Get a FREE prequel novella to the Shadow Knights series - Shadow Knights: Origine - by signing up for my mailing list at www. subscribepage.com/michaelwebbnovels or scan this QR code

Did you forget what happened in the last book? I've got you covered!

Go to michaelwebbnovels.com/book-summaries to get short summaries of each of the previous books in the series.

CONTENTS

PART III
LAST STAND

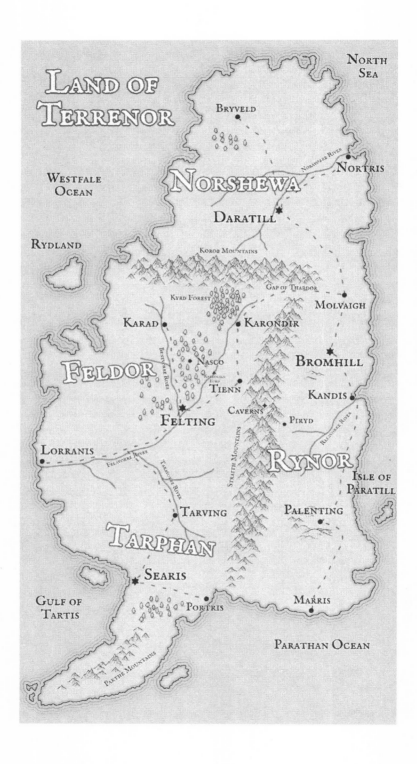

PART I

REBUILDING

1

GARRONTS

Lia hugged her knees to her chest. She pulled them toward her, wishing the effort would keep her from shaking, but the trembling wasn't from the cool air of the empty cavern. Her heart ached. The knights were rescued. Her parents were safe. Raiyn was alive. All it took was sacrificing her own freedom.

She stared across the chasm at the tunnel where she and the others had shown up days before to rescue the knights. They had waited, trapped on the same square-shaped plateau where she currently sat. Yet she harbored no hope of their return. They would all think she was dead.

I should have been dead.

She had tried to find her pure connection to the origine again, but the power eluded her. The constant presence of the glowing, red crystals sucked away any hope she could muster.

All she could do was wait. Wait and think about the others fleeing through the mountains back to safety. Think of what they may do next in their attempt to stop Danik. And think of the Marked Ones and what they would do with her.

Talon Shadow. I can't believe it.

The founder of the Shadow Knights had turned to the devion and found a way to prolong his life, hidden in the mountain stronghold for hundreds of years. Now, something had brought him and his followers out of hiding.

A red glow grew in the corridor across the pit. Lia inhaled and stared, wishing her father would somehow round the corner, carrying a torch and a plan for escape. Her smile turned down as Gralow and another woman entered the chamber and stared back.

"Cross the bridge," Gralow barked after lowering the wooden board that dangled from the far side.

Lia considered refusing, but nothing would be gained by remaining in the open-air cell. She extended her arms for balance as she padded across the span, keeping her eyes on the plank instead of the gaping void below.

Both of the marked ones' red crystals glowed when Lia set her feet on the solid ground of the far side. They fixed ankle chains to her legs. A short length of metal links ran between each foot.

The woman left the room first, carrying the torch, and Gralow pushed at Lia's back. "Move."

Lia winced, stumbling forward.

The anklets chafed her skin. Her natural stride was too long. The metal pulled on her legs, shifting and rubbing with each step. She shortened her pace, forcing choppy, awkward steps. Running for her freedom was out of the question.

The marked ones led her through twisting tunnels and past passageways. Lia tried to keep track of each intersection, but the similar-looking paths grew muddled in her head.

Natural light ahead teased her eyes. It had been days since she'd seen any, and the familiar glow gave her a spark of hope. After turning the next corner, they spilled into an immense chamber, and Lia's eyebrows raised.

Sunlight poured into the massive room from an oculus in the cavern ceiling. A ring of evenly spaced columns spread around the room. On the far side, a network of wooden scaffolding rose nearly to the ceiling, encasing an unfinished stone statue.

Next to the entrance she'd just walked through, water gurgled in a bubbling fountain that pooled in a murky basin. A group of gray-clothed women filling containers with liquid stopped chatting when she arrived. Other groups of men and women dotted the large space. All eyes were on her.

Her breath caught at the sight of a familiar young man huddled in conversation with some others. Danik Bannister argued with a marked one while Cedric and Nicolar stood at his side. Nicolar noticed Lia first and elbowed Danik. Lia glared when her former friend's eyes found hers. Danik's posture shifted. His neck seemed to retreat, and his face turned away.

Her blood boiled as air hissed through her teeth.

Gralow pushed against her back. "Keep moving."

Lia stared at Danik, but her choppy steps followed the woman in front. Her shoulders slumped when they stepped into another glowing-red passage, leaving the natural sunlight and the image of her old training partner behind.

"What was that room back there?" she asked.

"The Hub?" Gralow replied.

"Yeah, what do you do there?"

His only answer was a grunt.

"What is Danik doing here?"

"Enough questions!"

The outburst made her jump, but she held her tongue. She followed the woman through another maze of passages. They angled down a slope and entered another open room.

A metal gate blocked most of her view, but above it, a vast chamber extended past the gate. Two marked ones stood at attention with red crystals hanging from their necks. Two men stood beside them with someone else in chains.

Lia squinted in the dim light, then gasped. "Dayna!"

The fellow shadow knight offered a grim smile and nodded.

"Quiet!" Gralow punched Lia in the side, the impact sending a shudder of pain through her body.

Dayna looked in about as good a shape as Lia: scraped, dirty, and slumped in hunger. At least the injury she'd received in the back didn't seem to bother her anymore.

A grinding noise began as the metal gate rolled to the side. Lia craned her neck to see what lay beyond. When the gate had opened, the guards pulled her forward and her jaw dropped.

An open area stretched down a corridor the width of the old Shadow Knights' common room. Along the center of the passage, a group of empty wooden tables and benches clustered together. Both sides of the cavern walls contained open doorways where glowing-red passages led elsewhere. Four lanterns hung on the walls, giving a yellowish-orange color to the otherwise red cavern. Crystals dotted the chamber like she saw in the other passages.

To the side, tools and parts filled rows of shelves. Lia spotted hammers, awls, shovels, and pickaxes. Some contained varying shades of rust, and they all looked like they'd seen years of use. A larger tunnel extended into reddish darkness past the tools.

"Rasmill!" Gralow shouted. "I've got two more for you."

A beast of a man emerged from a room next to the tools, his neck looking as wide as his bald head. The gray outfit he wore barely contained his massive shoulders and chest. "Ah . . . the shadow knights." He flashed a grin, revealing graying teeth with a wide gap in the front.

"Keep their anklets on." A mirthless chuckle rumbled from Rasmill's throat. "Not that they'll make a difference."

The woman with him bent down to work on Lia's anklets while another marked one did the same with Dayna. The eyes of the other shadow knight simmered with a robust level of fear.

Chains jingled, and Lia looked down. The metal bands around her ankles remained, but the limiting length of chain was gone.

Gralow walked with the other marked ones back through the gate, calling over his shoulder. "They're all yours."

The metal barrier resumed its rumbling and closed with a clang. Rasmill shuffled to the gate and turned a key into a lock. The click bounced through the silent space before the man returned the key ring to his pocket.

"Is it just you?" Lia craned her neck around.

Rasmill laughed. "What? Are you ready to pick a fight and bust your way out?"

Lia swallowed. It was exactly what she was considering. She looked at Dayna, who shook her head.

Not yet.

"I'm Rasmill, the mine boss." He pointed toward the doorway he had come through. "You'll meet the other guards in time. They're in the office. Rules are simple—do what you're supposed to, and you'll be fine." He turned away from the gate and shuffled toward the rest of the cavern without instructions of what they were to do next.

Lia looked at Dayna. The other knight shrugged, then they followed.

Rasmill pointed back over his shoulder. "Stay away from the gate. You touch it, you'll lose a hand. You do it again, you'll lose your arm. You keep at it, you'll continue losing body parts. You'll stop on your own when you decide you want to keep whatever you have left."

Lia swallowed.

"You'll have a lot of freedom in the mines during the day. You may be tempted to run—thinking you can somehow escape. You would be wrong." He pointed at an object hanging from the cavern ceiling.

Lia hadn't noticed it before because the suspended cage blended into the rock wall. A shape slumped against the bars, as still as the rock itself. She angled her head and squinted. "Is that . . . a man?"

"That's right," Rasmill said. "That's Penner. Last week, he thought he might stay in the caves and search for a way out of here. He didn't come back after the shift was done—didn't find a way out, either. Days later, he stumbled back, starving. He lost an eye as penance."

Lia's stomach turned.

"Now he'll think long and hard about trying a stunt like that again."

"You want people to mine for you," Dayna said, "but you chop off their hands and gouge out their eyes? Doesn't that prevent them from being able to do anything? Why would you choose that as punishment?"

A wicked smile ran across Rasmill's face. "You misunderstand me. *We* don't punish anyone."

An icy wave rushed through Lia at the tone of the confusing statement. She waited for the mine boss to expound, but he moved his attention to the tables in the center of the room.

"This is the mess area. You'll eat once each morning. You can complain all you want about the food, but I suggest you eat it because you're not getting anything else."

Lia lifted her hand. "I'm sorry . . . you said you don't punish anyone . . ."

"Right." Rasmill nodded, then pointed back at the office. "There are four marked ones, but we're just here to keep the peace."

"So, how did that guy lose his eye?"

Rasmill stared, his dark gaze beating into her. "His captain dug it out with an awl."

A queasy feeling rushed through Lia's insides.

"The teams punish their own." He pointed up to the cage. "Penner's 'friends' did this to him."

Her heart sped. She spun, glancing at the glowing red doorways dotting the cavern. *What is this place?*

"Those doorways are the team barracks. That's where you'll sleep. During the day, you mine, and after that, you rest. That's pretty much it."

She nodded past the tables where glowing red light shimmered off the surface of a body of water. "What's back there?"

"A lake, but it's a dead end. We use the open area to the side as a boneyard for broken mine carts, tools, and lanterns. If you ever want to stretch your legs, feel free to follow the path around the lake."

A dull sound of distant voices perked Lia's ears. Her head turned to a large passage near the tools.

"Sounds like the teams are done for the day."

"What are these, uh . . . teams?"

"There are five," Rasmill said. "The Mountain Wolves, Blood Panzils, Bears, Valcors, and Garronts. The teams usually have twelve to fourteen workers, but the number varies, depending on when we last recruited and who we've had to reap."

Lia's brows pinched together. *Reap? What's that?*

The voices from the passage grew louder and more distinct. She stared ahead and waited, curious to see what sort of people would come from the tunnel. Despite her interest, a tremor shook her.

Glowing lights cast hard shadows. The brightness grew in intensity as more dark shapes projected on the wall. Lia braced for what was to come—blood-craved psychotics, monsters with protruding fangs, spice addicts gone mad. After a moment, a crowd of workers spilled around the corner, and Lia sighed, her shoulders falling.

The men appeared normal, with ragged clothes hanging from their bodies, hair mussed and dirty. Most held pickaxes or shovels over their bowed shoulders, and some carried lanterns swinging by their sides. The men stopped at the storage area where they deposited their tools, sloughing them off their shoulders as if unloading a heavy burden. Faces sagged and chests heaved, exhausted from whatever work they'd been doing.

The man at the front of the line stopped when he turned toward Lia. "New recruits," he muttered. "Two of them."

"And girls at that!" another man said. "Ha! Bridgebain, what do you bet you're getting at least one of them?"

A short-haired, clean-shaven man shoved the one who spoke, and a round of cackles echoed from the surrounding men.

Rasmill held up his hands and allowed the men to gather and settle. Lia estimated around sixty to seventy in the group.

"Yes, we have two more for your teams," Rasmill said. "They have special value to Talioth, so treat them well."

Several men snickered.

"Kilock." He pointed to Dayna. "This one will be a Mountain Wolf."

A rough man with arms crossed over his chest grunted.

"And the little one goes to . . ." Rasmill paused, and all eyes turned to the clean-shaven man near the front. "The Garronts."

The man hung his head. A handful of groans sounded while most men laughed.

"Quotas go up for all teams. One half more per teammate, starting today."

An explosion of discontent filled the room. Men raised their fists as they shouted, cries of outrage piercing the air.

Rasmill rested his hand on Lia's and Dayna's shoulders and raised his voice to be heard over the crowd. "You have these two to thank for that. Their friends caused some trouble for the rest of us, and now production needs to increase."

The crowd hushed as scowling faces filled the room.

Rasmill headed back toward the office, leaving Lia and Dayna behind. "Show them the ropes, men. They need to produce, starting tomorrow."

Lia looked at Dayna. "Good luck."

Dayna forced a smile. "Yeah, you too."

Lia stood still as grizzled men walked past her. Some scowled, others smirked, but most ignored her.

The beardless man with the short hair passed. She waited, expecting something. He didn't look at her or greet her, but he beckoned with a finger. Lia jerked to attention and followed.

The second doorway on the right contained a carving of a garront over the lintel. She glanced around the cavern and spotted similar carvings above the other doors: a vicious wolf, a nasty blood panzil, and a bear standing on its hind legs. She chuckled at the last one. *I assume that's supposed to be a valcor*, she thought. It looked nothing like one. A curious gold-colored emblem was displayed above the poorly carved image.

She followed the man through the garront door, and a musty smell hit her nose. Traces of body odor combined with moldy hay and fermented waste. A lantern hung from a wall hook, splashing light through the room. The barracks contained seven pairs of bunked beds with wooden frames. Sheets covered the straw mattresses. Three columns of merged stalactites and stalagmites were spaced through the room.

Several men already lay collapsed on their beds, their limbs splayed, appearing exhausted.

"Move it!" A man shouldered into Lia, pushing her against the wall. "Men coming through."

The man following him laughed and threw a wicked look at Lia.

"Come here, girl," the clean-faced man said, standing next to the central column.

Lia crossed the room, dodging other men who did *not* move out of her way. Heat creeped up her neck while she stood before him. She felt all eyes in the room on her.

The man's lips formed a grim line, but he didn't strike her as mean. The only clean-shaven man she'd seen, his short, groomed hair also stood out.

"Lia." She cleared her throat. "Lia Stormbridge." The last name didn't seem to spark any recognition from the men.

"I'm Christopher Bridgebain, team leader of the Garronts. You can call me Chris."

"Team leader? What does that mean?"

Someone behind her sniffed.

"It means I'm in charge of this sorry excuse for a team." Chris gestured around the room. "If you don't pull your weight, I'm the one who comes after you. If you act like you're sick and need to stay in bed, I'm the one who *convinces* you that you're not."

"Got it," she said. "So, you're the guy who cuts off hands and gouges out eyes."

Chris stiffened. "If I have to . . . Yes, I will. I take it Rasmill filled you in on the rules." He leaned into her. "Work hard. Do your part. And don't do anything stupid like trying to escape. If you follow those rules, we won't have any issues. Got it?"

Lia swallowed. "Got it."

"What are we supposed to do with her?" a man asked. "I hope they're not measuring our team on having eleven now because that wouldn't be fair."

A few grumbles of agreement echoed around the room.

"Maybe she can make our beds and tidy up while we're off at

work." A man with straight, black hair sauntered toward her, speaking in a pinched voice.

Chris raised a hand against the man's shoulder. "Cool it, Vekko. You too, Jarno. She'll mine like we all do. We just have to hope they take it easy on our quota." He turned back to Lia. "Like I said. Do what you're supposed to, and you won't have any issues. But if you step out of line . . . I won't get in these guys' way."

The one named Vekko glared at her.

"Yeah, you better listen to Bridgebain," a young man with brown, shaggy hair said. "He's the only one of us who's worth his weight in the mines. Without him, we'd lose every week."

"We *do* lose every week, Waylon," another man said, "even with him."

"Oh, yeah," Waylon laughed. "In that case, I say, 'Welcome, Lia.' After all . . . someone has to be chosen."

"Where are you all from?" Lia asked. "Before you got here?"

No one replied, a tense silence building.

"We don't talk about that. The past is the past." Chris motioned her toward the opposite end of the room, where two empty bunks sat on either side of a passage with a faint-red glow. He hit his hand against one of the wooden frames. "These bunks are both free. Take either bed."

Lia stepped closer and a pungent odor reached her nose, making her want to retch. She doubled over, covering her mouth. "Ugh, what is that stench?"

Laughter bounced across the room from the other men.

"That would be the latrine." Chris pointed through the door. "It's around the door to the right. Don't worry . . . sleeping so close, you'll get used to it. To the left is our bathing pool. It's nothing fancy, but it keeps the grime off. We clean once per week to keep the barracks from getting too rank."

Lia glimpsed Vekko and Jarno staring from their beds. She loosened the hand from her nose and tried to breathe through her mouth. "Is there a . . . women's pool anywhere?"

Chris chuckled, his shoulders bouncing.

"I think I'll skip the bathing."

The leader raised an eyebrow. "We'll see how you feel about that when your stench draws *them* to you."

"Them?" Her breath caught at the way he emphasized the word. "Who's *them*?"

He blew a soft laugh out his nose, then hit her on the shoulder. "You'll see. Welcome to the Garronts. Now don't get us killed."

2

FREE TO TRAVEL

Talioth stepped onto the stone ring that ran around the fountain, then turned to face the others gathered in the Hub. Gurgling water bubbled behind him, but the crowd remained silent, waiting on him. Except for the guards on duty in the mountains and those in the mines, the entirety of their community gathered—over sixty people.

Danik, Cedric, and Nicolar stood out like ravens in a flock of snow sparrows. Their eyes shifted, and their hands moved constantly, as if they couldn't figure out how to hold them.

A faint smile tugged at Talioth's face. *They have no idea what they've gotten into.*

"Thank you for gathering," Talioth said to the group.

Polite nods spread through the room.

"Our efforts these last two days have not been in vain. The Chamber Room is nearly cleared. It will take a bit more work to shore up the central column, but it should be usable soon. The entrance passage is open again. We built additional supports and removed the rubble. We are free to travel in and out as we need."

He caught a glance between Danik and his men.

"Did you determine what happened with the Core, yet?" a marked one called from the crowd.

Talioth frowned. "Unfortunately not."

A rumble grew.

"The shadow knights did something that impeded the crystal's impact. Not the power flowing through us, but its ability to absorb the origine and block its use. Thankfully, the effect was temporary. It was only a few minutes before the Core's powers returned, however . . ." Talioth paused, the uncomfortable truth churning in his gut. "Its strength is not what it was."

"What do you mean?" a voice called out.

Talioth glanced at Meliand, who gave a curt nod. "The light is weaker, despite the recent siphon of one filled with the origine. We need more power."

"What about the two shadow knights we captured?"

Talioth nodded. "We will use them soon. Their power should help. In the meantime, replacing crystals is our top priority. We lost many necklaces in the fight. Once we're supplied again, we will focus our efforts on tracking down the shadow knights who escaped."

He glanced at Danik. The newly crowned king adjusted his feet and rested his hands on the sword at his hip.

"What if we can't resupply the Core?" a woman asked. "What if it drains and we can't find the shadow knights?"

Mutters rumbled through the room.

"Marked ones." Talioth's raised hand settled the crowd again. "We've come a long way in the last three hundred years. We discovered the origine, killed King Vitrion, and founded the Shadow Knights. Do you remember that hideous place where we lived in Karondir?"

A few chuckled.

"Meliand chopped food. Gralow stood guard. Valdok sharpened weapons, and Balakolt would—" He stopped, the memory of his companion turning a knife in his gut. The pause dragged out, filling the room with an awkward energy.

"Soon, we realized there was more out there. The origine limited us, but the devion . . . It set us free."

Smiles dotted the faces in the crowd.

"We moved here to the caves to embrace the power. It's given us long lives and incredible abilities. We have dominion over everyone, everywhere. We can do anything we want."

"Except leave."

The lone voice stirred the crowd. Talioth glanced toward it to find Cedric with his hands folded over his chest.

"You're trapped here, right?" Cedric challenged. "Subject to the leashes of these crystal necklaces? What's the point of a long life if there's no pleasure in it?"

Talioth's eyes narrowed. "Pleasure is found in numerous ways. Once you embrace the devion, you'll learn the satisfaction that comes from being in its presence."

"'Being in its presence?'" Cedric scoffed. "Sorry, but I'll take a castle feast with strong liquor and girls on either side over sitting on rocks in a stuffy cave any day." The knight of power turned and stomped off.

Danik and Nicolar glanced at each other, then after their departing ally. For the moment, they stayed put.

Talioth turned back to the crowd. "We do what we do to survive. It's my promise to you that we'll do everything we can to keep this power for another three hundred years"—He nodded toward the departed Cedric—"when men like him are long dead and buried."

The crowd dispersed after the meeting. Some turned down passages, and others gathered into groups in the Hub. Danik and Nicolar approached the fountain as Talioth stepped down from the ledge.

"I'm sorry about Cedric," Danik said. "He can be blunt and tactless."

Talioth nodded. "An attribute that can be displeasing at times but refreshing at others."

"But mostly displeasing."

Talioth's mouth pulled up in a grin.

"He is right about our need to leave, though. This isn't our home. We belong in Felting. I have a kingdom to run. We're making plans —" Danik's words cut as if he censored himself. "We need to return. And we need more of those necklaces."

Talioth frowned. "We already gave you five."

"I lost mine in the battle—buried in the cave-in. And while the others cover our current group of knights, we have several more recruits who will need them in short order."

"These necklaces are valuable. They don't grow on trees."

Danik gestured around him. "There are, what, thirty glowing red crystals in this room alone? There are probably fifty more along the passage between here and the exit to the caves. How valuable can they be?"

Talioth narrowed his eyes. "You don't understand."

"What if we stop using the devion?"

A laugh erupted from Talioth.

Danik frowned at the outburst. "What? If we go back to the origine, then we could leave, right?"

The marked one shook his head. "The devion is part of you now. It fuels every part of your body, whether you're using it or not. That mark is proof."

Danik touched the black scab on his neck.

"If you stop using it, you will die." Talioth fought to not smile as he watched the king from the lowlands squirm under his gaze. He beckoned Danik and Nicolar forward. "Come with me, both of you."

He crossed the wide floor of the Hub. The two pairs of Feldorian boots followed him. When he arrived at the scaffolding, he headed up the ramp.

Wooden boards rumbled under his feet. The incline rose from the floor of the cavern, winding back and forth as it climbed higher and higher. The structure swayed when he halted at the top. He leaned against the flimsy rail and waited for the knights of power to arrive next to him.

"I never wanted to stay here when we first discovered these caves," Talioth said, looking over the people far below. "The Call brought us here, but all we found were rudimentary tunnels and that huge crystal. Everything you see now, we've built—carved from the rock itself."

"Like this?" Danik pointed behind them to the nearly finished statue.

Talioth chuckled. "You think it looks like me?"

Danik nodded. "It's pretty good."

"Your friends freed the slaves we had working on this."

"As I told you, if you had killed them in Felting like you were supposed to, none of this would have happened."

Talioth gritted his teeth.

"The Core would be whole. Your statue could be finished."

"Pfff!" He waved his hand. "I don't care about the statue. I could grab men from the mines if I wanted it finished that badly.

"Why are you building it if you don't care?"

"It was never for me. The others insisted. They wanted to commemorate me, and I didn't mind."

Danik gazed at the statue, the corner of his mouth curling.

"Over time, the caves became our home," Talioth continued. "Our numbers grew. We farmed. We built living quarters. We no longer had to fight against the Call. As long as we kept the Core powered, our people were safe. Now, we don't even miss it. Once you stop resisting, you'll find the same contentment here as we did."

"Well . . ." Danik said. "That's great for you, but like I said, I have a kingdom to run."

"Where are the shadow knights now?"

The question made Danik jerk upright. "Um, uh . . ." He glanced at Nicolar while he fumbled with his words. "I don't know."

"It may not look like it, but our lives are in danger—all of us, you included. The weakening of the Core—upsetting the balance of power—it's driving us to a place that's not sustainable. My wife died not long ago. She was my joy, the light of my life." He paused, choking on emotion. "We're used to the power from the Core keeping us alive, but it's waning. And my people are looking to me to save them. I *need* to save them, Danik. But to do that, I need to know where the knights are."

"I told you, I have no idea."

Talioth released his anger. "Lies!"

"I'm not lying!"

Talioth pointed in his face. "You were part of them for how many years? Don't tell me you don't know where they are."

"I don't! And I don't have to justify myself to you."

Nicolar stepped forward and lifted an arm between them. "Calm down, both of you."

Talioth's chest rose and fell, his blood remaining hot.

"He's not lying," Nicolar said. "We've been searching for them for the last several weeks, to no avail. We want them dead as much as you do."

"We must have those knights. The Core needs the origine they use."

Danik ran a hand through his hair and blew out his breath. "If we knew where they were, they'd already be dead."

"Fine," Talioth said. "We have two of them here. We'll see what they know. Who knows . . . maybe their sacrifice will be enough to stabilize the Core. If you are going to leave, then leave. The entrance is open—no need for you to hang around here."

Danik executed a slow nod. "And the necklaces?"

Talioth sighed. "How many did you need?"

"For me and the other trainees . . . twenty-three."

His eyes narrowed. He clenched his teeth together as he stared at the two men. After a long pause, he looked over the railing to the Hub floor.

"Meliand!"

The older woman looked up.

Talioth nodded to Danik and Nicolar. "They're leaving. Get them the necklaces they need, then escort them out."

3

A NEW MINE

Lia's back ached when she sat up in her bed. She had slept little the night before. The lumpy hay left her tossing and turning, and men traveling back and forth from the latrine woke her each time she fell asleep. With no sun to go by, she had no idea when it was time to get up, so she waited until the other men stirred.

No one spoke to her. She offered smiles, but no one returned them. When they mustered to leave the room, she followed, last in line. Three teams already ate in the mess area. She spotted Dayna on the far side of the room. Her fellow knight spooned something from a bowl and brightened at the sight of her. She smiled and gave a subdued wave. The men sitting nearby glanced at her with scowls. Dayna's welcome seemed little better than what Lia had received.

Lia followed her team through a narrow passage to the kitchen, where a marked one behind a wooden table ladled food into bowls. She picked up an empty bowl and was met with a wet sloshing sound as a ladle of gruel slopped into her bowl. A fair portion of the sludge splattered onto her wrist. She jerked back, expecting a burn, but the food was already cold.

Great. Cold porridge.

With no one waiting after her, she paused for a moment to inspect the meal. It looked mushy and smelled like eggs that had sat in the sun for too long. She moved a spoonful to her mouth and tasted it. Her tongue curled, and her lips writhed in protest.

"You have a problem?" the guard who had served her asked.

Lia shook her head and forced herself to swallow. The gruel slid down her throat, fighting all the while to claw its way back up. "No. Thank you." She exited the kitchen.

Her team sat together, huddled around either side of a long table. Vekko occupied the end, spreading his body wide, blocking the last seat and the possibility of her joining her teammates.

Perfect.

She turned to where Dayna sat and eyed the open seat across from her. She smiled and headed in her direction.

If they don't want to welcome me onto their team, then they won't feel hurt if I don't sit—

Lia's legs caught. Her body continued forward, but her feet couldn't keep up. She fell, tumbling toward the ground with no way to stop it. She let go of the bowl to catch herself against the rocky cave floor. The dish hit the ground and shattered. Cold gruel filled the air, flinging onto her face and splatting across her clothes.

Peals of laughter filled the air, the echoes hitting her from all directions. Lia remained on the ground, a hot flush rushing across her face. Her palms stung, scraped against the cave floor. Her knees ached from where they hit the rocky surface. She stood, keeping her head down. Porridge dripped from her hair, falling in loud plops onto the ground. Lia bent and scooped up the pieces of her broken bowl. The howling assaulted her back as she returned to the kitchen, broken shards of pottery in her hands.

"I'm not sure what to do with this," Lia said, standing before the server with the broken dish pieces.

"You don't get any more," he barked.

"That's fine. I'm just looking for where to put this." She glanced around the room but saw no obvious place to set her load. "I guess I'll just . . ." She leaned forward and extended her arms over the table. She hoped he might give her a sign that it was the right thing to do, but he only raised his eyebrows. ". . . set this here." She dropped the remains on the table.

The man scowled but didn't respond. Instead, he lifted a lid from another dish behind the counter.

An incredible smell filled the air, brightening her eyes. Cooked sausage links piled high in the uncovered dish. Her mouth watered. "What are those for?"

"Not you. It's for the Valcors." He nodded to the side.

"Get out of our way, new girl!" a man yelled next to her.

Lia jumped. She hadn't realized a new team had arrived. They lined up, waiting for her to move.

"We sure are lucky we didn't get this long-haired piece of garbage for our team," a tall man with a thick neck said.

"Not that we need luck," another gibed, sending the rest into a fit of laughter. The one who spoke nudged the guy next to him. "What do you think, Bronson?"

Bronson, a middle-aged man with slicked black hair, approached. "You know, sweetie, that food is meant to be eaten, not worn."

More laughter.

Lia turned on her heels and rushed out of the kitchen. Tears threatened to spring to her eyes, but she fought them back. *Can't let them see me cry.*

Back in the mess area, she walked toward where Dayna sat. Partway there, she stopped. *Where is she?* She looked at the faces and the backs of heads but couldn't find her. A line of people caught her attention. Her heart sank. The Mountain Wolves had finished eating and already headed toward the mines.

Dayna looked back at her with a knowing look. She mouthed, "I'm sorry."

Lia walked to where her team sat. She hovered next to Vekko, but the man wouldn't look up.

Jarno shrugged from across the table. "Sorry, there's not enough room here."

Lia sighed, then turned to the closest open table. She sat facing her team, watching while the rest of them ate.

It didn't take them long to slurp down the bowls of sludge. No one grimaced at the consistency or taste. As thankful as Lia was to not have to eat it, she would have much rather gotten food in her. Something told her she was going to need it.

"Garronts, let's go," Chris said, rising and leading the team. As if following a well-practiced habit, they piled their empty bowls in a bucket next to the kitchen.

Lia followed. When the group stopped at the tool supply, most of the others took pickaxes, but a few picked up shovels. Lia selected a pickaxe. It had a long and smooth wooden handle. The metal head contained plenty of dings and gouges but was sturdy.

A few men snickered, drawing her attention to Vekko's haughty grin. "Best grab a shovel. Save the axes for the men."

Lia's jaw clenched as the team turned away. She stared at the pile of shovels leaning against the wall. Her grip tightened on the pickaxe. The heavy wooden handle dug into her shoulder. She hiked it up higher, then huffed and followed the others.

Her team headed into the large tunnel past the tools. Despite being rested, their shoulders slumped the same way they had the previous day. It was as if they'd been beaten down before they'd even begun. The tunnel continued straight for a short distance until it opened into another vast cavern. Glowing crystals set into the wall at regular intervals, and lanterns supplemented the light. The ceiling stretched high, past the distance the light could reach. Multiple passages jutted in every direction. Empty, four-wheeled wooden carts piled together at the entrance to the area.

Next to the carts, five red boxes rose from the cave floor, standing out from their surroundings. Lia stepped closer. Markings on the side were drawings of their team animals—Garronts on the far right box.

Two teams already worked in different sections of the open chamber, pickaxes pounding into the cavern walls, making familiar tinking and thunking sounds that look Lia back to her time in Tienn.

"Wolves and Panzils are already here," Chris said from the front of their team. "We'll head to the Kardrian Passage."

The men trudged on as one unit to the right. Those carrying shovels grabbed a wooden cart apiece and rolled them until the team entered a narrow corridor. Walls tightened around them for a moment until space opened up again. The right wall soon disappeared, replaced by a scree slope that descended into darkness. The path itself grew wider, and the Garronts came to a halt.

Chris leaned closer to the wall as if inspecting it while the men waited on him. "Lowell, show Lia how it works."

An older man startled then frowned in her direction. A curved spine left him with a hunch, and thin wisps of gray hair curled on his head.

"Eleven teammates makes seventeen," Chris called. "But with the new quota . . . we need twenty-two by the end of the week."

The men groaned.

"And here I thought our three yesterday was a respectable start." Waylon looked at Lia with a sideways grin. "Maybe Miss Priss can bring us back from our deficit."

The men dispersed, spreading out along the passage. Those with axes began pounding away at the rock. The men with shovels positioned their carts as if waiting on rubble to scoop into them.

"Come with me," a gruff voice called.

The words snapped Lia from a stupor. She blinked to find the man named Lowell waving for her to follow.

He led her to the end of the line of men and stopped at the wall. "You don't have any idea about how this works, do you?"

"Yes, actually, I have some experience. I spent a few days mining in Tienn."

Lowell's eyebrows raised. He glanced along her arms then shrugged. "I guess you don't need me to instruct you then." He raised his pickaxe and slammed it into the wall, dribbling chips of stone to the path.

Lia mimicked his movement. Her swing dug into the rock. "What are we, uh . . . looking for?" Lia pulled the axe back. "Baltham?"

Lowell shook his head. "Crystals."

Lia stopped mid-motion and turned to him. "The red ones the Marked Ones wear around their necks?"

Lowell struck the rock again then sighed. "Similar. We mine the raw crystals. They do something to them to make them glow."

Lia ran her eyes down the passage, noticing the spaced-out crystals. "All the ones in the cave walls, they have to . . . *activate* them?"

"Something like that."

"Wait . . . So you're mining twenty-two of these per week? And that's just your team? What do they do with them all?"

Lowell stopped and rested a hand on his hip. "Do you want to work or ask questions?"

"Can we do both?"

He groaned. "Fine." His axe dug into the wall. "I don't know about the crystals. They always want more, though. The glowing ones in the walls go out and need to be replaced. Sometimes a few are out in a cluster that they haven't fixed yet. It can get pretty dark."

Lia took another swing with her axe, chipping off a small rock. "Tell me about all these teams. What's the deal there?"

"That's how they motivate us. It's a competition. Whichever team collects the most crystals in a week receives the golden pickaxe."

"To mine with?"

Lowell chuckled as he struck the wall. "No, it's an emblem that goes above the barracks."

The gold-colored emblem she saw returned to her mind. "The Valcors won last week?"

Lowell nodded. "They win every week."

"Is there a prize?"

"Yeah. Better food."

Lia's eyes grew. "Oh! I saw the sausages earlier."

"Yeah. It's coveted, but . . . we Garronts can't afford to hope. It only creates disappointment."

"So . . . if we're competing for the most, what's with the quotas?"

Lowell's face fell. "That's the real motivator for teams like us. We may never beat the Valcors, but if we make quota, we can avoid the weekly reaping."

"Rasmill mentioned something about that. What is it?"

He stopped to take a breath and leaned on the handle of his axe. "The mining is bad enough, but the reaping is the worst part of the week. If teams don't perform, the marked ones choose a member from that team."

Lia waited, expecting more, but Lowell seemed to be done. She leaned forward. "What happens to them?"

He shrugged. "No one knows. They take them away and we never see them again."

A lump formed in Lia's throat. "So . . . if we make quota, then we avoid it?"

"That's right."

Lia glanced along the row of men as they chipped away at the wall. "That's why everyone is so hard on each other. If the team doesn't mine enough, anyone on the team could be taken."

"Exactly. Unfortunately for us . . . the Garronts are far from the best team in the mines."

"Why's that?"

Lowell laughed. "Look at us. I'm so old, I can barely lift my axe. Half the men on our team could blow over in a stiff wind. And now they give us—" He gestured toward Lia.

She bit her lip but didn't respond.

"Look." He pointed down the line at the men who had lowered their axes and inhaled in deep breaths. "See how they're resting already? We're only two minutes into a full day of work. We can't keep up with the other teams. We had a full team of fourteen members after the last resupplying, but we haven't met quota four out of the last six weeks. Now we're down to ten—eleven with you."

Lia hefted her axe and dug it into the wall with a full swing. A chunk of rock tumbled down. She leaned in and touched the wall, rubbing her fingers along the rough surface. "What type of rock is this?"

"Mostly peredite. You'll run into some borlium and shalfix."

"It's soft."

Lowell nodded. "Peredite is manageable to dig through. That makes our job easier."

"What about the crystals? How do we find them without cracking them?"

Lowell chuckled. "Don't worry about that. A direct hit from the pickaxe couldn't scratch one of those things. With the soft rock, the crystals roll right off the wall when you find one."

Lia slammed her tool into the wall again, sending a jumble of stones skittering down. She sucked in air as she readied the axe again, pausing to take a few deep breaths. Her heart raced. Sweat already beaded on her forehead.

She longed for the comforting presence of the origine. Not only would it make the work much easier, but with the power, she'd be able to break out of the mines and escape.

After the brief pause, she swung the axe again. The pick glanced off the rock, not even denting it. Her arms felt fatigued. Her heavy breath had already returned.

This is going to be a long day.

An hour into the work, a man with a shovel and a cart wheeled up to Lia. "Is that all you've cleared?" he asked.

Lia looked down at the pile of loose stones she'd knocked free. Her back ached, her arms felt weak, and her lungs struggled to fill her body with the oxygen it needed. She wiped her forehead with the back of her hand.

"I told you to get a shovel," Vekko sneered from the other side of Lowell. "At least then you could have been productive."

She frowned. Her pile was at least as large as Lowell's. She turned back to the wall of the cavern, grunting as she attacked it with a full-body blow. A lone, small rock skittered to the floor.

"Crystal!" echoed through the corridor from down the line.

Lia jerked her head to see Waylon raise a dull, red object with a tired smile on his face.

The leader, Chris, stepped off the wall and glanced farther down the passage. "Go!"

Waylon jogged up the corridor, leaving his axe behind. Chris and another teammate followed, gripping their pickaxes with both hands as they ran.

The sudden effort struck her as odd. "What's that all about?" she asked Lowell.

He checked each direction down the passage before leaning toward her. "Did you notice the red boxes where we entered?"

She nodded.

"That's where we deposit the crystals."

"Okay, but . . ." She glanced around. The other miners had returned to work as if nothing were out of the ordinary. "Why the rush?"

Lowell's eyes grew. He moved his head in a tight shake. He raised a finger to his lips before he turned his attention back to the wall.

The hairs on Lia's arms stood on end. An unsettled feeling swept through her. "What do I do when I find a crystal?"

He paused and turned to her. "You let the team know . . . then you get it in that box."

LIA DIDN'T FIND A CRYSTAL. Their team only deposited two that day, dropping them even farther behind in their weekly quota.

At the end of the day, she trudged back toward the barracks with the rest of the team. Her feet stumbled against invisible objects in the path. Shadow Knights training gave her a strong overall fitness, but it failed to prepare her for the specific rigors of swinging an axe all day. Without the origine—like she had in Tienn—she felt lacking. She braced one hand against her back while stretching it. Her numb arm ached from the effort.

Behind her, Vekko and Jarno mumbled something about a girl being bad luck, but Lia tuned them out. She dropped her axe in the tool supply area, then stumbled after the others toward their barracks. She looked around, hoping to see Dayna, longing for a chance to talk with her fellow knight, but the other teams disappeared into their rooms.

Just as well, she thought. *I'm exhausted.*

She rested her hands against the barrack walls and bunks to keep from falling. When she arrived at the far end of the room, she collapsed onto her bed, letting herself sink into the straw.

4

RETURN TO THE GLADE

Raiyn blew out a deep breath as he scanned the Glade. The waterfall ran as it had when they left two weeks before. Butterflies still danced in the meadow, and the wooden homes waited, untouched. The afternoon sun poured over the rim of the rock walls, lighting up the trees, the field, and the stream that meandered through the enclave.

"Wow!" Bridgette shook her head after exiting the tight entrance passage. "I had no idea."

Veron waved the group forward. "Come on."

Raiyn kept an eye on the path but felt his gaze drawn to the side the farther they traveled. The sight of Lia's house brought an ache to his chest. Her empty hammock swung in the breeze from the second-floor deck. Tears blurred the edges of his vision. His breath shuddered.

Ahead, Veron turned toward the same house. Chelci wrapped an arm around him, leaning her head against his shoulder. After crossing the footbridge, they came to a halt in the training yard and gave the others a chance to catch up.

Veron cleared his throat and wiped at his eyes. "Why doesn't everyone take some time to settle in? Pair up and pick a house. Chelci and I will be in that one." He pointed at a house to the right. "And Raiyn's in the one by the waterfall." Veron turned to him. "You all right sharing with Brixton?"

Raiyn glanced at the grizzled mountain man, who nodded at him. "Sure thing," Raiyn confirmed.

The crowd dispersed: Gavin and Bradley leaving for the house in the middle, Ruby and Salina heading to the one on the far right, and Bridgette walking to Lia's old place.

"You stayed here?" Brixton asked, falling in step as they headed up the hill.

Raiyn nodded. "Only a couple of nights. I ended up in Felting's dungeon, then hiding out in various places for the rest of the time. It's been a wild last few weeks."

"How old are you?"

"Twenty-one."

Brixton released a short laugh.

"What is it?"

"Twenty-one seems like a lifetime ago."

"What were you doing at my age? Marching off to save Terrenor from bad guys, like I've been?" Raiyn managed a mirthless chuckle.

Lips pursed, Brixton hesitated.

Raiyn's eyes widened. "You did?"

"Ha! Um . . . not quite. I was, er—" He hung his head, watching his feet as they crunched along the path. "I was on the other side."

"You were the one being saved *from* the bad guys?"

"Um . . . no. I was *with* the bad guys."

"Oh." Raiyn tensed, his legs feeling awkward. He spoke with a waver in his voice. "Do, uh . . . Veron and Chelci know about that?"

Brixton's laugh burst from him, as if his entire body pushed it forward. The hearty chortle bounced off the stone walls of the Glade, sending a trio of birds fluttering from a distant branch.

Raiyn raised his eyebrows and paused, watching as the bearded man howled.

"Yeah," Brixton said, hooting and wiping at his eyes. "I'd say Veron and Chelci know *quite* well. They're better at forgiveness than anyone I know, and that's the only reason I'm still alive." He tossed his head toward the house. "Come on. Show me this place."

Raiyn led up the rest of the path and held the door for Brixton to enter.

"This is great." Brixton nodded as he stepped inside.

"Yeah, the other knights built it over the last few years, or something like that." Raiyn set his pack down next to the bed he'd used before. The sheet on it lay rumpled in the same position it had been in when he left previously.

Brixton dropped his pack by the other bed, then sauntered to the corner where the raised basin with the bamboo spout sat hip-high. "What is . . . Whoa! This is something."

"It was Chelci's idea."

The corner of Brixton's mouth curled, and he issued a soft laugh. "I believe it."

A quiet pause filled the air. Raiyn watched the grizzled man as he appraised the room. "What were you doing in the mountains?"

Brixton raised an eyebrow. "Did Lia or Veron tell you about me?"

Raiyn sat, shaking his head.

"It's a sad tale for another time. This place, however . . ." He nodded as he turned in the room. "Much nicer than that cave I was in."

"Yeah, I imagine. What about back when you lived in Felting? You did . . . live in Felting, right?"

"For a time. I grew up in Karad. And . . . I lived pretty well."

"Did you know Lia? Before you left?"

"A bit. I met her when she was young, but she wouldn't have remembered me."

Lia, Raiyn thought. His shoulders drooped, and his chin fell toward the floor.

"Were you together?"

Raiyn's head lifted. The thought of their conversation on the icy mountain trail filled him equally with excitement and sadness. "I— I'm not sure. I think so."

"You think so?"

"It was new. We had only just told each other how we felt." A faint smile pulled at his mouth while a lone tear pooled in the corner of his eye. "Yeah, we were together—for a moment. She was incredible. She was rebellious before I arrived, but all I saw of her was kindness and talent. When she spoke, you listened. You *wanted* to follow her." He shook his head. "But she's gone, and there's nothing I can do. It doesn't seem fair. All my life, I've been beaten down, and the one time something goes right, it's stripped from me."

"I'm sorry," Brixton whispered.

"What's even worse is that now that she's gone, I feel like I need to pick up where she left off—like I need to be the leader she was. But I don't see it in me. I don't think I'm built that way."

Brixton held his gaze. The older man's brows formed deep creases. "People say you learn from mistakes. With the amount I've made, I must be a genius by now."

Raiyn laughed through his nose. "You have some wisdom for me, then?"

"I see a leader in you, Raiyn, and I saw how you stood with the others in the caves. That took a lot of guts. I imagine you might be more capable than you realize. About Lia . . . I could tell you it's going to be okay, but that wouldn't mean anything. I could point out the fact that you're young and assure you you'll find someone else, but that's not what you want to hear, even though it's true. I could remind you that Lia died nobly to save you, me, and the other knights, but that does little to take away the sting."

Raiyn nodded. "What, then? What've you learned?"

Brixton stepped forward and stopped next to the bed. "I learned it stinks." He rested a hand on his shoulder. "I can't make it better, and I won't pretend everything's all right. And for now . . . it's okay to not be all right."

Pent-up tension released in Raiyn's body like a flood. Quiet tears trickled from both eyes. He wiped at his face and sniffed. "Thank you," he managed. The firm grip on his shoulder from a man he barely knew comforted him in a way he wouldn't have thought possible.

. . .

RAIYN AND BRIXTON were the last to return to the main hall. Salina chopped some greens while Bradley stirred a pot that hung over a flickering fire in the hearth. Gavin pawed through the pile of weapons at the end of the room, and the rest of the knights sat in a casual configuration around the tables. Continuing to blow steam off a mug of tea, Chelci's eyes flicked to the door when they entered.

"That's everyone," Veron said.

The chatter in the room stopped. Gavin and Bradley ceased what they were doing and crossed the room to join the others. Salina set down her knife and wiped her hands on her pants.

"Rooms all right for everyone?" Chelci asked, her head turning through the room. "Anyone need anything?"

"They're perfect," Bridgette said. "You did a great job."

"We're good," Brixton confirmed.

"Good," Veron added. "A few ground rules for the Glade. We rotate duties as we did in Felting: cooking, cleaning, wood chopping, training, and guard duties."

"Hopefully not three each night again," Gavin said.

Veron shook his head. "The crack in the rock is the only ingress point. One knight should be sufficient."

Heads nodded around the room.

"Since we've lost our funding, we'll need to add hunting and gathering duties. The woods are teeming with life, but we need to remain deep in them so we're not discovered. If the wrong people find this location, we could be in trouble."

"What about—what was that boy's name?" Chelci asked. "He knew where this was, right?"

"Marcus," Raiyn replied, a knot turning in his stomach at the reminder of the spy. He glanced at Veron. "He died in the caverns. I saw it."

"Would he have told anyone about the Glade before then?"

Raiyn shrugged. "It's possible, but unlikely it would have come up in the time they had together."

Veron nodded. "I agree. We *should* be safe from them, but still . . . we need to stay on guard. Hunting should sustain us for now, and in a couple weeks, we should plant wiether vegetables in the field."

"So, what do we do about the marked ones?" Bridgette asked.

Silence filled the room. The tension grew with each second it lingered.

"They'll come after us again, won't they?"

"Their power is growing weak," Chelci said. "They need to 'siphon' the origine from us—whatever that means."

"It's with that enormous crystal," Veron said. "They drag the origine out of us, and our lives give them energy."

Bridgette sighed. "That means they'll keep coming for us."

"I'm afraid so."

"Do we bring the fight to them?" Gavin asked. "We know where they live. That gives us some sort of advantage."

Raiyn's hands grew clammy at the thought of returning to the caverns.

"They know that, though," Veron said. "They'll be under heavy guard."

"Besides," Gavin added, "how are we supposed to kill them?"

"Can you repeat what you did with that crystal, Veron?" Brixton stood to the side, and all eyes turned to him. "Didn't you . . . suck their power away, or something like that?"

Veron nodded. "I don't understand it, but . . . possibly. It returned the origine back to me for good, but it only took theirs away for a short while. That's all dependent on us getting to it, though."

"Don't forget the guard," Chelci added.

Veron blew air through his nose. "As dangerous as they are, the Marked Ones aren't our top priority. It's unlikely they know where we are, and there's a decent chance they'll stay in their caves for a while. Meanwhile, a more pressing threat is out there."

"Danik," Raiyn breathed.

"That's right," Veron confirmed. "Danik. The ranks of the Knights of Power are growing, and they don't appear content to hide in caves. Besides wanting to wipe us out, they'll likely try to expand their power, reaching to the other kingdoms. The larger they get, the more difficult they'll be to subdue."

Chelci chimed in, "And the longer we wait, the more the people of Terrenor will suffer. We'll need to act soon."

"But the primary worry is what we saw in the caves," Veron said.

"The necklaces?" Raiyn asked.

Veron nodded. "Not only is Danik's group growing in size and wanting to kill us, but they now can shield us from using the origine."

"How do we fight that?"

Veron sighed, blowing air in a long stream. "I don't know." He glanced at the others. "Any thoughts?"

Mutters grew in the room as knights shifted.

"Maybe set a trap?" Gavin suggested. "Lure them to a specific place with the promise of us being there."

"They'd be on alert," Chelci replied. "And they'd use those necklaces. I'm not sure how effective we could be against that."

"Maybe we could lure them without them realizing we're doing it."

Chelci nodded. "How?"

Neither Gavin nor anyone else answered.

"Do we know where they sleep?" Bridgette asked.

"Danik's in the castle," Veron confirmed. "I'm sure he'll be heavily guarded."

"Guarded by knights of power? Or regular men?"

A pause followed Bridgette's comment.

Veron's face lightened. "That's a good question."

Chelci added, "If it's regular guards, they won't be shielding the origine. We could take them out."

The momentary lightness faded as Veron's shoulders slumped. "But Danik knows we've escaped. He doesn't know where we are, so he won't attack. That means—"

"All he can do is defend," Chelci finished. "He'll have men with the devion guarding him, asleep or awake."

Veron pushed against the table, rolling his neck. "We need to figure out how to fight them *without* the use of the origine."

"Is that possible?" Gavin asked. "We tried to fight Talioth's men at the training center, and we all know how that went."

"Lia did it," Raiyn said, drawing heads toward him. His heart twisted at the mention of her name. "I helped, but it was mostly her. She killed that Valdok guy without the origine."

"That's right," Veron said, a catch weaving through his words. Chelci set her hand on his leg. He lowered his chin in an extended pause before continuing. "She did. But I don't think we can count on being able to duplicate that."

"I wish one of us was in their group," Gavin said.

Veron raised an eyebrow. "In the Knights of Power?"

Gavin shrugged. "Wouldn't that be great? I'm not sure how they recruit, but if it worked, we could know all of their schedules and their plans."

"They'd never trust any of us, though." Chelci nodded toward Brixton. "Brix could have had a shot, but they would have seen him in the caverns."

"Could we get one of them to turn?" Gavin asked.

"Possible, but unlikely," Veron said. "Plus, it would be a risk for us to contact one of them."

Raiyn raised a hand. "I know who we can use."

Everyone turned to him.

"We need someone they trust who knows what they're up to. Someone already ensconced in their world. He's not a knight, but . . . I believe he can help."

5

INTERROGATION

The command sounded distant and fuzzy, like someone calling to her from underwater. Lia rustled, vaguely aware she needed to do something. She tried to open her eyes, but they wouldn't respond.

"I said, get up!"

The voice was back, clearer, but still muddled. She blinked several times and tried to move her lips to respond when a wave of cold water crashed over her.

"Ah!" Lia jumped from her bed, her heart racing and eyes blinking.

Chris set down a bucket and shook his head. The other men laughed behind him as they exited the barracks. "I don't care how tired and sore you are. Your team is counting on you to contribute. It's time to go. Move it."

Lia's legs barely felt capable of holding up her body. Her joints were stiff and sore as she walked after her team toward the kitchen. Her stomach growled while she waited in line. To her dismay, the serving ladle slopped out the same gruel as the day before. Whatever happened, she would make sure she didn't spill hers. She needed the energy.

Last for her team, she followed to their group's table. Jarno sat in the last seat, spreading his body like Vekko had the day before. Lia's face fell until she noticed Dayna lifting her chin and motioning to the open seat next to her. A smile pulled at Lia's face.

Finally, someone friendly to talk to.

"Stormbridge!" a voice bellowed from along the corridor.

Lia turned toward the open gates and found Rasmill standing with two marked ones.

He beckoned with an open hand. "Come on!"

"But," she muttered, looking at her bowl of cold slop. "I haven't eaten yet."

"Leave it! Let's go!"

Lia looked at her food, then shoveled spoonfuls into her mouth. Her cheeks puffed. She struggled to force the food down while taking slow steps toward the gates. She paused at the bucket next to the kitchen, hovering with another spoon. She tried to swallow what was in her mouth so she could take one last bite, but the food wouldn't go down. The slimy porridge thickened in her throat, making her gag.

"Don't make me come over there!" Rasmill warned.

A coughing fit projected most of what was in her mouth across the wall of the cave. She retched, losing any hope of retaining the nutrients she needed. With her breath labored and stomach lurching, she set the mostly full bowl in the bucket before turning to walk toward the gate.

"Next time, you come when you're called," Rasmill warned when she arrived.

One of the other men held her in place while the other knelt by her legs. A metal clinking sound brought a sinking sensation to her heart. She looked down and cringed at the fresh length of chain shortening her stride.

"Come on," a guard ordered, pulling her toward the gate.

Lia shuffled along. As she passed through the gates to the mine, a disconcerting feeling rushed through her. *Will I ever be back here?* As much as she never wanted to return, she cringed at the thought of what might cause that to come true.

The two marked ones led her through the cave system. They proceeded up an incline until they passed back through the Hub, then into another passage on the far side. She felt the hum before she even entered the room. When they rounded a corner, Lia's eyes widened at the sight of the massive red crystal hovering over a circular, black pit.

This must be the one Father spoke about.

She gaped.

"Impressive, isn't it?"

Lia's head jerked to find Talioth standing to the side.

"I remember how I felt the first time I laid eyes on it."

"And when was that?" Lia asked. "Three hundred years ago?"

His smile grew. "Yes, in fact, it was."

Farrathan's hilt jutting over his shoulder caught her eye. "Talon Shadow. You save Terrenor by defeating Vitrion, then you embrace evil by turning to the devion, and now you cling to whatever power you can, no matter how many lives it costs."

"Oh Lia, how naïve you are. It's not good versus evil. The origine is power to help others, and the devion—"

"Is to help yourself?"

He smiled. "Precisely."

"How noble of you."

"I never said I was noble."

"Selfish then."

His smile waned. "Tell me Lia . . . in Felting, did you ever eat a meal at suppertime? Let's say . . . chicken, maybe some vegetables?"

She didn't reply.

"I'll wager there were people that evening who went hungry. Maybe people who lived in the poor area of the city, or maybe people right across the street from you."

Her mind flashed to the Merryweather family, scrimping to put a measly meal on the table.

"Why didn't you give away your chicken?"

Lia stared for a long moment. "I had to eat, too."

"But they were starving. Some of them might have died. They

needed that chicken. Are you telling me you had no issue eating a juicy platter of meat when someone down the street was about to die of starvation?"

"We can't save everyone."

"You can't?"

"We have to take care of ourselves."

The grin on his face grew impossibly large. "Of course, you do, and so do we. We act to take care of our needs. We're trying to live, just like you."

"There's a difference," Lia said, her blood heating. "We don't kill or enslave people to feed our need for power."

"You *do* kill people! Ones who make your lives difficult. You decide who is good and who is bad, then you kill whoever you choose to."

Lia was quiet for a moment. "What do you want with me?"

Talioth's head cocked. "How was your first day in the mines?"

She chuckled. "I loved it. Nearly at the top of my mining experiences."

"Is there anything I can do to make your time there more pleasant?"

She paused. "Are you serious?"

He folded his hands in front of his body. "What would you like?"

A flurry of ideas ran through her head. *Better food. A better place to sleep. A chance to leave. Will he give me any of them?* She stared into his eyes. "Take off my anklets."

"Ha!" he scoffed.

"You ask us to mine. You want those crystals so much. I can get them for you, but I need to use the origine."

He pursed his lips as he looked into her eyes.

"I'm exhausted ten minutes into a day's work. I can barely lift the pickaxe. But if you let me use my full capabilities, I can power through ten times what I can do in a day now."

"It's a valid argument," he shook his head, "but no. The anklets stay on."

"Why do you need the crystals?"

"What we do with them is our business."

"With five teams, you're collecting over a hundred crystals per week. What can you possibly do with all those?"

He sighed, his shoulders slumping. "One raw crystal is worthless. We need ten to create a miniature version of this." He pressed his hand against the large crystal. "Once we fuse them into smaller Cores, we use them for our necklaces, cavern security, and simple lighting."

"What about this one?" She nodded to the large one at the center of the room. "Is this like the mother crystal? Do all your powers come from it?"

His mouth curled at the corner.

"It is, isn't it?" She turned to the glowing red object with a new appreciation. She tried to step forward, only to be held back by the marked one holding onto her. "What would happen if I grabbed that sword over your shoulder and shattered it, huh? Would you fall, weak and helpless?"

His short laugh told her it wasn't so simple.

"I'd offer to let you try," Talioth motioned over his shoulder, "but we'd all be impaled with sword shards after it shattered into a thousand pieces. And I, for one, am not ready for *you* to die . . . yet. Plus, you may be surprised by what this crystal actually does."

"What does it do?"

His mischievous smile turned her stomach as if there was an important piece of information she was missing.

"Fine, then tell me about the Gharator Nilden."

Talioth's slack jaw and raised eyebrows gave Lia smug satisfaction.

"How do you know about that?" he asked.

She knew nothing about it other than the cryptic messages they'd read in the book. "Life magnet, right? What does that mean?"

The Marked Ones' leader narrowed his eyes.

"It's the black marks, isn't it?"

"I've had enough of this. Gralow!"

Lia froze. Heavy footsteps rumbled the floor. She turned her head as one of the larger marked ones entered. Stringy hair draped against his face, and a gray beard framed his chin. His massive arms and shoulders concerned her. She took a step away, her foot clinking against the restraint.

"Chain her to the wall," Gralow said, his deep voice thick and husky.

At the far end of the room, an alcove tucked into a corner with four metal rings fixed into the wall and loose clamps hanging from each ring.

The guard who had brought her there fastened the clamps to each leg, pulling them apart, stretching to where her thighs burned. He took one of her hands and raised it to the side. She cringed as the cold metal clamped around her wrist. Soon, the other arm followed, stretched in the opposite direction. The lengths of chain were short. She pulled against the restraints, but her limbs wouldn't budge.

Gralow stepped closer, a hand's width from her body.

Lia cringed at the vulnerable feeling. She tried to lower her arms, but the rattling chains only taunted her.

The marked one inspected the cuffs around her limbs, one at a time. Lia felt the heat coming from his skin and smelled the odor from his body. Appearing pleased with the restraints, he nodded and stepped back.

Lia hadn't noticed the leather satchel over his shoulder until he set it on a table and unlatched it.

Talioth sauntered forward. "Valdok used to be our interrogator of choice, but you put an end to his life in Felting. Thankfully, Gralow is just as ruthless."

"I'm not telling you anything," Lia growled.

"That may be the case, but for all our sakes—yours most of all—I hope not."

Gralow rolled open the satchel, and Lia cringed. Filled with metal objects of various shapes and sizes, she shuddered at the thought of how they were used.

"You are about to go through an incredible amount of pain. I wish it weren't the case, but we've found it to be very helpful for making people talk."

Lia sucked in a breath.

"I'm going to ask you some questions. If I don't like your answers, Gralow is going to have some fun. Then, I'm going to ask again, giving you another chance. Whenever I like what you say, your day gets better. Whenever I don't like it, it gets much worse. If you remain silent, the pain will only grow. Don't think death will save you." He leaned forward and whispered. "You won't be so lucky."

Her heart raced. She glanced at Gralow, who sported an evil grin over Talioth's shoulder.

"First off, I want to know where the Shadow Knights are."

Her mind jumped to the Glade. She pictured them arriving there and settling in. She imagined them cooking and training together, hidden in their forested community. *No, I could never betray them.*

She tightened her jaw, clenching her teeth. Her eyes lifted to meet Talioth's. He stared back with a smoldering intensity. Her lips parted as if to speak, but she closed them again, flashing a faint smile.

Talioth stepped to the side.

Slam!

A fist like a stone slammed her stomach. Lia gasped. She tried to collapse forward, but the chains held her up. A deep ache rolled through her body, sending spasms of pain. She gulped to take in air, but it felt like breathing through a lattice of knives. The pain lessened, and she lifted her head again.

Crack!

Gralow's fist smashed against her jaw. White spots danced across her vision. Her face felt fractured, like it had broken from the blow. She groaned. A warm, coppery taste filled her mouth. Rolling her jaw only made the pain increase.

Talioth stepped in front of her. "Is this fun? Do you want to continue?"

She spit, bright red saliva splattering across the marked one's gray clothing.

His eyes narrowed. "Tell me where the Shadow Knights are."

"I don't know," she croaked, sending a fresh wave of pain through her mouth. "I haven't seen them in days."

"Where is their hideout?"

She didn't answer.

"Where would they go after they left here?"

"They said—" She sucked in several breaths. "They said something about—" More breaths. "They wanted to take a vacation—get some sun. Visiting the beaches of Searis, I think."

Her chuckle felt good, despite the pain.

Talioth scowled. "Gralow." He stepped aside again.

More blows landed on Lia's body. She cried out and grunted as the man pounded on her. When he stopped, bloody drool dripped from her mouth, and blurry vision marred her focus.

"Had enough yet?" Talioth asked.

She shook her head. She tried to spit on him again, but the blood just dribbled down her chin.

"I'll ask again, where are the Shadow Knights?"

She took in a deep breath, then blew it out. "You can pound me all you want. I'm sure this is only the beginning of the pain you can inflict. I imagine soon I will wish I were dead, but no matter what you do, I will not give them up. I turned my back on the knights once. I will never do it again."

She lifted her chin and breathed in, puffing out her chest. Through much effort, she kept both eyes open as she stared at Talioth.

"Let's try something new then," the marked one said. "I want to know what happened in the Chamber Room when the ceiling collapsed."

Lia traced her memory back to the moment of blackness. Drained of energy, she had expected to die. Out of nowhere, origine had flooded through her, giving her the strength and healing ability to survive. She held her breath. *He can't possibly learn that.*

"What did you do to summon the pure connection?"

Would he even be capable of that sort of sacrifice, to make it work?

He stepped closer. His face contorted before he shouted, "How did you do it?" His hot breath tingled the pain in her face.

"If I knew—" She winced at the pain the words caused. "I still wouldn't tell you."

Talioth stared for a long moment.

Is that it? Will he let me go?

The marked one turned to Gralow with a grim curl of his lips and nodded.

Lia's eyes flicked to the side. Gralow held two knives, one short and straight, and the other curved with a slender tip. Her pulse quickened.

He stepped forward, touching the tips together. A faint metallic scrape covered the low hum of the crystal until he stopped and held the curved blade to her cheek. "Now it's time to have some fun."

WITH GUARDS CARRYING HER, Lia floated down the corridor of the mining complex. She tried to move her legs, but they didn't work. The door to the Garronts' barracks approached, blurry and shifting, but she couldn't tell which of the three of them was right. The guards carried her through the middle door.

She winced when they dropped her on an empty bed, but the jostle was no worse than the constant state of pain she was already in.

"Drink this." A man held out a vial. "The boss wants you able to work again, and this will speed your healing."

Lia held the object. Her mind told her to be wary of anything they gave her, but her resolve was tired of fighting. She downed the liquid.

The guards stomped out, leaving her alone in the empty barracks.

She lay her head back on the pillow, pressing her eyes shut and wishing the pain would go away. After a moment, a fuzzy sensation trickled through her body. She welcomed it. It made her tired, but the nerve endings that had been on fire mellowed. Soon, the haze took over, and she welcomed the tendrils of sleep that grasped for her.

"WHAT'S THIS? What do you think—"

"Whoa! What happened?

"Vekko, hold up. Can't you see she's—"

"I don't care! She skips a day of work and then takes my bed!"

Lia was only vaguely aware of the voices. Her eyes wouldn't open, but she heard the muddled shouts around her. Rough hands gripped her and pulled. She tumbled from the bed, landing on the hard cave floor.

She told herself to open her eyes and find her bed, but the pull of slumber was too strong. Whatever she had drank left her unable to wake. She drifted back to the blackness.

6

IMPROVEMENT

Her third morning waking in the barracks was Lia's roughest yet. She couldn't see out of her left eye. In a panic, she felt for it and learned that the swollen skin around it obstructed her vision.

Rustling bodies told her the others were waking. Anticipating a bucket of cold water helped her work to a sitting position.

A vague recollection of falling asleep on the floor came to her mind. She rubbed a hand along the post of her bunk, searching her memory for how she got into it. A bandage wrapped around her arm. She touched it gently, curious about when and how it had gotten there. A basin of water beside her bunk caught her eye. At first, she thought the red tinge was from the lighting of the room, but a closer inspection proved it was the true color. A bloody rag lay to the side.

Lia raised her eyes to scan the room. *Someone took care of me.* No one looked her way.

She stood, using her arm to steady the dizziness.

"You get one day," Chris barked, the attention startling her. "If you need it."

Lia's insides jumped with excitement. She could hardly imagine walking, much less a full day of arduous labor. Her limbs celebrated as she sat back on the side of her bed. Her mind embraced the idea of taking a full day to rest.

A mutter across the room drew her attention. Men looked at her with angled eyes. They grumbled to each other, shaking their heads.

Lia's stomach dropped. *Their teammate, once again missing out on a day of work.*

Through much effort, she stood again. "Thanks, but I can work." Her words felt like a knife in her gut, but she spotted some nods and raised eyebrows.

She finally consumed a full bowl of the sloppy porridge. Sitting on her own, she tried to imagine it was Ruby's stew as she swallowed each mouthful. The wishful thinking did little to help. She kept an eye on the Mountain Wolves' door, but Dayna's team had either already left or hadn't gotten up yet.

As she approached the tool storage, Vekko's words about her not being productive haunted her. She eyed the shovels. The work would be easier even without her injury. No need to break anything up, just digging up the rubble the others busted. She walked toward a pile of shovels when a whispered taunt reached her ears.

"Girls can't mine. We'll see if she realizes it yet."

She didn't even need to turn to see who it was. Vekko's pinched voice was unmistakable. She leaned forward and wrapped her hand around the smooth shaft of a pickaxe, lifting it to a smattering of laughs behind her back.

Her ears felt hot. She lifted the tool to her shoulder, flexing her arm. She passed a stationary Vekko and Jarno, knocking each with her shoulder. "You guys going to work today, or are you just going to stand there?"

Unexpected chuckles came from other men. "Yeah, Vekko," Waylon said, "you just gonna stand there?"

Lia managed a smile as she walked toward the mine, shuffling along with their team.

The Garronts passed through the main cavern with the boxes again and entered a new corridor. The passage was narrow and dark, lit with faint crystals and the two team lanterns they brought with them. Lia worked between Lowell and Waylon.

"You going to be alright?" Lowell asked. His gruff nature seemed to have softened.

Her forehead pinched. "Of course. I'm fine." She tried to sound confident, but inside, she trembled.

She readied the pickaxe and addressed the tunnel wall. Pulling the tool above her head in an arcing swing, she slammed the sharp tip into the stone. The impact jostled her arms, making them scream. She took three quick breaths, then swung again. A grimace flashed across her face. Her jaw ached and her body trembled. Small stones tumbled down the wall, collecting at her feet.

That's good, she thought. *One swing at a time. One rock at a time.*

She gave herself time to breathe and made sure her arms could rest, but she kept at it. Blow after blow, stone after stone, she continued to work. Her injuries maintained a steady thrum of pain until they dulled into a vague, numb ache.

"It's all right to take breaks."

The words jolted Lia out of her axe-swinging trance. She turned to Lowell. "Huh?"

The older man sat, leaning against the cave wall with his axe next to him. "Breaks? You've heard of them?" He extended a water skin.

Lia looked down the line of workers and found they all took a moment to pause from work. *How long was I going?* She puffed out air. "I guess I was lost in the motion."

"Yeah, I could tell."

She accepted the water and took a large drink. The cool wetness soothed her fatigued throat. She smacked her lips and exhaled before passing the water to Waylon.

Lia groaned as she lowered herself to the ground. "Now I'm in trouble. I'm not sure I'll be able to make it to my feet again." Lowell and she both laughed.

"I'm surprised you're out here," Lowell said. "Must have been a rough day yesterday."

"It wasn't the best, that's for sure. The team dislikes me enough already. I didn't want to give them another reason."

"What happened?"

Lia stared forward at the opposite wall of the mine shaft. After a long pause, she shook her head. "They wanted replies to questions I couldn't answer."

"Couldn't or wouldn't?"

"A little of both. Thank you, by the way."

Lowell cocked his head.

She motioned to the bandage on her arm. "I'm guessing you were the one who helped me last night?"

He raised his eyebrows and shook his head.

"You didn't take me to my bed? Clean my wounds? Put on these bandages?"

Lowell chuckled. "Not me." He nodded down the line.

Lia followed to see their leader, Chris, checking on each worker. "Really? Chris?"

Lowell nodded. "He spent an hour cleaning you up. Chris is a good man. He can be brusque, but he cares about the team."

She stared at their leader and his short, brown hair with a fresh appreciation.

". . . which is saying a lot, because few do."

"What do you mean?"

"Us Garronts are hopeless. Our men are old and weak. We're behind on our quota every week. It's just a matter of time before everyone here gets taken away."

"Taken away . . . as in, from the weekly reaping?"

He nodded. "If we get chosen, we're taken and probably killed. If we don't, we stay here forever and continue mining as slaves, eating mush and living dreadful lives. Even the best-case scenario—winning the golden pickaxe—still leaves us as slaves, just with better food."

"I see what you mean. How long have you been here?"

"Me? It's been . . . a year, probably. I stopped keeping track long ago."

"Where'd you come from?"

"We don't talk about that."

She frowned. "What? That's stupid. Come on."

He didn't answer.

"What about the others?" she pried. "What do you know?"

Lowell sighed. "Jarno and Vekko came together, along with some men on the other teams. They were from Failhill, a village in south Rynor—got here not long after I did. Chris was here already when I arrived. He's from Cairn—Thurman and Harold, too. Waylon's been here for around a season. I'm not sure where he came from."

"Not sure? Or can't remember?"

Lowell didn't answer.

"Why don't you talk about your pasts?"

Lowell stared at the ground for a long moment. "Too many feelings tied up in it. It's easier to shut it off and block it up—you know?"

"You're saying some of these guys have been here for years, but you don't even know about their lives?"

Lowell shrugged. "Not much."

"What do you do all the time? What do you talk about?"

"We mine. We talk about—well . . . mining. We pick on each other and talk trash about the other teams.

"How did all this happen? I mean . . . what brings you all here?"

"Raids mostly. The marked ones go out a couple times a season. Often they'll grab in a couple people from a farm, but sometimes they bring in entire villages—small ones tucked in corners of the Straiths."

"What about you?"

His mouth shut. A pensive furrow formed on his brow.

"Don't wall off your past. It's part of who you are."

He nodded but remained silent.

"Tell me."

"I'm from Bromhill," he said, finally. "I was an apothecary—ran my shop for thirty years."

"Bromhill? I can't believe they attacked there. Wouldn't that have raised a warning to Rynor?"

He shook his head. "I was up in the mountains. I take a trip at the end of each suether, hunting for herbs: antispurn, turnfoil root, toad-grass, all sorts of stuff. It's abundant at the change of seasons, and I can collect enough for the entire year. I had just settled around my fire one evening when they came out of nowhere. My wife, she—" He paused, chin quivering.

"You're married?"

He nodded then swallowed. "Marcy. We've been married for twenty-eight years. I think of her every day. She probably thinks wolves or bears killed me. It's better she thinks that than knows the truth."

Shuffling feet drew their attention to the corridor. Another team rounded the corner, carrying their tools and pushing carts.

"Sleeping in late today, Panzils?" Waylon taunted as the other team walked by.

"Don't even start, Waylon," one of the other team members quipped. "We could beat your output with one arm tied behind each of our backs."

"Or with one eye closed?" he joked back.

Lia noticed who Waylon's comment jabbed at. The man from the suspended cage walked with them. A gray bandage wrapped around his head, and a large patch pressed over his left eye. His thin limbs looked like he'd been a few days without eating. He let his head droop as he trudged forward, following the feet in front of him.

"Come on, Garronts," Chris said when the last of the Blood Panzils had passed. "Back to work."

Lia groaned as she stood. "Thanks for sharing, Lowell."

A faint smile washed across his face. "It feels good. You know . . . to talk about her. Thanks for asking."

Lia only understood how much she had needed the reprieve when she began working again. Fatigue returned. Her shoulders and arms ached with each swing of the axe. Her injuries from the day before stung with each exertion she made.

I should have taken the rest day.

As the day marched on, each strike into the rock seemed weaker. The number of breaths she took between hits increased, but her pride and stubborn work ethic kept her going. One time, her axe missed the rock, and her legs collapsed under the momentum of the tool. She cringed at the snickers down the tunnel from her team. It took her a minute to get back to her feet.

Not long later, after driving her axe into the wall, a hollow sound answered. A cluster of rocks tumbled down, but one looked different. It wasn't the gray stone she'd been chipping away at all day. The rock contained a smooth surface with angled facets. Lia held it close to her face to get a better look. Holding it to the light of the nearest lantern revealed a red reflection. *Is this . . . ?*

"You found one," Lowell breathed.

"This is a crystal?" Lia held it toward him.

The man nodded. "That's it. Take it to the box."

Lia stood still and stared into the shiny surface. "It's not glowing."

"That's just how they are. You need to go, Lia."

Lia's mind raced. *If they use these crystals to subdue us, could it be possible to use one against them? Would that be embracing the devion? But how do you get it to glow?*

"Whoa," Waylon said on her other side. "Chris, she's got one!"

The leader stood straight, then motioned to Thurman next to him. They stepped away from the wall and nodded their heads up the passage. "Come on, Lia. Let's go!"

Lia took quick steps forward, continuing to gaze into the chunk of raw mineral. "But what if we get ten of them? If we could fuse them like Talioth talked about, we could—"

"Lia!" Chris' commanding voice startled her from her trance. He gestured forward. "You need to run!"

She picked up her pace into a slow jog. "I don't understand. What is it that's such a big deal? Why do you have to get rid of them?"

"Just go!" Chris and Thurman stood aside to let her pass.

The jogging motion aggravated her wounds again. She winced as her body bounced hard against the cave floor.

"Move faster. Come on!"

Lia lengthened her stride. They passed another dark passage, and she glanced down it. *What am I running from?*

Pain shot down her leg, a sharp twinge that forced her to limp. A stitch formed in her side. The urgency of her teammates kept her moving, despite not knowing what she ran from.

At the next passage, a rancid scent wafted out of the darkness. Lia slowed. The smell reminded her of rotten flesh, like an animal carcass left to bake in the sun. "What is that?"

Chris pushed her forward. "Keep going."

A growl echoed through the passage, bouncing off the walls to surround her. The guttural rumble turned her insides watery as the glowing red crystals embedded in the walls dimmed.

Chris pulled on her arm, backpedaling as he held his axe toward the passage.

Lia's limp grew more pronounced. She hustled as fast as she could. The dimming lights spread up the corridor, overtaking their group. The rumble grew louder. Lia imagined a beast barreling up the shaft to run them down.

Lia's hope surged as she stumbled into the main cavern. Two teams turned in her direction, drawn by the change in lighting and the oppressive growling.

"Drop it in the box!" Chris shouted.

Lia surged forward, eyeing the red boxes. The longer she ran, the farther they seemed to be. The cavern grew dim. The stench pressed in on her as she stumbled forward, barely able to make her way. The boxes drew near. She stretched out her arm, pushing the crystal as far away from her as possible.

Her hand rested on the box, and she pressed the object through a slit on the top. The crystal dropped into the container, and she spun.

Thurman and Chris held up their pickaxes and turned toward the gloom. Like smoke blown away by the wind, the darkness dissipated. The crystals in the wall resumed their full glow, the growling sound stopped, and the smell faded.

Lia's eyes flicked from side to side, her chest heaving. "What . . . was that?" she asked between breaths.

"What are you Garronts trying to do?" someone from another team yelled, "get us all killed?"

Chris's and Thurman's shoulders relaxed. They ignored the taunt.

She turned her attention to the box. It was square at the top, but it continued with a long tube extending into the cave floor. "Where does the crystal go?"

Chris shrugged. "I don't know. Away. That's all that matters. Come on." He led them back toward their team's passage.

"Are you sure we want to head back in that direction?" Lia asked.

"We'll be fine, now."

His assurance did not make her feel comfortable. The thudding of her pulse pounded in her head. Her shoulders rose and fell. The sudden sprint left her wounds from the previous day aching and raw. Her limp was more pronounced on the much slower return trip.

When they disappeared into the side tunnel, Lia's nerves grew heightened. Only a faint trace of the odor remained, but it was enough to keep her on edge.

Chris turned to her with a red face and a hard edge to his voice. "What do you think you were doing?"

Lia jumped back at the sudden change.

"We told you to run, but you stood there!"

"I-I'm sorry," Lia sputtered. "I didn't realize what was going to happen."

"When I tell you to do something, you do it. All right?"

She nodded.

"I gave you the chance to take the day off, but *you* chose to be here."

"I wanted to—"

He pointed at her face. "If *you're* going to be here, you listen to what I say!"

"I'm sorry!" Lia held his stare for a long moment. "What is it we were running from?"

"It's bad luck to speak of them."

"Of what? How am I supposed to know why I'm running?"

"You run because I tell you to."

"What is it?" she shouted.

Chris glanced at Thurman, then back at Lia. He sighed. "We call them fiends. If you're carrying a crystal, they will find you and kill you in seconds—no exceptions."

"But, what—"

"Ah!" He silenced her with a raised finger. "That's enough." He motioned for them to continue. "Let's get back. Good job finding a crystal."

WHEN LIA DRAGGED her body back to the mining camp, she had doubts about her legs' ability to hold her. She tossed the pickaxe down with a thud. Most of the cuts she'd received the day before had reopened. Her bruises felt deep, like they ran through her body, punishing all parts of her tissue, muscles, and bones.

She trudged past the mess area with her sights set on the Garronts' door. When she reached the entrance, a heavy shoulder bumped into her, smooshing her against the wall.

"Watch where you're going, girl."

She couldn't even tell who it was. Her face scraped against the cave wall, opening wounds that had never healed in the first place. She pressed her hand against her face, trying to quell the sting. Her fingers came back bloody.

She stomped through the doorway, ignoring the barbed looks and laughter from the men. Her bed called to her. She weaved through the bunks and cavern columns to find it. She needed rest. Her body couldn't take much more. She came to a halt just before her bed. Vekko stood before it.

"Let's get something straight." He pointed at her face and stepped forward. His low voice sounded even more menacing than yelling. "You found a crystal today, but don't think that means you're pulling your weight. It means you got lucky. I carved out twice as much rock as you did. Odds are, my work will pay out for our team long before yours will, so *you* need to get your act together."

Lia nodded.

"If you're going to be on our team, pick your butt up when you're tired. Keep swinging your axe when you feel weak. Right now, you're telling me you're not capable of handling this. I don't care that you're a girl, but I care if you drag us down. If that happens, you better hope you're the first to go." His eyes narrowed to slits. "Otherwise, I'll kill you myself."

Lia sat on her bed after he left, her legs groaning as she dropped to the mattress. She placed her head in her hands. Her teeth clenched together as she thought about what Vekko said. She was doing the best she could. *Gralow tortured me yesterday, and I can't use the origine. What else am I supposed to do? What more do they want?* A flash of anger ran through her as she thought through the day. *I did have as much rock as Vekko! I may be injured and new, but I'm contributing as much as anyone else! What is he—?*

She inhaled and blew it out. The truth hit her.

They don't care about that. All they want is to paint me as a target so they're not the ones chosen in the reaping.

If she could get access to the origine, she could blow them all away. If she could get off the metal bands, she'd have a chance.

She clenched her teeth. A rush of heat surged through her body —anger. Not at the Marked Ones or the other people on her team, but at herself. She *could* do more.

Lia stood too quickly and had to steady herself against the bunk. Once her vision settled, she walked across the room.

Vekko and Jarno eyed her as she passed their bunk. She stared but continued past to exit into the main cavern. She heard a vague whisper of, "What's she doing?" from someone in the room.

The main cavern felt eerie. The light was no different from any other time, but the energy felt more subdued. Distant voices echoed out of barrack doors. Groups of men gathered around tables, talking, laughing, and breaking out cards. A few turned to look at her. She scanned the groups to see if Dayna might be out, but she had no luck. *She's probably already in bed.*

Ignoring the curious glances, Lia turned away from the tables and walked toward the boneyard. As much as Vekko's words hurt, she saw the truth in them. Her lungs used to have more capacity. Her arms used to be stronger. She'd been taking shortcuts in her training for the last year, and she hadn't even trained at all in weeks. She'd grown so used to relying on the origine that her fitness struggled without it. Swinging an axe all day wore out her shoulders, but even more, it raced her heart and left her out of breath.

She stopped at a broken mine cart. The wooden slats had splintered, and the wheels had been removed, lying sideways against it. Lia picked up a wheel. It was as wide as her hips and weighed as much as a sandbag back in Felting. She heaved it to her waist, then bounced her knees to raise it on her back.

Bruises on her shoulders screamed at her to drop it. Her legs felt like they would buckle under the added weight. Her exhausted arms balanced it with what little strength they had left.

Muttering voices picked up from the mess area. Lia caught a few cackles and calls for others to come and look. She didn't pay them any notice. With the wooden wheel on her shoulder, she walked to the edge of the lake. The surface was still, like glass. She scanned from side to side, taking in the size of the body of water and the narrow path that ran between it and the cave wall. It looked larger up close.

Her ears burned at the chatter behind her, but she didn't turn. *If I'm going to earn respect, I need to be the best of them. I need to be in better shape . . . and it starts now.*

Gritting her teeth through the aches in her body, she eyed the trail and began to jog.

7

TRUTH FOR THE KNIGHTS

Danik's hard-soled boots clacked across the stone floor of the Hall of the King. The emptiness of the chamber caused an echo that heightened his nerves. A lone lantern threw long shadows across the open chamber, bathing the throne on the dais in flickering orange light.

Nicolar walked with him, carrying an armload of necklaces like the ones they both wore. The leather cords hung with dull, red crystals clicking together at the bottom. A thin, black scarf—matching Danik's—ran around his neck, looping once, then falling over his shoulder. "How do you think they'll respond?" he asked.

"They'll be fine." Danik spoke with confidence, partly to convince himself.

"When they signed up, they didn't expect all of this. None of us did."

"What do they want?"

A pause filled the air along with stepping feet. "Money," Nicolar answered.

"And what do we offer?"

"Power."

"That's right, which leads to money. The rest are mere trifles to deal with."

Nicolar nodded. "Make sure to relate to the new guys. They're intimidated by you."

"Intimidated? Ha! That's stupid."

Nicolar's eyes narrowed as he glanced at him. "You *are* the king."

Danik's foot caught on the ground, making him stumble. The words still sounded strange to hear. "Yeah. I forget that sometimes."

"Talk with them. Help them feel that you're glad they're there and part of the group. They'll be more eager to fight for you if they feel included."

Danik nodded as Nicolar turned the handle on the door in the back corner of the room and pulled.

Heads turned toward him when Danik entered the cramped private chamber. A dozen men sat or stood around the chairs at one end while another group gathered near the drink table. Cedric leaned over the table of spirits with a drink and a bottle paused in mid-pour. A black scarf wrapped around his neck, and a red ring stained his nostrils.

"Go ahead, please," Danik said, flapping his hand. "Pour me one, too."

The room used to fit the original knights of power with no trouble, but the more people they added, the tighter the space grew. Danik could choose a dozen other larger rooms in the castle, but he enjoyed the atmosphere . . . and the abundant supply of drinks.

"What'd you find out in the mountains?" Broderick asked, standing from his chair. "This idiot won't say a word."

"Idiot?" Cedric barked. Liquid splashed to the floor as he jerked two glasses off the surface of the table. "I've been back for—"

"I asked Cedric to not say anything," Danik interrupted, accepting a glass. "I wanted to address it when we were all here." He took a long drink, smacking his lips as the liquor burned down his throat.

"Looks like everyone's here," Nicolar said.

Luc stood by a nearby chair, his bald head and bushy, black beard setting him apart from the crowd. "Luc," Danik extended his hand. "Good to see you again. How's training going?"

The muscular man shook his hand. "It's going great, Your Majesty. My control is better than before. Just ask Mirko; I beat his butt every time, now."

"Hey!" Mirko—the large, dark-skinned man next to Luc— narrowed his eyes. "I'm doing just fine."

"I trust you haven't added any more star tattoos yet," Danik said.

Luc ducked sheepishly. "No, not yet. But I'm ready to kill if you require it."

Danik took a few steps to a group he hadn't met yet. "You all are the new crop from the Red Quarter?"

A red-haired man in his early thirties took a half step forward. "Yes, Your Majesty. Still learning, but eager. I'm Monty."

"I'm Kauno," another greeted. Then Parkas. Then more names Danik forgot the moment they were spoken.

He kept a smile on his face as he turned to face the rest of the room, swallowing more of his drink to ease his nerves. No one spoke. The only sound in the room was the muted flutter of lantern flames.

"We're back, and it was a productive trip." Danik nodded to Nicolar.

The man with the messy goatee pulled the necklaces off his arm and distributed one to each person.

"Take care of these because they're the only ones you get."

"You brought us souvenirs?" Broderick chuckled.

Danik fingered the smooth crystal hanging at the end of his own necklace. "Not quite," he muttered. "For any of you not up on your history . . . a man named Talon Shadow founded the Shadow Knights around *three hundred* years ago after learning to use the origine. Eventually, he realized what we have—that the origine is limiting and devion is where true power lies. In the mountains, I discovered something about power. We have only scratched the surface of our abilities." He shook a balled fist in the air and scanned the room. "Do you want power?"

Mutters of affirmation rumbled from smiling faces.

"I can give it to you. I found something in the mountains that proves how great we can be."

"What is it?" Alton asked.

A grin grew on Danik's face. "I found Talon Shadow."

Blank looks stared back. "I'm sorry . . ." Broderick said. "What?"

"That's right. The three-hundred-year-old embracer of the devion is alive and kicking, and quite capable, despite his age."

Monty raised a hand. "Are you saying we can live three hundred years?"

Danik shrugged. "Possibly. It's not just Talon, either. There are sixty or seventy of them there, some from the original Shadow Knights group."

The red-haired new recruit smiled, his eyes lighting up. Excited chatter filled the room.

"What about these necklaces?" Luc asked, holding the end of his. "I'm guessing they do something?"

"Ah, yes, they do." Danik lifted the leather cord, holding the crystal out. He concentrated his focus and touched the power within. The dull red glowed, growing brighter. The room filled with an eerie light. Men close to him stepped back, holding a hand out to block the light.

"What are you doing?" Broderick asked.

"These crystals have unique powers that will help us in two ways. You know those pesky shadow knights who were supposed to be dead? They're still alive—most of them. They'll be coming for us, so we'll need to stay on our guard. While their feeble origine doesn't compare to the strength of the devion, they can still be dangerous." He shook his fingers, bouncing the glowing crystal. "Unless this is activated."

Broderick crept closer, staring at the light. "Does it . . . hurt them?"

"It blocks the origine."

Broderick's eyes grew. "Do you mean . . . ?"

"Meaning, when this is glowing, they can't use their power. But we can use ours."

Around the room, men slipped the necklaces over their heads, chuckling and grinning.

"How do we make it glow?" Luc asked.

"We'll work on that in training. And the other thing it helps with —" Danik glanced at Nicolar.

The other man's mouth formed a thin line. He nodded.

"After using the devion for a while, you'll notice a . . . pull of sorts."

Lines formed across several men's foreheads.

"The source of the power—the caverns in the Straith Mountains where we went—it draws you in. It's called Gharator Nilden, meaning life attractor."

"That's what we've been feeling." Broderick looked at Alton. "Both of us, for several days."

"Does it go away?" Alton asked.

Nicolar looked down and shuffled his feet.

Danik cleared his throat. "It doesn't, um . . . go away, that we know of."

A rumble grew in the room.

"But that's a benefit of these." He jangled the necklace again. "When you're wearing it, the pull is satisfied—meaning you're free to go wherever you want."

Luc cocked his head. "You're saying we might live for three hundred years, but we have to either stay in a cave in the mountains or wear one of these at all times?"

Danik swallowed a lump in his throat. "Yes."

Luc nodded. "I can live with that." Other men muttered in affirmation.

Relief rushed through Danik, but he had one more piece of bad news to weather. He gripped the end of his scarf. "Another thing I learned . . ." With slow deliberation, he unfurled the loops of the fabric. The men watched with raised eyebrows and cocked heads. When Danik removed the last wisp of fabric, gasps filled the room.

"What is that?" someone asked.

Nicolar and Cedric followed suit, whipping their scarves off of their necks and exposing the dark black marks that stained their throats.

"What happened?" another said.

"When the black mark first showed, I was afraid." Danik raised his chin, exposing his mark to everyone in the room. "I thought I was dying or poisoned. I covered it up with powder in shame."

Broderick and Alton touched their necks where a trained eye could discern the discoloration peeking from behind a thick layer of powder.

"In the mountains, I learned what this is." Danik emphasized his words. "Pure, unbridled power. Our bodies aren't made to handle the incredible abilities we wield. When we channel the devion, the raw energy we produce has to escape our bodies." He tapped the rough patch on his neck. "It escapes through here."

"We're all gonna have those black marks on our necks?" Luc asked.

Mirko crossed his arms. "Doesn't bother me."

Luc pushed him. "Sure. If I had skin as dark as yours, I wouldn't care, either."

Several grumbles rolled through the crowd.

Danik raised his hand and waited for their attention. "Yes." He swept his gaze through the room. "You *get* to have black marks on your necks."

A few mouths opened but didn't speak. Faces scrunched up with lines of curiosity.

"Weeks from now, these black marks we'll all share will be the envy of Felting. They will identify you as one of the Knights of Power. When you walk down the street, people will stop and stare in awe at who you are. Men will buy you drinks at the tavern. Women will want to be with you. Children will play in the squares with replica marks drawn on their necks out of soot." He touched his neck. "This mark will make you a legend, and everyone will know who you are. I will no longer hide it. I proudly display the proof of my power.

Broderick and Alton rubbed at their necks, smiles growing as dark marks emerged from the powder that had covered them.

The grumbling quieted. "When do we get them?" Luc asked.

"Any day, now," Nicolar answered.

"One more thing," Danik said. "Once you use the devion, there is no turning back."

The room quieted.

"If you decide the black marks and necklaces aren't for you. If you determine you don't want the incredible power and the ability to live for hundreds of years. If you try to give up your connection to the devion, you'll find your lifespan cut short . . . significantly."

"You mean we die?" someone asked.

Danik nodded, then swept the crowd with his eyes. "Anyone have any concerns?"

Heads shook, but no one spoke.

The tension in his arms relaxed. "Good." The smile that came to his face felt natural. "Now that I understand this power better, I've been thinking about what we use it for. The ability this crystal provides frees us like never before, and I say we use it."

Curious eyebrows raised around the room.

"What do you have in mind?" Broderick asked.

"Felting loves us. They've seen our power and welcomed us with open arms."

Luc raised a hand. "I thought unrest grew in the city?"

The hairs on Danik's arms prickled.

"All that talk about the trade economy and coin problems."

"The counterfeiting will be under control soon." Nicolar's declaration made several men jump. He glanced at Danik and nodded. "It's creating inflation issues, but we'll stamp it out."

"The arena games were a hit. They showed off our power. It gave the people entertainment. They loved the valcor, despite—" Danik stopped, unsure of where he wanted to go with the statement.

"Despite it not killing the shadow knights?" Luc finished.

Danik's eyes narrowed until he forced a smile. "Yes, despite that.

The rest of Feldor has yet to see our power, yet they support us because Felting is the capital. They'll fall in line. Tarphan is weak. I saved their king's life, and I can take it just as easily. Rynor is no different. With a half dozen of us, we can walk into Searis or Bromhill and force their allegiance. No one can stop us."

Wicked laughter filled the room.

Rankin raised a hand. "What about Norshewa? Will we take all four kingdoms?"

Danik paused until he shrugged. "Sure, we'll get to them, too." He gestured to the room. "We are the Knights of Power—a force without equal."

A hearty cheer sounded in response.

"We number twenty-five men, and I value every one of you. With this number, we'll be unstoppable. We'll train during the day until your skills are finely tuned. We'll meet here once a week as a group to celebrate our wins and discuss our next moves. For now"—he gestured to the drink table with his glass—"the night is young, and the liquor supply is vast. Help yourselves."

Merry laughter filled the room as men grabbed glasses and poured flagons. The sound of sloshing liquid filled the air. The newer recruits gave Danik a wide berth, nodding in deference as they passed him. The men who had been there for weeks acted more familiar.

Danik took a drink until a meaty slap hit him on the back and jostled the contents of his cup.

"Quite an accomplishment, doing all that you have in only a handful of weeks," Luc said, drink in hand. "Leaders usually do nothing but talk, but you back it up."

"Just wait," Danik said. "There's lots more to come. Fame. Riches. Power."

Luc nodded, his bushy beard hitting his chest. "I look forward to it."

Monty, the red-headed recruit, caught his eye as the man lifted a glass.

Danik stepped toward him. "So . . . Monty-from-the-Red-Quarter, what did you do before joining?"

The recruit's eyes widened for a moment. "What did I . . . ?"

"For work. How did you get by?"

His mouth seemed frozen. A low hum was all that snuck out.

Danik chuckled. "I know what goes on in areas of the Red Quarter."

Monty's body shifted but remained tense.

"It's all right. I don't care about whatever petty life you lived before this. It all pales compared to what we're doing as knights of power. Everyone deserves a chance to start fresh, right?"

A faint smile showed on Monty's face. "Yeah, I guess."

Danik raised his eyebrows, waiting for an answer.

"I . . . took things to get by."

"*Took* things, like . . . ?"

A sheen of sweat glistened on Monty's brow. "Weapons. Jewelry." He swallowed. "Coins."

Danik lifted his chin and stared down his nose. The red-haired man's chest expanded, growing along with the whites of his eyes. Danik puffed a laugh through his nose and grinned. "Relax. Like I said, you start fresh, here."

Monty's shoulders fell, releasing the tension they held. "Thank you, Your Majesty."

"What led you down that path?"

The man's hairy hand wiped the sweat off his forehead. "I had a job at Foley's Transport—the warehouse by the docks."

"I remember the name. Didn't it burn down?"

Monty nodded. "Ten years ago. I was out of work"—he snapped his finger—"like that. Had no family, so I didn't need much. I'm sure I could have found another job, but . . . that night, I saw a man carrying a rack of beef into a salt cellar." A grin formed on his face. "It was too easy. I never looked back." He tipped his glass, pouring a healthy portion of drink into his mouth.

"With the man . . . did you . . . ?"

"Kill him? Oh no. Just broke the cellar lock that night. Turns out the fool kept his change purse hidden behind a loose board in the cellar, too. I showed up for a bit of food and ended up buying some new outfits." Monty chuckled.

"So, you didn't kill him. Have you ever?"

Monty clammed up.

"Relax." Danik grew bolder at the sight of the other man's hesitation. "As a knight of power, you will be required to kill in service of the kingdom. I couldn't care less about your past squabbles, but I care if you know how to handle yourself."

"In that case . . ." Monty's eyes twinkled. "Yeah, I've killed. Plenty. I'm skilled at it. I'd sneak in at night, take what I wanted, and leave no witnesses if anyone spotted me." His body perked up, and his voice grew louder. "One time, I discovered a back room of a cobbler shop that had a box of silver bars. The gray-haired dolt stumbled in while I was cleaning him out. He didn't even cry out before my knife punctured his windpipe. Another time, I found a man decked out in full soldier gear. He had a shelf of bronze trinkets I wanted. I pounced from a shadow and struck him down." He straightened his tunic. "Yeah, you could say I know how to handle myself."

The pride with which Monty spoke left a twinge of guilt in Danik's gut. *Attacking unsuspecting people in their homes isn't the same as fighting enemies.* He considered the fact that he planned to attack peaceful cities—filled with unsuspecting people. *Is it different?*

"Often they freeze up and don't know what to do. This one time— it was about nine or ten years ago—I hit this house, but the idiot man and woman didn't even try to flee. It was like they expected me to show up or something. It was strange."

Danik's twinge of guilt morphed into a watery foreboding. *A man and a woman?*

"I shouldn't have hit the place at all—couldn't find even a copper pintid. All I left with was a handful of jerky."

Danik's throat felt stuffed with cotton. "And the people?"

Monty scoffed. "I didn't even have to fight them. A quick slice to their throats and they were down." He mimed a finger running across his neck, then followed with a burst of laughter.

A deep thud pounded in Danik's ears. "Did they have any children?"

"The couple?" Monty's eyes drifted to the ceiling. "I remember a comment about a son being away, or something like that. They insisted I kill them and leave."

Danik's breath grew ragged. He clenched fists at both sides.

"I remembered it because—it was odd. The hovel was filled with these—" He paused, his face contorting. "I don't know what you'd call them. They were miniature carvings of . . . houses, I guess."

Blood raged through Danik's veins, willing his body to lash out.

"They were carved out of something—I'm not even sure what. It felt creepy—these house models hanging around."

"They were gourds," Danik breathed.

Monty leaned in. "What?"

Danik spoke through gritted teeth, his breath seething through the gaps. "The carved houses . . . they were made out of gourds."

"Gourds?" Monty's face scrunched in question. "Yeah, I guess that could have been it. How did you know that? Did you—" He cut off mid-sentence. A tense moment hung in the air as the red-haired man's face drained of blood. "Did—did—did—" His words seemed stuck on his tongue.

Danik's chest puffed. He spoke deliberately. "I know . . . because those were my parents." His sword ripped from its sheath, metal screaming in the air. The devion flooded his body, heightening his senses and the strength of his limbs.

Monty attempted to counter the move, but his inexperience showed. He reached for the weapon hanging at his hip but fumbled instead.

A clean swing of Danik's blade cut through the man's neck, severing his head in a smooth motion. Blood splattered across the nearby men. Monty's body crumpled to the ground, and his head of red hair rolled as it hit the ground.

Danik's breath heaved as he spun. The room was silent. The other men's faces turned down, looking away.

"I'm sorry." Nicolar raised an eyebrow. "Your parents?"

"He killed them." A heavy catch sounded in Danik's throat.

Nicolar lifted his glass. "We didn't want Monty, anyway. Twenty-four men will be plenty."

Danik nodded, scanning the room. His heart continued to pound. "Yes . . . twenty-four will be plenty."

8

NO MORE HIDING

Danik stood at the head of the oval table with his hands on the back of the chair before him. Nicolar and Cedric paced the room on either side, passing the handful of royal guards who were little more than window dressing, given the power of the devion. All three knights of power wore their necklaces with the crystal pendants hanging in front of their chests.

Danik made eye contact with each high lord as they passed the double doors of the Advisors Council chamber. He kept his chin up, displaying the black stain on his neck for everyone to see. Kennith Stokes nearly tripped when he saw it. Marie Windridge gasped and set her hand on her chest. Magnus Hampton flinched. After the initial sighting, each entrant averted their eyes and said nothing.

Herman Miligan was the last to arrive, feet shuffling. His pale face implied he was still recovering from an illness. With his head cocked, he stared as he walked around the table and pointed to his own neck. "You've got something . . . here, Your Majesty."

Rebuking hisses sounded around the table.

He glanced around at the others. "What? There's some sort of black—"

Danik's laughter cut him off. "It's all right, Herman. Take a seat."

The High Lord of Justice eased into a chair, his eyes betraying his confusion.

"It's good to have you back, Your Majesty." Bilton's voice retained its usual confidence, despite Danik's black stain that should have left the man confused.

"Thank you, Geoffrey," Danik said. "And thank you all for joining me. I'll start by addressing this." He tapped the mark at the base of his neck. "You'll begin to see this on all the knights of power. What it is does not concern you. It's a sign of strength, identifying us for who we are. It will be proudly displayed, visible for anyone to see, and that's all you need to know."

He glanced at Cedric. The knight strolled passed the nearest balcony column and nodded at him, black stain showing.

"I learned a lot in my travels over the last couple of weeks. Most notably, I discovered the truth behind what the shadow knights were up to. The Norshewan heir that the valcor failed to kill had infiltrated the Shadow Knights organization and converted them to his cause."

A quiet rumble grew around the table.

"The knights had been working with Norshewa to overthrow the throne of Feldor." He shook his head. "I was in their midst and didn't even realize it. Traitors, every one."

Pinched expressions adorned the faces of the high lords. Hillegass leaned toward Windridge and muttered something under his breath.

Danik cringed but continued. "They attacked us out of nowhere in the mountains. We killed two of them."

"Veron?" Bilton asked. "Chelci?"

"No, but their daughter is taken care of." Guilt twisted his stomach, but he pushed it out of mind. "The rest remain alive—exiled and in hiding, waiting for their chance to attack again. They will come for us. They will assuredly come for me. We will station one knight of power with the royal guard at all times."

"I hear you have twenty-five knights now?" Quentin, the advisor, said.

"Twenty-four. One didn't work out." The memory of his parents' murderer stirred up his blood, but he kept his face composed as he sat. "Give me updates. How are things in Felting?" He glanced from side to side, waiting for the high lords to speak up. No one did. "Miligan, what's new in the justice department?"

The aging high lord covered a cough as he sat straighter. "Little change, Your Majesty. We had hoped that seeing criminals killed in the arena would discourage crime, but there doesn't seem to be an impact."

Hillegass laughed. "A starving man will steal to feed his family regardless of potential consequences."

A few nodded around the table.

"Either way," Miligan continued, "the dungeons are less crowded, which is a pleasant change. Unfortunately, we've seen a resurgence in child gangs."

"I wonder why," Windridge muttered.

Danik bristled. "Something to add, Marie?"

The High Lord of City Affairs stared at Danik, pausing as if weighing her words. "I believe . . . closing the orphanage was a mistake." She folded her hands on the oval table. Her erect posture did little to help her rise out of her chair. "These children are learning nothing except how to fight and thieve. No one cares for them. No one models good behavior. They're left to fend for themselves. If the goal is to nurture a new generation of criminals, then we should consider it a success."

Danik pressed the tips of his fingers together under the table, straining his muscles and willing his blood to calm.

"Merchants are complaining about it," Stokes added. "The gangs. We could use more constables patrolling the markets."

Danik tapped his chin. "If ragged children are the greatest worry we have, then I'd say Felting is in a pretty good spot." He smiled before his laugh pervaded the air. "Use the constables. Have them take any troublemakers off the streets. I hear there is plenty of room in the dungeons."

"Your Majesty," Nicolar said from the side of the room. "The dungeons would get them off the street, but that requires guards and food. They would remain a drain on the kingdom's resources. Perhaps it's worth considering a more permanent option?"

"Permanent, as in . . . ?"

Nicolar answered by raising an eyebrow.

Danik's blood turned cold as his suggestion became clear. "We're not monsters, Nicolar."

As the words left his mouth, his chest tightened. *I'm not a monster*, he reiterated. *I'm not.* He wouldn't kill orphans, but eliminating shadow knights was necessary. That was about survival.

Windridge squirmed in her seat.

"We will add more patrols." Bilton nodded. When no one else spoke up, he cleared his throat and continued. "As far as the army goes, we maintain our state of defensive readiness. If called upon to advance elsewhere, we will be ready . . . despite the lower-than-usual numbers of our forces."

"And with our twenty-five knights of power, we will not need as many," Danik added.

"Twenty-four," Nicolar interjected.

"That's right. Twenty-four." Danik swallowed, hoping the rush of blood didn't redden his face. He glanced down the table and lifted his eyebrows. "Who else?"

Magnus Hampton lifted a hand. "The state of the treasury is . . ." He waggled his hand. ". . . average, which is a marked improvement from where we were weeks ago. While not happy about the tax increases, people have accepted them. At a minimum, there are no more revocation requests from the guilds."

"That is encouraging," Danik said. "See, I told you the people just needed time. Good work, Hampton."

The High Lord of the Treasury returned a proud smile.

"However," Danik added. "I heard something else."

The smile faltered.

"I hear there is a counterfeit ring spreading false coins throughout Feldor and devaluing our currency."

Magnus' jaw tightened as his face froze.

"Copper, yes?"

Magnus nodded. "Pintid and tid. Thankfully, we've yet to find any argen or sol. We learned of it the day you left for the mountains."

"It's already driving up prices in the markets," Stokes added. "Merchants are trying to keep up with the inflation, and customers are furious."

"Who is responsible?" Danik asked.

"We don't know yet," Magnus said. "A crime syndicate from the warehouse district is our best guess, but . . . we don't have any leads. The stamps look identical."

"How do you know they're counterfeit?"

"The metal gives it away. We add ferric shavings to the coins from the treasury. A savvy merchant could check with a magnetized device, but most wouldn't bother taking the time even if they had one. We checked to make sure no molds are missing. All modern presses are under lock and guarded in the treasury's basement. Anything decommissioned has been dismantled and burned."

"What about your employees?" Danik asked. "Or the guards? Could any of them be the culprits?"

"It's possible, but most of them have been there for decades, and they live simple lives—ones that an infusion of coins would shine a harsh light on."

"Come by the constables' office tomorrow, Magnus," Miligan said. "They can help if they know what to look for."

Hampton nodded.

Danik scratched his chin. "It's not enough. We *must* put a stop to this." He turned. "Geoffrey, get some of your men and dig into it."

Bilton raised his eyebrows. "The army?"

Danik held his gaze, emphasizing his point. "This is critical. If the kingdom falls apart economically, we'll lose the remaining approval of the people. We can't let something like this ruin the progress we've made. Do you understand?"

The High Lord of Defense recovered. "Of course, Your Majesty. You can count on me."

A moment of silence lingered while Danik considered the problem of the coins.

Hillegass cleared his throat. "The Department of Trade set new goals for our export ratio with Tarphan and Rynor. We—"

"No need." Danik lifted a hand. "Trade is about to change, so your goals will be obsolete."

The high lord's eyes shifted to the other men around the table. "What do you mean? Change, how?"

"We have twenty-four knights who are more capable than any army that ever existed. I am no longer content to let this power sit unused while the rest of Terrenor ignores us. We don't need four separate kingdoms. We only need *one*, united and ruled by us, and the Knights of Power will make it happen!"

A nervous hum grew in the room.

"I'm sorry," Bilton said. "Are you declaring war on the other kingdoms?"

Danik exaggerated a nod. "I am."

"But . . ." Bilton looked around at the others while the hum built into muttering. "We barely have enough men in the army to defend ourselves, much less launch an assault against the rest of the continent. How would we—"

"The size of our army is of no concern," Danik said. "A dozen knights could cow a kingdom into submission."

Bilton leaned forward. "You've planned this out? You have an attack strategy? Only a fool would take on something like this without a proper plan and resources."

Danik clenched his jaw, his blood heating. "Of course, I've planned it. As you say . . . I would be 'a fool' not to. First, we'll head to Tarphan."

"King Constantine is weak and sickly," Miligan said. "Right? That should make their kingdom ripe for new leadership."

"He used to be weak," Danik said. "Poisoned by his advisor, until I saved his life. Constantine owes me everything. It will be simple to gain an audience for me and a handful of knights, then the choice will be up to him."

"Consent to our rule or die?" Bilton asked.

Danik shook his head. "We can't transition power and allow him to live. If he calls on his subjects to follow us, he can die in a quick and painless method. Otherwise . . . it will not be so pleasant for him. Either way, he must go."

Bilton nodded, appearing deep in thought. "What about Rynor? Bromhill may not be as welcoming, and they have those high walls to protect themselves."

Danik laughed. "Those pitiful walls may keep out your army, Geoffrey, but they'll do nothing against the Knights of Power. King Tomas insulted me weeks ago. I'll show him what sort of 'figurehead boy' runs this kingdom. He may not willingly meet with us when we show up, but he will relent."

"Then do you head north to Daratill?"

"Norshewa?" The king paused for a moment. "Possibly."

"I hear they're already amassing their army."

"It could prove more challenging, but . . . nothing we can't handle. We'll see where we are after conquering the other kingdoms. Who knows . . . maybe Norshewa will come to us."

"What does this accomplish?" High Lord Hillegass raised a wavering hand. "Why conquer these lands?"

Danik scanned the table, taking in all the eyes watching him and waiting on his word. "Because we can."

Hillegass opened his mouth, but no words followed.

"I am more powerful than any past ruler, and I'll show the other kingdoms what Danik Bannister is capable of. Rynor mocked my name. Tarphan used me to solve their problems. It's time for us to take charge."

A faint tug registered in Danik's chest, like a string wrapped around his heart pulling toward the window. He gulped a breath and turned his head. Through the open archways, past the balcony, the Straith Mountains loomed in the distance. Jagged peaks reached to the sky, topped with white blankets of snow. Peaks that hid a cavern filled with crystals.

He pressed against his chest, feeling the hard facets of the red crystal at the end of the leather necklace. The strength of the pull was nothing like it had been before he received the necklace, but it was there all the same.

"Sir?" Bilton pulled his attention back to the table. "Is everything all right?"

A clammy feeling filled Danik's hands. Sweat prickled the pores on his forehead. Swallowing the knot in his throat, he forced a smile. "Yes, of course. Everything is perfect."

9

ALLIES

Brixton's stomach turned as he walked up the long stone path lit by lanterns. The fountain in front of the house bubbled as merrily as it had when he'd first been to the old Marlow home many years before. The three-story building ahead flowed of polished stone, with steps leading to its front door.

He couldn't shake the memory of riding with his father to meet Chelci for the first time. He had been young, naïve, and selfish. The mistakes he made from that point forward had haunted him ever since. The years he'd spent hiding in the mountains hadn't helped, so it was time to try something new.

Mounting the steps made his hands sweat. He'd volunteered to help, but the gesture was easier to make in the safety of the Glade than when faced with actually doing it. With his heart in his throat, he clanked the knocker on the front door.

Brixton pulled at his tunic, then ran his hands through his hair. He gasped at the short length. *I'd almost forgotten.* Chelci cutting it had left a pile of hair on the floor that looked like a small mammal. He ran his hand over his face. Missing the beard that he had grown for years, the smooth skin felt naked under his fingertips.

A click and a groan preceded the large wooden door swinging open. Brixton dropped his hand and straightened his posture.

A woman appeared in the cracked doorway with raised eyebrows. Her dark hair was tied up in a bun, pulling back the wrinkles on her face. "Can I help you?" she asked.

"Yes." Brixton cleared his throat, thankful that the woman wasn't someone he recognized. "I have a matter to discuss with High Lord Bilton. Is he at home?"

"The high lord doesn't receive visitors at this hour. You'll need to come back tomorrow."

The door began to close until Brixton slapped his hand against it. The woman's eyes grew.

"I'm sorry," he said. "I don't mean to be forceful, but the matter is urgent and requires his immediate attention."

"I have no doubt." Her voice took on a harsh tone. "They're always urgent. And it will *still* be urgent when you see him tomorrow."

She pushed again on the door, and Brixton had to press harder to keep it from closing.

"Any trouble?" another voice said.

The woman looked over her shoulder. A man joined her and opened the door a crack wider, staring at Brixton. His brown beard speckled with gray, pulled down in an exaggerated frown. His thick neck and broad shoulders suggested he wasn't someone to mess with.

"He wants to see the high lord," the woman said, "and I told him to come back tomorrow during the daylight."

"It's important," Brixton added. "It can't wait until tomorrow."

The man's hand rested near his hip, drawing Brixton's eye to the sword hanging there.

"Back off," the man said, his voice a growl.

The door gradually closed, despite Brixton's weakening attempt to keep it open. "Tell him—" He grasped to think of something as the crack drew to a close. "Tell him . . . Wesley's betrayer is here!"

The pressure against the door stopped. A sliver of the man's face showed through the gap. "What does that mean?"

"Just tell him and let him decide! Trust me. He'll want to see me."

A pause caused his hope to surge. He kept a loose hand on the door, waiting for the verdict.

"Wait here," the man said after a long moment. He closed the door.

Brixton exhaled, letting the tension in his body melt away. Muted footsteps faded inside the manor. He tapped his feet on the stone pavers while he waited. The night air held a humid warmth, but a faint breeze kept it comfortable.

I can't believe I'm back here, he thought. Felting held so many memories for him: his schooling days in King's Academy, the time he spent courting Chelci, and his brief period as Commercial Envoy of Terrenor. He cringed at the memory of the crimes he'd committed and the way he'd used others for his own advancement.

No more.

The forgiveness Veron and the leaders of Feldor showed him was difficult to swallow. He tried for years to accept it and move on, but it took his time in the mountains to realize his life could still have a purpose.

What if Bilton won't see me? An even scarier thought turned his stomach. *What if he's still holding on to what I've done in the past?*

A sound at the door turned him back around. The knob twisted, and the wooden barrier swung open, revealing the woman again.

"The high lord will see you now," she said, stepping out of the way and keeping her eyes on Brixton's feet.

Brixton forced a smile, but his nerves didn't feel relieved at the victory.

He entered the foyer, the familiar grand room where he'd first met Chelci and her family. He followed the woman through the corridor to enter the sitting room, where Geoffrey Bilton stood on the far side.

The high lord wore a plush, blue robe tied with a sash. His chin lifted high, barely allowing Brixton to see his narrowed eyes. He stared, shadows from his still body flickering across the room from the light of the lone lantern hanging on the wall.

The servant ducked her head and backed out of the room.

"When they told me, I didn't believe it could be you, but I had to see it with my own eyes." Bilton didn't move.

Brixton took a cautious step forward, raising a hand. "I know you and I have had our differences over the years. I probably deserved death for what I did, but somehow I remain alive. I'm sure you still hate me, but I hope you will hear me out."

Bilton shifted his weight, the hilt of a dagger poking out of the folds of his robe. "What do you want?"

"I'm not here for myself. I'm here because we have mutual friends who need your help. Friends that you helped a few weeks ago." Brixton spoke the last words slowly, adding emphasis. His eyes flicked to make sure no servants lingered in the shadows. "If you care about their cause, we need to speak." His heart pounded as he waited for a response.

The high lord pursed his lips. "Who?"

Brixton leaned forward and whispered, "Veron."

Bilton's chest expanded as he sucked in air. Finally, he gave a slow nod.

"Can we speak privately?"

"I don't like this." Chelci paced the training room, stopping to peer out the window each time she passed the door. "It shouldn't take this long. There's no guarantee Bilton won't turn us in. He could overpower Brixton and show up here with a dozen of Danik's men and their glowing crystals. We should have gone ourselves."

"Be patient," Veron said, tenser than he cared to admit. "We're too well known to go ourselves. Brixton can handle it. Bilton won't turn us in, even though he acted like he was on Danik's side."

"He stuck out his neck for us earlier," Raiyn said. "He's the one who got us into the ball and set the plan in motion to rescue Veron."

Chelci set her hands on her hips. "The ball where you were nearly captured? The plan for moving Veron that didn't work?"

"Well . . ." Raiyn shrugged. "I spoke with him. He seems to be on our side."

"Lia felt the same way." Veron nodded while a tense quiet hung in the room. "She was convinced, so I think we should trust him."

Chelci walked again, wringing her hands out.

Veron chuckled. "Raiyn. Do you know where Chelci and I met?"

"At this house, right?" the young knight replied. "You were a servant?"

"How'd you know?"

"Lia told me, the night we first met with Bilton."

Veron pointed at Raiyn's feet in the center of the room. "It was here, in fact. I stumbled upon her training. She was the most amazing thing I'd ever seen. Beautiful. Determined. Fierce. She swept me away."

Chelci flashed a tender smile at Veron that made butterflies flap in his chest.

"She still does every time I look at her."

Footsteps outside the door reached his ears. Veron spun, muscles rigid. He pulled his sword and stood in line with Raiyn and Chelci, tucked into the deep shadows at the far end of the room. Light danced on the window from outside as the steps grew closer.

"Be ready," Chelci said, the leather grip of her sword creaking.

Veron dropped into a crouch, sword up in dragon stance.

The door opened with a jerk. Geoffrey Bilton entered first, carrying a lantern, and he waved Brixton in after him. "We should be safe to talk in here." Bilton set the lantern on a wall hook, but his hand paused.

Veron held his breath, feeling his heart thump in his chest. The flickering flame rustled the silent air, thick with tension.

The high lord spun, twirling his robe and pulling out a knife.

Veron held his stance, muscles tense and ready to pounce.

Raiyn took a half step forward and raised a hand. "High Lord Bilton, it's us."

The strain on Bilton's face melted. His shoulders relaxed, and he put up his weapon. "I wasn't sure if I'd ever see you all again. Chelci, it's good to see that you're safe. I trust that book led you to her?"

"It did," Veron said. "Thank you for your help at the ball. I heard how you stuck your neck out for me."

"You're welcome. Danik was furious about your escape. Now, he's telling everyone you're all traitors to Feldor, trying to help Norshewa take over."

Raiyn groaned. "Yeah, that sounds like what he'd say."

"I heard about Lia." Bilton's face turned down, and the room grew silent. "I'm so sorry."

"What else is Danik saying?" Veron asked, pushing the thought of his lost daughter away.

"They have these black marks on their necks."

"From the devion," Chelci said. "It has something to do with how the power interacts with their bodies." She chuckled. "I'd bet Danik didn't know about that before he dove in."

"He has twenty-four knights of power now."

"Twenty-four," Chelci breathed, turning to Veron. "How do we stop a group that size?"

Veron's heart sank. "I don't know, especially now that they have those crystals."

"What are those, by the way?" Bilton asked. "Danik said nothing about them."

"They block the origine. *They* can still use the devion, but *our* power is inaccessible."

The high lord's eyes grew. "Yeah, that would be a problem. His new goal is to take over Terrenor."

"Like Bale?"

"Sounds very similar. He doesn't plan to use the army though—at least not primarily. He wants to use the knights for more strategic strikes. He thinks he can force their surrender without having a battle."

"And he's probably right," Veron said. "Twenty-four devion-powered fighters could do just about anything. Does he trust the army?"

Bilton blew out a long breath. "I *think* so, but it's easier for him to rely on the loyalty of a couple dozen men. One or two of them turning would be snuffed out. If I were to turn with a few of my captains, the rest of the army would follow us. And devion or not, fighting against the numbers of the Feldor army would be a challenge, even for Danik.

Veron frowned. "You may be surprised. What about allies for us?"

"I'm not sure. Tienn doesn't seem to be supportive of Danik. I can't tell about Lorranis or Karad. Baron Devenish in Karondir is his most vocal opponent."

"Rodrick always was a good friend to us. That's great to hear. How quickly is Danik planning to act?"

"He didn't say. I got the impression some of the newer knights need a few more weeks to train before they're ready to go anywhere. But Danik was interested in acting sooner rather than later." Bilton raised his eyebrows. "So, what's your plan? Are you all trying to stop him?"

Veron turned to Chelci. The grim look on her face matched how he felt. "We're trying," he said. "We have to try."

"Any thoughts on how to get to him?" Bilton asked.

"That's why we're here. We must find an element of surprise."

"What do you mean?"

"We can't take them in combat. Not only do they outnumber us, but if they block the origine, we're no different from ordinary citizens."

"Well—" Bilton started. "I don't know about ordinary citizens. You *have* trained for years, even without the origine."

"Still . . ." Veron continued. "Against the devion, it's nothing. Can you think of anywhere Danik or his knights are going to be? Somewhere we could get a jump on them? Or somewhere that they have to take off those necklaces?"

Bilton held his chin while his eyes drifted to the wall. "I don't know about the necklaces. I'm guessing they sleep and even bathe with them on. If we plotted out a few places where they'd travel, you could lie in wait and get the jump on them."

"If they're not expecting it, we could take out a couple," Veron said.

"But no more than that," Chelci finished. "What if we targeted Danik?"

"The guys he's with are ruthless," Bilton said. "I'd guess if we kill Danik, Nicolar and those others would swoop right in and take his place."

"I agree," Veron said. "We need to get them all at once."

"Danik has guards from his knights on him at all times, not just the usual royal guards—even when he's sleeping."

Veron frowned. "Anything else?"

Bilton pressed his lips together, then shook his head. "I'm not sure. Let me give it some thought. I have a few people I trust, too. I'll talk with them and see what I can put together."

"All right," Veron said. "We'll wait on word from you. If you come up with any ideas or anything we can do, let us know."

The high lord's brow wrinkled. "There is something I could use some help with, if any of you are available."

"What do you need?"

"There's a counterfeiting ring in Felting wreaking havoc on the economy. High Lord Hampton can't figure it out, and Danik is furious."

"That's a good thing, right?" Raiyn smiled. "Danik being upset?"

"Yes, but this is hurting the people of the city. Market prices are skyrocketing. The average person can barely afford the basic necessities anymore. Inflation is hurting everyone, the lower class most of all. Danik cares because stability means cheerful people, and unrest leads to revolt. Although we have different motives, our goals align, in this case."

"How can we assist?" Chelci asked.

"I have a lead to follow up on, but I imagine it could involve some . . . nighttime surveillance, which is not my strongest suit if there are any building-climbing or roof-jumping activities. If one of you with your origine power could join me . . . ?"

"I can help," Raiyn said. "I can try, at least. I'm not as experienced as either of these two, but . . . I'd love to pitch in."

"He's good," Veron added. "He can do it."

Bilton nodded. "Great. I'll see what I can find out about Danik and his men. Raiyn, why don't you come back tomorrow afternoon?"

The knight nodded.

"Do what you can to help, Raiyn," Veron said, "but make sure no one recognizes you."

"I will," Raiyn replied.

"If a knight of power identifies you, there will be no running away. He'll activate his crystal and will have you in chains as fast as you can blink."

"Don't worry. No one will see me."

10

LIFE IN A TEAM

The soreness remained, but at the end of Lia's fourth day in the mines, some of it had lessened. Despite the improvement, her body still had progress to make. Her wounds from her time with Gralow still cracked and bled whenever she strained them or scraped something against a fresh scab. Her legs and arms felt weak from an entire day of hard labor. To add insult, dirt from the mines and the constant bleeding gave her clothes a thick layer of blood and dirt.

She tossed her pickaxe down in the tool storage, thankful to be done with the mines for the day. However, she was not done with work. The boneyard at the other side of the cavern called her attention. She followed her team past the mess area. When she was about to continue past their door, Chris waved his arms to usher everyone inside the barracks.

"Team meeting, everyone," he ordered, leaving little room for debate.

Lia sighed with relief. *No workout yet.* She entered the barracks and wound her way through to sit on her bed.

"Tomorrow is Weekterm," Chris said once everyone had arrived. "That means quotas are due."

"There's no way we're getting nine more by tomorrow," a man named Stewart whined. "Why should we even try?"

"Are you willing to offer yourself to be reaped?"

Chris' stare made the other man shrink back.

"Any of you?" He turned to take in the entire room. "Anyone want to volunteer to be the next to go so you can take the day off tomorrow?"

No one said a word.

"I didn't think so. We're going to give it our best, and we're going to do that because we can. We may not get nine, but if we don't, it won't be because one of us gave up. Tonight, you're bathing. You all reek, and I'm tired of being around your stench."

Jarno raised a hand. "I'll help the new teammate. I can show her how it's done."

Lia's stomach turned as a few men laughed.

A pungent smell caught her attention. Being near the latrine, she had grown accustomed to it, but this seemed stronger, closer. She wrinkled her nose and sniffed as she leaned over her bed. *What is it? Maybe*—"Ugh!" She recoiled from a yellow spot on her pillow. The musty smell now contained a fresh layer of urine. She looked across the barracks and noticed a few heads turn away and snicker.

Her blood boiled. She fought to keep herself from stomping through the room, demanding to know who did it. *No, I won't give them the satisfaction.* Pinching the pillow by the corner, she lifted it off her bed and tossed it on the floor. The pillow on the empty bunk above hers looked clean. She held it to her nose. *Much better.* She tossed it on her bed.

Jarno paused by her bed and made a show of removing his shirt. "What do you say, dear? You ready to get clean?"

Lia's only reply was to walk toward the exit to the barracks. His hold on her arm stopped her.

"Sorry about the pillow. I heard someone saying how they needed to go but couldn't make it to the latrine. You know how it can be."

She wanted to smack him in his lopsided grin. Instead, she jerked her arm away and continued toward the door, his laughter following her.

She took a deep breath when she exited the barracks, thankful to be out of the dirty, sweaty, and urine-filled room. The cart wheel called her name, resting where she'd dropped it the day before. She lifted it to her shoulders and began her run.

Each step felt labored. Lungs struggled to find oxygen. Shoulders drooped. Her back hunched. She fought to keep her head and chest up. Her legs threatened to collapse, but she kept them moving. After the first lap around the lake, she spotted several figures looking her way from the tables. She eyed the trail, then proceeded on another lap. By the time she finished the third, her legs could barely function. She worried she would tumble into the lake and not have the strength to pull herself out.

Her jog turned into a walk. She stumbled to the busted cart and dropped the wheel off her back to the ground. It thudded, then rolled to a stop. Lia lifted her arms, extending them in a stretch. She angled them, pulling against each side of her body.

The thought of her bed felt inviting. Even the chairs in the mess area would be a welcome relief. She took a step in that direction until she stopped. The memory of Vekko trying to shame her stuck in her mind. She looked back at the cart wheel for a long moment. She breathed in, then blew out a long breath of air.

I must be an idiot to do all of this.

She stepped back to the wheel. Setting her feet apart, she squared her shoulders and rested her hands on each side of the heavy object. She took a deep breath, then lifted, standing full and pulling the wheel to her hips. Pausing, she bounced her legs and lifted the wheel above her head, pressing until her arms fully extended. "Gah!" she yelled before lowering the wheel back to her hips, then down to the ground.

She lifted it again: to her hips, above her head, then back to the ground. Over and over, she repeated the motion. Her heart thumped faster and faster. Already tired from the run, her legs burned. Pressing the wheel above her head took more and more effort. Her body begged her to take longer between efforts, but she kept pushing. She breathed through the moves, ignoring the discomfort of her pounding pulse.

After countless repetitions, she pressed the wheel above her head, but it wouldn't move. The heavy wooden object hovered just off her head with her elbows bent. She tried to straighten them, but the wheel wouldn't lift. Her arms felt dead, drained of any power that remained. A low roar grew in her chest, then built through her throat. It clawed its way out of her mouth as the wheel creeped higher. Her elbows straightened. With a final growl, she reached full extension.

An exhausted smile crept over her face. She dropped the wheel, letting it clatter against the other broken pieces of wood. She bent over, resting her hands on her knees while she sucked in air. Her eyes closed, waiting for her pulse to settle. When she straightened, she caught several heads looking away from where people sat around the tables.

Sweat mixed with dirt and blood across her face and arms. Lia wiped it out of her eyes as she walked toward the mess area. She found an empty table and sat while her heart continued to recover.

"You must be thirsty after that." Lowell approached, carrying a flask.

Lia nodded, accepting the container. She gulped the water, letting the liquid fill her exhausted body.

"Is the mining not enough of a challenge?"

She frowned. "What do you mean?"

"I'm worn out every day. The last thing I want to do is more work, but you"—he pointed toward the lake—"you're running and lifting. I can't imagine having that much energy left over."

She laughed. "It's not extra energy, believe me."

"Why do you do it?"

She paused, staring at the table.

Why?

The question was simple, yet critical.

What am I trying to do? Why am I training like this?

"The men say I'm not contributing," she said. "Even though I'm doing as much as them."

"So say something."

She shook her head. "It wouldn't matter; they already know it. Instead, I'm going to be the best one on the team."

He chuckled.

"Plus, I haven't given up hope of getting out of here. I have a family out there somewhere, and Raiyn. I miss them all. I haven't always been the best daughter or the kindest person. I was only just recently making amends for that, and now I'm here—stuck. But I have more to do."

"You want to get to your family again."

She nodded. "But also . . . we were working toward something—something important. It's as critical now as it's ever been, and I need to help. But to do that, I need to survive." She looked toward the lake. "And if the word is I'm the weak link, I won't make it long."

"You look to be in good shape. Even so, your body's still getting used to what we do. It will improve in time. Plus, you had those injuries—"

"Excuses don't help. I need to stay alive, and to do that—at the moment—I need to find crystals."

Lowell leaned back. "So you have a reason for all of this. You're training to be a better miner."

She shrugged. "Basically, yes."

He chuckled. "We all thought you'd snapped—gone crazy."

She smiled. "There may be some of that going on, too." She scanned the room. "So tell me more about this place. What would it take for someone to break out of here?"

A frown formed. "No one breaks out. You remember Penner?"

"The guy in the cage?"

He nodded. "He tried—took a lantern and searched the caves, looking for a way out. The glowing crystals don't extend past the area we've excavated, and his lantern oil soon ran out. Stayed out there in the dark for two full days until marked ones found him."

"And his team took one of his eyes."

"He left the Panzils high and dry. They had to keep up their team quota without him, but they didn't make it—lost a good miner that week. The punishments are to keep people from trying to leave because it's the ones left behind who pay the price."

"What if everyone left at once? One big escape?"

"How?" He shrugged. "The caves don't lead anywhere. That gate's the only way out, and it's locked."

"But there's a key."

"Have you seen what these marked ones can do? How fast they can move?"

Lia's shoulders slumped. "Yeah."

"Even if you somehow steal the keys from Rasmill, there are always guards posted outside the gate. You roll that thing open, and you'll be dead before you know who stabbed you."

"What about the crystals?"

"What about them?"

"They give the marked ones power. Has anyone tried to use them in any way?"

He shook his head. "We get rid of them as soon as we can."

"Talioth said they needed ten to fuse them. I guess that's what makes them glow and gives them power?"

Lowell shrugged. "I don't know anything about that, but good luck collecting that many without getting killed by the fiends."

Lia leaned forward. "Tell me about them."

He shook his head. "We don't talk about them."

"Argh," she groaned. "Why not? What are they? Where do they come from?"

He didn't answer.

"At least tell me this—"

His raised hand stopped her. "It's no good." He stood and nodded toward the barracks. "I'm going to head in. I don't know about you, but I could use some sleep."

Lia sighed but nodded. She moved to follow Lowell when a voice stopped her.

"Lia?"

A smile crossed her face as her fellow shadow knight walked between the tables toward her. "Dayna!" They met in a tight embrace. She ignored the sharp pain where the hug pulled at her partially healed injuries. "I thought you might be asleep."

"I have been every other night at this point. Did I hear you were out here training?"

A rush of warmth filled Lia's face.

"Did something I teach make it through to you?"

"Don't rub it in." Lia laughed then paused as she looked toward the barracks. "How's your team been?"

Dayna's face turned down. "They've been . . ." She looked over her shoulder. "All right."

Lia caught the hesitation. "Come on. Walk with me." Lia led the way past the tables toward the main gates. When they arrived at the tool storage yard, she tried again. "So, how are they, really?"

"Ugh, they're awful!"

"Mine, too!"

"They trip me and push me around. They even piled a bunch of crushed rocks in my bed yesterday."

"Someone peed on my pillow."

Dayna's face contorted. "Disgusting! Is that why you're out there training? To get away?"

Lia sighed. "Everyone says I'm the worst on the team, even though I don't think I am. Our team is struggling and, without the origine, it makes me a target. I almost got taken out by one of those fiends yesterday."

"I heard about that."

"Do you know what they are?"

Dayna shook her head. "Not much. Just that they're drawn to the raw crystals—the smell of the mineral, I think."

"Interesting. Not the glowing ones, though? Those don't bother them?"

Dayna shrugged. "I guess not. That's why you have to get rid of them as soon as you find one. They say there are dozens of the monsters lying in wait in the darkness."

"This place is strange," Lia said. "I wish I understood more about the marked ones and these crystals."

"Thanks for coming to find us."

Lia blushed.

"Last I remembered, you were running off with that idiot, leaving the Shadow Knights behind."

"Ugh. Don't remind me."

"Then you return and try to save us. Great job killing that marked one in Felting, by the way. Next thing I know, you show up in the barren mountains and rescue us."

"It was my father and Raiyn, too."

Dayna held her eyes. "Thank you, Lia."

She nodded. "I, uh . . . I saw you get stabbed. Did they let you heal?"

"Yeah, after the others left, the marked ones lowered their crystals for a moment to let me heal. It's strange. It's like they want us dead but prefer us alive and captured. I haven't quite figured it out. I was lucky none of that debris landed on me. How about you?"

"Not sure if you were conscious at the time or not, but I was the one who brought down the column."

"Really?"

"I busted it with a hammer and the ceiling fell."

"It didn't . . . crush you?"

"Eh . . . it kind of did."

Dayna raised an eyebrow.

"Do you remember that conversation we had in the common room not long before I left Felting?"

Her eyes floated up and to the side as if searching the recesses of her brain. "The one about your parents fighting Bale?"

Lia nodded. "Do you remember what you said about the pure connection?"

"I mentioned how—" Her words stopped and her eyes widened. "Did you find it?"

Lia's mouth pulled up at the edge. "I think so. I was wiped out and about to die. Then, suddenly I was filled with origine, bursting with it. It was incredible. I expected to be dead, but I wasn't. I pushed my way out of the rubble."

"What caused it?"

"Sacrifice, I think. In Norshewa, my father was willing to die for my mother. I was willing to die to save the others. That's when it started." She gestured to the glowing crystals around the cave. "Not that it would even do any good here. I lost it as soon as Talioth came closer with his glowing necklace. Honestly, it feels hopeless."

"Hey." Dayna shook her on the shoulder. "Don't give me that."

Lia's shoulders slumped. "While I was out there lifting that wheel, I was thinking . . . doing well here just means staying a slave for longer. There's no way out, so does it matter?"

"Hey, I thought I was going to die weeks ago, but then you somehow appeared. I may not have made it, but six of our group did. Sure, things look bleak here, but you never know who might come through those gates."

Lia shrugged. "I guess. I assume the rest of the knights think we're dead, though. They're not likely to be showing up."

"Don't give up, Lia. Keep going. Keep trying." Dayna nodded toward the lake. "You want company for the training tomorrow? I could probably use it, too."

Lia smiled and then nodded. "Yeah, that would be great."

11

WEEKLY REAPING

"One hour to go," Chris called down the line. "Come on, Garronts. We need five more!"

Lia wiped her brow with the back of her hand, then turned to Lowell. "Is that possible?"

"Possible?" Lowell replied. "Yes. Likely? No."

She pounded her axe into the wall. "How do they decide who to take?"

"Rasmill makes the final decision, but he's always talking with the team leaders for input."

"Chris decides who dies, then?"

Lowell nodded. "He has a say in it. It's based on who fits in with the team and—of course—output."

"Great," Lia muttered.

"Hey, at least you found one this week. I worked all week, but I haven't brought in any."

Lia's stomach turned. She exhaled a long breath. *What's the point?*

Her legs were exhausted, and her arms ached. Despite the pains, she lifted the pickaxe and continued on her task, the never-ending chipping at the cave wall.

With only one hour left, their team quota seemed hopeless. Her swings lessened in power. Her rests between strikes grew longer. She entertained what it would be like to stop for the day. Soon, the only thing that kept her going was the men on either side who continued to work.

A chunk fell from her wall after a solid hit, and a different reflection caught her eye. *A crystal!*

She picked it up and studied it to make sure. Memories of the fiend flooded into her mind, spiking her adrenaline.

"Lowell," she whispered.

The man turned, and she tossed the mineral to him. "Go!"

He caught it with wide eyes.

"I got one!" Stewart's voice called down the line.

Lia spun and raised her hand. "Lowell has one, too!"

"Let's go!" Chris called, pulling Thurman with him like before. "Both of you!"

Lowell held the crystal and stared at her. His mouth parted, but he said nothing. After a beat, his mouth pulled up in a half smile, and his eye twinkled. He dropped his axe and ran, hot on Stewart's heels.

"Two more down," Lia muttered. After a smile, she groaned. She could slack off for an unachievable five crystals, but only needing three more was possible—especially considering it might save someone's life. She lifted her axe again.

Lia worked along with the others, chipping and sweating until their mining shift was done. Her and Stewart's late finds were encouraging, but the team failed to add any more crystals for the remainder of their day. Spirits were low when Chris called them off the line and ordered them to head back.

The Garronts were the last team back to camp. The other teams watched as they sloughed their way forward with drooping shoulders and bent necks.

"Looks like the birds failed for another week," someone quipped from where the Valcors gathered.

Lia walked with her team to the last table. She caught Dayna's eyes across the room. The other knight's face turned down.

"Now that we're all here . . ." Rasmill paused to bring attention to their team's late arrival. ". . . we can begin the reaping."

The conversations around the tables faded. The tension built, like a thick fog hanging over the teams.

"With forty-three crystals mined this week—"

A hoot burst from a member of Team Valcor.

"—the golden pickaxe remains with the Valcors. Nice work, Bronson."

Their team burst into cheers. High fives slapped around, and several men hit their team leader on the back. The rest of the teams sat in stony silence.

"Team Blood Panzil took second with thirty-three."

A less enthusiastic celebration rose from the team sitting behind the Valcors.

"Bears came in next at thirty, skirting past their team goal of twenty-nine." Rasmill turned to the last two teams. "But the others were not so lucky."

Lia's stomach churned. The men on her team fidgeted while most of the room looked either at them or the Wolves.

"The Garronts missed their quota by three crystals. As punishment, you must surrender one of your members for the reaping. This week's sacrifice is . . ."

Lia's heart pounded in her chest. Her hands felt cold and clammy.

"Lowell."

She gasped and jerked her head. The kind, old man bobbed his head in quiet acceptance. His thin, gray hair bounced along with the motion.

The rest of the crowd muttered. Their conversations formed a dull background drone, but Lia focused on him. A faint glimmer of a tear fell from the corner of his eye. She imagined his wife, Marcy, still holding onto hope that he might return one day. She would never know that her wish had turned impossible. As much as Lia hated to see him chosen, she breathed a faint sigh of relief that it wasn't her.

"Dayna."

The name of her friend startled her from her reverie. Lia turned to the rest of the group and found everyone looking at the other shadow knight.

Rasmill continued, "If you all want to avoid two people chosen in the future, you need to do better work in the mines."

Wait! What?

"Lowell and Dayna, come with us."

This can't be happening!

Rasmill's three other guards wove through the crowd to escort the two chosen workers. Dayna stumbled forward, held in the firm grip of one of the men.

"No!" Lia yelled, turning heads in her direction. She surged forward and hit the guard. His devion-powered reflexes batted away her attack, leaving her flailing her arms through the air.

"Lia," Rasmill said, "I almost forgot. Talioth asked for you to come, too."

She stopped her attack and dropped her jaw. "What?"

His lips twisted into a sneer. "He wants you to watch."

THE FARTHER along the passages they walked, the more Lia's stomach sank. Although she wished for something different, their eventual destination grew apparent. When they rounded the corner to the room with the large crystal, Talioth and a dozen marked ones waited on them.

Lowell stared agape at the black pit underneath the crystal, but Dayna's disinterested eyes gave away that she'd been there before.

"Welcome to the Siphon Chamber." Talioth gestured. "Lia, it's good to have you back."

Her eyes flicked to the end of the room where the metal rings lay fixed in the stone.

"Did you miss it? You've been wanting to return, haven't you?"

She stared at him, blood running hot through her veins.

"You know, we didn't even learn how to siphon until around a hundred years ago. It was by accident, in fact. We were threatening a worker with this pit when it just kind of happened. It was a lucky thing because our power had dwindled dangerously low. But now, we can recharge. All it takes is . . ." He paused while a smile grew on his face. "Your lives."

Dayna struggled against the hands holding her, to no avail.

Talioth stepped closer. "It's Dayna, isn't it?"

She didn't answer.

"Shadow knights are the true gifts, Dayna. Siphoning one of you brings in ten times the energy of a regular man." He clenched a fist in the air. "When the Core grabs hold of you, it sucks every ounce of strength from your body. It flows out of you, stripping your breath, your mind, and your soul, leaving you a shriveled empty husk of a person. Pleasant, huh?"

"Are you going to kill all of us?" Dayna asked.

"I'm going to kill *you*." He chuckled then turned to Lowell. "And you. However, you both still have a chance. Your fate doesn't lie in Meliand's grip, but rather in the stubbornness of your friend."

Lia's stomach dropped. She swallowed and tried to take a step back when he looked at her. The firm grip on her shoulder kept her in place.

"That's right. Your friend, Lia, controls your fate today. If she wants to keep her secrets, she will watch you both die horrible, painful deaths. But if she decides she doesn't want to selfishly hide what she knows, you both get to live another day." He moved into Lowell's face. "How does that sound?"

Lowell's jaw quivered until he clenched it tighter.

"Let's see how much she cares about you." Talioth motioned. "Start with him."

Lowell tried to jerk away but went nowhere. Two sets of arms pulled him forward, guiding him to kneel in front of the pit. His body shook. Spurts of breath shuddered from his mouth. Meliand slid behind him and grasped his head in her hand.

Lia's heart pounded in her chest. "Leave him alone!"

Talioth grinned. "You do care after all. That's good because his life is in your hands, Lia. Tell me where the other shadow knights are?"

Faces flashed in front of her eyes: Gavin, Bridgette, Ruby, Salina,

Bradley, Mother, Father . . . Raiyn. Her mouth clamped shut. *No. I could never tell him.*

"Your friend here is going to have his life sucked away, all because you won't talk.

Lowell's head was fixed, staring forward, but his eyes angled toward her. Meliand's hand gripped tighter, digging into his gray hair.

"Tell me, Lia!"

His shout caused her to flinch.

"His death will be on you!"

An ache tore at her insides. She stared forward and managed a faint shake of her head. "I'm sorry," she whispered.

Talioth paused, then grew rigid. "Very well." He nodded at Meliand.

"No!" Lowell shouted.

The crystal pulsed, and a hum filled the room. The glowing light grew in intensity, forcing Lia to squint and turn her head away. A faint rumbling shook the ground. Lowell's shouts were barely audible over the reverberation in the room. Lia clenched her teeth until the light faded.

Lowell had slumped forward. His hair appeared thin and brittle. His wrinkled skin looked like it would crack with the slightest touch. A low moan escaped his lips until Meliand pushed him forward. His broken body tumbled into the gaping pit, fading into the blackness.

Lia covered her mouth to stifle a cry.

The central crystal looked brighter than it had been before, but not by much.

"Next." Talioth motioned to Dayna.

The shadow knight lashed against the guard holding her. She threw elbows and kicked. Her body writhed, pulling limbs in each direction. A flailing head attempted to crush the closest man's face.

The guard kept his hands on her shoulders, looking unconcerned with her attempts to break free. His hold kept her pinned like a grip from a vise. With little apparent effort, he wrestled her forward toward the pit. A smack echoed in the room when her knees hit the ground.

"Leave her be!" Lia said. "You already have whatever energy you got from Lowell. Save her for later."

"I'd be happy to," Talioth replied, "as soon as you talk. I shared plenty with you the other day. It's time for you to reciprocate."

Lia's chest rose and fell, her lungs working to keep up with her pounding heart.

"If you still won't share where the knights are, I'll give you another chance to talk about the pure connection. Tell me what you know."

She gulped. "I know nothing. I already told you that. It just . . . happened."

Meliand positioned behind Dayna and placed her hand on her head.

"Lia," Dayna croaked. Her head jerked straight from the marked one's sudden grip. A tear fell down her cheek.

"Dayna, I-I—" Lia's voice choked with no words to finish the thought.

"I don't know where they are, and I don't know about that connection," Dayna said. "Whatever you *might* know . . ." Her eyes adopted a fierce intensity, and her upper lip trembled. Her voice grew forceful. "Don't tell them a thing!"

A seething whistle came from Talioth's clenched teeth. His lips turned up in a snarl. "Drain her!"

Lia's stomach sank as the crystal blazed to life again. She lunged forward with a desperate desire to pull her friend away, but the guard's tight grip held her fast.

The light blazed even brighter than before. The roar of the crystal mixed with the shout that tore from Dayna's throat as her back arched. Dust fell on Lia's head. The walls trembled. She covered her face, unable to watch.

When the light faded again, she struggled to pull her hand away. It shook, pressed over her eyes. Needing to know the result, she pried it away.

Dayna's limp body slumped in the same way as Lowell's. The skin that had seemed so full of life moments before looked gray and cracked.

A tear rolled down Lia's cheek, and a choking feeling caught in her throat. She watched helplessly as her friend fell forward, following Lowell into the abyss.

"It's a pity," Talioth said. "You could have saved them, but you chose not to."

Lia stared at the pit, her jaw hanging loose.

"Take her back to the mines."

The guard pulled on her shoulders, forcing her back in the direction she had come.

Lia's legs tottered forward, numb. Her eyes glazed, unseeing as the corridor moved past.

"Don't get comfortable," Talioth called, his voice low and menacing. "Your turn will come."

12

COUNTERFEIT SEARCH

The dreary sky and spitting rain created the perfect excuse for Raiyn to hide his face in his hood. He followed High Lord Bilton, his feet making pattering sounds as they stepped through shallow puddles. He kept his face down, avoiding eye contact with anyone, in case someone might recognize him.

"It's up here," Bilton said over his shoulder.

Down the street from Turba Square, Bilton ducked under the sloped wooden awning of a shop with the name *Heirloom* carved into a sign above. Airy scarves of varying colors draped over displays. Pewter and copper trinkets filled tables. Tucked in the back—farther from wandering hands—tables of jewelry lined the shop from one end to the other. Earrings, necklaces, bracelets, and hairpins shone in gold and silver with various gems helping them stand out.

"Welcome to Heirloom," a man said, standing behind the jewelry tables. "Looking for a pretty necklace for your wife?"

"Are you Bernard Tarragish?" Bilton asked.

The man nodded. "That's me."

"I'm Geoffrey Bilton, High Lord of Defense. I need to speak with you."

Bernard straightened and his eyes widened. "High Lord Bilton. Of course. How can I help you?"

Under the awning, the sprinkle of rain couldn't reach them, but Raiyn still kept his hood up. He stood at Bilton's side, observing the interaction.

"You were found with a bag of counterfeit tid last week," Bilton said.

"I had no idea!" Bernard held shaking hands up. "Honest! I already spoke with the treasury and turned 'em over."

"I am aware. I discussed it with High Lord Hampton."

"Please don't take me to the dungeon. I had nothing to do with—"

"Relax." Bilton raised a hand, pausing while the shopkeeper exhaled in rapid breaths. "I'm only here to talk."

The visible tension in the man's shoulders did not lessen.

"I need to know where the coins came from."

"I told the others, I didn't know who it was. Never seen him before."

"Describe him."

"He was"—he pointed at Raiyn—"about his height. Brown hair with a pointy goatee. He wore bulky clothes—burlap—and carried a sack over his shoulder. He looked to be about forty, but it had just gotten dark, and I couldn't see him well."

"What did he buy?"

"Necklaces. Bracelets. A bunch of rings. Gold and silver. Some jewels. He liked the thick ones rather than the delicate designs."

"Easy to melt down," Raiyn said.

Bilton nodded. "Easy to move elsewhere."

"He paid with a thick pouch of tid. It was odd, so I asked him about the coins. He said he runs a gambling hall in Karad. Seemed feasible, so I didn't question it. The coins looked real to me."

"Where did he go?"

"When he left?" Bernard shrugged. "Dunno. Stuffed it all in his sack and headed that way, toward the river."

Bilton paused.

"Did you notice anything else?" Raiyn asked. "Identifying marks? Symbols on his clothes? Rings?"

"Yes!" The man snapped his fingers and pointed. "He had rings on his right hand—pinky and pointer fingers. I remember because I thought it odd he was buying so many rings when he already had two."

"What'd they look like? Anything unique?"

"Not particularly. Silver, both of them. No gems."

"Were they smooth? Shiny?"

"No. They had bumps—small ones circling the ring."

"Good," Bilton said. "What else?"

Bernard shook his head.

"Did he say anything more?" Raiyn added.

"Sorry. I can't think of anything else."

Bilton nodded. "If you think of more, leave word for me at the garrison." He made to leave.

"B-b-but"—Bernard extended a hand to stop them—"I turned in the coins. I thought there might be some . . ." His words faded.

Bilton inclined his head forward. "Some . . . what?"

"Recompense?" The vendor's shoulders lifted while a hopeful smile covered his face. "I lost a lot of expensive jewelry to those coins."

"We can't pay money for trading in counterfeit. It's on you to make sure coins are real before selling your goods."

"I-I know, but . . . my family. We need that money."

The high lord sighed, his eyes drifting up to the wooden awning. "File a report with the constable. Ask them to validate with the Treasury Department how much you lost." He glanced at Raiyn. "We plan to catch this guy, and when we do . . . I expect to make back what you and others have lost. Hopefully, we can get most of it back for you."

Bernard's smile broadened. "That would be incredible. Thank you for trying, and good luck to you!"

Bilton led back into the street with Raiyn a step behind. Despite the drizzle, men and women came and went, wearing hoods and walking with purpose. A stopped wagon blocked much of the path while a man with tools worked on one of its wheels.

When they were a safe distance from the vendor, Bilton turned his back to a stone wall where a portico blocked the drizzle. "What do you think?" he asked.

"It's not a lot to go on," Raiyn said. "A goatee, brown hair, around my height—that could be hundreds of men."

"Two rings. That's unique. We could set up city checkpoints on the main roads. A quick inspection where we look for rings to match the other descriptions."

"If he's still wearing the rings."

Bilton frowned. "True. It's worth a try."

Raiyn glanced down the street. The tall buildings of the warehouse district peeked above the other rooftops, marking the area where Felting ended at the river. He rubbed a hand across his face.

"What is it?"

Raiyn blinked, turning back to the high lord. "Gold and silver . . . if you wanted to trade it for real coins, what would you do with it?"

"Probably melt it down and sell the raw material."

"And where would you do that?"

Bilton shrugged. "Could be any blacksmith shop."

"Not just any shop though, right?" Raiyn felt his body heating from excitement. He leaned outside of the portico and pointed down the street. "See, there's one down there. It's too public. It's open and airy, visible to anyone passing by. You think someone would use that shop to melt down piles of stolen jewelry?"

A crease formed on the high lord's brow. "No, I guess not."

"He'd need something different—something enclosed." He nodded farther down the street. "Like something in the warehouse district."

A smile grew on Bilton's face.

"Bernard said the man left his shop and headed toward the river."

"And it was at night."

"I'll bet he's using one of the warehouses at night, when no one else is there."

"That's a good thought," Bilton said. "You up for a watch tonight?"

"You going to join me?"

Bilton chuckled. "I'm probably too old to be helpful, but sure."

Raiyn nodded. "Sounds like a plan."

An echoing crack filled the air, and the man working on the wagon kicked at a splintered mess of wooden spokes. "Stupid wheel!" he shouted.

The horse hitched to his wagon snorted in response. The vehicle listed to the side, the compromised wheel crumbling under the weight of it. In the narrow street, the stuck vehicle blocked over half the space, creating an obstacle for other men and women to go around.

"You need a hand?" Raiyn called.

The man's shoulders rose and fell. He was short and stout, wearing a rust-colored tunic that looked like it had faded years before. His pudgy, red face turned toward the portico. "You good at changing wheels?"

Raiyn kept his hood up as he stepped into the rain. "Never done it before, sorry."

The man sighed and leaned against the uneven wagon rail. "This piece cracked on me. I've got a spare, but I'm struggling to get this one off." He nodded at the ground where a splintered piece of wood lay soaked in a puddle. "My lever broke."

"What did that do?"

"Raise it off the ground." The man gestured up with his palms. "So I could remove the old wheel and put on the new one." He sighed and leaned against the wagon. He lurched as if he tried to push the vehicle, but it didn't budge.

"You need me to hold it up while you swap the wheels?"

The man laughed. "Hold it up? You ever lifted a wagon, son?"

Raiyn glanced at Bilton, who stood just behind him. "With us together, we should be able to lift it. How long would swapping the wheels take?"

"Not long. If you think you can do it, that would be a tremendous help." He squatted to scoop up his broken material.

"You up for assisting, sir?" Raiyn asked.

Bilton's face strained, showing his hesitance. He leaned in closer and lowered his voice. "I don't mind helping, but my back is not what it once was. I can act like I'm helping but . . . do *you* think we can hold it?"

The high lord's inclined head and pointed question told Raiyn that the effort would fall mostly on him . . . and his ability to use the origine. "Sure. We'll help."

The man stood, flashing a smile. "I can't thank you enough. My name's Ferran."

"I'm Geoffrey," Bilton said, avoiding his recognizable last name.

"And I'm . . ." Raiyn swallowed. ". . . Crabtree." He pointed toward the cart. "We should be good to hold it."

Ferran pointed to the corner of the wagon. "You want to try? See how it feels?"

Raiyn approached the wagon and bent his knees, placing his hands where they could grip.

"Keep your hands wide." Ferran pointed to the back side of the wagon. "The supports are loose and have been known to break."

"Sure." Raiyn kept one hand along the back side of the wagon and the other around the corner.

Bilton squeezed down the narrow passage and moved to the opposite side of Ferran. He readied himself with his hands along the sideboard.

Raiyn sensed the power of the origine ready to fuel his muscles. A tingle ran through him. He adjusted his hands, feeling the wooden grain against his skin. With a nod to Bilton, he lifted.

The wagon was dense—much heavier than he expected. His legs strained under the weight. His hands struggled to hold on. His jaw clenched as he focused on holding the weight. He glanced at Bilton. Bulging muscles lined the older man's arms.

"Impressive." Ferran ran a hand through his wet hair, slicking it back. "You good to hold that for a minute?"

Bilton's eyebrows raised as if letting Raiyn make the call. Raiyn took a second to consider how much origine he'd need. "Yeah," he forced through his tight jaw. "We've got it."

Ferran jumped into action, pounding on the axle arm with a dented hammer. The metal rod slid with each strike, moving farther and farther until it popped out and clattered on the street.

Raiyn shifted his feet and adjusted his hands. An itch on his covered forehead soon turned into a drop of sweat sliding between his eyes. He wrinkled his nose and tossed his head with a puff of air from his nose. The deep-set hood shifted, falling back a bit to allow him to see better. Rain misted onto his face.

Ferran braced his feet and set his hands on the felloe of the broken wheel. He paused to look at Raiyn. "Last chance. Once I take this off, you can't just drop the corner."

"All good," Raiyn said, clenching his stomach to push the words out.

The short man pulled on the rim, sliding the wheel off the wagon's axle. It hit the ground with a thud, then tipped until it crashed at an angle against the nearby stone building. Cracked spokes fell loose. "Now I just need to put on the new one," he said.

Losing the broken wheel didn't make a difference in the cart's weight. Water dripping down Raiyn's arms ran over his hands, making his grip slick. He shuffled his stance to attempt a better hold, but the change didn't help. The tingling origine flowed through him, strengthening his muscles. He did his best to balance the power and not spend too much.

After squeezing past Bilton, Ferran grabbed the new wheel that leaned against the front of the cart. Holding the oversized wheel against his chest, his shuffling feet crept back.

Raiyn groaned. *Come on. Hurry up!*

"Can you slide behind me?" Bilton asked, his words strained.

"I'm not . . . sure." Ferran stepped carefully, as if trying out the space. "Nope." He took a step back and dropped the wheel. Pushing the object in front of him, he rolled the spare through the narrow gap and walked behind it.

A tremor began in Raiyn's arms. He wiggled his fingers, trying to circulate blood. His strength held, but he wasn't sure how long he could maintain it. A deep breath flooded his lungs with oxygen. He focused on the air as he blew it out, hoping the exercise would calm him. It didn't. He sensed the level of origine remaining and felt the blood draining from his face. *It's too low!*

Ferran positioned the wheel in front of the axle, then paused. "Sorry." He took in some deep breaths. "Just need to catch my breath a moment."

"So . . . you just need to throw it on now?" Raiyn asked.

"That's it."

He managed a weak smile through the pain.

The man grabbed the edges of the wheel and lifted the wooden object off the ground.

Raiyn watched, anticipating the relief that was soon to come.

The circular hub of the wheel wobbled through the air as Ferran struggled under its weight. He took a lurching step forward, missing the axle. "It sure is bulky," he said with a laugh. The wheel centered again. He leaned forward, setting the hub over the axle. "This . . . should . . . do . . . it." The wagon driver stopped pushing. A frown formed.

"What's wrong?" Bilton asked.

"It doesn't fit."

A sinking feeling rushed through Raiyn's body. "What?"

"It won't—" Ferran pushed against the wheel, straining. "—go on the—" He dropped the wheel to the ground and exhaled. "Something's wrong."

"Can we, uh . . . set it down, then?" Raiyn asked.

Ferran stared at the balanced wheel with his fingers on his chin. "It should work. It got it from the same guy who—Wait . . . was it the same guy?"

"If we're careful," Bilton began, his arms trembling, "will it hurt it if we lower it?"

"The axle will crack," Ferran said. "Give me a second."

Raiyn's fingers ached. He'd lost feeling in the part of his hand where the wood pressed against it.

"Ah! I've got it." Ferran shook his head. "How stupid of me."

"Is it going to work?" Raiyn asked.

The short man grabbed the hammer and bent over next to the wheel. "I forgot to knock out the spacers. This will only take a moment." He banged at the hub of the wheel, a dull thunk filling the air.

"You going to make it?" Bilton asked, looking at Raiyn with deep furrows in his brow.

Raiyn pulled more from the origine and managed a quick nod. He felt the supply of power running low. *I can't hold it for much longer!* "Gah!" He craned his neck toward the sky, wincing against the strain in his body. His hood fell back farther, exposing his face to the direct drops of the rain. He relished the cool sensation, taking the moment to appreciate the distraction from his ebbing strength.

A clattering sound made him open his eyes. An object fell to the street from the hub of the wheel.

"Was that it?" Raiyn asked.

"That's the first one. Only two more."

Raiyn groaned through gritted teeth and raised his head. As his eyes drifted up the road, his veins turned into ice. Down the street, two men walked their way. One had shaggy, black hair with a messy goatee, and the other smirked with long, brown hair framing his face. Swords hung on both of their hips, but it wasn't the weapons that concerned him. It was the necklaces that dangled in the center of their chests. The necklaces with red crystals set in the center.

Raiyn turned his head toward the wall. Nicolar and Cedric would recognize him in a heartbeat, and there was nowhere to hide. He longed to hide deep in his hood, but his hands were occupied. He tried lightening his hold with one hand. The wagon groaned, threatening to crack.

"Hold on. I'm almost done," Ferran said.

Raiyn resumed the two-handed hold. He tossed his head, shrugging his shoulders to try and fling the hood up.

A clanking sound filled the air. "Only one more," Ferran said.

The knights of power grew closer. They spoke between each other and didn't seem to have noticed Raiyn yet. He continued to attempt to raise his hood. The weight of the wagon pulled at him while his upper body flailed. *Come on, hood. Get up*—It slid back. His heart dropped. The hood had fallen all the way, resting on his back and leaving his entire head exposed. He turned and looked down. Straining his neck to keep his face as obscured as possible.

"Almost there . . ."

Footsteps drew closer, clacking against the stone street. The voices of the two men grew pronounced.

Raiyn's heart pounded. *Should I drop it and run? Should I fight?* All he had brought was a dagger, and that would hardly be sufficient against two knights of power. He also remembered their crystals and how they would remove his ability to use the origine if they activated them.

The origine struggled to sustain the strength he needed. Holding the cart up had taken all he had, and his muscles were nearly spent.

I can't just wait here. I've got to—

"Got it!" Ferran exclaimed in sync with the last spacer hitting the ground.

"Be quick," Raiyn muttered. He kept his face turned as far away as possible as the cart driver dropped the hammer and grabbed the wheel.

"Now, I just need to . . ." the man talked to himself as he hovered the wheel in the air to fit it on the axle. "Hmm . . . that should have made it to where I could . . ."

"Bilton!" a man said in a thick Norshewan accent.

Raiyn held his breath, his insides turning to jelly. A pain filled his neck as he twisted his head to its limit.

"Nicolar," Bilton said. "Cedric, hello."

"What are you doing?"

"Aha!" Ferran shouted. The wheel slid home on the axle, settling in with a satisfying clunk. "Whew! You can set it down now."

Raiyn dropped his hold before the man had even finished his sentence. The wagon crashed to the ground, but the new wheel remained intact. Raiyn pulled his hood up and ducked to the ground in one motion. "Here," he said to Ferran, forcing a rasp into his voice. "I'll help with the axle arm."

Blocked by the wooden slats of the wagon, he struggled to manage his exhaustion. His chest shuddered as he gasped for air. He reached for the metal rod, but his arm was too weak to hold it.

Ferran chuckled. "It's all right. You're tired. I can get this."

Bilton cleared his throat, stepping back from the wagon and flexing his hands. "I was, uh, helping this man. He had a broken wheel."

Nicolar chuckled. "The High Lord of Defense is reduced to fixing carts."

"High Lord of—" Ferran paused with the rod pressed against the hub. "I had no idea. Thank you, sir." He turned to Raiyn. "What does that make you?"

Raiyn stayed crouched, ducking his head.

Bilton spoke up, facing the knights. "We're done here, so no need for you to stop."

Raiyn watched from under the cart. The men's legs scooted by the wagon on the opposite side. His neck heated as he listened to their steps pass by and then fade in the opposite direction.

"Are you all right?" Ferran asked.

Raiyn lifted his hooded face and offered a faint smile. "Sorry. I'm just winded. You're right, that was heavier than I expected." He snuck a look behind him, peering from around the edge of his hood as the knights of power disappeared around a corner.

"We should go," Bilton said.

Raiyn stood. The effort of nodding left his vision spinning. He rested a hand on the cart for balance and used it as a guide for him to walk.

"I can't thank you enough," Ferran said. "I could never have done that on my own."

"It was no trouble." Raiyn gave a half wave as he joined in step with Bilton.

"Whew," the high lord whispered. "That was close."

13

NIGHT TRACKING

"You do this often?" Bilton leaned over the edge of the building, keeping his body far away from the drop while craning his neck. "I don't think I'd ever get used to this height."

Raiyn chuckled. "I haven't done much of it myself. Mostly training." He thought of the night he and Lia climbed up the side of the castle and snuck into the library. "But the drop doesn't bother me."

"You have the advantage of not dying if you fall, though."

"True."

A warm breeze curled over the edge of the roof. Most of the city consisted of dark, jutting walls and roofs lit by the half-moon shining in the clear sky. A few lights shone inside buildings, but most remained as black as the night. The Felting wall penned the buildings in with the castle on the far side. Across the street from their rooftop perch, a row of larger buildings blocked the view of the river with narrow alleys between.

"So, you think it's one of these?" Bilton asked.

Raiyn swept his eyes up and down the street. "It's more of a guess."

"During the day, people fill these warehouses. Carts leaving to make deliveries. Men and women laboring inside. But at night . . ."

"They're quiet," Raiyn finished. A frown pulled at his face. No light shone along the street, despite the windows. "I guess I was hoping we'd see something."

"You knights do this often?"

"I can't say I have, but the other knights—yeah, they spend a good bit of time hanging out on rooftops. Good places to watch from. Easy to jump from roof to roof. Easy to remain unnoticed."

"At least this one had a ladder for me to use to get up here," Bilton said.

A cat yowled on a nearby roof, but the silence returned.

Despite the darkness hiding him, Raiyn felt exposed. No other shadow knights were there to fight with him if a problem arose. Bilton was a warrior in his own right, but not to the degree needed against someone using the devion. As Raiyn scanned the streets, every glowing light in a window made him think of a red crystal. He shuddered at the thought of facing a knight of power with his abilities taken away.

Was this a bad decision? he wondered. *I probably shouldn't have been so quick to insist on helping.*

A comforting thought ran through his head. *Lia would have volunteered.* It confirmed that his instinct had been right—to help. The memory of her brought an ache to his heart, but he smiled at the thought of continuing her legacy.

"I'm curious," Bilton said into the silence. "All that stuff Danik said about you. Is it true?"

"He said a lot of things, most of which weren't true. Which part—"

"Bale." A thick silence followed the name. "Are you really his son?"

Raiyn nodded. "Unfortunately, yes."

"I thought they killed all his wives and descendants in the aftermath."

"The others, yes. At least that's what we heard. My mother stole us away in the night before they got to us."

"But your siblings . . . ?"

Raiyn shook his head. "I was too young to keep anything more than a vague memory of them, but news reached us."

"Have you considered going back?"

"To Norshewa? No." He shook his head for emphasis. "No."

Bilton leaned back, his arched eyebrows catching the light of the moon.

"I've tried to forget that part of my life. I was young, so it was easy, but . . . it was nothing but pain for my mother. The land is cold and brutal. Why would anyone want to live there?"

"You realize you're the last living heir of Edmund Bale, don't you?"

Raiyn swallowed, then nodded.

"That means . . ."

Bilton didn't finish his sentence, but Raiyn knew the rest. "I know what it means," he said. "I could never do that. I don't want that."

A curl of smoke in the moonlight caught his eye, and he straightened.

"What is it?" Bilton asked.

Raiyn pointed. "What's that building used for?"

Bilton followed where he pointed. "Coopers and Ale? They make casks and barrels."

"Carpentry?"

"Yes, but I bet they also melt iron to form the hoops."

"At night?"

"Hmm. Probably not. If I'm not mistaken, they closed down several weeks ago. Problems with their taxes or something."

Raiyn grinned. "Yet smoke rises from their chimney. I say we check it out."

Bilton climbed down the ladder first while Raiyn monitored the warehouse. The smoke continued to rise above the building, but no one entered the street. Raiyn followed next, touching down next to the puffing high lord.

"Let's go," Raiyn whispered. He crossed the street, dancing from shadow to shadow, then hugging the building on the far side. Walking in a crouch, he stopped at the alley separating the closest building from the cooper's warehouse. He nodded ahead. "The window."

Scuttling across the alley brought them to a dingy window covered by a patina of grime. Raiyn rubbed his fisted hand in a circle, bringing a bit of clarity to the frosted pane. The cavernous interior looked nearly black, but a glowing orange light shone around a corner.

"Someone's in there," Bilton whispered.

Raiyn pressed the glass. The pane tilted, filling the night with a faint squeak. His breath caught, but a hissing sound registered somewhere deep inside the warehouse that more than covered the noise. He pushed the pane farther, creating a space large enough to squeeze through. "Come on," he whispered, lifting a leg into the opening.

A wooden board creaked when Raiyn dropped into the building. He crouched, frozen. The noise from the glowing area continued. When Bilton had made it through, Raiyn waved them forward.

He stalked like a cat, walking on the balls of his feet. The hissing sound abated, replaced by a metallic clanking and something dropping onto a hard surface. Raiyn stopped behind a row of storage shelves. He ducked and peered between the stacked goods.

A furnace glowed ahead. Curls of steam hung over a workstation where a man used a sieve to fish objects from a basin of water. They clinked on a pile of similar items, shimmering in the light from the furnace.

Raiyn's eyes shifted to the high lord crouched next to him. He leaned closer and mouthed, "What is that?"

"Coins," Bilton mouthed back. "It's the counterfeiter."

The man in question wore bulky leather clothing and a mask that covered his entire face. He dunked the sieve in the water again and fished around. When it lifted out of the water, it dripped, empty. He tossed the sieve down and pushed the pile of coins into a heavy bag. They clinked together until the bag bulged, stuffed with the newly minted coins.

Bilton set his hand on the hilt of his sword, then stepped back from the shelf.

"Should we take him now or follow wherever he goes?" Raiyn asked.

Bilton's eyes glanced around the room. After a moment, he nodded. "Let's see where he goes."

Past the shelf, the unknown man sloughed off a heavy cloak and removed the protective mask he wore. A head full of brown hair and a pointy goatee shone in the glowing light. He lifted the bag, grunting as he held it in his arms and hugged it against his chest. Two silver rings displayed on his right hand.

"It's him," Raiyn whispered.

The man kicked a creaky metal door shut to the furnace. The light dimmed to near black. His plodding steps headed toward the front door to the warehouse.

Raiyn pulled at Bilton's sleeve and snuck across the floor to the window where they'd entered. The front door of the warehouse opened with a groan. Raiyn slid out the window, then jogged to the front of the alley. Pressing against the stone wall, he leaned forward to peek around the corner. The man with the goatee headed down the street, away from the alley.

Bilton arrived, breathing heavily. "Is he there?"

Raiyn motioned him forward.

The high lord peeked around the edge of the building.

"Can you follow in the streets?" Raiyn asked.

Bilton nodded.

"Stay back so he doesn't see you." Raiyn pointed to the buildings across the way. "I'll head back up and keep an eye from above."

"You can do that?" Bilton asked. "Jump across buildings?"

Raiyn laughed through his nose and grinned. He pointed down the street. "You better get a move on."

Bilton left the dark alley and crossed to the far side of the street. Despite his age and lack of stealth training, the high lord appeared to have good instincts. He kept to the shadows, stepping to the nearest corner and watching before surging to the next dark area.

Raiyn left the man to the streets and ran for the ladder they had just used. It only took him a moment to return to the roof of the city, where moonlight illuminated a clearer picture than it did in the canyons of the narrow streets. Using the origine to speed up his legs, he jogged over the peak of the roof and down the sloping tiles on the opposite side.

When he approached the edge, the gaping blackness that fell two stories to the alley below gave him no hesitation. He sent the power to his legs and leaped through the air. Wind pulled at his skin, ruffled his hair, and ripped at his clothes. He sailed through the air, flying through the night, and landed in a soundless crouch, absorbing the impact on the roof tiles with his muscles.

Two more buildings came and went. Twice more, he leaped. When he peered over the edge, the head of the goateed man showed up where he'd expected it to. Raiyn grinned. Glancing back down the street, he found Bilton slinking through the shadows, safe in the distance. Raiyn tracked the man through the city, leaping across streets and alleys when needed and hiding behind ridges and chimneys.

The man below managed his burden well. He didn't slow as time dragged on and seemed purposeful in his walk. He skirted Turba Square and kept to the alleys instead of the main streets. The homes grew larger and nicer the farther they traveled.

Raiyn readied himself to leap over a gap in the buildings when the man below did something unexpected. He turned right.

A frown pulled at Raiyn's face. He hurried to the closest corner of the roof and looked down another street. The path down the new alley remained straight, ending back the way they had come. *The exact street where we came from. Why wouldn't he have taken that route to begin with?*

He spun back to the target and peered closely. The man's steps continued straight. Steady rhythm, no variation. Raiyn pinched his brows and craned his neck.

With his hands full, the man scratched his chin against his shoulder, working hard to appear casual. He stole a glance behind him before continuing forward.

Raiyn spun and spotted Bilton continuing through the shadows, giving the appearance of a breezy night stroll.

He knows he's being followed! Should I apprehend him now?

The street led through an arched passage under a building that stretched across the path. The man with the goatee approached the tunnel.

Looking back down the street, Raiyn waved his arm. The high lord paused and looked up at him. "Get him, now," Raiyn mouthed, pointing ahead to where the man disappeared into the darkened passage.

Bilton broke into a jog, seeming to understand the gesture. While the high lord approached from behind, Raiyn surged ahead to cut the man off on the far side. He sprinted across the roof, sending a gust of wind in his wake. On the far side of the building, he stopped, perched on the edge, ready to drop.

Any second now.

His muscles stretched taut, flowing with the power of the origine and poised to act. The opening into the street yawned below him. His breath labored, but he kept his eyes on the backside of the tunnel. The second stretched out into two, then into more.

Where is he?

Muffled voices drifted up to his perch. Questioning. Angry. A clash of steel followed.

Raiyn jumped. Gravity pulled him down, fluttering his clothes and hair. He hit the street, softening the fall with bent knees. The black tunnel pulled him forward, running. The faint silhouette of a body lay prone on the street, but the rest of the passage was empty.

"Bilton!" Raiyn ran and crouched beside the fallen high lord.

"I'm fine. I'm fine." Bilton struggled to sit up, his head craning in each direction.

Raiyn spun, pulling his sword in a smooth motion. "Where is he?" The tunnel was empty. The moonlit streets contained no one in either direction.

"I don't know." Bilton winced as he struggled to his feet, holding out his sword. "He was just here."

Raiyn jogged along the tunnel, inspecting the wall. His feet skidded to a stop at a door. He grabbed the knob and twisted.

Locked.

A keyhole set into the wood taunted him. He pulled, but the door wouldn't budge.

"I didn't expect it," Bilton said, limping to his side. "I was trying to catch up when he jumped me from the shadows. Do you think he went in there?"

Raiyn glanced down either side of the tunnel and noted the empty streets on either side. "I'm sure of it. And I'll bet he has a key."

Bilton stepped forward and pressed a hand against the stone wall. His head pivoted on both sides while his mouth remained agape. "That can't be right. This is—" He cut himself off as if he didn't believe what he was about to say. "This leads to the constables' warehouse."

"Constables?" Raiyn frowned. "But that means . . ."

Bilton nodded. "That means our circle of suspects has narrowed."

"Plus, we know he has brown hair, a goatee, and the rings."

Bilton grinned. He held out his sword where a trace of red glistened along the edge. "We also know he has a nasty cut along his right upper arm."

14

A POWERFUL WEAPON

The stone wall grew more uncomfortable the longer Danik sat on it. It could have been the surface, but more likely it was the setting. The old Shadow Knights center churned up conflicting emotions every time he returned.

The sun hung above the mountains in the east, shining its warm light on his face. In the courtyard below, Broderick and Cedric took the knights of power through training exercises meant to build stamina, reinforce sword form, and strengthen their bond with the devion. The men formed loose lines attacking the air in response to Broderick's demonstrations.

"They're getting better every day," Nicolar said, mounting the last few steps to join him on the wall.

Danik nodded. "Should be ready soon—maybe a week."

"You still set on hitting Tarphan first?"

"I think so. They should be easy enough to take down. We'll need to leave a few knights behind to make sure they're following the rules."

"What rules?" Nicolar asked.

Danik raised his eyebrows.

"What rules do you want them to follow?"

Danik took in a deep breath, then blew it out. "I haven't decided."

Nicolar paused. "What do you hope to achieve by conquering them?"

Danik's eyes lifted toward the south. He stared over the city, past the Felavorre River, into the rolling hills beyond where Tarphan waited.

"Money? If so, then we need to outline a plan of taxation. Strength? Then we need to set expectations for their army."

"I want respect." Danik's voice sounded weaker than he intended. "I want them to know I'm in charge."

"You do that with all the above. Have a firm hand and a straight spine. You give them no room to doubt that you're in control. Make an example of someone—the king, his advisors. Kill anyone loyal to Grint."

Considering another mass of killing turned Danik's stomach. "We need stability to keep order."

"Find new leaders, ones who will be loyal to you."

A thought ran through his mind. "Do you think I've been careless with the leaders here?"

"In Feldor?" Nicolar cocked his head. "It would have been safer to start fresh than to risk old loyalties rising. But you're doing a good job of rewarding those you need to keep loyal. I suggest you keep a close eye on Bilton, Hampton, and the other high lords, though."

"I do . . . and I will. If any of them act shady or give me a reason to doubt their commitment, I won't hesitate to replace them, too."

"For Tarphan, you'll also want to make their kingdom a better place than before you arrived."

Danik felt his brows pinch together. "How so?"

"Resources and security—that's what they want. Food, drink, a good economy. They also don't want to worry about thieves or murderers."

Danik nodded.

"Remember when I commented about the problem of filling Felting's dungeons with thieves?"

"We were talking about child gangs, Nicolar."

He turned up his palms and shrugged. "If you want to make a difference in Tarphan's—or anyone's—economy, I suggest a tougher stance on the people who drain society. If they don't contribute, they're pulling everyone else down with them."

The logic made sense, but the savage suggestion made Danik queasy. He didn't want to discuss it anymore, so he dismissed it. "I'll keep it in mind."

An invisible pull tugged at him. His breath caught and his lungs shuddered. His chest felt like it jerked forward, but nothing had moved. He glanced in the direction of the pull—the Straith Mountains.

"You feel it again?" Nicolar asked.

Danik clenched his teeth and nodded.

"I felt it once, too . . . yesterday. It was weak, barely registered." Nicolar touched the crystal that dangled in front of his chest. "These make it merely an inconvenience."

"Yeah, much better than it was before." Danik nodded toward the men below. "We should do more training with how to use the necklaces to block the origine."

Footsteps on stone turned his eyes toward the steps as High Lord Bilton's head came into view. His eyes contained a shade of red at the corners.

"Good morning, Geoffrey. Rough night, last night?"

Bilton paused. "You can tell?"

Danik pointed to his own eyes. "The red gives you away."

"Yes. Well . . . it was a late one. I was tracking down the counterfeiter."

"Oh? Did you find him?"

"I did, but he slipped away."

A surge of excitement, followed by disappointment, ran through him. "Who is it?"

"I don't know. I found where he works and have a general idea of his looks. That should at least slow him down for the moment. I expect to have him captured within the week."

Danik inhaled, letting the news simmer. "Do whatever you have to. Find him. I want this man to pay."

The high lord nodded. "I will make sure of it."

"Is that why you came here this morning, or do you have other news?"

"I wanted to inform you of my progress, but also, I wanted to know if you have any more details of your plans for war?"

The question raised the hairs on the back of Danik's neck while Nicolar's eyebrows lifted. "You want to know my plans?" Danik asked. "Why?"

Bilton's face screwed up in question. "Why? I'm the High Lord of Defense." His mouth hung open while he glanced between the two men. "If you're declaring war on a neighboring kingdom, I don't care how capable your knights are, our army needs to be ready. We'd need to prepare supply lines. We'd need to activate our reserves. I have a lot of work to prepare for whatever we may be called to do."

Danik pursed his lips. "Of course. And when it's time for you to know, you will know."

Bilton's shoulders remained tense. He turned to the men below. "What about your men?"

"What about them?"

"Do they know what's going on?"

Danik's blood heated in his veins. "What I talk about when I meet with my men is none of your concern."

"When do you meet? I'll join."

"What are you getting at, Geoffrey?"

"What am I getting at . . . ?" Bilton tossed his hands. "Nothing! You expect me to lead the army to serve your purposes? All I ask is to be kept apprised of your plans so I can prepare in advance to do my job." Bilton turned to leave in a huff.

"Wait!" Danik said, stopping him. "I'm sorry, Geoffrey. You've been nothing but supportive, and I don't mean to insinuate anything different. I am meeting with my knights once a week, but it's a closed-door meeting. I want them to be themselves."

Bilton raised an eyebrow but didn't reply.

"I assure you, when I have more information, you will be the first to know."

The high lord offered a slight bow. "Thank you, sir."

Danik stared at the back of the man's head as Bilton descended the stairs. "Did he seem pushy to you?" he asked when the high lord was out of earshot. "I may just be on edge."

Nicolar shrugged. "Possibly, but . . . it could be passion for his job."

"From what I know of him, he's always been zealous."

"Still . . . it wouldn't hurt to send him a reward of some sort—to keep him loyal."

Danik nodded. "As soon as he catches that counterfeiter."

The group of knights below paused from their training routine.

"For now, it's time to practice." Instead of taking the steps, Danik leaped off the wall. When he hit the ground, the nearby men jumped back, shouting and raising their weapons. A grin formed on his face. "Good work, Broderick. Now it's time to train on how to use these." He lifted the crystal hanging against his chest.

A rumble grew in the crowd as men glanced at each other.

"When used properly, the power from this crystal blocks the use of origine. In regular combat, this serves no purpose, but if you run into one of the traitorous shadow knights, it could mean the difference between a dangerous fight and slapping a mosquito."

The men laughed.

Danik inhaled and focused his devion strength into his core. He closed his eyes until the crystal materialized in his mind. A low hum reached his ears. A glow warmed the backs of his eyelids. When he opened his eyes, his necklace radiated a red light. The surrounding men watched his chest with eager expressions. "You try," he said. "Spread out."

The men returned to their rough formations and stood with their feet shoulder-width apart.

"Close your eyes."

The men obeyed.

"Use the devion, but only a faint amount. Search inside yourself.

The crystal will feel like a friend ready to take your hand and pull you forward. Welcome it with your mind. Grasp hands. Let it strengthen you. When you connect with its raw power, your necklace will illuminate."

A handful of crystals glowed around the courtyard.

Danik smiled. "Good. A few of you have it. The crystal wants to bond with your power. You'll sense it waiting for you, protecting you."

More lights shone.

"How does this work against shadow knights?" a voice called out from a short man with thick arms and a shaggy beard on the far side of the courtyard. The crystal around his neck pulsed with a strong red light. "Does it create a barrier?"

"Not exactly," Danik said. "What was your name?"

"Immo, Your Majesty," the man bowed.

"I'll demonstrate, Immo. Crystals off, everyone. And give us some space." The glowing lights from the rest of the necklaces dimmed, and a path formed between the two men.

Danik pulled his sword and nodded for Immo to do the same. "I'm going to use the origine to come at you, and I want you to use the crystal to stop me." He pulled from the dusty ability he hadn't used in several weeks, and a laugh bubbled up. The power was weak. Its supply felt paltry compared to what he'd grown used to. *How was I ever content with this?* he thought.

Immo held his sword up. "So, you're going to attack me, and . . . What am I supposed to—"

Danik surged forward with the power of the origine. The muscles in his legs contracted, and his body flew across the courtyard. He cocked his sword back, ready to strike.

It took a moment for Immo to register the danger. Danik had crossed half the courtyard before the other man moved. First, the shorter man's sword adjusted, then his body crouched, but Danik continued forward. Despite paling in comparison to the devion, the origine was a powerful ally. A few steps from the other man, Danik doubted whether the other man would do what he needed to do.

A faint glow teased the crystal.

Danik continued forward.

Immo held his sword with two hands. The glow strengthened.

Only a few steps away, Danik lunged with his weapon. When time was nearly out, the short man's crystal burst into a full glow.

Danik lost his footing. His legs gave up. The power that had flowed through him, powering him forward, had disappeared. His gut seemed empty, and his body felt impotent. As he fell to the ground, Immo snapped into action, forming a blur to Danik's eyes.

He hit the dirt and skidded to a painful halt, turning to raise his head toward the sky. Immo stood over him. The man's shaggy beard bounced with his heavy breathing. A deep crease ran across his forehead. His necklace hung down, dangling over Danik. The glow of the crystal pulsed with intensity, filling the air with a dull hum. Danik's eyes traced not one, but two blades pointed at his chest, pinning him to the ground. He glanced at his own hand, where he had held a sword seconds before. *Empty.*

Danik nodded. "Excellent."

Immo backed up and exhaled. A relieved grin formed. "Whew! It works."

"What does it feel like?" Cedric asked.

Danik gathered himself to his feet. A courtyard full of men stared at him, listening. "It's like air fills your lungs until you're punched in the gut and lose it in an instant. It's as if you're covered in warm blankets that are ripped off. When you meet a shadow knight, this is what you will do to them. It leaves them no different from any common soldier, but you retain the ultimate power of the devion." He turned to Immo. "Nice control of the devion, too."

"Immo's been one of our quickest studies," Nicolar said. "He shows incredible strength and promising control, especially for only training for such a short time."

Immo handed Danik his sword back. "I don't get it, sir."

"What don't you get?" Danik asked.

"The Shadow Knights. I don't understand how they became traitors, and I'm confused about why we need to kill them."

A lump formed in Danik's throat. "As I've said before, they turned on Feldor. They were tired of taking orders and wanted to be in control, so they killed King Darcius. Thankfully"—he motioned to Nicolar—"we were there. We ran them off and killed a few of them. But we must remain vigilant because they could strike back."

Immo shook his head. "It doesn't sound like the knights I've grown up hearing about. Is stopping them what our job is going to be?"

"Your job as knights of power?" Danik paused and glanced around the courtyard. The rest of the men listened with rapt attention. "We have lofty ambitions. Uniting the kingdoms is our first priority. The intention is to create stability for our subjects and prosperity for all. But yes . . . the Shadow Knights are our number one enemy, and stopping them—killing them—is one of our primary objectives."

Immo glanced at the ground and managed a weak nod.

"Is that a problem?"

He glanced up at Danik. "I thought this group was—I don't know—something different. I don't think I want to kill shadow knights." With his shoulders slumped, he held the hilt of his sword forward. "I'm sorry, sir, but this isn't for me. I can't be a knight of power."

Numbness washed through Danik as he took the sword. He'd never considered that someone would want to leave. "But you're already trained."

"I know. I just can't do what you want me to do. Thank you all for the chance, but I need to drop out."

Danik stared at the man, blinking several times. "You've been given a chance few others will ever have. If you leave, there is no coming back."

Immo nodded. "I understand. I've been thinking about it for a few days . . . and I'm sure."

"A word," Nicolar said into Danik's ear.

They stepped to the side as Immo clasped hands with a few other men and exchanged mumbled words.

"He can't leave," Nicolar whispered, standing out of earshot of the others.

Danik turned his hands up. "What should we do? Put him in shackles? Force him to stay?"

The thin line of Nicolar's mouth left no room for humor. "He knows everything. What's stopping him from starting up a one-man crime group in Karondir? Or killing the baron of Marris to place himself in power?"

A thumping resonated in Danik's head. "We would stop him." His weak words fell flat.

"You would travel to Marris? What if he trained his own group of devion-filled fighters? We know he can't give up using the power. You heard Talioth; he'd die."

The suggestion turned Danik's stomach. It wasn't the fear of one man leaving that bothered him. It was the realization that, once someone was trained as a knight of power, they couldn't let them go. "What do we do?"

Nicolar pulled the pointy tip of his goatee. "Leave it to me. I'll take care of him."

"Take care?" A sinking feeling swept through him. "No. We can't do that."

"We must." Nicolar ignored Danik and turned to the crowd. "Immo! Come with me." He wrapped an arm around the short man's shoulder and walked him through the exit of the courtyard. His voice grew softer as they passed into the hallway beyond. "Let's take a walk. I'd like one more chance to convince you to stay."

Danik watched the dagger on Nicolar's hip bounce with each step until the two of them disappeared around the corner. An ache tugged at his insides. Not the pull that drew him toward the mountains. This one was deeper and more unsettling. *We can't ever let these men leave.*

15

TENUOUS ALLIANCE

Veron's eyes swept across the dark street, noting every cracked shutter and stack of crates that someone could hide behind. The sun had set, but the night was still young. Laughter and glowing light emanated from each tavern they passed. A drunk man staggered down the street, using his arm to steady against the wall of the closest building. In an alley, a group of men and women in ragged clothes huddled around a makeshift fire burning on the cobblestones.

A typical night in the Red Quarter.

Brixton walked with him. The blond man kept a hand on the hilt of his sword, his body jerking at each howling animal or sound in the night.

"Are you all right?" Veron asked.

"Sorry," Brixton replied. "I'm a bit jittery. It's been a while since I've done something like this."

"Take a deep breath. Being jumpy won't help." Veron glanced up, spying two black shapes leap over an alley next to them. "And don't forget, we have people watching over us."

Brixton's head turned to the rooftops. "You've seen them?"

"They're pacing us."

Veron slowed as he caught sight of the two-story building. A sign proclaiming *Brookfestin Traders* hung askew over a set of double doors. The doors looked solid, but it didn't matter. The wall beside the door had long ago collapsed. Moss grew down the stones with interspersed black streaks. Windows free of glass formed open rectangles along the side of the building. The higher up his eyes traced, the more pronounced the sag in the stones became. Decomposed thatching covered part of the roof, but holes littered the rest.

Veron slowed to a stop and leaned his back against the building. He scanned the street, specifically the path along which they'd approached. A man and woman walked in the opposite direction, but no one appeared to follow. He waited longer, staring into the shadows. None of the shadows moved.

"Do you think this is a trap?" Brixton whispered.

"If I thought that, I wouldn't be here," Veron replied on instinct. The thought was already in his head, but hearing Brixton ask it gave him pause. "There's always a chance, but we have to take risks. Bilton has come through so far, and it's worth the risk. But if it *is* a trap . . . we're all dead."

Content with the path behind them, he ducked into the gaping hole in the wall. Moldy, thick air greeted him inside the husk of the building. Wooden planks covered the floor, broken in sections. At the far side of the ground level, an orange glow beckoned them forward.

Veron stepped cautiously, and Brixton followed. Sporadic holes on the second floor above revealed a crumbling roof and a starry sky. He scanned for the others but saw nothing. Each creak of the wood increased his tension. His muscles remained taut, ready to spring into action should something go wrong.

Turning a corner revealed a flickering lamp sitting on a dusty table in the middle of a room. Three hooded figures lingered at the far edge with their faces obscured. A panicked tingle rushed up Veron's spine. His mind conjured an image of glowing crystals and Danik jumping out of the shadows. He rested his hand on a short knife tucked into a sheath at his waist when the first figure lowered their hood.

Bilton stepped forward. His face held a nervous smile, mixed with what looked like relief. "I was worried that you wouldn't show."

"Sorry. We needed to be cautious." Veron's hand remained on his knife while his eyes flicked to the other two figures.

The aged face of Stanley Hillegass presented itself when the next hood fell. A hopeful smile covered his face as he crossed the room and clasped hands in a tight shake. "Veron. I didn't believe it when Geoffrey first told me. I'm sorry about everything Danik has done— the spectacle at the arena and the hanging at the square. I would have tried to stop it, but—"

Veron stopped him with a raised hand. "I understand, Stanley. There's no need to beat yourself up over it. I appreciate you being here now."

The other figure stepped forward with his face displayed.

"Magnus Hampton." Veron shook hands with the younger man. "Thank you for coming."

"Danik is running this city into the ground. If there's anything you can do to—" He stopped mid-sentence and stared slack-jawed over Veron's shoulder. "Brixton?"

"Magnus," Brixton said in an icy voice.

"I thought you were gone."

Brixton stepped forward to stand by Veron's side. "I was, but now I'm back. Is Mila well?"

Hampton's eyes fell to the floor. "You were here when your mother passed, yes?"

Brixton nodded. "I left just after."

"Mila died in childbirth. I'm sorry."

Brixton exhaled and averted his eyes. He managed a nod. "I'm sorry, too."

A tense moment of quiet filled the dilapidated room. Bilton cleared his throat. "I brought these two in because I trust them, and we all share the same goals—eliminating Danik and the Knights of Power."

"My wife runs a charity down the street," Hillegass said. "I suggested this was a good place to meet, where no prying eyes or ears would intrude."

"We risk a lot by meeting," Veron said. "Danik's men are more powerful than ever, and we must be cautious."

"We heard about the crystals and how they block your power," Hillegass said. "Danik doesn't seem to fear anything anymore."

"I need to know we can trust you."

"You can," Hampton replied.

"Why now?" Veron danced his eyes between the men. "Why didn't you stand up to Danik from the beginning?"

Hillegass turned his hands up and shrugged. "What were we to do? We couldn't hope to fight him and his crew. It was clear Danik lied from the start, but it was either resist and die . . . or play along. But now, you're here. The Shadow Knights are back, and there's hope again."

"We need stability," Hampton said. "The economy is in upheaval. Feldor is already a mess, but he's preparing to take over the other kingdoms on top of it, as if adding more to rule will make things better."

"It's also for my daughter," Hillegass said.

"What do you mean?" Veron asked.

"Geneva is eighteen. She has beautiful, long brown hair and olive skin. She's not married yet and turns the heads of everyone she meets. Unfortunately, she's caught the eyes of a few knights of power —one in particular—Cedric, the shaggy, creepy one. She tells him to go away, but he won't listen. I've talked to him and Danik about it, but they just laugh it off. She rarely leaves the house anymore for fear that he'll find her."

"I'm sorry about Geneva," Veron said. "We agree with both of you. Danik and his men need to be stopped. We hope to do it, but we'll need your help."

Two bodies dropped through holes in the ceiling, landing in a crouch.

Bilton, Hampton, and Hillegass jumped backward, suppressing yells, but Veron only chuckled at the sight of Chelci and Raiyn.

"You scared me," Bilton said with his hand on his chest.

"Sorry about that." Chelci walked to Veron's side.

"The building and the surrounding area are clear," Raiyn said. "It's only them."

Bilton raised an eyebrow. "You didn't trust us?"

Veron shrugged. "You, yes, but we didn't know who else would be coming. Plus, it never hurts to be cautious." He opened his stance to address everyone present.

The three men looked back, waiting for him to speak. Hesitation pulled at his gut. Sharing too much with the wrong people could commit them to certain death. *We have to take the chance.*

"You're right about the crystals," Veron said. "They block our power, but the knights of power will still have use of the devion. This leaves us no different from anyone else and highly vulnerable. For us to kill Danik and his men, we need to take them by surprise—ideally, without their necklaces. Getting Danik alone would be great, or maybe a handful of them. Either way, we need to strike before they're able to activate their crystals."

Bilton raised a hand. "We have an idea, but it may not be possible."

Veron raised his eyebrows to encourage the high lord to continue.

"Their knights meet once a week."

Veron's hope deflated. "I'm not sure we could take on that many at once, even with surprise."

"Where do they meet?" Chelci asked.

"There's a meeting room at the back of the Hall of the King," Hillegass said.

"The one with the drinks?" Brixton asked.

The High Lord of Trade nodded.

"I know the room well."

"All twenty-four of them will meet together, and no one else is allowed."

"Twenty-three, now," Bilton corrected. "One knight didn't work out. I believe they killed him."

Magnus Hampton chuckled. "If we wait, maybe they'll kill themselves off."

"What are the access points to the room?" Veron asked.

"One door," Brixton answered. "That's it."

"Windows?"

"One to the courtyard garden, but it doesn't open."

"A direct attack would be futile," Veron said. "They'd see us coming."

Brixton raised a finger. "We could poison the drinks." He squirmed as he stood. "It's worked before."

"Good thought," Veron said, "but I don't think it would work. Lia drank poisoned water in Nasco, and she recovered. With the devion, the men could likely push it out of their system. The rest wouldn't drink as soon as they noticed something was wrong, and all of them would know someone in the castle was trying to kill them."

"What about the air?" Chelci asked.

The group turned to her.

"What do you mean?" Veron asked.

"What if we poisoned the air?"

"How would we do that?"

"Philbius powder, ethydriline, and kotoric acid."

Raiyn pointed at her. "Yes! Lia mentioned it while hiking in the mountains."

Chelci nodded. "She and I talked about it in Searis. If you combine them, they're supposed to kill in seconds. I'll bet Gavin will know about them."

"Do you think that would work?" Veron asked. "If we pumped the gas into their room?"

"It would hit them all at the same time," Chelci said. "And if they tried to heal with the devion, it would keep entering their lungs. The devion can only do so much. I think it would work."

"This may be our best shot." Veron turned to the high lords. "Any thoughts on how to get us into the castle undetected?"

16

HOPELESS

Lia's arms swung her pickaxe, but her body didn't participate. Her legs remained stationary, her muscles hardly flexed, and her mind was anywhere but present. The metal tip pinged off the wall, but not even a small chunk of rock broke free.

She collected the axe handle again, breathing evenly. Her arms raised the tool to a useless height, then let the pick fall into the cavern wall again. Nothing.

"Are you trying to avoid hurting the wall's feelings?" Waylon joked.

Lia didn't reply. The purpose that had fueled her the day before drained when Dayna and Lowell died. She went through the motions of mining, but there was no motivation or spirit behind her work.

"If you keep that up, the result at the end of this week will be predictable."

"I don't care," she said. "None of it matters."

Mining crystals leads to mining more crystals. Success only brings more work, more darkness, more gruel. *What's the point?*

Waylon paused a moment before returning to his section of the wall. With a forceful swing, his pick dug into the rock, knocking a chunk of stone loose.

"Take a break, everyone," Chris called from the middle of the line of workers.

Lia let her axe fall to the ground, then turned and leaned against the wall. Her hair mussed against the stone, and a sharp corner dug into her leg. She didn't adjust.

"Remember, a new week starts today," Chris continued. "We were close last week—as close as we've been in a while. I think this week will see us get back up there, even with the increased quotas."

"What does that give us?" Harold asked.

"Twenty crystals," Chris answered.

A few mutters rumbled down the line.

"We had nineteen last week. Twenty is doable."

"But now we're a person down," Jarno grumbled.

"We can do it. Each of you keep digging, and we'll find what we need. We have six days to get there."

"And then what?" Lia said, her voice dropping to a thick monotone.

Chris stepped toward her. "What do you mean?"

"What's next, if we make quota?"

The team leader narrowed his eyes as if he read her thoughts. He flashed a smile then spoke to the entire group, "We haven't seen it in a while, but quota means victory! It means each of you lives another week! Who knows, if we can keep improving, maybe we can knock the Valcors off their top spot and take the golden pickaxe from them. Bronson and his team are bound to have a bad week."

The smiling team nodded.

"The marked ones want to tear us down week by week. Let's not give them what they want."

Lia laughed. "Aren't we doing that already? They want crystals, right?"

Chris looked at her with nostrils flared before he addressed the entire team. "All right, everyone, break's over. Let's get back to work." He picked up his axe and bored a hole through her with his glare of warning.

Lia shook her head. She struggled her way to her feet, taking double the time of the rest of the men. She rubbed her hand along the smooth handle of the pickaxe. *How many loads of rocks has this thing broken apart? How many crystals has it found?*

"What have you been doing all day?" Vekko stopped the debris cart behind her. "This is pathetic. You shouldn't even count as a team member."

Lia looked down at her pile of rubble—at least where a pile of rubble should have been.

"I'm the one on shovel duty, meanwhile you're standing around scratching your butt. No wonder we're not meeting our quotas."

Lia's blood heated. Her grip tightened on the handle of the axe.

"You realize what happened to Lowell, right?"

Her eyes flicked toward him.

"We mined nineteen crystals last week. The week before that, our regular quota was only seventeen. That means that you showing up and doing whatever stupid thing you did is what caused our quota to increase. That's what caused us to miss our goal."

Lia clenched her teeth together.

"If we didn't miss our goal, Lowell wouldn't have died." Vekko moved closer. "And that means you're the one who killed him."

"Gah!" Lia shouted, lunging with her pickaxe raised.

Vekko's eyes grew. He stepped back, raising his shovel in defense.

"Lia!" The shout reverberated through the tunnel.

She stopped, axe above her head, muscles taut and ready to strike. Her team stared.

Chris shook his head. "Back off! We're all on the same team here."

Lia blew out a breath and lowered the axe.

Vekko gathered his composure, then slid the cart behind Waylon. "I guess I'll work here." He lowered his voice. "Since he has debris to clear. By the way, Lia"—he sniffed twice then wrinkled his nose—"you stink."

Lia ignored his barb and turned back to the cave wall. She took in slow and steady breaths, waiting for the repetitive mining sounds of the rest of her team to resume. Finally, she readied her axe with both hands. She lifted it to her shoulder, then swung the metal head in an arc. It collided with the wall, making a faint clinking sound. Nothing chipped off the wall . . . and she didn't care.

LIA TOSSED her axe into the tool storage. It hit the pile of others, then fell askew on the ground. She left it where it lay. Despite barely working all day, her body ached. It wasn't the deep sore and fatigue she'd felt during her first week. It was a weakness of spirit. Her energy had felt drained all day, even though her body could do more.

She scanned the mess area out of habit while she walked down the cavern passage. A fleeting moment of hope ran through her until she realized she wouldn't find her target. Dayna would not be waiting for her.

Lia's footsteps slowed when she approached the doorway to the Garronts' barracks. The discarded items in the boneyard caught her attention next to the lake. She stopped.

Dayna was going to train with me today.

She had been looking forward to the thought of Dayna ordering her around again. As much as she chafed at it during Shadow Knight training, the prospect had sounded like a fresh breath of familiarity. But without Dayna to motivate, her drive waned.

I should train.

She stared at the cart wheel. Her body swayed from side to side.

"Hey, girl!" A man from the Blood Panzils called to her. "You going out there to sweat and lunge some more? If so, I'm going to watch."

The men standing around him laughed.

Lia's stomach twisted. Ignoring them as best as she could, she lifted her heavy feet and stepped toward the barracks with a drooped head.

Before she entered, Chris exited the door, blocking her way. "There you are." He nodded toward the tables. "Let's talk."

Lia sighed but followed. The men from the Panzils lost interest.

Chris walked to the closest table and sat on the bench. He waited until she sat opposite, then folded his hands before him. "Where are you at?"

"What do you mean?"

"Are you just waiting to die?"

Lia shrugged.

"Yes?"

"What does it matter? Die this week. Die next week. What's the difference?"

"A full week."

"Yeah, but a week of what?"

"Life."

She scoffed. "This isn't life. This is . . ." She gestured around the cavern. ". . . drudgery. What's there to hope for?"

Chris paused. He watched her with soft eyes and a gentle smile. "Every day I walk to the mines thinking about two things. Do you know what they are?"

Lia shrugged.

"The village I come from, Cairn, sits in the foothills of the Straiths, close to Palenting."

"I thought you all didn't talk about your past lives?"

"Do you want to hear or not?"

She didn't reply.

Chris' smile grew as his eyes drifted. "When you enter Cairn, the third house on the left is a small two-room cottage. Tulips bloom early suether in the front garden. When you leave the windows open, the scent wafts through the house along with the fresh mountain breeze. The thatched roof hangs over in extended eaves, so rain doesn't get in, even in the strongest storm. There's a window out the back that looks down the valley. It's green and rolling, and in the distance, a waterfall tumbles over a rocky ledge.

"There's a boy in that house named Tobin. He'll be nineteen now. I picture him helping Catherine, his mother: chopping firewood and working in the garden. He liked a girl named Grace." A soft laugh puffs from his nose. "I wonder if they're married by now."

"Your son?" Lia asked.

Chris nodded, his gaze still roaming. "It's been two years since I've seen him. Thankfully, I was *traveling* with Thurman and Harold when the marked ones caught us. No one else from the village has turned up here, but the fear of it sometimes keeps me awake at night."

He tapped his fingers against the table. "Every crystal I find is one less that the marked ones will need. Every week we meet quota and keep our teammates is one less person they need to replace. Every day when I mine, I do the best I can, because that helps make sure marked ones never stumble into Cairn and take my son."

Lia swallowed hard. "What's the other thing?"

Chris turned back to her.

"You said you think about two things every day."

He nodded. "The other thing I think about is that *this* day may be the day."

"What do you mean?"

He gestured over his shoulder. "The Marked Ones can't do this forever. Despite their powers, they're still human. Terrenor is vast with lots of people. Word will get out. You had a group that escaped, right? *They* know where this place is. What's stopping them from spreading the word, getting help, and coming back?"

A dozen thoughts of why it would be difficult for the knights to storm these caverns ran through her mind, but the thought perked her interest.

"Every day I wonder . . . will this be the day someone shows up to take them down? Will it be tomorrow? And that's why I have hope, Lia. I do what I can to make it to that day when we'll be set free. I look forward to walking down the path into Cairn and spotting those thatched eaves. I want to see my wife again and hold her in my arms. I want to hug my son, maybe—" He paused and moved his hand under his nose. "Maybe hold a grandchild."

Chris blinked and averted his eyes. They turned red and glistened at the corners. After a moment, he cleared his throat and turned back to Lia. "The thought of *my* family may not motivate you, but what do you have? I challenge you to find something that keeps you going."

Her mind jumped to the Glade. She pictured her mother and father and the other knights. The image was pleasant, but the realistic hope of joining them seemed too far-fetched.

Chris rose. "Think about it. And remember, we're a team. If you give up on yourself, you're giving up on us all."

She nodded as he walked away. "Thanks."

"Lia."

She turned to him.

Chris stood in the doorway with a hand on the lintel. "As long as you have breath in your lungs, you have life to live, so make your moments count."

Lia froze as the team leader disappeared. *Make your moments count.* She pictured Raiyn saying the same words in the snow as they stared over the ravine.

Raiyn. Her heart thumped faster. *He's still out there. What if I could show up for him?*

She stood and moved toward the barracks, her blood running warmer, and a boost of energy loosening her limbs.

Is it worth hoping for?

She glanced past the door to the wooden wheel lying askew on the boneyard floor. It called to her. A snicker over her shoulder told her she held the attention of the Panzils again. Heat crept up her neck. The door to the barracks waited for her. Her bed sat inside. *I can rest—take it easy—avoid caring.*

A sigh escaped her lips. "I must be a total fool," she muttered. Angling left, her feet led her past the barracks. Loose rocks crunched under her feet. She stopped when she reached the wheel. Tuning out the catcalls behind her, she took several deep breaths, preparing herself to work.

"Wait!"

The call stopped her as she prepared to lift the object.

Waylon and Thurman jogged up. "You want company?" Waylon asked.

She cocked her head. "Are you serious?"

Thurman nodded. "We've seen how your strength has been

growing since you arrived. We thought . . . maybe we could train with you."

Lia's mouth pulled up at the corner. "That sounds great."

Waylon turned his hands up. "What do we do?"

She crouched and lifted her wooden wheel, heaving it onto her shoulder. "Grab something heavy, then come with me."

17

UNDETECTED

With his eyes closed, Raiyn tried to keep his breath as shallow as possible. When he exhaled, the warm air blew back into his face, bringing an overwhelming smell of stale hay and manure. Brixton's elbow poked into his side, and Veron's feet pressed against his own. The hard wooden boards underneath him jostled back and forth as the cart bounced over cobblestones and potholes.

"You alright?" Bradley whispered.

"I'm good," Chelci replied.

"Good," Raiyn repeated with Veron and Brixton.

"We're coming up to the gate now."

Raiyn made himself extra still to prevent the hay piled on top of him from shifting. He strained his ears but heard nothing over the rolling wheels and crunching footsteps.

"Whoa!" a voice called. "What's this?"

The cart rolled to a stop.

"We were called to help with the stables," Bradley replied.

"The king's stables?"

"We should be on the list. Name's Birchfield."

Raiyn's stomach clenched at the silence that followed.

"Hold on," the unknown voice said.

Footsteps faded, but the cart didn't move.

Was this wise? Raiyn thought. *What if we're captured before we even get into the castle grounds?*

His mind raced with ideas of what to do if their ruse didn't work. His sword was pinned by his side, but he could pull it at a moment's notice.

"Let them through," the guard called.

Raiyn exhaled, letting his chest fall. The cart resumed its jostling as the wheels rolled once more.

"So far, so good," Brixton whispered.

The cart continued rolling for several minutes until it came to a stop once more. The hay rustled.

"Come on," Gavin said. "It's clear."

Raiyn sat up and pushed the hay away from his face. He blinked his eyes open and spluttered to knock loose strands off his mouth and face.

The wagon had come to a stop, shaded by the roof of a stable. Stalls lined both sides of a dirt path. Heads of horses peeked over rails, staring with large, unblinking eyes. One whinnied. Harnesses and saddles hung on hooks. A pile of blankets sat folded on a shelf. Shovels and pitchforks leaned up against a wall.

"That was a new experience," Brixton said, pulling hay off his clothes.

Veron and Chelci waded through the straw and hopped off the wagon. Raiyn and Brixton followed.

"No one?" Veron asked.

Gavin's mouth quirked into a hint of a smile. "Two knights of power walked right by us."

"Really?"

"Whew!" Bradley said. "That had me sweating."

"They had their crystals around their necks and swords on their hips," Gavin said. "They didn't recognize us, though. I think Danik's the only one who would have identified us."

Raiyn walked to the edge of the row with the others. Safely

through the castle's outer gate, they had arrived at the king's stables. Peering out from where the roof ended, the castle loomed above them with its towers stretching to the sky. He pointed across a garden courtyard at a row of windows. "Is that it?"

"That's the Hall of the King," Brixton said. "The lone window on the far end marks the meeting room."

Veron pointed at the next door on the opposite side. "And that's the door to the kitchens."

Brixton nodded.

Gavin tossed hay aside and pulled out a wooden box from the wagon. "According to Bilton, this should be our first clear window of time. We need to get in and prep the room. I could use a few of you to come with me."

Raiyn volunteered along with most of the knights.

"We'll stay here." Veron pointed to himself, Chelci, and Brixton. "It's best we stay out of sight."

After checking to make sure no one passed, they crossed the path. Raiyn kept his head down but walked with purpose, acting like he had every right to go to the door. Bradley reached it first. Raiyn's nerves amplified as the knight grabbed the handle. The door swung open. Raiyn sighed, his shoulders relaxing. Gavin entered first, carrying the bulky wooden box.

Inside, the large kitchen stretched into the distance. Countertops and basins filled with dishes and empty platters. Dried meat hung on hooks, and a cold hearth sat unoccupied at the far end. A mixture of spice and fruit filled Raiyn's nose. He imagined the feasts that had been prepared in the room.

"Come on." Gavin turned to a small door on the right side of the room. "We only have about thirty minutes until workers arrive."

Bradley opened the door and held it ajar for the others to enter.

The room beyond the door was larger than Raiyn expected, with a low window along the side. Six knights fit with space to spare. The room looked to be the storage space for banquet dishes. Plates, bowls, and fine goblets stacked on rows of shelves. According to High Lord Bilton, none of it would be used that night.

Gavin set the box down and rummaged through its contents. After a moment of clanking glass, he pulled out a drill with a corkscrew bit and a wide t-handle.

"Near the floor or ceiling?" Bradley asked with his hand on the wall. The meeting room waited on the opposite side. "Will it matter?"

"The gas should spread either way," Gavin said. "I'm thinking near the floor, by the center of the room. There's no way they'll notice it."

"Here." Raiyn held out his hand. "I'll start. I've worked plenty with drills."

Gavin passed the drill to him and moved out of the way.

The handle was thinner than drills Raiyn had used at the lumberyard, but the function was the same. He crouched on the floor and ran his hand along the stone wall. A section of mortar was thicker than others—just wider than the bit of the drill. He pressed the sharp point into the hard surface and pushed. The point dug into the mortar, chipping off small flakes. Using both hands and a bit of origine, he jabbed the point multiple times until the bit had enough depth to gain traction. With one hand guiding the bit and the other pushing against the handle, he turned the drill. The blade caught. Scraping sounds filled the room as he labored. Dust fell on the floor, and the drill pressed into the wall.

He relied on the origine to push and turn through the hard surface. Sweat itched his forehead and trickled past his eyes, dropping to the floor. His heart sped up from the exertion, but he only pushed harder.

A hand rested on his shoulder, and Raiyn stopped drilling.

"Take a break," Gavin said. "That was good work."

Gavin, Salina, then Bradley each took turns at the drill until the tool punched through the far side.

"Got it!" Bradley whispered. A sheen of sweat covered his red face. He backed the tool out, pulling a pile of dust back through the hole to drop on the floor.

Raiyn lay his head against the floor and peeked through the hole.

A grin formed on his face at the sight of light on the far end. "It's good. Clean all the way through."

Bridgette found a broom and swept the pile of dust under a cupboard.

Gavin put the drill back in the box and took out other objects. He set three glass jars on the ground, taking care to balance each one before moving to the next. One contained a white powder, and the other two were half-filled with clear liquid.

"Be careful with these. They're not mixed yet, but they can still do damage." He tapped the one with clear liquid. "Especially the kotoric acid. It will eat your skin down to the bone in a heartbeat."

He removed one more object from the box. The large glass cylinder contained a narrow top with a cork stopper. One end contained a long, metal spout that had been clamped to the cylinder, while a bellows connected to the opposite side.

"How does that work?" Raiyn asked. "We mix the three chemicals in there, then use the bellows to pump it through the hole?"

Gavin nodded. "Pretty much. We'll barely even need the bellows, though. When these mix, the reaction is . . . intense."

"What do you mean?"

"The gas will shoot out the spout."

"How will we do it when it's time?" Bradley asked.

"We'll need to work together," Gavin said. "And quickly. Can you, Ruby, and Salina each take one of the chemicals?"

The three knights nodded in sync.

"We'll start by pouring in the two liquids. I will use this"—he lifted a metal rod—"to stir them together, then we'll add the powder as quickly as possible, and I'll stopper it again with the cork." He pointed at Bridgette. "While we do that, can you hold the spout up to the hole?"

Bridgette nodded.

"We want it as deep as possible. And use these." He held up a handful of rags. "Wrap the spout and use them to seal off any gaps."

"Will those be enough to stop the gas from reaching us?" Bridgette asked.

"Gas wants to fill the space of its container. With the clear opening into the other room, it will flow in that direction. We should be safe. Nothing more than a trickle would get in here, which would disperse in the air. When the last of the liquid evaporates, we'll run out of here."

"How quickly will it work on Danik's men?" Raiyn asked.

"It's called borlic gas, and it works fast," Gavin said. "The first breath is supposed to smell like raspberries. The second breath gives you a splitting headache." He paused to set the glass cylinder back in the box. "There is no third breath. You hemorrhage from the mouth and nose, then your spine breaks from the force of the spasms."

Raiyn shuddered.

"Raspberries, huh?" Bradley said.

Gavin shrugged. "So I hear. As soon as his men realize something is going on, it will be too late." He patted the jars of chemicals. "And we have enough here to fill that room. It shouldn't take over ten seconds for all of this to react. Raiyn, we'll need a signal to know when it's safe to go. Can you watch from outside? Hide in the courtyard and tap on this pane when they're in place next door?"

A surge of nerves ran through Raiyn. "I can do it."

They packed the chemicals and glass container back in the box and covered it with a cloth in a corner of the room. The kitchen was still empty, and the six knights hurried out the back door.

Walking with the other shadow knights, Raiyn felt a sense of pride in his involvement. Kicked out not long after he'd first started, this was his first chance to work on a mission with the full team.

Veron exited a stall when they arrived back in the stables. "How'd it go?"

Chelci and Brixton followed.

"Perfect," Gavin said. "We bored a hole straight through, materials are ready, and we have a plan for mixing everything."

"I'm going to signal from the courtyard when it's time." Raiyn turned to Gavin. "How should I signal?"

"Two slow taps for us to get ready," the older knight replied. "Three fast when it's time to go."

"What if there's a problem?"

"Like what?"

Raiyn shrugged.

Gavin paused. "If something unforeseen goes wrong. Five fast taps and we'll abort and evacuate."

Brixton raised a hand. "If we want to use it, there's a drawbar for the meeting-room door in the Hall of the King."

Veron cocked his head. "Really?"

"My father and I considered using it with Bale, but . . ." he shrugged. "I believe it was used as a holding room years ago."

"Could be risky," Chelci said. "What if they hear us put it in place or try to use the door before we're ready?"

"Hmm," Veron mused. "And if they sense danger they could break through it with the devion. But buying a second or two of time could make the difference."

Chelci nodded. "I say we do it."

"I agree," Veron confirmed. "Once they all arrive, Chelci, Brixton, and I can enter the castle and bar the door. As soon as that's set, we'll tap for you, Raiyn. Then you pass the signal down to them." He stopped and glanced along the line of people. "Everyone good?"

Heads nodded through the stable.

"We've got about six hours to wait, now. Bilton will signal us when the kitchen is clear. It shouldn't be long after that when Danik and his men meet."

The day dragged on with knights trying to look busy, taking turns pushing hay around and alternating resting inside an empty stall. Raiyn clammed up when a servant arrived mid-afternoon with a horse to drop off, but Chelci stepped up and handled it with the grace of a pretend stable hand. The sun dropped behind the rest of the city, and lights dimmed through the window to the kitchen.

"Should be soon," Veron mused, peeking over the wooden barrier. Despite the hours of waiting, he remained poised and ready to act.

The knights had all given up simulating work. Most sat in the hay, leaning against the walls while a few paced. Raiyn stood near Veron to keep an additional eye out. A lone lantern hung on the stall with the shade pulled to only permit a sliver of light to escape.

"What will we do when it's done?" Bradley asked.

"Assuming we get them all . . . we should be safe," Veron said. "No one else in Feldor can oppose us, and I expect any shifted loyalty will switch back once Bilton, Hampton, and Hillegass stand with us. We're to meet Bilton at the cistern near Turba Square, after."

"Then we'll only have the Marked Ones in the mountains to worry about."

Groans filled the stable.

"One issue at a time," Chelci said. "If we can clean up the Knights of Power first, at least then we can restore order in Feldor and prevent the other kingdoms from meeting the same fate. Talioth didn't seem concerned about ruling—only about draining our power."

"Maybe we can enjoy a few weeks of rest in the Glade." Gavin's head leaned against the wooden board at his back. A smile covered his face. "I could go for some peace for a bit—maybe some gardening."

"I'm looking forward to some training time with you all." Raiyn glanced across the group. "You have so much knowledge to pass along. I feel like I've barely scratched the surface."

"We'll train with you," Gavin said. "You've proven yourself to everyone here."

Salina chuckled. "If we have a mission to Norshewa, it could be fun to have him along. You never know when someone like him could be useful."

Raiyn laughed and shook his head while a flush crept up his neck.

"What are you looking forward to, Brixton?" Veron asked.

The blond man looked up, caught in the other eyes of the group. "I'm thinking about looking up Matthew and Emma again—seeing if they could use help at their bakery."

"I met them," Raiyn blurted, surprising himself by his volume. "Sorry, just excited about someone I know."

"I bet they would love to have you back," Veron said.

Brixton nodded. "The mountains were peaceful, but baking is relaxing in a different way—warmer, too."

Raiyn tensed at the sight of Veron's alert posture. He followed the Shadow Master's gaze toward the castle wall. The rest of the lights in the kitchen had been extinguished, and their signal of a red flower was displayed inside the window, glowing in the moonlight.

"Are you ready?" Veron asked.

The knights stopped talking and turned to him.

"It's time."

18

THE TRAP

Gavin opened the kitchen door for the second time, his nerves heightened to a new level. His eyes flitted in each direction, but the room was empty. A salty tang of spiced soup mixed with the lingering smell of roasted fish. He swept across the floor. Shadows led the way, created by the lantern Bridgette carried. He held the door as the other four knights entered the storage room, then shut it behind them.

Bradley brought the box from its hiding place, and the group removed its contents. The glass containers clinked as they set them on the stone floor.

"Do you think anyone's there yet?" Bridgette whispered.

Gavin leaned toward the floor, angling his ear toward the hole. He shook his head. "Nothing."

He positioned the mixing cylinder by the hole, removed the cork from the top, and placed a funnel in the opening. The knights readied their chemicals. Bridgette wrapped her rags around the container's spout.

A deep thudding filled Gavin's chest. "This is our shot."

Grim lines reflected on the faces of the others. "Do you think it's going to work?" Bradley asked.

Gavin inhaled a deep breath. "I do. It has to work."

"THERE THEY ARE," Chelci whispered, pointing.

With his head peeking over the stable fence, Veron followed her finger. The light of a torch shone through the hall window.

Nebulous bodies obscured by the distant window arrived, the lights multiplying as more torches entered the hall. A mass of men crossed the Hall of the King. Their raucous conversation passed through the walls of the castle to reach where the shadow knights hid in the stable.

Veron turned to the faint form next to him. "You ready for this?"

Brixton appeared to gulp before he replied in a faint whisper, "Ready."

Veron looked past Brixton. "Raiyn, those bushes at the far end should be perfect."

The young man nodded, his face determined and shoulders squared.

"We'll signal at the window when the brace is in place, then you can pass it to those in the kitchen."

The line of bodies continued through the room until the torch-light faded. Soon, the hall dimmed, and the meeting room brightened with a warm light as lanterns were lit. The transparent windows revealed a packed room. Men gathered around the supply of liquor, pouring glasses.

Although obscured by the aged panes, he recognized Danik standing at the center of the group in a royal-looking, purple robe. The black on his throat gave a sinister impression.

Danik, why did it have to come to this? Veron had poured years into the young man, training him as best he could. The rejection felt like a stab to his chest. A hand rested on his shoulder, and Veron flinched.

Chelci's fingers offered a soft caress. "You all right?"

He nodded. "Yeah. Sorry, just lost in my thoughts." The room was full and no one else crossed the hall. "Let's go."

Veron exited the stall first. He crept to the front of the stables, keeping in the shadows. His neck craned in each direction, ensuring the path was clear. He moved with purpose—a mix between a casual stroll and a hurried walk as they crossed the garden courtyard.

Raiyn curled off when they neared the building, heading toward the bushes by the windows. Chelci and Brixton stuck with Veron, heading for the door at the far end. He crouched as he neared, transitioning to the balls of his feet. A glance along the line of the building saw Raiyn duck into a cluster of shadows against the castle, below the last window.

Veron rested his hand on the door handle. His pulse beat fast, the gravity and the danger of what they were about to attempt weighing on him. The power of the devion gave him pause. The thought of the crystal necklaces caused his throat to run dry. *If any of them catch us, we'll be dead.*

He turned the handle, the relief of the door being unlocked fighting with the sheer terror of what they were about to attempt. He paused to take a deep breath. "You two with me?" he asked, hoping their assurance would fill him with more confidence.

Brixton said, "Yes," and Chelci gave a light squeeze on his arm.

After one more breath, Veron tensed his arm to pull the door, but a noise inside made him freeze. Hurried footsteps and muttered words passed by the door. Someone was late. The tardy arrival rushed down the hall until the far door opened, bringing more light into the hall. Laughter burst from the room until the door closed behind.

"Whew," Veron exhaled. His sweaty hand remained frozen on the turned handle. "That was close."

After waiting a moment longer, he pulled the door open.

The Hall of the King held an ominous silence, broken by the muted conversation coming through the door at the far end. The throne on the raised dais was visible in the faint light coming through the wall of windows.

Veron crouched as he rushed across the room. Pretending to be a stable hand no longer worked. If any of the men exited the room, they would be caught.

They stopped at the door. Veron stood aside while Brixton inspected the frame. Chelci leaned to the window and tapped twice, slow and soft. *Get ready.*

Waiting by the door felt interminable. Brixton rummaged around at a hole built into the wall, but it was so dark that Veron couldn't make anything out. "You need help?" he whispered.

Brixton shook his head, his fingers digging into the frame.

Sweat formed on Veron's brow. They were exposed, standing with nowhere to hide. *We need to go!*

Finally, Brixton backed up, pulling something with him. A faint scrape reached Veron's ears. He cringed, the hairs on his arms standing on end. Jumping in, he found the metal bar that emerged from the hold in the wall. It was heavy—thick and sturdy. He lifted the end, eliminating the scraping sound as Brixton guided it across the opening.

When extracted, the bar rested into two grooves on either side of the door. It fit snugly. He pressed down, seating the brace, but making sure it didn't clang into place at the same time. When he felt the bar hit home at the bottom of the grooves, his anxiety increased. *We're in this now.* He nodded toward Chelci, who stood beside the window. She rapped three times in quick succession.

RAIYN HELD HIS BREATH. His ears strained, listening for the signal. A surge of laughter came from the next window down, and his nerves heightened. *Will they knock loud enough? What if I miss it and they're waiting for me?*

The triple knock arrived, faint but clear.

His arm flinched, and he sucked in a breath. With the stone wall on one side and a row of bushes on the other, he scrambled forward on hands and knees. His fingers pulled at the ground. His knees sunk into the dirt. He sensed the glowing light bathing the bushes and area around him as he passed under the window. He kept his head down and back low so they wouldn't see him.

Past the lit window, the next one was much darker, with only a faint light reaching the window. Raiyn raised his hands to grab the sill. With a jump, he lifted his chin and held himself in place while his feet dangled off the ground. Lit from a sliver of lantern light, Gavin's face stared back with raised eyebrows. A solemn nod from the shadow knight was the last he saw before he dropped. Raiyn reached back up, knocked three times on the glass, then ducked into the safety of the bushes once more.

HE HAD EXPECTED THE SIGNAL, but when Raiyn appeared in the window, it still made Gavin's stomach twist. The thick wall distorted and muffled the noise in the adjacent room, but the hole near the ground added a bit of clarity. Danik's men had arrived, and it was time to act.

"Go," Gavin said.

Bradley poured the kotoric acid through the funnel first. The clear liquid fizzed as it hit the base of the empty glass container. A vinegar-like smell wafted through the air. As soon as he finished, Ruby tipped in the ethydriline. A gurgling sound filled the room as large bubbles billowed inside the glass. The fizzing bubbles grew nearly to the top until they settled. The vinegar smell turned pungent, irritating Gavin's nose.

When Bradley and Rudy had cleared, Gavin pulled out the funnel and inserted the metal stirrer. He whisked it, churning the clear liquid. The bubbles continued to settle until only liquid remained, forming a line near the halfway mark of the container. He continued to stir as he looked at Salina, then at Bridgette. "You ready?"

Salina nodded. She held the philbius powder at an angle, the white, flaky contents ready to go.

Bridgette wrapped her hand around the rags, pressing the container's spout into the hole in the wall and plugging up any potential points of leakage. "Ready," she whispered.

Gavin's stomach clenched in a ball of nerves. His stirring had settled into a slow spin. He didn't want to take the object out for fear of what came next. *There's no turning back from this.*

"It wouldn't hurt to hold our breaths," he said.

The five knights all took a collective breath, their chests puffing out. With a flick of his wrist, Gavin pulled out the stirrer and set the funnel back with his other hand.

Salina moved, dumping the powder into the funnel. The smooth material slid down the channel and fell into the waiting concoction. A faint gurgle bubbled as the first flakes hit the liquid.

Gavin shook the funnel, trying to drop the chemicals in as fast as possible. As soon as the majority had passed through, he tossed the funnel aside and slammed the cork in place.

The bubbling grew, slowly at first. The light sound built into a deep rumble. Glass clinked against the stone floor as the container shook. Gavin's hands gripped the sides to keep it steady. Bridgette clenched tighter on the rags. In a rush, the reaction reached its full power. The surface of the liquid simmered as if boiling while a cloudy substance filled the top half of the container.

Bridgette's arm jerked as the gas rushed into the nozzle. She brought in her other hand to hold it steady.

Gavin watched the contents of the container. The level of the liquid dropped as the bubbles turned the chemicals into the deadly gas. At the halfway mark, he pushed against the bellows on the side, continuing to hold his breath as a precaution. The cloudy material flew into the spout, disappearing into the wall.

A nervous grin pulled at his lips. *It's working.*

WITH HIS BACK to the castle wall, Raiyn stared across the courtyard at the stables. The city wall rose behind it, and stars twinkled in the night sky. He turned his head toward the glowing light of the meeting-room window.

He couldn't help but count in his head. He gave it twenty seconds for the chemicals to be mixed, then he started over at zero. Gavin had said it shouldn't take more than ten seconds to react once mixed.

Two . . . Three . . . Four . . .

The light didn't waver in the room—not that he expected it to. He thought perhaps staggering bodies could throw shadows around.

Five . . . Six . . . Seven . . .

Perhaps someone would cry out. At the first sign of something wrong, maybe a yell would reach through the window.

Eight . . . Nine . . . Ten.

Raiyn pictured the gas. He imagined what the room looked like— twenty-three knights of power drinking and talking with no idea the room had filled with an invisible killer.

They won't reach the third breath.

He paid attention to his own breathing.

One . . .

An unreasonable fear that the gas could reach through the walls in a concentrated form left him taking shallow breaths.

Two . . .

Adrenaline pumped through his veins. He struggled to breathe regularly. Fighting against the need for oxygen, he finally inhaled.

Three . . .

He stopped counting and held his breath. His ears trained toward the window, using a faint amount of origine to enhance his ability. He heard nothing.

"How long will it take?" Brixton whispered.

Rather than risk answering, Veron only shook his head.

Brixton held the center of the brace while Veron and Chelci took the ends. They each leaned their weight forward, pressing against the bar. If the poisoned knights made a disoriented dash to attempt an escape, Veron hoped their bodies combined with a bit of the origine would make the difference.

On the floor, a line of rags had been stuffed into the crack of the door. It blocked the light and would hopefully do the same for any traces of the gas that tried to escape.

Veron held the power of the origine at the ready. It simmered in his gut, warming him from the inside.

The hairs on the back of his neck prickled, but he wasn't sure why. He glanced across at Chelci. Her eyes held a suspicious fear as they stared back.

"What?" he mouthed.

"It's too quiet," she whispered.

NOTHING, Raiyn thought as an unsettled feeling built in his chest. *I should hear something, right?*

No one screamed or pounded on the door. No glasses shattered or tables crashed. His subconscious counting had long passed the point at which chaos should have erupted.

Gavin and the others should have run out by now . . . right? A glance at the kitchen door revealed nothing.

He crept closer to the meeting room window, craning his neck to see what he could glimpse. The corner of the room came into view. He continued forward. He spotted the door that would have Veron, Chelci, and Brixton barricading the other side. A small corner of a rag peeked out from the bottom. He stepped closer. Half the room was in his sights, but he had yet to find anyone.

Did they leave?

Impatient and nervous, he stepped forward again. He sucked in air when he spotted the backs of two men. They faced the wall, staring. Terror rushed through Raiyn's body.

What are they doing?

He stepped forward, taking step after step through the dirt. The rest of the men came into view. He needed to stop. He needed to duck out of sight, but the scene before him drew him in. It was bizarre— nothing like what he had expected. He couldn't move. He couldn't run. His limbs felt frozen in horror.

He couldn't breathe.

. . .

GAVIN CONTINUED to pump the bellows, grinning as the gas disappeared into the hole in the wall. The liquid level fell lower. Lower. He leaned closer to the cylinder to get a better look. The act of bending forward put pressure on his lungs, activating his body's impulse to take in a fresh breath.

It should be fine to breathe, but still . . . We're almost done.

His racing heart had diminished his ability to hold in the oxygen he needed. He activated a bit of the origine to help his body cope.

Bridgette's face caught his eye. Her lips pressed together, the pink color fading to a hint of blue.

She's struggling, too.

Bradley motioned with a hand and pointed toward the door. His cheeks puffed large, and his eyes flicked to the others.

What does he want?

Gavin glanced at the door. Nothing was there. Unsure of what the man wanted, he turned back to the job at hand. He pumped faster, watching the level of the clear liquid. A stronger urge to take a fresh breath racked his body, forcing him to use more of his power. He straightened to lessen the pressure on his lungs, but the movement only made it worse.

The sound of Bridgette exhaling made him freeze. His eyes flicked to her, scrutinizing her reaction as she sucked in a breath. She smiled, looking pleased with the infusion of oxygen into her body.

Gavin followed suit. He blew out his stale air and breathed in a fresh supply.

Normal. Fresh. Safe. He smiled.

The other three knights echoed his example.

He turned back to the container as the last dregs of liquid disappeared from the glass bottom. He grinned and finished with two pumps of the bellows for good measure. "Let's go." As the words left him, he froze. He stared at Bridgette.

Her shoulders were tense and her chin trembled. The fear in her expression caused Gavin's stomach to turn, and that's when it hit him.

Raspberries.

The scent was unmistakable. It filled his nose, sweet and fruity, singeing the fine hairs lining his nostrils. The shock was like a hit to his gut. His mind clouded over. His focus evaporated. Rather than run from the room, dragging the others with him, his body reacted in the opposite way than he intended.

His lungs sucked in another breath.

19

BEST LAID PLANS

Raiyn's jaw shook. He stared through the glass, his eyes locked on the men inside. Rags covered their faces. Some stood and watched, but several of them crouched beside the wall. A long, round object ran along the wall, near the floor. Where he imagined the drilled hole would have come out, several men held the object in place, flush against the stone. Others supported the tube along its length, and several more men pressed the opposite end of it against the wall, close to the window.

Another hole!

His heart thumped.

Raiyn leaped away from the window. He lunged toward the darkness and reached up to the pane of the storage room. His knock rattled the window, a frantic five taps. With the echo of the taps still ringing in his ears, he grabbed the sill and pulled himself up.

The sight through the window turned his stomach. The lantern had fallen on its side, and its shade had knocked open. Five knights lay on the ground, motionless. Their limbs didn't twitch. Their chests didn't move. Blood trickled from each mouth and nose. Crooks in their spines contorted their torsos into unnatural shapes. Each set of eyes remained open, still and lifeless. Gavin looked toward the window, his dead eyes unable to see Raiyn. In the corner of the room, tucked by the floor, another bored hole opened up with a small pile of undiscovered rubble. The lantern's light illuminated a faint wisp of white smoke curling into the room.

"No!" Raiyn muttered. His fingers lost all strength, and he dropped back to the dirt. He tried to breathe, but the air felt caught in his throat. He hunched over and set his hands on his knees. A retching impulse racked his body. He wanted to heave but pushed the urge away. *This can't happen. The plan. The knights. How did they know?* He jerked his head up. *Veron!*

Raiyn rushed across the window, leaving all pretense of secrecy behind. He had his sights on the dark panes of the Hall of the King, but his legs stopped as he passed the glowing clear panes of the meeting room. Locked in an inexorable pull, his head turned.

Standing a hand away from the window, Danik stared at him. His purple robe flowed off his shoulders, his mouth forming a hard line. The dull crystal hanging around his neck surged to life, thrumming with a warm red glow.

"Something's wrong," Chelci whispered, leaning in. "I can feel it."

Leaning against the door, Veron felt it too, but abandoning their post without reason didn't feel like the right call.

"I'll check outside," Brixton said. "You two keep holding the brace since you have your power thing."

A sinking feeling hit Veron. He turned to Chelci with a gasp. "It's gone," he breathed. "The origine."

Her eyes grew wide.

He lessened his push against the brace while staring at the door. "They must be . . ." He trailed off.

"They know," Chelci added. "They know we're here."

Five fast knocks slammed outside against the window. Through the pane, Raiyn waved.

It took a moment for the significance to register. "Abort," Veron breathed. "We need to get out of here."

Before he had let go of the brace, something pushed the door from the opposite side, rattling the wood and pressing against the metal support.

Chelci backed away. "Let's go. Now!"

Veron brought up the rear while all three ran across the hall toward the door at the far end. He strained to find the origine, but the power was cut off.

A castle-shaking crash boomed behind them. Veron glanced over his shoulder while continuing to run. The metal brace looked bent. "They'll be through in seconds! We need to go!"

Another crash shook the door and rained bits of loose mortar down on the floor.

The exit door they headed toward flew open a moment before they arrived. A distraught Raiyn stared back, waving them forward. A pained look covered his face. "It was a trap!" he sputtered, his eyes red. "The knights, they're—they're all dead!"

The words shook Veron to his core as he emerged outside. His legs turned weak. "What?" His question came out of reflex, hoping to get a new response.

Another bang shook the room they had just left.

"They knew our plan," Raiyn said. "They made another hole and sent the gas back into the storage room."

Veron looked down the wall of the castle to where the kitchen waited. Despite Danik and his men being a room away, bent on capturing and killing them, he wavered. A sharp pain stabbed into his gut, but no physical weapon was there.

"They're gone, Veron. We can't help them," Raiyn said. Another loud boom from inside the castle made him jump. "Danik saw me! He's coming!"

Chelci grabbed his arm. "Come on!" A thick sorrow laced her cry. She pulled him in the opposite direction. "We need to get outside the radius of their necklaces."

In a daze, Veron stumbled in the direction she pulled. Leaving the knights' bodies behind didn't sit well, but he knew what would happen to the rest of them if they didn't flee. He forced himself to focus and deal with the problem at hand. His tottering legs strengthened, building to a run. They hurried down the narrow path, trapped between the city wall and the stone bricks of the castle.

"This leads to the front gate, right?" Brixton asked.

Veron's feet skidded to a halt. "We can't go there. Someone betrayed us, so we should assume they'll be waiting."

"Where do we go?" Raiyn asked.

A crash filled the air. Veron looked back as a chair blasted out the window of the meeting room, scattering glass into the path.

"Veron!"

The hopeful way Chelci said his name told him what she tried to communicate. He reached inside and found the power of the origine, simmering and ready. *We're far enough!* "Raiyn, help me with him!" Veron turned to the towering city wall and ran an arm around Brixton's back.

Raiyn stepped on the other side and added his support.

"On the count of three, we jump."

Brixton blanched, staring up at the wall. "Up there?" He placed his arms over their shoulders.

"Three, two, one . . ."

Veron's legs pressed into the ground, shooting him up. His arm clenched against Brixton's ribs. His enhanced muscles made the man's weight negligible, and the trio soared into the air. His clothes rippled in the wind. Air blasted against his face and hair.

The top of the wall was wide enough for two men across, which gave them plenty of room to land. Brixton hit the surface hard, falling to his side. Chelci landed a moment later, and all four of them crouched low in the shadows. Veron crept forward to peek over the edge.

Far below, Danik leaped through the broken window, landing on the ground. He checked both ways before running in their direction. His crystal shone, giving the path a red glow.

"It's gone again," Chelci said.

The power faded, like water pouring from a pitcher.

"Where do we go from here?" Brixton asked. "Run along the wall?"

Veron shook his head. "They'll spot us. We need to drop down on the other side and disappear into the forest."

Chelci started, "We can't—"

"I know. We have to hope they disperse, taking their crystals far enough away again."

Danik had run past them, but more men gathered outside of the meeting room. One ran around through the Hall of the King to open the barred door. Soon, knights of power filled the area between the castle and the wall, each one with a glowing red crystal.

Danik addressed the group. "Split up. They'll want to escape, but they may hide to throw us off. Half of you check that direction, and the rest of you follow me. Check every door and window. Look behind every bush. Someone tear through those stables. A couple of you run the city wall in case they made it up there."

Veron sucked in air. He turned to Chelci and her wide eyes.

"What do we do?" Raiyn asked. "Can we jump down?"

Veron backed away from the edge to fade deeper into the shadows. He checked through the crenel on the opposite side. The shadowy branches of the forest swayed in the breeze on the far end of a cleared field. The grassy ground looked like a blanket of darkness far below—too far. He checked again for the origine. *Nothing.*

He shook his head. "We'd break our legs."

Men jogged down the path, heading toward the front gate. Some headed in the opposite direction, following the path around the other side of the castle. A man pulled his sword and entered the stable, tearing through the stalls. Horses nickered and stomped.

"They were here!" he called.

Two men stood in the path and stared up at the wall. They pointed and spoke to each other. Their crystals pulsed, casting a red glow on the ground.

"Don't do it," Chelci whispered. "Don't jump."

When one pointed farther down the wall, Veron's hope surged.

Pulling their blades, they jogged up the path toward where a set of stairs ran from the far side of the stable to the top of the wall.

"Will that be far enough away?" Raiyn asked.

"We'll see," Veron replied. "Get ready."

"What do I—" Brixton began.

"Be ready to jump," Veron said, "one second after I do. I'll take care of the rest."

The man in the stable finished his search and joined the men heading toward the stairs. They took them two at a time, jogging as they ascended, growing farther away with each step.

Veron rested hands on the merlons and set his foot in the crenel. Brixton took the closest one to him, with Chelci and Raiyn on the opposite side.

"Not yet," Chelci said.

Veron's heartbeat sounded like a drum in his ears. He searched inside for the power he needed, but it remained inaccessible.

The men continued, nearly to the top.

"It won't be far enough," Raiyn said.

The first man arrived at the top and waited. When the next one arrived, the first pointed in Veron's direction before tossing his thumb the other way. They muttered between each other while the last man took the final steps.

Like water breaking from a dam, the power flooded into Veron. "That's it!" he whispered. "Jump!"

Without a pause, he leaped off the backside of the city wall, falling to the dark ground below.

BILTON'S HEAD swiveled as he walked through the castle halls and up the stairs. High Lord Miligan prattled on about his need for sleep and the importance of rest for the constables in the justice department, but Bilton heard little of what the man said.

Veron and the others had failed to meet at the cistern. Bilton feared the worst but realized they could have called off the plans or gone into hiding once it was complete.

Having given up waiting, he received a late-night summons at his house for an Advisors Council meeting. He hurried to the castle and arrived at the same time as the other high lord.

"What do you think?" Miligan asked.

Bilton turned his head. "I'm sorry?"

"About the constables? How none of them matched your description of the counterfeiter?"

Bilton continued forward, unsure of how to respond.

"Were you not listening that whole time?"

"I'm sorry, Herman. I have a lot on my mind."

Miligan's scoff gurgled with wet phlegm. "As if I don't." His breath was heavy, and a gloss of sweat covered his forehead. "Just because you have Danik's ear doesn't mean you're above it all."

"I don't think I'm above anything," Bilton said. "And I don't feel close to Danik, to be honest."

"Oh yeah. In this meeting, let's see how many times he talks to you compared to me, shall we?"

Bilton frowned. "Sure. Let's see."

They approached the double doors of the meeting room at the end of the hall. No men guarded the entry, and Bilton's nerves trembled with anticipation. He peeked his head through and found only a few of the usual crowd alone in the torch-lit room.

Kennith Stokes and Marie Windrige sat at the oval-shaped table, chatting with shoulders drooped and bags under their eyes. Stanley Hillegass paced the floor on the far side of the chairs. The High Lord of Trade tapped his fingers together and muttered, seeming oblivious to the others.

"Geoffrey and Herman," Windridge greeted. She covered her mouth while her face stretched into a yawn. "Any idea what this is about?"

Miligan shook his head. "Where is the king?"

"We were just wondering that," Windridge replied. "It's curious. He usually has at least a few of his men around."

Bilton fought back a smile. *Curious indeed.*

While Miligan settled into a seat, Bilton joined Hillegass. "Did you hear anything?" Bilton whispered.

The High Lord of Trade paused his pacing. "You didn't?"

"No. What is it? What'd you hear?"

"A few hours ago, the—" He paused as the door opened.

Quentin Cotterell and Magnus Hampton entered. Hampton's jaw formed a firm line. His eyes found Bilton's, but they flitted away after a second.

"What happened a few hours ago?" Bilton whispered to Hillegass.

The man paused, then shook his head. "We shouldn't be talking."

"What?"

Hillegass grabbed a chair and sat as Hampton and Cotterell did. Positioned at the top of the oval, Bilton was the sole person standing. He rested his hands on the back of the high-backed chair and looked around the table. The Advisors Council was ready, but neither the king nor any of the knights of power had arrived.

Hopefully, that means they never will.

Bilton opened his mouth to speak but paused at the sound of boots in the hall—several pairs. With a firm push, the doors flew open, and Danik entered. Lines creased in his forehead. His scowl drew the corners of his eyes down, and a faint red hue colored his skin, except for the place on his neck where the black mark displayed as dark as ever. Behind him, Nicolar and Cedric followed with angry looks.

Bilton's heart sank.

"Thank you for coming this late," Danik called. "Something happened and it couldn't wait until morning to be discussed."

The room was silent, all eyes on him.

"Earlier tonight, we thwarted an assassination attempt."

Gasps echoed around the table. A knot twisted in Bilton's stomach.

"The traitorous shadow knights returned, and they attempted to kill me and all of my men."

"The shadow knights?" Windridge echoed. "I can't believe it."

"Part of their plot to help Norshewa overtake Feldor, no doubt.

First, they needed to unseat me from power. Next, they would march the Norshewan army south to occupy these lands."

"What happened?" Quentin asked.

"During our Knights of Power meeting, they tried to trap us and poison us with gas—a bold but foolish move. Thankfully, we're all right."

"Was it your—" The advisor paused to tap against his neck. "Your power that saved you?"

Danik touched the black spot on his own neck. "No, although our ability would have been enough to keep us safe." He stepped farther into the room, strolling along the length of the table. "Knowledge is power. When you gain information, what you do with it can either help or hurt you."

Hillegass kept his eyes fixed forward while the king passed behind his chair. One hand trembled on the surface of the table until he covered it with the other.

"Someone heard whispers of this threat. They *met* with these traitors and engaged in dangerous conversations." Danik passed behind Bilton. "But it wasn't just one of you, it was *three* of you."

Bilton's dry throat refused to swallow. The hair on the nape of his neck prickled. He kept his hands on the back of the chair, sweat staining the wood.

Danik stopped pacing and stood beside him. "Stanley Hillegass, Magnus Hampton . . ." He turned and met Bilton's eyes. ". . . and Geoffrey Bilton."

He couldn't breathe. *Do I run? Do I try to fight?* He knew what they were capable of. The attempt would be futile. He wanted to object— to claim it wasn't true. His mouth opened, but the words caught.

The king stared for a long moment. His mouth opened, poised to proclaim Bilton's death.

Will he kill me before I realize he's moving?

Danik's eyes softened. The lines on his forehead smoothed, and a faint smile came to his face. He looked at Hillegass and then at Hampton. "To you three, I thank you."

The tension in Bilton's body eased. *What does he mean?*

Danik continued walking and stopped behind Hampton's chair. "Loyalty means a lot. You three took it upon yourselves to mislead the shadow knights and set up a trap."

Trap?

"When Magnus came to me and told me of your plan—what you three did, luring the knights into a false trust, I beamed with pride."

Bilton's eyes flicked to Hampton, who stared back. His gaze held a restrained intensity that reflected their shared knowledge. Bilton felt like someone had kicked him in the gut, knocking out his breath.

"I thank you for your trust. You three will be rewarded for this act."

"Th-thank you, Your Majesty," Hillegass said with a pale face.

Hampton wore a look of satisfaction. "Yes. You are too generous."

Bilton cleared his throat to push away the terror in his voice. "What of the shadow knights?"

"They were *supposed* to be captured." Danik glared at Nicolar.

His right-hand-man shrank back, averting his eyes toward the table.

"There was some . . . misunderstanding about how to handle it."

"What happened?" Bilton asked.

Danik swallowed. "They're dead."

The kick in Bilton's gut doubled in intensity.

"At least most of them. Veron, Chelci, and the Norshewan traitor survived." His face softened as he paused. "I worked with them for years. They lost some good people, and it's unfortunate it had to end this way."

The room remained quiet as the king ruminated, lost in his thoughts. After a moment, he snapped back to the present.

"I imagine we'll see more desperate acts from these last three as they foolishly try to wrest back power. Bilton, send scouts along the main roads with sketches of what they look like. We need to know where they are."

The high lord nodded.

"In Felting, knights of power will remain on alert for as long as is needed. We will keep this attack quiet. No one in Feldor needs to know. We can't have anyone thinking the leadership of their kingdom is at risk." With a clap of his hands, he started toward the door. "That is all for tonight."

Cedric and Nicolar followed, and the three men left the room with silence in their wake.

Marie Windridge rose. "That was unexpected."

Miligan and Stokes exchanged a furtive look while Cotterell left the room as soon as possible.

"Magnus," Bilton said, drawing the man's gaze. He nodded toward the arched balcony openings while his heart pounded. "Do you have a minute?"

Movement near the door caught his eye. Hillegass hurried to exit the room. "Stanley, can we speak, too?" Bilton asked.

The high lord waved a dismissive hand. "Sorry, it is late, and I must be off." He didn't even break stride as he left the meeting room.

Hampton sniffed as he rose. "He has nothing to discuss. I'm free to talk, though."

Bilton walked with Hampton to the balcony. The flickering torch failed to penetrate the gloom that marked the edge of the platform where darkness had replaced the sky. The stone walls held onto the day's heat, creating a warmth despite the chill in the air.

"What was that, Magnus?" Bilton asked.

Hampton turned and held his gaze. "You know what that was."

"You turned on them!" He checked over his shoulder, aware of the volume of his words. "You turned on me."

"I *saved* you," Hampton said. "It wouldn't have worked."

"It *could* have."

"They were doomed either way. Do I feel bad? Of course I do. But you've seen what the devion can do. The plan was futile. This way, we're heroes instead of martyrs."

"I've seen what it can do. I've seen what *they* do. That's why we needed the shadow knights to stop them. And now—" He ended with a shake of his head and a groan. "Now there's little hope."

"You heard what Danik said, didn't you?" Magnus asked. "He said we'd be rewarded. I'm not proud of it, but sometimes you have to forget about impossible ideals and grab hold of what's in front of you." The younger high lord moved to leave.

"Wait." Bilton grabbed his upper arm.

"Argh!" Hampton gritted his teeth. He jerked away, covered his arm with his other hand, and hissed.

"What is it?" Bilton leaned closer and stared at the man's arm.

"Nothing." Hampton shook his head. "Just a cut."

"From what?"

"My chef had a knife and didn't see me walking by. It was stupid."

The hairs on Bilton's neck stood on end again. "A chef?"

"Yeah."

The memory of attacking a mysterious man at night rushed into his head. He stared at the arm—the upper right portion that Magnus held. "Show me."

Hampton flinched. "It's foolish, really." He motioned to the long sleeve of his tunic. "It's tough to roll up, plus I need to leave so I'm not late."

Bilton grabbed the younger man's arm again. "Leave?" Bilton narrowed his eyes. "You *just* said you're free to talk, and you can't have anything you're late for at this hour."

"Geoffrey, let go."

"Show me."

Hampton stopped struggling. After a bitter look, he rolled up his right sleeve. Fabric folded over itself until a tight diagonal scab displayed across the upper portion of his arm.

Bilton mimed a slow-motion move of slicing with a sword. The path of the imaginary blade crossed Hampton's arm at the same angle as the cut. "Chef's knife, huh?"

Hampton's eyes narrowed. He didn't answer.

"I remember you were planning to meet with the constables. I'll bet you stole a key when you were there, and that's how you got away in that tunnel," Bilton hissed. "It was you. You're the counterfeiter."

A shrug jostled his frozen position. "So what if I am?"

The admission took Bilton aback. "You can't—" He couldn't think of how to finish his sentence.

"Why not? Danik's running this place into the ground. Why not make some money before it all burns down?"

Bilton scoffed. "You sure have changed since your wife died."

"Yes, I have. I spent most of my adult life trying to be good and where did it get me? Alone. Miserable."

Bilton turned to leave. "I'm turning you in."

"No, you're not. Because if you do, I'll tell Danik what really happened at that meeting in the Red Quarter."

Bilton stopped.

"He'll hear how it wasn't all three of us working against Veron. How do you think Danik will react when he hears that you *actually* tried to have him killed?"

Bilton pinched the bridge of his nose and sighed.

"You owe me," Hampton said, "for saving your life. You and Stanley, both."

The memory of the other high lord's nervousness came to Bilton's mind. "You're blackmailing him, too?"

Hampton shrugged. "I wouldn't call it blackmail, but we came to an arrangement."

"What does he have that you want?"

"A wife."

"You're going to take his wife?"

"Ha! No." A weak smile crossed his face. "Have you met his daughter, Geneva?"

PEEKING from behind a tree at the edge of the woods, Raiyn scanned the darkness. After the initial pass of the two knights of power walking the city wall hours before, he'd seen no one else. The city gate to their west had remained quiet.

Content that they were safe for the moment, he turned toward the deep forest. He jogged in a crouch, his silent feet padding along the ground until he rounded a boulder tucked well out of sight from the city. The others flinched when he arrived, but relaxed when they saw it was him.

"Nothing," Raiyn said.

"I don't think they're coming," Brixton said.

Veron and Chelci exchanged a look. Both of their eyes were red, like they held back a wave of sorrow. Chelci's hand trembled as Veron took it in his.

"What do you think happened?" Raiyn asked. "Did Bilton or those other guys turn us in?"

"Could have been any of the three." Veron's weak voice was barely audible.

"Or all," Brixton added.

"I spent some time with Bilton," Raiyn said. "I don't think it would be him."

"I agree," Veron said. "But we can't contact him. We can't take that chance. "

"What do we do now?" Raiyn asked. "Regroup at the Glade?"

"To what end?" Chelci asked, her voice thick with emotion. "Hide? Farm?"

"Make a plan." Raiyn glanced between Chelci and Veron, noting the hopelessness in their eyes. "There must be something we can do. We can't let Danik win."

"They'll be guarded at all times. And we only have three knights now. Without someone on the inside—" Veron paused and shook his head. "I'm not sure what we could hope to do. They're too fast, too strong, and too many. Maybe we can go to Karondir. It sounds like Baron Devenish would be sympathetic to our goal."

An idea flooded into Raiyn's head. His heart beat fast at the possibility and the danger. He opened his mouth to speak, but the implications turned his stomach. "We need something they won't suspect," he forced out. "A weapon they're not prepared for."

Veron raised his eyebrows.

"We need something that allows us to attack in a way they couldn't possibly defend."

"Such as . . ."

Half of Raiyn's face pulled up in a nervous grin. "Bravian Fire."

A quick inhale of air from Veron and Chelci preceded a chuckle from Brixton. "Yeah, that would be nice," he said.

The others turned to Brixton.

"Norshewa supposedly discovered it," Veron said.

Brixton's eyes grew wide.

"Danik's men are fast, but they're not *that* fast." Veron looked at Chelci. "It would create possibilities."

"Wait," Brixton raised a hand. "Even if they discovered it, it's going to be heavily guarded. They won't give it to us. It doesn't matter what you tell them about Danik or Talioth, they won't care. Norshewa is out for themselves."

"They'd have to give it to me," Raiyn said.

Veron held his gaze, his eyes filled with understanding. "Are you sure you'd want to do that?"

Raiyn nodded. "It's time. We don't have any other options. This may be the best chance we have."

Veron's mouth formed a grim line. Chelci rested her hand on his shoulder.

"I'm sorry," Brixton said. "I feel like I'm missing something. Why would Norshewa *have* to give it to you?"

Raiyn took a deep breath and then blew it out, trying to settle the trembling in his arms. "Because I'm their rightful king."

PART II

TAKING ACTION

20

TAVERN PROBLEMS

A hazy knock reached into the recesses of Danik's mind, thudding like a distant drum. *What is that?* He pushed it away, grasping at the sleep that threatened to leave him. *Knock, knock.* Again.

"Your Majesty?"

The voice was closer. Clearer. He blinked and lifted his head. The room was still dark. He wiped at his face. A guard stood at the door with a lantern.

"What time is it?" he grumbled.

"It's . . . early. I'm sorry, but your presence is required."

"Why? What happened?"

"There's been a, um . . . an incident. I was told to fetch you. I'm sorry, but that's all I know."

Danik frowned to show his displeasure until he realized the guard wouldn't be able to see it. With a huff, he threw his legs over the side of the bed and rose.

THE KING YAWNED as he stumbled along the road. An orange light peeked over the mountains in the east, indicating dawn was near. Most of the city remained dark, yet to rise with the new day.

"How much farther?" he grumbled.

"It's just ahead," the guard leading him replied.

The familiar sign of Fetzer's Tavern materialized in the dark street. Two city constables stood on either side of the door. Danik's gut confirmed it must be their destination.

Entering the street from a side alley, Nicolar arrived with an escort of his own. "They got you too, huh?"

"What is this?" Danik asked. "Why are we here?"

"Apparently, there's been a problem with Cedric."

"Cedric?" Danik glanced at the tavern door. "What happened?"

"I'm not sure."

A constable at the door squirmed. "Thank you for coming." He grabbed the handle and pulled the door open. "They're inside."

Danik entered first. The still-lit lanterns on the wall kept the room looking the same as always. Tables, chairs, and booths filled the room, but the usual rowdy patrons were gone. The circular throwing target hung in the corner with knives stuck in it. Two more constables stood in the room, pressed close against the wall. Their tense shoulders relaxed as Danik entered.

In front of the far row of booths, Cedric paced. Red spice powder ringed his nostrils and covered his upper lip. Sweat beaded on his forehead. He wiped it with the back of his hand—a hand that held a knife. Dried blood coated its blade. He muttered as he walked, alternating between laughing and whimpering with the black stain on his neck displayed prominently. Lost in his chaotic ramblings, he seemed oblivious to the king's arrival.

The source of the distress caught Danik's eye. A body lay on the floor, facedown and wearing a barmaid's uniform. The braided brown hair gave her away. *Clara.* Although he'd never taken the time to get to know her, Clara had served him drinks for years. Her skin was pale and still. A red gash cut across the visible portion of her neck, and a congealed puddle of dark red stained the floor.

Danik's blood ran cold. *Did Cedric do this?* His neck flushed, the warmth creeping up his face. *Cedric, one of my knights of power.*

Behind Cedric, a man huddled in a booth, rocking in a slow rhythm. He pressed his back against the wall with his knees brought to his chest. His head drooped against his legs while his arms wrapped around them. Dried blood covered his cream-colored tunic.

An older man with bleary eyes and disheveled hair walked out from behind the bar, keeping to the far side of the room.

Danik recognized the tavern owner. "Louko, what happened here?"

The owner cast a nervous glance at Cedric while he joined Danik and Nicolar. He kept his voice low. "Your Majesty, there was a problem last night. Cedric here was being, uh . . . *friendly* with Clara."

Nicolar frowned. "He's always like that. He means nothing by it."

"This was worse than normal. He was loud and obnoxious, upsetting the other patrons. He'd been"—Louko flicked his own nose—"using. Clara started avoiding his table, so he followed her around the tavern, grabbing at her skirt. It was late, so I told him we were closing and he needed to leave, but he wouldn't listen. I tried to push him toward the door, but he stood there with a smirk on his face." Louko pointed toward the bar top, where glasses hung upside down from a wooden rack on the ceiling. "He grabbed one of those glass mugs and stared at me while he crushed it with his bare hand."

Danik winced.

"The shards sliced into his fingers and palm. Blood dripped onto the floor. He laughed at it. He held his hand up and cackled while it healed before our eyes. I've never seen anything like it. It was . . . horrible. The room cleared out at that point. I sent someone to fetch the constables."

"What happened to Clara?" Danik asked.

Louko swallowed. "Her husband arrived soon after." He nodded to the man huddled in the back of the booth. "He confronted Cedric."

"I can't imagine that went well."

The owner shook his head, then pointed to the corner. "Cedric pushed him against the target and made him stand there while he threw knives, threatening to switch him with Clara if he didn't stay put. It's a wonder a knife never skewered him. Cedric was shaking with each throw. When he covered his eyes with one hand while readying to throw with the other, she tried to stop him." He grew quiet as his gaze drifted to the body on the floor. A tear ran down his cheek. "She got a blade in the neck. Bled out straight away. Cedric threw her husband in that booth and threatened to do the same to him if he moved. That was hours ago, and he's been there ever since."

Footsteps approached as the constables against the wall joined them. "We arrived just after that," one said. "Tried to subdue him, but he grew increasingly erratic, wavering between tears and fits of rage."

As if on cue, Cedric bellowed a string of insults directed seemingly at no one.

"Cedric," Nicolar called.

The pacing man stopped and looked at them as if recognizing their presence for the first time. His dilated pupils looked like black orbs. His crooked grin made him look crazy. "Nicolar. Danik. I'm glad you're here." He sniffed and pulled at his nose, the knife coming close to his eyes. "This woman was a threat. She wanted to take your throne, but don't worry, I stopped her."

Danik swallowed, but the lump in his throat wouldn't go away.

Cedric waved the knife toward the man huddled in the booth. "This one tried to kill me. We need to throw him in the dungeon, so I held him here until . . ." He stopped and cocked his head. "Until what? I don't know."

"Until we showed up," Danik answered, his stomach churning. "So we can let him go."

Cedric's face turned red. "Let him go? No!"

Danik flinched. "You're high on spice, Cedric. You're not thinking clearly. Use the devion. Flush out the effect of the—"

"He assaulted an officer of the king! A quick death is too gentle for him. He deserves—" Cedric wobbled. He extended an arm to brace himself against a booth. "We need to torture him—find out what he knows."

"He doesn't know anything," Nicolar said, his flat voice lacking emotion. "Wipe away the spice, Cedric."

Cedric froze, his eyes wide. He held up the knife. "Oh yes, he does. I'll show you. I'll get him to talk."

"Cedric, no!" Danik shouted.

A dizzy spell seemed to take over Cedric. "All we need is—" He teetered. "We need—" His eyes rolled back, and his arms slumped. The knife fell to the floor, followed by his body.

Danik stepped forward and knelt. The knight lay unconscious but breathing. "What a mess," he muttered.

"You're safe now," Nicolar addressed the man in the booth. "You can get up."

The grieving husband lifted his head. His face trembled, eyes locked on Clara's body.

Danik shook Cedric's arm, but the man didn't respond. "We should take him to the prison. Keep him locked up while he sobers."

"You two," Nicolar called to the guards who had escorted them there. "Take him to the training facility. Wake Luc so he can monitor him."

Danik frowned. "The training facility?"

Nicolar nodded, then lowered his voice. "It's best we keep him out of sight for the moment while we let this blow over. One of our knights of power in the city prison wouldn't be a good look."

"But . . ." Danik's argument faded as the guards arrived. He moved aside while the men scooped up the unconscious body.

Nicolar stood and nodded toward the constables. "Take care of the man and do something with this body." He pulled at Danik's sleeve. "Come on. We need to get out of here."

Danik's legs felt hollow as he stumbled toward the door, pulled by Nicolar. He cringed as the constables dropped a sheet over Clara.

The cool air infused life into his lungs, making him realize how stuffy the tavern had become. Nicolar pulled his hood up and motioned for Danik to do the same. He complied.

"I don't like it either," Nicolar said, breaking the silence of their footsteps padding up the street. "He messed up, sure. It happens, though. We expect a lot from these knights, and they need to let loose sometimes."

"Let loose?" Danik's mouth hung open. "He killed that woman—for no reason. We can't let that happen."

"What do you want to do, huh? Execute Cedric—one of our strongest knights of power?"

"Well ... no, but—"

"Don't forget, almost two weeks ago, *he* was almost killed by the Shadow Knights and their poison gas. All of us were. That's tough to deal with. He's coping the best he can."

"He's got to kick the spice habit," Danik said. "We *cannot* have men who can't control themselves."

Nicolar sighed and nodded. "Of course. Of course. I'll speak with him once he's clean. It won't be a problem again."

Danik stewed as they walked. *This group is getting out of control.* That the necklaces didn't completely solve the pull from the caverns troubled him. And the size of the group continued to create more problems.

"What is it?" Nicolar asked.

Danik glanced at him. The other man's lips pursed, pulling his goatee to an exaggerated point. "I'm worried we're overextending ourselves."

Nicolar raised an eyebrow.

"At first, I wanted as many men as I could train. The more the better. We'd be able to conquer anyone, do anything. But the more knights we have, the more liability. What if others don't work out?"

"Like the short guy? Immo?"

Danik nodded. "We can't just . . . train people, then eliminate them when they want to leave."

"There will always be differences in opinions. This is not a social club where they can hop in and out. If they commit, they're in. There's no getting out. It's too dangerous, Danik."

"I know. I know. I just think ... with a manageable number of people, that's a smaller risk. Also, we have the black marks and the cavern pull to deal with." He tugged at the crystal hanging around his neck. "What if these necklaces stop working? What if some break or get lost? That invisible force from the caverns is going to bring us back to the mountains."

"Then we'll go and get more of them. You saw how many they had in those caverns. They were glowing everywhere. I don't care what Talioth says."

"But they're barely doing the job now! It's a mess is what it is, and it's only going to get worse." The scene they'd just left flashed into his head. "And then Cedric! The fool can't stay away from spice. Our knights can't wander the city acting like this."

"Why not?"

Nicolar's stern challenge brought Danik to a halt. "What do you mean?"

The older man stepped toward Danik with narrowed eyes, pointing at his chest. "These men dedicate their life to you—to serving your interests. You give them the ultimate power and ask them to use it for *you*. Do you really expect them to moderate their behavior in their free time?"

"We still have laws," Danik said. "There are conduct expectations."

"Conduct?" Nicolar bellowed a laugh. "Are you serious? Why don't you come to the training center tomorrow? I'd happily let you lead a training session with these killers on which fork to use at dinner and whether or not to lift their pinky when they drink tea."

"That's not what I mean."

"Wake up, Danik. Give them some latitude."

Danik clenched his teeth at the informal address and the disrespect with which the man spoke. "You will call me by my title."

Nicolar's eyes narrowed. "Wake up . . . Your Majesty. Don't pump these men up, telling them they're the most powerful beings in Terrenor, then pull the rug out from under their feet by putting them in restraints."

Danik chafed at the rebuke, but he saw the truth in Nicolar's words. *I would feel the same way. I would want to have some freedom to be myself.* He realized the grim truth. *I did feel the same way . . . under the Shadow Knights.*

When Nicolar continued forward, Danik walked with him. "You have a point," Danik said. "I can allow some freedom, but . . . what Cedric did tonight—"

"Not acceptable," Nicolar said. "Agreed."

"Good." Danik's stomach settled, feeling back on the same page. "Maybe we can give Cedric something to do to keep him occupied."

"I think that would help. You have anything in mind?"

"At some point, we're going to need more crystal necklaces. I'd rather plan ahead than wait for us to need them. I'm thinking we could send Cedric back to the caverns to collect a dozen more. Maybe take a few of the new recruits with him."

Nicolar nodded. "That's a great idea."

"By the time they're back, our latest trainees should be ready. Then we can begin the plan."

"The plan to take over?"

Danik grinned. "Exactly. Conquering Terrenor."

INCREASED TRAINING

C*rack!*

The pickaxe knocked a sizable chunk of debris to the ground. Lia grinned as the angular, shiny block settled to a stop. She placed her axe against the wall and scooped it up. "Got one!"

"Another?" Waylon stared from the next spot down. "That's, what . . . three today?"

She nodded and jogged down the corridor. Chris and Thurman fell in step behind her.

"We might not need to train tonight," Chris said. "All this running we're getting today."

Lia glanced over her shoulder. "No one's making you show up."

The team leader grinned. "I'll be there."

They passed a side cavern where the Mountain Wolves labored. Their team's glowing red faces glanced up as Lia flew past. She rounded the corner in the main cavern, maintaining full speed. The team boxes waited ahead. She slowed as they neared, then dropped the crystal into the Garronts' receptacle.

The Valcors worked against the far wall of the main chamber. A worker hit Bronson on the shoulder. The leader turned and glared at Lia. She waved and flashed a smile.

"This is a great start for the week," Thurman said as the three made their way, walking back toward their tunnel. That makes . . ."

"Eight . . . in one day," Chris finished.

"Incredible. We have to be ahead of the Valcors. Granted, it is only the first day."

"Spirits are high. Energy is strong." Chris nodded. "I feel good about it."

"We made quota the last two weeks," Lia said. "Five crystals to spare last week and three the week before. That helps with the spirits, I think."

"I thought the evening training sessions would tire people out more, but you're right, Lia, they only give them more energy."

Leaving the light of the large room, they ducked into the smaller side corridor.

"I still wish there was something better we could do with these crystals," Lia said.

"Like what?" Thurman asked.

"We could start sandbagging after we reach our quota—save them for next week."

"We can't—"

"I know." She held up a hand. "The fiends. But if there were a way we could save them back, we could try to harness their power. Get ten together, then do . . . whatever the marked ones do with them."

"It's too dangerous," Chris said. "We'd risk everyone's lives by holding on to even one."

Since Dayna's death, two weeks before, Lia had racked her brain for ideas about how to escape. She'd thought through the impacts of storming the gates, attacking the guards, even hiding in the caves. None of the scenarios played out well in her mind. She continued to return to the idea of stockpiling crystals, but that held obvious drawbacks.

"What if we train to fight them?" she asked, taking in the sight of the Mountain Wolves they passed.

"The fiends?" Thurman asked.

"Yeah. They're the reason we have to get rid of the crystals as soon as possible. But if we could fight them off, maybe we wouldn't need to."

Chris and Thurman exchanged glances.

"What is it?"

They didn't reply.

"What are these things like? They've got to have weaknesses." She glanced between the two men, but neither said anything. "Come on! I know you don't like to talk about them, but ... surely—"

"I've never seen one," Chris blurted.

"Me neither," Thurman added.

Lia stopped walking. Her head jerked forward, and her mouth froze, pursed together. "What?"

Chris shrugged. "I haven't."

"You've been here two years?"

He nodded. "I don't know anyone who has. At least not anyone alive."

"No one?" Lia's stomach dropped.

A shout echoed down the corridor at their backs. "Find it!"

"It was here. I-I kicked it somewhere!"

Lia and the men turned, leaning their ears toward the passage where the Mountain Wolves worked.

"Bring that lantern! Hurry! Come on! Everyone help!"

"You think they're talking about a crystal?" Thurman asked.

"Find it, Reuben!"

Lia stepped toward the passage. "Sounds like it."

"We should get out of here," Chris said, moving in the opposite direction with Thurman.

Lia took another step. "I wonder if ..."

A low rumble reverberated ahead.

"Lia!" Chris said. "Let's go!"

Her feet remained rooted.

"I hear it!" A Wolf yelled. "Get that crystal out of here!"

"They're in trouble," Lia whispered to herself. The rotten stench she'd smelled before wafted along the passage. Motivations to learn more about the fiends warred against her desire to flee as well as protect.

"Found it!" someone shouted.

The red crystals dimmed. Scrambling sounds poured through the tunnel as the growl increased in volume.

"Go! Go! Go!"

Lia stepped closer to the voices.

"What are you doing?" Chris pulled against her shoulder.

"Hold on." Lia sloughed his hand off. "I'm curious."

She moved faster. The lip of the Wolves' tunnel came into view. The light was dimmer when two men careened around the corner, running at a full clip toward the main cavern.

A blood-curdling roar shook the walls. Lia cringed and ducked to the side as she continued forward. The smell left her light headed. *I need to see it!* The passage grew even darker. Lia could barely see her hand, but she stumbled along.

A shriek tore through the corridor. "Watch out!"

Lia moved faster, holding a hand over her nose to block out the odor. A bellowing sound surrounded her. Screams filled the darkness ahead. Close.

Where is it?

She extended a hand, feeling the black space. She tripped and scraped over rocks, fighting a gag reflex from the stench. Her eyes squinted, tested by an unfamiliar sight. A blue glow teased the darkness.

What is that?

She stepped forward. Ripping and snarling sounds should have sent her running, but the light drew her in. Closer. Closer. The blue emanated from an object, something floating in midair. A faint shattering sound replaced the snarls, and the cave fell silent. No roars. No growls. No ripping or shouting. After a moment, the blue light vanished.

Lia blinked against the light as the red glow returned. She shaded her eyes, then spun toward jogging footsteps. Chris and Thurman skidded to a halt beside her.

"Are you all right?" Chris asked.

She nodded. "I'm fine."

"Did you see anything?"

Lia turned up the passage. Two lumps lay on the ground.

Chris pointed. "What is that?"

She stepped forward. The glowing red crystals reflected off a liquid that covered the floor and walls. The lumps looked like—Lia gasped. "It's the two Wolves."

Thurman made a muffled straining noise. "I think I'm gonna be sick." He stumbled in the opposite direction.

A coppery smell filled the air, mixing in with a faint hint of sulfur. Lia leaned in for a closer look, and her stomach turned. One arm was missing, severed at the elbow, while strings of flesh comprised the other. The man's clothes had been shredded. A gash tore from his side up to his chest, leaving entrails scattered across the outside of his corpse. His unidentifiable face was a mangled, pulpy mess. The other man fared no better. Parts of both their bodies lay strewn across the ground. A drop of red liquid fell onto Lia's arm. She brought it close to her face. *Blood.* It covered the cave, splattered on the floor and walls and dripping from the ceiling.

A crushed object caught her eye. Lia stepped around the bodies and squatted to inspect it.

"What is that?" Chris asked.

She tried to lift it, but the item crumbled in her fingers. Shiny edges broke like hard-packed sand crumbling under pressure. It fell to the ground in dull-red crumbles. "I think this was their crystal."

Chris stepped closer. "That's impossible. It's-it's . . ."

"Destroyed. I thought we couldn't break these with a direct hit from a pickaxe?"

Chris didn't answer. He straightened and looked in both directions down the corridor. "What are these things?"

"There was a blue light."

"What do you mean?"

"In the passage, the red crystals dimmed, but something had a glowing blue light."

"Blue? The fiend?"

She shrugged. "I guess."

They both stared at the grisly scene. Lia's heart pounded. Without the origine to assist her, a beast like that would tear her to shreds, and there would be nothing she could do about it. She swallowed hard.

"So . . ." Chris began, "how do you feel about fighting them, now?"

A SOMBER CLOUD hovered over the teams as the groups trudged out of the mine. Wooden wheels clacked over the stone where the Mountain Wolves rolled two carts. Red stains marred the top edge and dripped down the sides.

Rasmill stood outside the mine office with his hands on his hips. "What happened?"

"We ran into a fiend," Kilock, the Wolves' leader, said.

"You should know better than to tempt them."

"Reuben lost the crystal. It was an accident. By the time he found it, it was too late."

Lia dropped off her pickaxe with the rest of her team.

"What's the plan, Lia?" Waylon asked.

The other Garronts glanced at her while they walked past the mess area.

"Hopefully not those buddy carries, again," Harold whined.

"I didn't mind those," Thurman said. "The shoulder crawls were what killed me."

Several groans sounded.

"Arm strength is getting better," Lia began, "but we need to work on stamina. Mining is repetitive and grueling over a long period, so we need to train for that."

She passed the barracks, then walked to the edge of the boneyard. She waited while seven other men gathered around. Their faces held an odd mixture of excitement and terror as they looked at her.

"Vekko! Jarno!" Chris called. "Join the team!"

The two other Garronts paused at the entrance to the barracks and looked their way.

"You're all idiots!" Vekko called. He ducked through the doorway with Jarno following and shaking his head.

Grumbles bounced around the group.

"Forget about it," Lia said. "We're all going to be mining circles around those two, soon. We can't want it *for* them. They have to desire it for themselves. Give it time."

Heads nodded.

She clapped her hands. "Tonight, we're going to start by getting our heart rate up. Then, when we're good and tired, the real effort begins. We'll work the legs, the shoulders, and your upper backs. If you stop to rest, you're running the lake. If you drop your load, you're adding more weight.

"You're going to want to quit. Your mind will tell you to stop, telling you it would feel better if you rested. Tonight, we're working through the fatigue. Your heart can handle it. Your lungs will do what is required. Your body will become an unstoppable force.

"When Jarno and Vekko are breathing with their hands on their knees, you'll be knocking crystals out of the rock. When the Valcors are taking breaks, you'll be digging in another shovelful of rubble. At the end of the week, when Rasmill totals up our work, we'll have such a crazy amount of crystals that they're going to accuse us of cheating."

The men chuckled.

"Let's do it," Thurman said.

"Line up," Lia said, motioning in a straight line and standing in the middle. She faced the far side of the boneyard. "Twenty sprints. Last one to finish cleans out the latrine."

"Where do you come up with all this stuff, Lia?" Waylon asked, his voice carrying a slight waver.

"My parents." She grinned. "I had an interesting childhood."

She glanced down the line of men. They toed the imaginary line, their legs poised, ready for action. A nervous energy emanated from the group.

"Go!"

. . .

LIA COLLAPSED ONTO HER BED, exhausted. She closed her eyes, breathing deeply to bring oxygen through her body. Her heart had finally slowed from the intense training she'd put the team through.

"That was great, Lia," Waylon said on his way past her bed. His words were light, buoyed by the grin on his face. "The toughest yet." He turned to the rest of the barracks. "Harold, I don't want you to be bored when you clean out the latrines, so don't worry . . . I'll make sure you have some work to do." He laughed as he ducked around the corner.

Harold turned to Chris. "That wasn't real, was it?"

The leader raised his shoulders. "You heard Lia."

"But—"

"Someone has to clean them. Next time, run faster."

The men laughed.

Thurman hit Harold playfully on the back, then shouted toward the latrine, "I'm next, Waylon!"

Vekko and Jarno sulked in the corner. Lia caught a nasty glare thrown her direction.

An unexpected savory scent reached her nose.

"What is that?" Thurman asked, heads perking up at the same time throughout the room.

Lia sat up, sniffing. Her eyes settled on Stewart, who sat on his bed, hunched over. The rest of the men turned in his direction.

"Stewart," Chris said. "What do you have?"

The man's head shrank into his neck as his ears turned red. His eyes shifted around the room. After a moment, he held a bundle of rags up. Something lay uncovered at the center.

Thurman stepped closer. "Is that . . . sausage?"

"Yeah."

The men pushed and shoved to get closer.

"Hey! Hey! This is mine!"

"Where'd you get it from?"

"I nicked it from the kitchen this morning. I've been saving it."

"There's enough to share. Come on!"

Chris laughed. "If you want to hide food, you need to find something that doesn't smell up the whole barracks and give you away."

The men forced their way in, making Stewart share his prize in tiny pieces.

It seemed forever to Lia since she'd eaten any food like that, but she didn't feel like fighting the others over it. *After this week, maybe we can have food like that.*

22

BOLD REQUESTS

Talioth stared at his cards. His eyes flicked to the five piles spread on the table. None of them looked right. He touched the star prince in his hand and paused. Shaking his head, he pulled out the saber king and tossed it on the pile nearest Centol.

"Thank you," Centol said with a grin, covering the card with a diamond king.

"Argh!" Talioth groaned. "What a waste."

"You should have known I'd have it."

"Gammit never suited me."

"Luckily for you, we play for fun. Back in Karondir, I used to send the city guards home broke."

They both drew cards and Talioth resumed staring at his hand.

Around them, slaves scurried through the room, filling the four oversized tables of the massive dining chamber with settings for dinner. Marked ones stood watch with readied weapons and crystal necklaces that didn't need to be used. Savory smells of simmering onions and potatoes wafted in from the adjacent room, teasing the meal that was to come. While red crystals in the walls gave the room a muted glow, most of the light came from the drilled holes that angled through the thick stone to the sky.

Meliand caught Talioth's attention. He dropped a diamond jester onto another pile and turned as she approached. The swishing of her unbound, gray hair waved in rhythm with an armful of necklaces—red crystals hanging from the end of blue leather cords. He nodded to her burden. "You got it done fast. Blue cords; nice touch. How many?"

"Thirty," she answered.

"Good. I asked Rasmill to up the quota in the mines again."

Centol played a star eight on a pile showing a star five. They both drew cards.

"I think you're right," Meliand said.

Talioth grinned as he slotted a star king into his hand. "Right about . . . ?"

"The increased power. I feel it—barely. Siphoning Dayna was a great boost, but there's been a small uptick since then. You really think Danik and his men killed one of them?"

"That's my guess. Nothing else would explain a bump like that." He tossed another card on a pile, then set his hand down and faced Meliand. "We're going to make it through this, I promise. Our people will be safe."

She managed a strained smile. "Do you think we should take the other?"

Talioth raised an eyebrow. "Lia?"

She nodded. "She's a liability. If she were to escape her shackles . . ."

Her unfinished suggestion turned his stomach. "Maybe. Not yet though." He picked his cards back up.

"You better wrap that up," Meliand said as she walked away. "Dinner should be soon."

Centol grumbled as he tossed down a seven. They both drew.

Shouting voices bounced through the cavern, coming from the opening that led to the Hub.

"What's that?" Centol asked.

Talioth set his cards down again and stood. The commotion grew closer.

Heathine rounded the corner. Her eyes flicked through the room until they found Talioth. "They're back," she said. "Some of Danik's men."

Talioth inhaled, letting his lungs fill with air.

Three men rounded the corner. Their haughty swagger and Feldorian clothing made them stand out. Marked ones followed them, necks craning with curiosity.

"Talioth!" the familiar man in front bellowed. His greasy brown hair fell on either side of his face. He scowled as he crossed the room. His trailing companions gawked.

"Cedric, was it?" Talioth fought to not show his sneer. "I thought you were off to enjoy—what was it? Strong liquor and girls? Did you miss us so soon?"

Cedric scoffed. "This place? Hardly."

"I see you brought friends."

He thumbed over his shoulder. "Alton's been with us since the beginning, and Rankin is a new recruit."

The one indicated as Rankin dipped his head. "It's good to meet you, uh . . . Talioth."

Talioth declined to answer and folded his hands before him.

Cedric shuffled his feet then cleared his throat. "We, uh . . ."

Talioth leaned forward and raised his eyebrows as if trying to pull the words from the man.

"We're here for more necklaces."

The leader of the Marked Ones kept his face impassive. "More? You mean the thirty we already gave you weren't enough?"

"Where do you keep them?"

Talioth stared. His eyes flicked to the wall where Meliand had hung up the recently finished set. "You don't need more."

"Don't tell us what we need."

"Then don't talk to me like a servant!"

Gralow and Rosalik approached with swords in each hand.

Talioth shook his head. He turned back to Cedric, then forced a smile. "I apologize for forgetting my manners. You are our guest." He gestured toward the tables where slaves began to bring out serving dishes. "Would you join us for a meal?"

Cedric's scowl lessened. He glanced at the tables, then over his shoulder at his men.

Rankin shrugged. "I could eat."

THE KNIGHTS of power dug into the food before the last of the marked ones had even taken their seats. Meliand raised her eyebrows, and Talioth shook his head. The various men and women in gray glanced across the tables as they settled, curious to observe the newcomers.

Gralow took a seat next to Talioth, resting a dagger on his lap. "Just in case," he whispered when Talioth raised his eyebrows.

"Ugh," Cedric said, grimacing after taking a mouthful of the boiled potatoes. "Have you all ever heard of salt?" The smacking noises he made while he chewed echoed off the cave wall.

Rankin laughed and pointed to the squash on his plate. "You should try these. They taste like warm snot."

Talioth clenched his fork, along with his teeth.

Meliand's hand touched his arm. "Breathe," she said. "They'll be gone soon."

"Do you not eat meat?" Cedric glanced around at the dishes table before settling back on Talioth. "Or do you bring that out later?"

"We do," Meliand said, speaking before Talioth had a chance. "But it's scarce in the mountains, so we save it for special occasions."

"I guess we don't qualify as special," Alton joked.

"Perhaps if we had known you were coming . . ." Meliand didn't finish her thought.

Voices faded into an awkward quiet. Nothing but the clinking of utensils and chewing of food could be heard.

"So, what do you do?" Rankin asked, wiping butter off his chin with his hand. "They said you just live in these caves and never come out? Doesn't that get old?"

"We get by," Talioth said.

Cedric's eyes fixed on Jennioth. Although nearly one hundred years old, her straight black hair and wrinkle-free skin kept her looking no more than twenty. "At least you have women here," he said, winking at her. "Maybe it wouldn't hurt us to stay at least a night or two."

Rankin and Alton laughed.

Talioth gritted his teeth. "As our guests, of course, you're welcome to stay the night."

"Any baltham in these caves?" Rankin asked.

Talioth paused after skewering a cooked carrot with his fork. "Not that we're aware of."

"Have you looked? Straith Mountains have loads of it. You might be surprised if you started mining."

"Oh, we mine." He chuckled. "But we have more important things to look for than chunks of useless metal."

Rankin scoffed. "Useless, ha! Clearly, you don't know the value of baltham."

Gralow leaned forward, barely parting his teeth as he muttered, "Clearly *you* agree with *us*. Otherwise, you wouldn't be here demanding more crystals."

A tense silence hung in the air. Cedric broke it by setting down his fork with a clank. "Speaking of which . . . Let's talk about those necklaces."

"We gave you plenty on your last visit." The edge in Talioth's voice left no room for debate, but the knights of power didn't seem to care.

"We need more," Cedric insisted. "We have one for each person, but the necklaces barely prevent the Call—your *Gharator Nilden* or whatever it is."

"It's not *our* Gharator Nilden."

"Then whose is it?"

"It is . . . whose it is."

"Pppbbt!" Cedric sputtered. "That's stupid. We have plans, and we need more of your glowy rocks."

"Do you intend to train more people?"

"What we do with them is our business."

"On the contrary"—he gestured to the entire room—"what we *all* do with them is *all* of our business."

A crease formed in Cedric's brow.

"The devion. The origine. It all comes from the Core."

The knight of power shifted his eyes around the room.

"Imagine you want to train ten people to rely on the devion. That's ten more people we need to make space for, and space is already tight. Or if you refuse to come here, you need your crystals to fend off the Call, but those necklaces don't last forever. Gharator Nilden does not rest. You'll need a regular supply of crystals, and *you* don't have any means to produce your own. Now imagine those ten people turn into thirty or . . . one hundred." Talioth raised his eyebrows. "What are you going to do, then? We sure won't have space for you all here."

Cedric leaned back in his chair, frowning. "What about the Shadow Knights?"

"What about them?"

"The origine. You say it comes from the Core, too? How does that factor in to this?"

"Think of a set of scales." Talioth held out two hands, one low and one high. "Imagine we want to use a great deal of power through the devion." He shook the lower hand. "We can do that as long as the power of the origine doesn't offset it." He lowered the high hand and raised the low one. "As more people use the origine, it balances what we're capable of. The more power they use, the less we can."

"So we *should* train more people to use the devion, right?" Rankin said.

"The origine limits the devion, but not the other way around."

"But there are only a few who use the origine, right?" Cedric said. "Aren't there way more of us?"

Talioth nodded. "While the devion has more power, the origine holds more weight in the balance of the Core. Everyone they train reduces our ability tenfold."

A light came on in Cedric's eyes. "That's why you want them dead."

"Correct."

The shaggy-haired man sat up straight and flashed a confident smile. "In that case, you'll be happy to know that we killed five of the eight who were at large."

Talioth inhaled quickly and turned to Meliand. Her steely gaze matched how he felt. "You *killed* . . . five?"

Cedric nodded.

"You fools!" He emphasized his words by pounding his fist.

The knights of power jumped back.

"What?" Cedric shrugged. "They wanted to kill us—you too, I'm sure. You just said . . . the more of them there are, the less devion there is to use."

Pressing his fingers against the bridge of his nose did little to help the head pain that had come on suddenly. "Killing them helps, but only a little."

"I thought you wanted to kill them all. Isn't that why you had them here?"

"To *siphon* them! We take the power they've used and transmit it back into the Core—thus increasing the power available for us with the devion. Killing one or two is fine, but *five . . . ?*" He shook his head. "This is catastrophic."

A rumble grew in the room as the other marked ones muttered between themselves.

Gralow leaned in and whispered, "Should we take them out?" He gripped the knife in his lap.

Talioth mulled over the question.

The shoulders of the men from Felting grew tense. They looked at each other, ignoring their food. After a long moment, Cedric extended his chin and broke the silence. "We need more crystals."

"We don't have any," Talioth replied.

Cedric nodded toward the wall where the fresh supply of blue-corded necklaces hung on a hook. "Then what are those?"

"Those are spoken for."

Cedric drummed his fingers on the table and held his gaze. He looked at the other men with him, then slid his chair back. The scraping of wood against the stone floor echoed in the quiet chamber.

"They're. Spoken. For," Talioth repeated, emphasizing each word. His tense muscles strained. His breath sounded loud in his ears.

The knights of power jumped to their feet. Powered by the devion, they ran in a blur toward the door.

Gralow's and Rosalik's chairs flew back. They rushed after the men.

A whirlwind of motion ripped the necklaces off the wall and disappeared through the passage.

"Let them go," Talioth called.

Gralow stumbled to a stop with Rosalik. They looked back at Talioth with wide eyes.

"You're joking, right?" Gralow edged closer to the exit. "We can run them down. They can't take—"

"Gralow." Talioth's calm demeanor lessened the tension. A broad grin stretched across his face. "Let them go."

23

NEW ARRIVALS

Despite the unappetizing noise of the slop filling the bowl, Lia's stomach growled at the sight of the food. Mining all day and training at night required as much fuel as possible to sustain the body.

Past the server, she noticed the nearly empty bin of cooked sausage. "What do you do with the rest of the sausage?" she asked.

"Forget about it," the marked one said.

"But the Valcors have already eaten. You don't toss it, do you?"

"I said forget about it! It's not for you."

She observed the scraps before she left the room and imagined ways to steal them and save them for later.

I'd need a container to store them in that would stop the smell. She passed between the tables, heading to her usual seat. *Then, I could keep them and have them whenever I wanted. I could—*

A thought came to her, causing her steps to stutter. *Would that work?* Her pulse beat faster. It was risky, not just for her, but for everyone.

"Vekko, stop being a jerk." Waylon's voice caught her attention. "Scoot down."

Lia stood over her usual empty table but watched as Vekko scooted down at the Garront's table.

Waylon motioned to her. "Come join us. There's plenty of room."

Vekko's scowl gave her a moment of pause, but a smile pulled at her lips. She left her table and joined the team. Waylon had made space between him and Thurman at the center of the table.

"Thanks," she breathed.

"As long as you don't make us run laps around the lake during the meal." Stewart's quip had most of the table chuckling.

Lia's heart surged as she sat. Where she'd been an outcast weeks before, she finally felt welcomed and part of the team. "Now that I'm sitting here, do I get to learn about you?" She filled her spoon and put it in her mouth.

The men's faces fell and turned away.

She swallowed. "Your families? Jobs? Where you lived?" She glanced down the table, but no one returned her gaze. She swallowed another spoonful, then cleared her throat. "In that case, I'll go."

The team lifted their heads, showing off raised eyebrows.

"I grew up in Felting. My parents are still alive and drive me crazy at times. Father is controlling and too focused on getting me to do what he expects, and Mother can be critical. They both instructed me relentlessly, hoping I'd be like them. I ran away from home for a few weeks, but that ended up being a disaster. Now, I regret the way I acted out. My grandfather was—" She paused, refraining from revealing she was the granddaughter of a king. "He was a good man but passed away recently."

"Were you training in a family business or something?" Thurman asked.

She chuckled. "Something like that, yeah. Lots of training. It never ended. I'd been getting more responsibility, too."

"Any guys in your life?" Waylon asked.

"I guess. Two, actually."

Several men chuckled.

"One was a lot of fun. We used to be more similar, but he ended up going down a dangerous path. I'm lucky I didn't follow him."

"What about the other?"

Lia felt her smile growing. "Raiyn's been a pleasant surprise. He's humble and sweet, and it seems that he likes me, too."

She swallowed another bite. "So . . . that's my motivation. I want to get back to my family, and I want to see Raiyn again. They probably think I'm dead, and I can't wait to prove them wrong. Who wants to go next?"

The men turned back to their bowls and filled their mouths with food.

Lia waited with raised eyebrows. "Come on. Anyone? Waylon? Thurman? Chris, surely you want to . . ."

The leader's shaking head caused her to fade out. He swallowed a mouthful, then his lips parted. He hesitated.

Lia leaned in, waiting for him to say something.

"How many crystals do you think we'll get today?" Chris asked.

She groaned. "You all are hopeless."

"We had eight yesterday. What will we do today?"

She exhaled a long breath. The rest of the men looked at her. "I think we can do nine," she said.

"Can you imagine that?" Waylon said. "If we could keep that up, we'd have . . ." His eyes looked distant as if his brain struggled to calculate. "Well . . . enough to take the golden pickaxe."

"Can you imagine the sausage we'd get?" Thurman asked. "What do you think, Stewart? You think it tastes good?"

"Shut it, Thurman," Stewart said.

The team laughed.

"You know," Lia swallowed her mouthful, then dropped the volume of her voice. "I was thinking about the sausage, and I had an idea."

The men around the table turned to her. She leaned forward. She opened her mouth to speak until approaching feet and turned heads caught her attention.

"New workers!" Rasmill bellowed.

Three middle-aged men approached with a line of marked ones.

Their shoulders slumped, and their eyes skittered around like nervous birds. Thin arms and torn clothes showed they'd received a lack of nutrition and care for some time.

Rasmill pointed to the two closest to him. "These two will be Wolves." He leaned closer to the men as if speaking only to them. "They had two of their team eviscerated yesterday, so they can use the help."

The two men glanced at each other, their eyes widening as the guards pushed them toward the Mountain Wolves.

"And this guy will join the Garronts."

Lia expected as much, having been the only other team to lose a member since she and Dayna had arrived.

The man had a thick beard and shaggy hair. Bony collarbones pressed against his skin where the neck of his tunic hung loose. His head drooped as he walked toward their table.

An awkward silence stretched until Chris addressed him. "You want food?"

The man scanned the table, his face puckering at the sight of their bowls. He shook his head.

"Suit yourself."

Lia slurped more spoonsful, keeping an eye on the newcomer.

"What were you going to say, Lia?" Waylon asked.

She turned to him.

"You had an idea?"

The rest of the Garronts faced her, leaning in and listening with eyebrows raised.

"Um . . ." Her gaze flicked to the newcomer. He stood to the side of their table but watched with a keen eye. She shook her head. "It was nothing. Never mind." With a large spoonful, she swallowed the rest of her meal.

Waylon raised an eyebrow. "Is something wrong?"

She wiped her mouth with the back of her hand as she stood. "Welcome!" She addressed the new team member, extending her hand. "What's your name?"

"Anton," the man replied, taking her hand. His voice sounded like a whisper.

"How old are you, Anton? Thirty? Forty? Three hundred?"

Anton's brows creased. "I'm thirty-four."

She stared for a moment, watching as the newcomer squirmed. Finally, she forced a smile. "Welcome to the Garronts. I'm Lia." She pointed down the table. "Here we have Stewart, Manne, Thurman, Waylon. Chris is our team leader. That's Harold, then Doyle. At the end is Jarno and Vekko."

The last two men scowled.

"We're the Garronts, and we're glad to have you on the team. Do you have any experience with mining?"

Anton shook his head.

"No problem. Stick with me today. I'll go over all you need to know."

THE GARRONTS DIDN'T GET the nine crystals Lia predicted, but seven was still incredible. The team worked hard, celebrating each deposit. The only challenge was the new guy. He struggled with the physical work, taking frequent breaks. His attitude was positive, though, and he seemed to appreciate the warm welcome and guidance from Lia and the others. Spirits were high while the team walked back.

Ideas spun through Lia's head about how to exercise the team. While their recent training sessions had been effective, she remembered how much she enjoyed variety during her time with the Shadow Knights. *I wish we had more equipment*, she thought as she eyed the material in the boneyard.

"Where do you think you're going?" Waylon said.

Anton followed Jarno and Vekko until he stopped at the barracks door and looked their way. His face drooped, heavy with exhaustion after his first day in the mines.

"We're not done. Get over here with the rest of us."

"But I—" Anton pointed after the team members who had retired.

Eventually, he sighed and trudged ahead to join the rest. "I thought the work was finished."

"The mining's finished," Chris said. "If you were on a subpar team like the Wolves or the Panzils, you could be done, but Garronts are held to a higher standard. Lia whips us into shape. It will be painful at first, but you'll learn to love the agony. We won't lose another member on my watch."

Anton's wide eyes took in everything.

"Lia, what do you have planned for us?"

"Well," she began, "we're short on wheels now that we have more people. I'm going to check with Rasmill to see if they have anything else we can use. You all start with a lake run. Chris, can you get them sweating?"

The team leader nodded.

"Three laps. If anyone falls behind, give them an extra."

"You heard her!" Chris shouted, bursting into a run toward the lake. "Let's go! Let's go!"

The regulars sprang into action, running after Chris, but Anton paused.

"It's all right," Lia said. "Just do your best. We all remember our first days, and they were exhausting. Keep up as best as you can. I'll be right back."

Anton nodded, then hurried in an exhausted-looking shuffle after the team.

With the team working, Lia jogged past the tables and around a group of arriving Bears. She ducked through the mining office doorway.

The room contained a low ceiling filled with bumps. A lantern hung on the wall, throwing shadows around the space. A shelf with books and stacks of paper rested against a wall. In the center of the room, cards littered a square table where Rasmill and the other three guards sat. Their cushioned seats looked more comfortable than anything else in the mines.

"Yeah." Rasmill looked up from his hand of cards. "What do you want?"

She threw a thumb toward the boneyard. "We're training with the new guy now, but we're out of heavy objects—wheels or cart pieces or the like."

"You all are idiots, you know that? Why don't you rest like the other teams?"

"We're *trying* to do our best."

Rasmill sighed. "What do you need?"

"Do you have any other broken equipment? Wooden carts or spare iron or anything like that?"

"Make do with what you have." He turned back to his cards.

"The better in shape we are, the harder we can work. The more we work, the more crystals we collect. Isn't that something you want?"

"Ha!" He scoffed but didn't refute the point. After a pause, he folded his cards and placed them face down on the table. "Come on." He pointed at the other guards and stood. "Don't even think about peeking!" He lifted the lantern off the wall, leaving the men behind in a faint reddish glow.

Lia followed through another doorway as Rasmill led the way. They passed through a bunk room. The beds looked and smelled nicer, and the chamber even contained two lounging chairs. *Why can't we have furniture like this?* she wondered. Something caught her eye, an object hanging on a hook from the closest bunk. The ring of metal contained four keys—the ones she needed to escape her metal cuffs and escape through the gate. She fought the temptation to lunge for them, knowing a devion-filled Rasmill would knock her out before she even discovered which key was the correct one.

Past the bunk room, a wide corridor split off multiple times into dark passages. Rasmill continued straight until the passage opened into a larger chamber.

The open area tripled in height and width from the previous tunnel. A dark passage continued forward, stretching into the darkness past where the lantern reached. Two decrepit mining carts lay against the wall.

"Something like those?" Rasmill asked, holding the lantern out toward the carts.

Lia inspected the closest one. The wood was covered in a thick layer of dust but appeared solid and heavy. The wheels groaned as she pulled. After a bit of persuasion, it rolled. "This is perfect. What is this place?"

"It's the old mine, way back from when they first started. They eventually abandoned it and moved to the one you work now. You're welcome to take what you want."

LIA PANTED when she finally stopped back in the boneyard after pushing the heavy cart. Shadows of running men jogged in front of glowing crystals on the far side of the lake. She grabbed the side of the cart and wrenched it back and forth. The wheels jostled side to side. The wood creaked. She leaned into it, and the axle snapped, wheels falling on either side. The wooden structure crashed to the ground, busting some of the wooden slats. Lia pulled against them, breaking the wood walls into pieces. When a chunk of wood had broken off, a small object clattered to the cave floor.

Lia stopped. *What's this?* She picked it up to inspect it closer. It was a small wooden box. It had been fixed to the outside of the cart wall, but breaking the planks had jarred it loose. The wood was smooth and light. Seams at the corners were invisible. A hinge at one edge looked rusted through. After popping a clasp, the top pivoted open despite the rust. Empty.

Lia's heart beat faster. She stared at the box, its purpose clear. A surge of hope rushed through her. She hustled to the side of the boneyard and set the box out of sight as the men of the Garronts jogged up.

"You found one," Chris remarked.

"Yeah." Lia returned to the busted cart. "There's an old mine through the office that has a couple of old carts. This should work fine. How was the warm-up run?" She glanced at the others, who continued to arrive. "How did Anton do?" The newest arrival brought up the back of the line but wasn't too far behind.

"He managed," Chris said. "Not bad for a first day."

Anton bent over, resting his hands on his knees. He sucked in air, wincing while his legs wobbled.

"Nice work, Anton," Lia said. "Trust me, in about a week, you'll be glad for this." She turned to the broken wood pieces. "We should have enough loads for everyone now. Grab a wheel or a plank, all of you. Thurman, don't let me catch you trying to use that tiny piece again."

The miner grinned and picked up one of the new wheels. "I was trying to save the good stuff for the others since there wasn't enough to go around."

"No excuse. I want to see twenty lifts all the way over your head back down to the ground. When you finish twenty, hold your load and jog a lap around the lake."

Groans rumbled through the group.

"Then . . . twenty more lifts and take a break."

She paused to let all the men gather their objects and spread out. Anton selected a board from the new cart. It was lighter than the others' but was good enough for his first day.

"All right . . . Go!"

Lia wiped the sweat off her face as she sat on the bed. Her arms and legs contained a welcome, tired sensation. Two days down. Four more until quota checks.

Anton stumbled across the room and made it to the bed across the aisle from hers.

"What'd you think of the first day?" she asked with a sly grin.

He held his head up through great effort. "You all are crazy."

Lia laughed.

"I think I'm too tired to even sleep."

"You'll sleep. Trust me. You think you're hurting now. Just wait until tomorrow."

Chris approached her bed. "Hey, can I have a word?"

She frowned. "What's up?"

He stepped closer and lowered his voice. "I know you're the only," he paused as if searching for the right word, "female in our group and we weren't always welcoming. I'm sorry about that, and I want you to know that we have your back."

"Thanks. I feel welcome now."

"And, uh . . . we want to make sure you feel comfortable doing . . . whatever you need to do."

Lia raised an eyebrow. "Okay . . . thanks. That's good to know."

Chris's hands fidgeted. He opened his mouth but hesitated in whatever he meant to say. "It's just that . . . you've been training, and . . . sweating a lot."

She leaned forward. "And . . ."

He dropped his voice to a whisper. "You need a bath."

A wave of heat rushed to her face.

"I know you've been avoiding it because of some of the guys, but I think it's time."

"How am I supposed to—"

"I'll block the way." He nodded toward the doorway. "I'm going to stand there, and no one will pass me until you're finished. You can take all the time you need, and no one is going to bother you. You have my word."

His smile offered her warm reassurance. Her feeling of shame passed, replaced by a sudden desire to scrub the weeks of grime and dirt off her. She tucked her nose toward her shoulder and inhaled. "Ugh! Yeah, I guess I've been ignoring it. Sorry."

"Don't be sorry. I understand why you waited." He nodded toward the passage. "There are scrubbers already in there and towels. I suggest using whichever one smells the best."

Lia stood and passed through the doorway. Glowing red crystals led around a corner. Before she disappeared out of sight, she glanced back. Chris stood in the doorway, facing toward the barracks. His arms crossed over his chest, and his feet spread wide, touching either end of the tunnel.

Someone else walked up just out of her sight. Chris held a hand up. "You gotta wait."

"Lia back there?"

It was Waylon.

"Yeah," Chris answered.

Chris scooted over as Waylon's back came into view. He stood next to Chris and crossed his arms, too.

Lia smiled. *They have my back.* She turned and headed toward a long-overdue bath.

24

NORTHERN ARRIVAL

The snow that had covered the countryside the last time Veron visited Norshewa had melted. Green grass and wild-flowers covered the ground in a colorful blanket of life. To the south, the snow-capped Korob Mountains stretched to the sky, dissolving into rolling hills with fir trees and fields of yellow and green at their base.

Humble homes of black obsulom grew prevalent as Veron and the others drew closer to the capital city of Daratill. Steep roofs formed sharp angles above the homes. Rocky walls separated roaming goats and cattle from humble gardens. A chill nipped at the air, despite the midday sun and late-suether season.

A man with gray hair and a rounded back stood from where he worked in the dirt. A burlap sack with shoots of green spilling out the top rested against his legs, clenched by a gnarled hand.

"Hello there," Chelci said, throwing an amiable wave in his direction.

The man's scowl and narrowed eyes left no doubt about his feelings toward the outsiders.

"Tough crowd," Raiyn said, shifting in his saddle. "Is everyone here so friendly?"

"Not many," Brixton said, "but there are some."

The four horses' hooves clopped against the dirt road as they passed the man.

"How long were you here?" Raiyn asked.

"Not long," Brixton said. "A week or two."

"What'd you do while you were here?"

"I worked with your father, trying to figure out my new role, but I wasn't here long enough to do much."

"He was here long enough to propose to me," Chelci said.

Brixton's face flushed.

Raiyn's head jerked in her direction. "Really?"

Chelci's shoulders bounced as she chuckled. "He did. It was beautiful, too. 'We're stuck in this barren winter wasteland together. We might as well get married. What do you think?'"

"It wasn't like that," Brixton objected.

Veron and Raiyn shared a laugh.

"I was trapped here, too," Brixton said, his face still beet red. "It wasn't the same as you, but still . . ."

"How does it feel to return?" Veron asked.

"It's strange. Bale is gone, and so is the snow—those are pleasant changes. Even so, it feels odd coming back after all this time." A shudder rolled across his shoulders. "It reminds me of the old me, and I don't like it."

"For me, it's like returning to a terrible memory," Chelci said. "Bale threw me in his tower to freeze and be beaten."

Brixton jumped in. "I tried to get him to—"

"It's all right." Chelci held up her hand. "I know. It's in the past. Still . . . the memories never go away."

Veron exhaled a heavy breath. "It reminds me of William."

"Your father, right?" Raiyn asked.

Veron nodded. "I only knew him for part of a season. Even missing a leg, he came with me to the frozen north to rescue Chelci." He laughed. "We knew one of us was going to die stopping Bale, and he fought me tooth and nail to be the one. He was something else."

"You should have seen him back when he had both legs," Chelci added.

"Wait." Raiyn's brows pinched together. He pointed at Chelci, pressed his lips together, and paused. "How did you know him with both legs if . . ."

Her laughter cut him off. "It's a long story."

"How about you, Raiyn?" Veron asked. "How does it feel being here?"

His head cocked and his eyes drifted toward the countryside. "I'm not sure."

"Do you remember it at all?"

"I have a vague memory of the snow, and I remember an impressive room with red-and-black columns."

"The Hall of Dignitaries," Brixton said. "Tough to forget that one."

"I don't remember much else. Being here makes me think . . . 'What if?' What if my father had lived? What if I'd grown up here? Would I have ended up like him?"

Veron adjusted in his saddle. "Do you . . . wish you had that chance?"

"No." Raiyn shook his head. "It's only a curiosity. I'm glad I didn't."

"What's this?" Brixton asked, looking up the path.

A sea of canvas tents spread between the road and the river. Soldiers in leather uniforms drilled in formation. Groups of men jogged together, and others sparred with swords. Red-and-black Norshewan flags of crossed swords over a bear rippled in the breeze, flying through the camp.

"The rumors were true," Veron said. "Not as large as Bale's army but still significant."

"Does this mean they're going to attack?" Raiyn asked.

"Marshaling isn't done just for fun. But . . . it's possible it's only for training."

Where the camp met the road, a group of eight soldiers stood on guard. They stiffened when Veron and the others drew near.

"Halt, foreigners!" a man shouted. He wore a gray jerkin with a head full of jet-black hair and a beard to match. He took a half step toward the road and drove the butt of his spear into the ground.

Veron pulled back on his reins. The four horses exhaled a chorus of whinnies.

"Who are you and what is your business here?"

Veron raised his hands as his horse came to a halt. "We come from the south—travelers journeying to Daratill." He pointed at the buildings along the street ahead of them. "Have we arrived?"

The man's eyes shifted between the travelers and his fellow soldiers, as if he wasn't sure of the right protocol. "Yes, this is Daratill. Why have you come?"

"We hear this is the jewel of the north, the most beautiful city. We had to see it for ourselves."

"Where are you from?"

"Feldor."

"And you've . . . come to see our city?"

Veron shrugged. "Want to see if it could be a suitable trading partner for my company in Felting. It seemed wiser to come now than in the middle of wiether."

The soldier frowned, then glanced between them. A nervous ball grew in Veron's gut until a chuckle escaped the guard's mouth. "That's a smart move," he said. "Wiether can be brutal." A smile formed, and his spear leaned against his shoulder. He pointed up the road. "This road leads through the city. You'll find the market, the riverfront, and a good view of the River Palace ruins. There are several inns along the way. Take your pick, but I'd recommend the White Horse Tavern. Brolin's a friend of mine. He runs it and charges fair rates. If you stay on the road, it will end at the castle. I hope that helps."

Veron bobbed his head as the man spoke. "Thank you. Indeed, that is very helpful." Deciding to press his luck, he nodded behind the guard. "What are you doing here? Looks like you're getting ready for a battle."

The man's smile turned sour. "Not at all. We're only . . . training. It's good to be prepared."

Veron maintained his smile. "Of course. Well, good luck to you, and thank you for the information."

With a flick of his reins and a soft kick, his horse resumed walking forward.

"I'm surprised he wasn't more suspicious," Chelci said when they were out of earshot. "He was friendly."

Brixton nodded. "Yeah, I thought our mission was about to end prematurely. There had to have been thousands of men there."

"They have nothing to suspect," Veron said. "They've been at peace for eighteen years. They may be about to breach that, but until they do, they've no reason to think we're here on anything other than a visit to establish trade."

Past the army encampment, the border of the city took shape. Black-stone buildings ran together along the street. The road grew more crowded with carts and people walking. Side streets led to more homes and shops. Without the snow to cover everything, the city looked dirty and bleak. The greenery that had grown up in the previous countryside was nowhere to be found. Ruts filled the muddy, rain-softened road.

"Any thoughts about what we'll say when we get there?" Brixton asked. "Gauging from my previous experience, I'm not sure announcing their true king has arrived will earn us a welcome reception."

"We should be cautious about mentioning the Shadow Knights, too," Chelci added. "There could be bad feelings around that."

"I thought Norshewa supported the Knights," Raiyn said. "Weren't they contributing money or something?"

"Technically, yes," Veron said, "but not much. I'm guessing they felt compelled to after their previous issue with Bale. I've communicated only briefly with King Darian and only via letter. He was cordial enough, but they've never called on the Knights for help."

Raiyn's forehead developed a deep crease. "What do we talk about, then? We need to explain more if they're going to give up something as valuable as Bravian Fire."

"We need to be wise about when and to whom we speak," Veron

said. "Too much information about the devion could leave them hungry to learn it for themselves. We need to find people who could be loyal and then decide how much information we can trust them with. If pleading as shadow knights doesn't work, we can bring up Raiyn's lineage."

"What do we do if it all falls apart?" Chelci asked. "If we lay our cards on the table and they refuse. Or even worse, what if we find that army back there surrounding us?"

"If it comes to a fight, Brixton, stay close and let us three do the work," Veron said.

"Ha!" Brixton laughed. "Like in the castle courtyard when we fought Bale? Or in the caverns against Talioth?"

The memory of Brixton fighting with him and Chelci brought a smile to his face.

"If it comes to it, I *can* fight, and I will."

"Fine. You make a good point."

Black stone ruins stretching over the river caught Veron's eye. Bale had resumed construction of the ancient River Palace once his slave workers from Feldor arrived, but Veron and his father put a stop to it before they made any noticeable progress. The partially constructed fortress was left spanning the river, with incomplete towers on each end.

Veron leaned toward Raiyn, whose horse walked next to his. "How are you feeling?"

Raiyn's body looked tense. He turned toward him with wide eyes. "Me? I'm . . ." He blew out a breath. "I'm fine."

"Nervous?"

"Yeah. A bit. What if I can't do this? What if they laugh at me or kill us on sight."

"If that happens . . . this will be a short trip," Veron joked.

"I've just never seen myself as a leader, and now I feel like the weight of Terrenor rests on my shoulders."

"I believe in you, Raiyn. You've sure proven yourself in my book. And remember, we're all in this together."

The young knight nodded. "I know. Thanks."

The group of four continued down the street, past a row of shops, to find the imposing walls of the castle looming ahead. A drawbridge crossed a frothing river with four guards posted where a portcullis peeked from the top of the gate entrance.

Veron dismounted at the bridge. He took his horse's reins and walked across. The sound of four horses clopping on the wooden surface resounded.

The guards formed a line. They kept their hands on the swords at their hips and spread out to block passage through the castle entrance. "What is your business?" a guard asked. The man wore a red-and-black uniform. His bare forearms rippled with muscles. His sharp jaw extended in a square shape, framed by a trimmed beard.

Veron continued closer, lifting his open free hand in a sign that he meant no harm. "We're here to see the king."

The guards laughed. "Sure you are."

"I'm serious. We've traveled from Feldor and have urgent news to discuss."

"I don't care if you're from the tip of Tarphan or if you came riding on the backs of norsh bears. No one demands an audience with King Darian."

"I've corresponded with him. He invited me to visit, and I'm here to take him up on his offer."

A scowl covered the guard's face. "Do you have that invitation?"

"I, uh, don't have it with me. We had to leave in a rush—the urgent news I mentioned. Tell him Veron is here and we must meet. If he's not available, check with General Ryker."

The guard stepped forward, pulling his sword free of its sheath. His bulging neck flexed with the massive shoulders on either side. "We're not telling either of them anything."

Raiyn moved to loosen his battle axe from its back sheath, but Veron stopped him with a hand on his shoulder.

The guard burst into laughter. "You want to try that, kid?"

"I'm not a—"

Veron silenced Raiyn with a quick squeeze. "Let it go, Raiyn."

"The king offers open audiences to anyone with a plea, but you must line up early if you're hoping to make it to him before sundown."

Hope glimmered in Veron's chest. "When is his next audience?"

The guard cocked his head. "Four weeks from tomorrow."

Raiyn blew out a frustrated sigh. "We can't wait that long."

"You look like you all have been living in a pit for weeks. You're filthy, arrogant, and out of place. If you don't have an invitation and aren't here with someone who can vouch for you, you're not getting in."

"Please." Chelci's plea was soft. She stepped closer, lifting open palms with compassion in her eyes. "You're doing your job, and you're doing it well. Your king should be proud of you. Still, we must get an audience with him. Please pass along the word that Veron is here and needs to speak with him. That's all we ask."

The guard ran his eyes up and down her body, leering. "Our concern is that we don't know you well enough." His mouth curled in a crooked grin. "If the lady'd be willing to spend some time entertaining us, maybe we'd feel differently about your lot."

The three guards behind him cackled.

Veron's hand balled into a fist as Chelci's shoulders tensed. She took a half step back.

"Come on," Veron touched Chelci on the arm. "We'll figure something out."

The lead guard laughed as they headed back across the drawbridge. "It's too bad. Could have been a good time."

"Idiots," Brixton muttered.

"Let's find a place to sit and think," Veron said. "Perhaps we need a more creative approach."

25

ENTERING THE CASTLE

Holding two mugs in each hand, Raiyn dodged chairs and people to make it to where Veron, Chelci, and Brixton sat around a circular table by the far wall.

From the sagging roof outside to the sticky floors and mildewy tables, the Roaring Boar Tavern struggled in the harsh northern environment. The small windows and dim lanterns created a depressing sensation of being trapped in a dungeon, despite the full sunlight outside. The other patrons didn't seem to mind, though. They ate, drank, and reveled with the enthusiasm of a merry group of partygoers.

Raiyn set the drinks down on their table with a clunk, sloshing foam over the sides. A basket of rolls already sat on the surface. "Ale is all they have. No water."

Chelci nodded, pulling a mug toward her. She leaned forward and sniffed the foamy top. The four of them each lifted their drink to their lips at the same time. After measured sips, Veron, Raiyn, and Chelci lowered their mugs.

While setting his ale on the table, Raiyn grabbed a roll and turned to Brixton. The older man's throat undulated while he made loud gulping sounds. Liquid sloshed in the clear mug as it tipped farther and farther. Raiyn's eyes grew.

After a long moment, Brixton lowered his mug, smacking his lips with a loud, "Ahh."

His eyes checked each of the other three. "Sorry." He wiped his mouth with the back of his hand. "Norshewan ale. It's been a long time. This is the one thing I missed."

"Clearly," Veron said with an upturned grin. He placed his hands on the table and leaned forward. "All right. Let's think of options. How do we get to see the king?"

"How'd you do it last time?" Brixton asked. "You came over the walls, right?"

Veron nodded. "On the western wall. Boulders next to the river give more height. An origine-filled jump would get the three of us up."

Brixton frowned.

"Sorry, Brix. I'm not sure we could jump that high while carrying you. It's taller than Felting's wall."

"You could leave me," Brixton suggested. "You don't *need* me to be there."

"But it would be helpful," Chelci said, "considering your time here and your background. Plus, leaping over the walls could get us into all sorts of trouble."

"I had to kill people last time," Veron said. "That would definitely start us off on a bad foot."

Chelci faced Brixton. "Did you learn of any secret entrances during your time in the castle?"

Brixton shook his head.

"We could forge a letter," Raiyn suggested. "They want a letter from the king. What if we wrote one somehow?"

Veron frowned. "We don't have the king's seal. Plus, after telling them we didn't have one, it would be suspicious if we showed up again with it magically appearing."

"What about barreling through the gate?" Brixton said. "Each of you three is skillful enough on your own to take those guards. With all four of us, we could practically walk right in."

"Again," Chelci said, "not starting on their good side. We want them to welcome us."

The door to the tavern opened, letting a stream of light in. A silhouetted man entered the room and walked to the bar with a slight shuffle. His crimson cloak draped over black leggings. Thin, silver hair seemed to light up, and heavy wrinkles identified him as being at least in his sixties.

With his mug halfway to his lips, Brixton sat up straight and watched. The man spoke with the bartender. The words were too quiet to hear, but Brixton leaned toward him.

"You know him?" Veron asked.

Brixton kept his eyes on the bar while a smile formed. The man with the silver hair finished his conversation and left out the same door he had just entered.

"Who was it?" Chelci added.

Brixton leaned in and dropped his voice. "If we're lucky . . . he's our ticket in. Come on."

Raiyn was the last to his feet. Leaving their drinks behind, they hurried toward the door. When they stepped outside, Brixton slunk to the side of the road. "Stay behind me and stay quiet," he said.

Raiyn lingered at the back of the group. Over Veron's shoulder, he glimpsed the unknown man who walked through the market toward the castle. Brixton watched from a distance but kept the man in sight.

"Are you going to talk to him?" Veron whispered, loud enough for Raiyn to hear.

"Not yet. I want to watch him first," Brixton replied.

"If you're trying to stay hidden, you're too exposed."

Brixton waved a hand over his shoulder. "Quiet."

The man with the silver hair paused at a fruit vendor stand. Brixton stopped, causing Veron to run into his back. Raiyn covered his face and turned away, wishing to be free of the awkward surveillance.

When the man turned down a side alley, Brixton hurried after on the balls of his feet. He peered around the corner before slipping into the alley. When Raiyn arrived, there was nothing to see.

Brixton glanced in each direction while he rushed forward. "He was just here," he muttered.

Veron shook his head but followed along.

"Do you know who it is?" Raiyn whispered to Chelci.

She shook her head.

A metallic scrape filled the air, followed by a harsh "Who are you?"

Brixton froze farther down the alley with a sword tip pressed against his chest. The older man emerged from a shadow, keeping his weapon against Brixton but eyeing Veron and the others.

"What do you all want?" he asked. "Why are you following me?"

"You're Desmond, right?" Brixton said, his words weak and wavering.

The man's eyes narrowed. "Who's asking?"

Brixton stood straighter and took in a deep breath. "Don't you know?"

The man leaned in until a sparkle of recognition flickered in his eyes. He sucked in a gasp. "Brixton?" Sweeping his gaze to the others, he stiffened at the sight of Veron and Chelci. "And I know these two."

No one spoke, leaving tension in the air. The man kept his sword tip against Brixton while his eyes flicked between him and Veron. Raiyn itched to snatch the axe from over his shoulder, but he didn't dare move.

After a stressful wait, the man's stoic face melted into a smile. "It's been, what, almost twenty years?" His sword pulled back, the smile growing. "Yes, it's me, Desmond Carvin. It's good to see you again. Chelci, we never met, but I'm sorry about what happened."

Chelci's mouth held a grim line.

"And this is Raiyn . . ." Brixton's sentence ended with an awkward catch in his throat.

"Yes," Raiyn said quickly, pumping the man's hand with vigor. "Nice to meet you, Desmond."

"This is quite a surprise," Desmond said. "What brings you to Daratill?"

Brixton's relieved face turned serious once more. "Are you still an advisor to the king?"

"To King Darian? I am."

"We have an urgent matter we need to speak with him about. Would you be able to get us an audience?"

Raiyn held his breath.

The advisor's brows pulled together as his head cocked. "An audience with the king? For four uninvited foreigners?" His concerned look melted into a smile. "Of course. It would be no trouble."

The clenched ball of stress in Raiyn's gut loosened. His shoulders relaxed.

"Come with me," Desmond gestured back toward the main road. "He should be done with his midday meal by now."

The group headed back up the alley. Raiyn felt renewed hope at their mission, but the feeling soured when he considered what part he had yet to play. Keeping his voice low from the back of the line, he called, "Veron."

Veron turned, then slowed to walk beside him.

"Who's this guy?"

Veron's eyes flicked ahead while they continued walking. "Desmond was one of your father's advisors. I only met him after the fighting was finished. From what I heard, he was pragmatic and wise. He saw through bad ideas and gave perspective to difficult decisions."

"Wise enough to live through the fall of Bale, I see."

Veron nodded. "I don't think he's as much a fighter as he is a talker. In either case, it's good that we found him."

The drawbridge of the castle came into view at the end of the street. Nervous anticipation filled Raiyn at the sight of the guards on duty. He continued forward, hoping the encounter would be smoother.

With his eyes trained on Desmond, the lead guard nodded when the advisor passed. "Sir," he greeted.

Desmond waved a hand over his shoulder, not breaking stride. "These four are with me."

When the guard looked at Raiyn and the others, he flinched. The man's mouth fell open, gaping like a fish out of water.

Brixton, Veron, and Chelci followed Desmond without saying a word. Raiyn touched his finger to his temple and offered a nod. "Have a good day," he said. He fought to keep his smug grin at bay.

The group passed under the portcullis. Ahead, an inner courtyard spread between the castle walls. A bridge above ran from the main keep to a tower that rose high in the sky. Desmond opened an iron door that was set into a wall, then ushered them inside.

Raiyn felt an odd tingle when he stepped into the castle's entrance hall. The scene was foreign, but a familiarity from the recesses of his memory prickled at his mind. He followed in silence, taking in the black stone walls, narrow windows, and tapestries. After ascending a flight of stairs, two guards stopped them at another door.

"Leave your weapons here," a young man ordered, pointing to a table pressed against the wall.

Raiyn followed the example of the others, removing the axe from his back and setting it down with a clunk. When the guard looked satisfied, he stepped out of the way.

The group passed through the door, and a grand hall spread before them.

"Welcome to the Hall of Dignitaries," Desmond said.

"Wow," Brixton breathed. "This takes me back."

"I remember it," Veron said. He turned his head toward the vaulted ceiling and gazed at a railing where a passage on the next level peeked in at the chamber.

Marble columns lined each side of the hall, alternating between red and black. A giant bear emblem with crossed swords was displayed on the far wall, the symbol of Norshewa formed from blue glass. Nostalgia swept over Raiyn.

With his boots clacking on the marble floor, Desmond walked toward a group of people who sat in gold-trimmed chairs at the side of the room.

"Desmond," a portly man called, his words muffled by a mouthful of food. "We weren't expecting you."

"No, Your Majesty, but something urgent came up."

King Darian, Raiyn thought.

The heavyset man was hardly the picture of discipline and training that Raiyn remembered his own father to be. His rounded chest stretched the purple tunic he wore to its limits, leaving a portion of his stomach peeking out. He leaned against the back of his chair as if the muscles in his stomach couldn't hold him upright. Likely in his mid-fifties, the man's bald head contained only wisps of gray hair. Grease dripped down one side of his face until he wiped it with his hand. The action prevented the liquid from falling off his chin, but an oily residue remained. Next to him, a half-eaten carcass of meat sat on a plate while flies buzzed around it.

The king's eyes fell on the visitors. "Is this your . . . urgent matter?"

"Yes, we have visitors from Feldor. Allow me to introduce Brixton Fiero, Veron and Chelci Stormbridge, and Raiyn . . . I didn't catch your last name."

Raiyn's jaw tightened as a wave of fear rushed through him. *It's not time.*

"Veron Stormbridge!" the king bellowed.

Silence filled the room. Darian rocked forward and pushed against the sides of his chair. He strained audibly as he lifted his body to a standing position. With his face red and breathing quicker, he lumbered forward with narrowed eyes.

Guards materialized from unseen corners of the room, pressing close with weapons drawn.

"The man who infiltrated our kingdom and assassinated our former ruler. You have a lot of guts showing up here."

"It's with good cause, Your Majesty," Veron said, his wary eyes shifting while he added a formal bow.

"And Brixton Fiero," the king continued. "The traitor who could have had it all. I remember your brief stay here in Daratill."

"Should we restrain them, sire?" a towering guard asked. His deep voice resonated through the chamber while his lip curled.

Darian flapped his hand in the air and scoffed. "There's no need, Beldrick. They're shadow knights. They could take you out with their bare hands before you even pulled out the restraints."

The guard stiffened.

The king laughed. A smile grew on his face while he extended his arms wide. "Besides, that was a long time ago. Norshewa is friends with the Knights."

Raiyn relaxed his hands that had balled into fists.

"Allow me to introduce my son, Alvin."

Darian opened his stance and gestured to a man in his thirties with thick black hair. The stiff collar of his crisp blue tunic reached his chin. Alvin looked at the group but remained seated while he shoveled a handful of nuts into his mouth. His puffy features fell short of his father's size, but he appeared to be on a path to catch up. He nodded, the crunch of his chewing filling the air.

"I've ruled for eighteen years, and Alvin has been involved in every decision I make. Once I pass on"—he leaned in and faux whispered—"which my physician threatens will be any day now if I don't drink less." He erupted in a jolly laugh and slapped a hand against his belly. "Alvin will make a fine leader, carrying on the proud Norshewan tradition of kingly succession, unlike you Feldorian fools who have to make things complicated."

The king gestured farther along the circle of attendees. "I trust you remember the general of our armies, Ryker Galliford."

A stately man in a well-pressed army uniform stood alert. His full head of salt-and-pepper hair and wrinkled face put him around the same age as the advisor, Desmond. The tallest man in the room, Ryker filled out his outfit with firm arms and a barrel chest. He walked forward, jaw tight and eyes locked on Veron.

"This is quite the surprise. I didn't expect to see you this far north," Ryker said. "And again, I thank you. You convincing Feldor to spare my life eighteen years ago has not gone unappreciated."

"I trust your days of assisting leaders in conquering Terrenor are over, then?" Veron asked.

Raiyn caught the subtle flicker of movement in King Darian's eyes.

Ryker was all smiles. "Of course. Assuming you came from the eastern road, you will have passed our camp."

"Yes, I *was* curious about that," Veron said.

"Training, organization, and discipline, that's all. Nothing to worry about."

Veron's smile appeared genuine, but Raiyn knew a mountain of doubt lay behind his pleasant facade.

"That's right," the king added. "Norshewa has no intention of repeating past mistakes. So tell me, shadow knight, what brings you to our northern kingdom?"

The room hung on the king's question. Raiyn held his breath.

"We need your help," Veron breathed.

"The all-powerful Shadow Knights need our help?" Darian's light-hearted chide punctuated his mouth curling at both ends.

"We are not all powerful," Veron said. "There is a group in Feldor that has killed King Darcius and taken over."

"We heard of his death." Darian's face fell. "I'm sorry."

"A young man named Danik leads a group called the Knights of Power, and their goal is to take over Terrenor."

"So, stop them. Isn't that what your group does?"

Veron's jaw formed a tight line. "We tried, but we were unsuccessful. We are all that's left of the Shadow Knights."

Darian's head turned in a curious appraisal.

"Danik and his men—" Veron stopped as if contemplating what to say. "They're more powerful than us, and they have double the numbers the Shadow Knights did at their peak. We can't stop them on our own."

"So, you want our help?"

Veron nodded.

The king's bouncing laugh filled the hall. "Shadow knights come to us—Norshewa—asking for help to put down their coup."

The other group of men joined the king in his laughter.

"Do you take me for a fool? I'm sorry, Veron, but our army is staying right here. If they're so dangerous, then we'll need our men close to home."

"Your army will be obliterated," Veron said.

The trickling laughter stopped. "Obliterated, huh? Nice try. You wouldn't want them for yourself if that were true."

"We don't want your army."

The king paused. He glanced at Ryker with a bemused look on his face before turning back to Veron. "I don't understand."

"Your army would be a nice distraction, but it wouldn't be enough to defeat them."

"But, what—"

"We need your Bravian Fire."

26

THE KING'S DECISION

A gasp punctuated the air. Thick silence followed, marked by twitching eyes and stiff torsos.

"Bravian Fire." Darian's nervous laugh appeared forced. "How ridiculous. You think we have discovered the legend? It's nothing more than a child's myth."

"I *do* think so." Veron's resolute face held no hint of doubt. "Danik and his men are capable of more than you could imagine. He *will* take over Norshewa, and there's nothing you'll be able to do about it. We're trying to stop them, for you and all of Terrenor, but we need the Fire. It's our last hope."

The king maintained his laughing mien, but Veron's words appeared to soften his resolve.

Raiyn waited with bated breath, hoping the plea would work. Back in Felting, the idea of claiming the Norshewan throne to procure the Fire seemed simple enough, but standing before the current king made the prospect feel infinitely more foolish.

Desmond leaned toward the king. "Sire." He nodded toward a quiet corner of the hall. "A word." The two men retreated with Ryker to the corner and engaged in whispered conversation. Alvin leaned in their direction but didn't bother to rise.

Veron brought Chelci and Brixton into a circle with Raiyn. "Don't mention who you are," he whispered, looking at Raiyn. "If this doesn't work, say nothing."

Raiyn frowned. "But how are we—"

"It's too dangerous. This king and his son are not about to sit back and let you push them off the throne."

"I agree," Chelci added. "Maybe we can work through Desmond or Ryker." She turned to Brixton. "How well do you know them?"

Brixton shrugged. "I hardly know either. We worked together for only a short time, and that was eighteen years ago."

Veron sighed. "Maybe we can find it on our own. If they'll at least grant us hospitality to stay in the castle, we can sneak out—"

"Agreed." King Darian's voice rang through the hall, cutting Veron off.

Raiyn frowned. He played the word over in his head to make sure he understood its meaning. "You agree?" he asked.

The king nodded. "Desmond reminded me that I wouldn't be here if it weren't for you. My throne, my rule . . . I owe you. The old Norshewa kept to themselves. They did whatever they wanted, regardless of the impact on the rest of Terrenor. Your coming here has reminded me that's not what I want. We will be different. We will help. Your rumors are true. We *have* discovered Bravian Fire."

Raiyn's eyes grew as he inhaled.

"And if that's what you require to stop this group, then Norshewa will do its part."

"What happened to the Fire being a myth?" Veron's lip pulled up in a grin.

Darian smiled back. "Myths are only myths until they're proven to be true." He waved them toward the back door to the hall. "Come with me." The king led the way, waddling toward the door.

Part of Raiyn felt relief at the Norshewans' purported willingness to do what they asked, but a nervous tingle ran down his spine.

"Would you permit us to retrieve our weapons?" Veron pointed toward the door where they had entered. "I feel exposed without them."

Raiyn raised his eyebrows while the king stopped and turned.

Veron continued, "If there is to be trust between us, we'd appreciate the gesture."

A smile washed over the king's face. "Of course." He motioned toward the men on either side of the original entrance.

The guards snapped into action, ducking through the door and reemerging moments later with their arms full of the weapons.

Raiyn strapped his axe onto his back while the others worked on their swords and daggers. When the gear was in place, Veron nodded.

The king clapped. "All right, then. Follow me."

Desmond and two guards walked after the king, followed by Raiyn and the others. Ryker, the king's son, and a few more guards brought up the rear. They passed down a hallway, then descended a winding staircase, using torches to light the way. A musty odor strengthened the farther they dropped. The steps grew damp where water trickled down the rocky walls.

"Do you think he's really taking us to it?" Raiyn whispered.

Veron turned over his shoulder while continuing down. He opened his mouth but hesitated. "I think—" He took several more steps. "I think it's good we have our weapons."

A lump formed in Raiyn's throat.

"Be alert and ready."

The staircase ended in a dim level with a low ceiling. Jars and vials filled a wall of shelves. Glass containers held grotesque objects floating in yellowish liquid. A cauldron hung from a wrought iron hook over a cold hearth.

"This is the alchemists' shop," the king said. "They study and experiment, testing metals and chemicals. Many of our weapons and armor over the years have come from this shop. Follow me."

Darian led them through a doorway into a similar room. It led to another, and then another. Dim hallways flickered to life by torches as the party passed storage rooms and multiple passages. A pungent odor mixed with a musty scent wrinkled Raiyn's nose.

"Did you know that many considered Bale to be unbalanced?" the king said.

Raiyn perked up, drawing his attention back from the curious labels on the shelves he passed.

"He controlled the army, to be sure, but many in the kingdom felt he was a danger to us all. Norshewa is an unforgiving land. We must spend a great deal of effort on resources and food. Bale stretched us thin. When a leader focuses on nothing but outfitting an army and conquest, the rest of the kingdom is bound to suffer. Those not reaping the rewards can grow bitter."

"We experienced some of that," Veron said, "back when we came for Bale. We ran into several people who didn't share his ambition."

They entered a room with a grinding wheel and a row of weapons in a vertical holder along the far wall. A ring of keys dangled from a hook.

The king held up a hand and stopped moving. "We're here."

Raiyn's pulse beat faster.

"Torches out," Darian ordered. "Don't want a stray spark to cut this visit tragically short."

The guards holding torches snuffed them against the floor. Hisses accompanied the transition to darkness.

Raiyn touched Veron's back to make sure he wouldn't run into him.

"That's dark," Brixton muttered.

"Sorry," Desmond said. "The Fire is highly reactive, so we take extra precautions." Feet shuffled ahead. "Keep straight. Your eyes will adjust."

Taking stuttering steps, Raiyn continued. Small windows near the ceiling let in a faint amount of light. He soon could make out general shapes, but he kept a hand against Veron's shoulder.

"This way," Darian said. "It's just ahead."

Veron's muscles tensed under Raiyn's fingers.

"What is it?" Raiyn whispered.

"I have a bad feeling about this," Veron answered.

Raiyn's nerves tingled. He moved his hand to his own shoulder and touched the haft of his axe. The origine simmered in his gut, waiting for his call for it to flood his body with power.

"How do the alchemists work in this light?" Brixton asked.

The king's voice bounced through the darkness. "They do what they must. Norshewans believe in achievement. Nothing great is accomplished without sacrifice." Feet shuffled to the side. "Hold on. Let me open this to bring in more light."

Raiyn slid the axe from its holder at the same time Veron pulled his sword. Origine rushed through him, heightening his senses and readying his muscles to act.

Metal creaked ahead. Something large moved, surrounding them with noise.

Raiyn dropped into a crouch, holding his weapon with both hands. The dim light provided nothing more than outlines of shapes.

A loud clang resounded behind him, causing him to spin. The passage was even darker. Another clang boomed in the other direction, and he turned back.

Flames jumped to life on either side of them. Guards held relit torches on the other side of latticed metal bars.

"What is this?" Brixton called.

Raiyn's heart pounded. He gripped his axe with both hands, pivoting. Veron and Chelci each held swords, but all four of them were trapped. Chiseled rock formed two sides of the cell while metal barriers blocked the other directions. Four crossbows held by shaking arms pointed through openings in the cell walls.

"Slide your weapons through the grate," Ryker barked.

Raiyn's eyes flicked to Veron. The Shadow Master didn't flinch. He held his sword up in a firm stance. His gaze pierced the cell as if his eyes could burn through the metal bars.

"This is a mistake," Veron said.

The king roared with laughter. "A mistake? The only mistake was you coming here to ask for help. Did you really think we were going to ally ourselves with the person who assassinated our leader?—the man we all rallied around, who was going to lead us into a new era of power and prominence?"

"What happened to Bale stretching you thin and the kingdom suffering? I thought he was a danger to you all?"

A wicked grin grew on Darian's plump face. "It's true that many felt that way. We call them cowards. Fools. Sure, we were hungry and cold, but Bale gave us hope in something greater. He provided a vision that gave us something to long for—something we still want to this day. Now, slide your weapons through the grate unless you want these crossbows to unload at your wife."

Chelci sucked in air but didn't flinch from her ready position. "Don't do it," she whispered. "I can handle it."

"You may get lucky and dodge four simultaneous bolts, but then we will reload while you sit there trapped. Do you think you'll get as lucky the second time? Or the third? Hmm?"

Sweat dripped down Raiyn's forehead. He wanted to wipe it away but didn't dare flinch. He stared at a crossbow that pointed at Chelci. The tense silence grew heavier.

"Fine," Veron broke the standoff. He straightened and lowered his sword.

"Veron, no!" Chelci whispered.

"We can't do anything in here." He stepped toward the bars and slid his sword through until a guard grabbed the other end. "Do it."

Brixton moved next, passing his to a guard against the rear grate.

Raiyn set the head of his axe against the metal. The tall guard, Beldrick, stepped forward and grasped the blade. "That's a good boy," he said with a sneer.

Raiyn had trouble letting go of the shaft. It took a sharp yank from the guard to wrest it from his hand.

Chelci was the last to comply. She shook her head as she tossed her sword through the bars. It fell to the stone floor with a loud clang that filled the corridor.

"Put your hands together and then slide them through the bars," Ryker ordered.

Chains jingled together as guards pulled out metal shackles. Raiyn's stomach clenched. The sight took him back to his time in the Feldan Arena when Danik tried to sacrifice him to the valcor. When the metal took away his power, he felt helpless.

All four in the cell hesitated. They stood back-to-back, facing the metal bars on either side.

"Don't make us use the crossbows," Ryker threatened.

Veron set a hand on Raiyn's shoulder. "It's alright," he said.

A gleam in Veron's eyes loosened the knot in Raiyn's stomach. "Wha—"

Veron teased the edge of his cloak, revealing a ring of keys tucked into his pants. "Play along," he whispered.

Raiyn's frown turned into a smirk that he promptly wiped away. He complied along with the others. His arms grated against the metal as he shoved them through an opening. Beldrick snapped a restraint around each wrist and affixed them with a tightened bolt.

"What about the Bravian Fire?" Veron asked. "Was that all a lie, or do you have it?"

Stepping closer to the light, King Darian held up his double chin and stared down his nose. "Oh, we have it all right, but you'll never receive it." He held out an open hand. "Now, hand it over."

Raiyn held his breath, terrified of what the king meant.

"Hand over what?" Veron asked.

"The *keys*."

The brief hope that buoyed Raiyn dissipated. His chin fell forward, and his shoulders slumped.

"Should we threaten with the crossbows again?"

Leather creaked as the men with crossbows raised their weapons once more.

Veron sighed. He fished into his cloak. A metal clinking sound filled the room as he tossed the ring of keys through the bars. A guard scooped to pick them up.

The king's chest puffed up. "For killing our king, Edmund Bale, I sentence you four to death."

Raiyn's stomach turned.

"There is no appeal. I am the law."

"What about the Knights of Power?" Veron asked. "I wasn't lying about them."

"Bale had it right," the king said. "It's our destiny to rule Terrenor.

You saw our army coming in. That's only half of our men, though. We *are* preparing to march south, and soon the rest of Terrenor will see our might once again."

"The Knights of Power are stronger than any army you can put together. You'll lose everyone trying to stop them—all the kingdoms will."

"I think that's a wonderful strategy. We'll let the other kingdoms kill each other, then Norshewa will swoop in to clean up."

"You need us." Veron's plea lacked his usual confidence.

Darian chuckled. "I *do* need you. Your death will be the motivator our army requires."

Raiyn rested his hands against the bars while the king, his guards, and the others left, taking their torches with them. Gloom returned to the cell with only a faint light from the small windows above. Raiyn turned to the others and sighed. "Well . . . now what do we do?"

27

THE BEST OPTION

Veron gripped the cell bars with both hands. He took in a slow breath, then pushed it out in the same rhythm. The chains between his shackles rattled. He closed his eyes, focusing, pushing out the rest of the world.

The tingle in his gut was barely a whisper. The origine hid from him, like a wisp of smoke trailing through his fingers. He pulled from inside, harder. The power grew slowly. It answered his summons, but only a fraction of what was possible.

His arms tugged at the bars. Teeth clenched together while a groan built in his throat. Stronger and stronger, the amplification grew while his body strained. Metal creaked. A low rumble filled the cell. The origine rushed from his stored well like a bucket of water dumped on the dirt.

A little more.

Veron grasped at what power he had remaining, pressing his eyes closed even tighter. The groan coming from him had turned into a yell. With a last gasp, he released his hold on the origine and slumped forward. His head hit the bars while his lungs sucked in air.

Chelci's hand rested on his shoulder. "It was worth a try."

Her soft tone told him all he needed to know. Still, he lifted his head to see for himself. His shoulders undulated in rolling heaves while his eyes opened.

The bars remained unchanged.

Veron groaned and pounded against the bar with the metal wrist cuff. "If only we didn't have these things!"

"I'm not sure we'd be able to get through those even without the restraints," Raiyn said. "Thanks for trying, though."

Veron rolled to his back and slumped to the ground. Chelci settled next to him while Raiyn and Brixton sat against the opposite wall. As the day progressed, rays of light from the top windows slanted across the room.

A chuckle from Chelci turned his head. "What?" he asked.

Her smile caught the beam of light. "Who would have thought?"

His forehead wrinkled. "What?"

"This. Me, you, and Brixton. Together. In prison in Daratill." She pointed across the cell. "With Edmund Bale's son."

He managed a weak laugh. "Yeah. Not me."

"So, how do we play our last card?" Brixton asked.

The other three looked at him.

"You mean Raiyn?" Veron asked.

Brixton nodded.

Veron turned to the young man. "What do you think?"

Raiyn breathed deep. "I've been thinking about it. This king won't be sympathetic to me announcing who I am, whether he believes me or not. All that would do is speed up the execution."

"Agreed," Chelci said.

"I see two possible ways to succeed. One is if we can find someone with influence who would be on our side."

"Someone with connections," Veron said, "who wouldn't tell the king but could rally people around them to support your claim."

"Desmond seems to have influence," Raiyn said. "At first, I thought we could trust him, but . . . I don't think that's the case anymore."

"Ryker's who we want," Brixton said. "He controls the army and people respect him. If he were on our side, that would be all the support we'd need."

Veron's shoulder fell. "I don't think we can trust him any more than Desmond, though."

Raiyn nodded. "I agree. Either of them is a fast road to an even quicker death. We should keep our eyes open for other possibilities, but I find it unlikely we're going to run into someone who's perfect."

"So what's the other way of success?" Chelci asked.

Raiyn blew out a deep breath. "Announce who I am where a lot of people hear it and might believe me."

Veron nodded. "At the execution."

"Exactly. That way, the king can't sweep it under the rug. We just need to hope there's a crowd."

"There will be a crowd. Darian wants to build favor with his people. If he can execute those responsible for killing their previous king, it shows his power. The sticking point will be, does anyone believe you when you speak?"

Raiyn's face tightened.

Chelci reached for Veron. He turned to her and smiled, squeezing her hand. "We've been in worse spots before," she said.

"You're right," he replied. "It's going to work out." The optimistic words ushered a long moment of silence into the cell.

"We must have hope," Raiyn whispered.

Leaning against the wall, Veron's mind hopped through the difficult situations he'd been in: with Slash in Karad, as a slave in Felting, fighting Bale in the courtyard, rescuing Chelci from Talioth. A pang of loss jolted him as Lia came to mind. He'd worked so hard to mend that relationship, only to lose her in the end. "Lia wouldn't have given up," he whispered. His jaw trembled and his sight grew blurry.

As if sensing how he felt, Chelci turned to him with a knowing smile and tears brimming in her eyes. Seeing her cry unleashed a wave of tears that wouldn't be held back. He buried his face in her neck. Choking sobs from both Stormbridges echoed in the cell. They held each other tight, tears falling to the stone floor as they set their sorrow free.

Releasing the grief left Veron lighter. When the tears stopped, he sat back up and wiped his face.

Chelci's hair tangled across her cheeks. She laughed as she pulled the strands back and noticed Raiyn and Brixton watching her. "I'm a mess. Sorry about that."

"It's fine," Raiyn said. "I understand."

"I know I've said it before," Brixton said, "but I'm sorry, Chelci."

Veron scooted to sit straighter, his eyes fixed on his old friend.

"Way back in Felting when we first met, I used you. I was deceitful and ambitious and only looking out for myself. I was blinded by trying to impress Bale and please my father. But I chose the wrong people to impress. I'm sorry."

A faint smile showed on her face. She sniffed and wiped her eyes. "Thank you, Brixton. It's been long forgiven."

"Being in this place," he gestured around him. "It brings me back and reminds me of who I was." His eyes fell on Veron. "And Veron . . . No one ever showed me kindness like you did. You were the only person who cared about me. Truly. I broke that trust. I sacrificed you to elevate myself."

The memory of waking up in the Karad dungeon entered his mind: the hopelessness and betrayal when he learned Brixton had turned on him.

Brixton shook his head. "It was meaningless, though. I can't believe I thought the titles and money would make me happy. I could never say it enough to reflect how awful I feel about it, but . . . I'm sorry."

"Things have a way of working out, Brixton," Veron said. "If you hadn't done what you did, I never would have met Chelci. I would not have found my father. And my—" He choked on his words and lowered his chin, fighting back the emotion that bubbled to the surface. "And my daughter would never have been born."

Chelci squeezed his hand.

Veron exhaled a slow breath. "You also helped create one of the greatest moments of my life." He pointed toward the ceiling. "Up there in the courtyard. I thought I was about to die with Bale until my wife showed up, alive, and my friend redeemed himself, fighting by my side. You two rescued me. What could be better than that?"

A clank echoed somewhere in the distance, jerking Veron to sit forward. He strained his ears, looking through the cell bars into the surrounding gloom. Footsteps padded through a passage and a light grew.

A man rounded a corner. Attired in a coarse brown tunic, his greasy, black hair fell over his eyes. He held a flickering torch and headed toward the side wall.

Veron watched, tense.

The man approached the rack of weapons and selected an axe. The blade was the length of his arm. Its tip scraped the low ceiling of the room as he pulled it from its holder.

"Hello there," Veron greeted.

The man's eyes flicked toward them for only a moment. He shook his head, then headed toward the far corner of the room where a grinding wheel waited with a chair.

Veron tried again. "What's your name?"

The man with the axe sat at the wheel. He placed the torch in a holder and moved his feet to set the wheel spinning. When it reached its full speed, he pressed the blade of the axe against the face. A grating sound filled the room while sparks danced off the wheel.

"Should I try with him?" Raiyn asked, barely audible over the noise.

Veron raised an eyebrow. "Tell him who you are?" He shook his head after a moment. "He's a lackey. He wouldn't be able to do anything. Besides, the word would probably make its way straight to the king."

"You, there!" Brixton called through the bars, loud enough to be heard over the grinding. "Do you know who we are?"

The man continued working as if they had said nothing.

"There is a group that will destroy Norshewa, and you won't be able to stop them. We're trying to help. We have a plan that will save your kingdom, but it won't work if we're killed." Brixton paused but still received no response. "If we die, Norshewa will as well."

Another torch rounded the corner, and Ryker's broad form entered the room. He paused at the sight of the man at the grinding wheel but then continued forward to the cell.

Veron stood at the bars, his fingers woven around the metal. He waited with his head cocked as the general drew close. "Have you come to fulfill the king's sentence?"

Ryker stopped an arm's length from the bars. A frown pulled at his face as he mulled over his words. "You are to be executed tomorrow."

A lump formed in Veron's throat. "All of us? I was the one who killed Bale. If we're meant to die, it should be just me. Brixton isn't a shadow knight, and Raiyn wasn't even with us."

"All of you," Ryker said. "Beheading. At first light. In the castle courtyard."

"Will it be a private audience?" Veron asked. "Or will there be spectators?"

"Word has already spread through the city that we caught Bale's killer. The courtyard will be packed."

Veron's eyes flicked to Raiyn.

"I wish—" Ryker paused, words appearing stuck on his lips. He stepped closer to the bars and lowered his voice. "I'm sorry about all of this."

Veron's brows pinched together. He pressed against the bars to make sure he could hear the words over the grinding noise in the far corner.

"I meant what I said before. I have changed. The king is bent on conquering, but I'm arguing with him every step of the way. I think it's foolish."

"So do something about it," Chelci said, quiet enough that the man with the axe couldn't hear. "Get us out of here."

Ryker shook his head. "I tried to convince Darian, but he won't be persuaded."

"You control the army, don't you?" she added. "They'll follow you."

"It's not that simple. Norshewa is a kingdom steeped in tradition. I have their respect, but they're loyal to their rulers. The king is revered above all."

"But *Darian* was appointed by committee, right?" Brixton asked. "There's no tradition around that."

"True, but that was necessary because you all killed the previous king."

"They respect the crown—the rightful ruler of Norshewa," Veron breathed. "And you're sympathetic to our cause." He turned to Raiyn with a raised eyebrow. "What do you think?"

Raiyn's wide eyes flitted between Veron and Ryker. "I'm not sure."

"It's your call," Veron said.

The general leaned in closer. "What do you mean?"

Everyone stood frozen for a long moment while nothing but the grinding of the axe filled the air. With his eyes locked on Ryker, Raiyn gave a tight shake of his head. "No. It's not the right move."

Veron blew out his held breath.

"What are you all talking about?" Ryker asked, his voice louder.

"Nothing," Veron said, bringing the attention back to him. "Think about it. The Knights of Power will take over your kingdom. You won't be able to stop them, even with your army. You need us, and we need your Bravian Fire. It's not too late for you to act—to save Norshewa."

Ryker swallowed. He paused until his head offered a weak nod. "I know. And I'm sorry. I'll see you in the morning." The general spun on his heels and disappeared down the hall.

"Why didn't you tell him?" Brixton asked as soon as the general was gone. "That was our perfect chance!"

All eyes turned to Raiyn. The young man's head shrank into his shoulders. "I wasn't feeling it."

"You weren't—" Brixton cut himself off with a groan.

"What if he was lying?" Raiyn asked. "Trying to win our confidence. We have no way of knowing if he was telling the truth."

Veron sighed. "You're right. We couldn't know for sure. It was a chance, but it would have been a risk. Even if he was being genuine, we don't know if telling him would have worked."

"He said that the courtyard will be packed," Raiyn continued. "I think that's our shot."

"As long as they believe you," Veron added, his heart refusing to place much confidence in the long shot.

On the far side of the room, the scraping sound from the axe stopped, and the grinding wheel slowed its spin. The man in the brown tunic rose to his feet. He carried the freshly sharpened axe with one hand and the torch with the other as he headed toward the exit.

"Wait!" Raiyn shouted.

The man flinched, pausing his stride.

"I need to speak with you."

Veron leaned toward Raiyn and whispered, "You're not telling him, are you?"

The man resumed his path, only a few steps from disappearing down the hall.

Raiyn shook his head toward Veron. "Please!" he called after the man. "I'm to be killed in the morning, and I'm only twenty years old. I have one favor to ask."

His shaggy black hair blocked his face as he entered the far passage.

"I beg of you!" Raiyn shouted. "The last wish of a condemned man. It's easy and will be no trouble at all!"

The man in brown paused, his body half in view and half around the corner. He turned to look at them, then ambled toward the cell. "What do you want?"

With his heart beating in his chest, Veron leaned toward Raiyn. "What are you trying to do?" he whispered.

The man drew closer.

Raiyn wrapped his hands around the bars of the cell and looked at Veron. His nervous smile matched the sparkle in his eye. He leaned back. "Grasping for hope."

28

THE ROYAL BARGE

Moored at the end of the dock, the royal barge drifted in the river. The single mast lay bare, the rarely used sail tucked away somewhere in storage. A roof covered most of the ample deck, providing shade for the empty seats. Danik walked up the gangplank.

"This is nice." Lisette entered the boat behind him, wide-eyed as she took in the luxury of the cushions and woodwork that filled the shaded area. Her sleeveless blue dress flapped in the river breeze, showing off her pale skin. "What does the king use this for?"

"For whatever he wants." Nicolar chuckled. "Right, Danik?"

Danik puffed through his nose in acknowledgment.

Magnus Hampton stepped off the plank to the boat deck. "My father had one for a while. We used it a lot when I was young." He turned and took the hand of the young woman who followed.

Geneva Hillegass kept her brown hair long and straight. Her smooth olive skin reflected her eighteen years of age. Her shoulders looked tight, matching the nervous look of her flitting eyes.

"What do you think, dear?" Magnus asked.

She nodded. "It's nice."

"You know, we held my first wedding at the palace. It was a grand affair, stuffy and crowded. I'm thinking ours should be something smaller . . . more intimate. Maybe on a boat like this. What do you think?"

She dropped her eyes to the deck. "Whatever you think."

Danik smiled. "You're welcome to use this, of course. If you decide, let Quentin know. He'll take care of the details."

Danik removed his sword belt and tossed his weapon on a table. He sat on a couch with red cushions next to the edge, where water lapped against the hull. The shade and the breeze kept the air comfortable despite it being the middle of a cloudless day. "Lisette," he patted the seat next to him. "Join me."

The young, red-haired woman sat next to him on the couch while the others found their own places to sit.

"Where is Quentin?" Nicolar added his sword to the table. "Is he coming?"

"I told him to leave us alone. I need a day without scheming and stress." He caressed the back of his hand along the pale skin of Lisette's bare arms. "A day of relaxing." Danik looked at the dozen servants who lingered on the periphery. "Cast us off. And where are our refreshments? I'm thirsty!"

The men and women wearing gray uniforms snapped into action. Three men worked on the ropes that attached the boat to the dock. One tied a line to a post at the far end. When the ropes were free, the barge drifted in the current. The shore drifted by until the long rope pulled taut, holding them in place. A woman at the far end pulled at a rudder that maneuvered the craft into the center of the river where the water split around them. The crew kept well inside the perimeter of the boat. Although a small lip would keep objects from rolling off into the water, the lack of railing would send an inattentive servant overboard.

Drinks came first—silver goblets filled with generous servings of dark red wine. Danik took a long swallow, smacking his lips at the smooth taste.

Nicolar sniffed his cup. "You don't have any firetonic, do you?"

Danik raised his eyebrows, catching the attention of the man who had served them.

The servant shook his head. "I'm sorry, Your Majesty, but we don't."

Nicolar batted a hand at the air. "Eh, don't worry about it." He tipped his goblet. A dribble of wine ran down his chin until he wiped it away. "Back in Norshewa, you could get it at any tavern. You're the king now. Bring it back."

Platters arrived. The servants placed a half-dozen bronze dishes on the various tables scattered between the seats. Fruit, nuts, cheese, bread, and meat filled the plates. Danik dug in, piling several chunks of cheese and thin-sliced meat on a hunk of bread. Nicolar and Magnus joined him, but Lisette and Geneva kept their hands folded in their laps.

"Eat up, ladies," Danik encouraged. "This is the best our city offers."

They gave in and picked at the food.

Magnus scooped a pile of nuts. "Bilton couldn't make it?"

Danik shook his head. "He was busy. Still trying to track down that counterfeiter."

Magnus coughed as if a nut threatened to go down the wrong pipe. "Excuse me." He cleared his throat. "Still working on that, huh? Reports have been down in the last couple of weeks. I wonder if the culprit was scared off."

"Let's hope so. We could use the stability at home before we expand." Danik took a large drink, then leaned his head back. He closed his eyes and let the river breeze ruffle his hair.

Nicolar leaned forward and spoke in a quieter voice, "Speaking of stability . . . Magnus and I were talking, and I think I have a way to boost the economy in Feldor."

"This was Nicolar's idea," Magnus interjected.

"I call it the Purification Act." Nicolar continued. "Before you say 'no,' hear me out."

Danik raised his eyebrows.

"The people who fill the Red Quarter don't contribute to society. Men are too lazy to work, but when their families go hungry, they expect the kingdom to provide. The elderly are even worse. They do nothing but talk and get sick. Do you have any idea how much money Darcius' elderly care initiative costs?"

Danik frowned. "Is that the program that gives out medicine and food?"

"Yes, and it costs a *fortune*. Do you know what's supposed to happen when bodies break down? They *die*. It's the natural cycle of life and death. Now, we're trying to avoid it, and the healthy people of Feldor are the ones paying the price."

"What does this act do?"

Nicolar held out a hand and counted on his fingers as he talked. "The sick, the poor, the sloths. Anyone who can't take care of themselves shouldn't be a drain on everyone else."

"You want to make it a crime to be poor?"

"No, but real life should have consequences."

"If we cancel those programs, I doubt anyone would appreciate walking through the streets with all the beggars that would line them."

Nicolar's eyes turned dark. "Don't leave them in the streets."

"What? You mean . . ."

"No one would miss them."

Danik's stomach twisted. He batted his hand in the air. "Enough of this. I said I wanted a day without plotting and scheming." He tipped his cup and took a drink, enjoying the earthy wine trickling down his throat.

Nicolar leaned back in his chair with a disappointed frown.

The group lounged for an hour, floating on the river. The plates remained full, refilled by vigilant servants as they grew low. Their cups never ran dry, despite Danik's attempt to make it to the bottom of his. The alcohol in the wine left him buzzing. His mind felt foggy. He could swipe it away with a touch of devion, but he let it remain—a welcome escape from the stress of being a king.

A round of laughter caused him to jump. He had let his gaze drift, looking toward the far bank of the river. Magnus and Nicolar leaned together, laughing as they clinked their goblets.

"What do you think, Danik?" Nicolar asked. "Should we train him?"

Danik racked his brain, trying to recall any words. A hazy fog was all he found. "Train for...?"

"The devion." Nicolar squeezed Magnus' upper arm. "He's got at least a few muscles hidden under his rich clothes."

Magnus' eyes were unfocused, as if he didn't follow the conversation.

Danik squirmed, cognizant enough to remember the over-crowded spot they were in. "I don't know. We have quite a few men as it is."

Magnus waved a hand. "It's fine. I think I like my neck spot free, anyway."

"Why do you only have men?" Lisette asked, breaking her long-standing silence.

"What do you mean?" Danik asked.

"In the Knights of Power," she clarified. "Why aren't there any women?"

A grin pulled at Danik's mouth, the curiosity amplified by his mental impairment. "You want to join? We'll make a space for you."

Her eyes widened, and her head shook. "Oh no, not me. I just—I was curious."

"We should have women," Nicolar said, leaning back in his seat and taking a drink. A faint slur marked his words. "They'd help the training center look and smell better."

Danik leaned closer to Lisette. "Why not? You don't want it?"

"I, uh—" She glanced between the men. "It's not for me, I don't think."

Nicolar laughed. "Not for you? You say that because you've never felt it. You've never tasted the power." He jumped to his feet and picked up his sword. "The strength of the sun fills your body."

"Faster than a sprinting deer," Danik added.

"Stronger than a roaring bear." Nicolar waved his unsteady weapon in the air as if striking an invisible opponent.

Magnus shrank back from the blade. "Watch it!"

Danik and Nicolar laughed, a drawn-out affair not shared by the others.

"Strong, as long as there is no metal," Magnus added. "Correct?"

Danik's laugh faded. His mouth formed a hard line. "That's right."

"What does that mean?" Lisette's eyebrows raised. "How does metal take away your power?"

Danik felt his forehead wrinkling. He looked at Nicolar, but the man only shrugged. Turning back to Lisette, a muttering of mumbles and half-words came out. "I have no idea," he articulated.

Nicolar and Danik burst into laughter again but with double the intensity. Danik's wine sloshed from his goblet, dribbling onto the deck. Nicolar extended his sword and tapped him on the side with the flat of the blade. Continuing to laugh, Danik batted the steel away, making the deck of the boat spin.

"No. No." Danik gathered himself and turned back to Lisette. "I'm sorry. It's like this—the metal does . . . something. I don't know what." He stopped, rifling through his muddled mind to determine how he could explain it. An unused boat anchor and length of chain caught his eye at the edge of the deck. "Like this."

Danik stood. His vision blurred for a moment, and he held on to his chair to help stabilize. With his feet steady, he wobbled to the end of the chain and pulled it off a hook attached to the deck. The metal links scraped across the deck as he dragged it to their couch.

"Give me your leg," Danik said.

Lisette looked frozen, her eyes appraising him with caution. After a pause, she extended her leg. Her dress slid higher. Smooth skin stretched up to her knee.

Danik rested a hand under her calf. "Inside, the ability feels unlimited. Nothing can stop you." He brought his other hand and draped the chain over her ankle. He wrapped a loose end again so that it formed a circle twice around her leg. "When metal surrounds you, it . . . impedes your power. You're not weak or helpless, but you can't use the devion that gives you extra strength." He wrapped the chain again and again, pulling it into a knot at the opposite end. A grin formed on his face. "Even like this, we're lethal fighters."

Waving a hand from shore, his advisor Quentin grabbed his attention. The man stood at attention where the taut rope connecting to the boat was fixed around the end of the dock. "Your Majesty," he called over the river. "A word."

Danik groaned. "Today isn't about business."

"Should we pull up and let him board?" Nicolar asked.

With his eyes on the dock, Danik tossed back another swallow of his drink. He smacked his lips. "Fine." He nodded to the servants.

The woman on the rudder steered them back toward shore while another pulled at the rope. In less than a minute, the barge bumped into the wooden dock and Quentin stepped onboard using a steadying hand from a servant.

"Thank you, Your Majesty."

"Quentin, as you can see, we are enjoying this beautiful day fine enough as we are. Was I unclear about wishing to be left alone?"

The advisor squirmed. "You were clear, sir, but I thought this was news you would want to know."

"Is this about that children's dinner you're making us go to tonight?"

"The King's Academy Feast? No."

"What is it then?"

Quentin's eyes moved to Geneva then Lisette. "Do you wish to find a more private loc—"

"Out with it!" Danik's sudden outburst washed a wave of dizziness over him.

Lisette bent forward, rattling the chain around the leg, but Danik kept his eyes on the advisor.

"The northern scouts returned this morning."

"From Karad?"

Quentin shook his head. "Rynor. They spotted a group of four traveling together."

Danik's eyes narrowed. "Four what?"

Quentin's eyes flicked around the crowd. "Four shadow knights."

The king sucked in air and tensed. "Shadow knights? Impossible, there are only three left."

"It was them," Quentin said. "Veron, Chelci, and the one from the hanging. They didn't recognize the fourth—around Veron's age with shaggy blond hair."

"Where did they go?"

"The scouts tried to keep up, but they lost the trail. They were heading north."

"North," Danik repeated. "Toward . . ."

"Norshewa."

Danik set his jaw, running an image of the traveling knights through his head. He turned to Nicolar. "Norshewa," he repeated. "It's your people. What do you think?"

Nicolar chuckled. "I haven't set foot there in ages. They do have an army already assembled, though."

"What would they do with an outsider? Someone with Raiyn's bloodline. He couldn't just . . . show up, could he?"

Nicolar shook his head. "First, they wouldn't believe him. Even if they did, it's a new regime now. Darian's not just going to step aside. He'd kill Raiyn as soon as he found out—" Nicolar raised an eyebrow. "Would Veron and them kill Darian to take over? To get control of the army?"

Danik stood and paced toward the edge of the boat. "They *could*, but I don't know that they *would*." A laugh from Nicolar turned his head. "What?"

The knight of power grinned. He held his free hand out, palm up. "It doesn't matter."

"What do you mean?"

"Even if they take over Norshewa. Even if the army pledges fealty to them, what are they going to do? They're going to march down the road. Then what . . . lay siege to Felting?"

It was Danik's turn to laugh. "No, they won't."

"Why not?" Magnus asked. "You think they wouldn't want to hurt the city or something?"

"No," Danik said. "Because as they're marching south, we'll hit them. Five knights of power would be a challenge. Ten would be better. But twenty or thirty?"

"It'd be easy." Lines formed on Nicolar's face.

"What is it?"

"It sounds too easy. What are we missing?"

Danik shrugged. "Why do we have to be missing something?"

Quentin's eyes flashed a glimmer of recognition as he looked out toward the river.

"What is it, Quentin?"

The advisor turned to hold his gaze and stared. "What? No, it's nothing."

"Quentin," Danik's voice dropped into a growl. "Do you know something?"

Nicolar turned to the advisor, angling his loosely held sword in his direction.

"Er, no, um—" Sweat beaded on the man's forehead. "I heard something, back when Darcius was king."

Danik winced.

"I heard—" His eyes flitted between the group. "I heard the Norshewans had . . ." He swallowed. "They had a plan to take over Terrenor. Like back when Bale was in charge. I'm sure that's why this army is mobilized."

"A plan to take over Terrenor. What brand-new information." Nicolar's sarcastic tone returned levity to the group.

Quentin chuckled, wiping his forehead with the back of his hand. "Yeah, I just remembered that."

Lisette continued to tug at the chains, making no progress in untangling them. She stood and stepped closer to the anchor where she had more slack to work with.

Danik took another large swallow, letting the wine wash afresh over him, dulling his senses. He raised his cup toward the advisor. "Thank you for the update, Quentin. It's good to know where the remaining shadow knights are. Seems like we'll have a bit of time before they return."

Nicolar tossed back a drink. "And then we'll finish them."

Danik grinned. "It'll be easy."

Nicolar leaned toward Magnus. "It'll be a lot easier if Danik can stop killing all our trainees."

The two men burst into a fit of laughter. Quentin joined in but sounded more restrained.

Danik's face felt warm. "Hey, that was only that one guy, and he deserved it."

"Da-nik the ki-ller," Nicolar teased in a sing-song manner.

"You killed that other guy. What was his name?"

Nicolar extended his sword and tapped Danik playfully with the flat of the blade. "Ki-ll-er."

Danik pushed the weapon away. "Immo, that was his name. He was your call."

"Kill-er. Kill-er" Nicolar stepped closer, tapping his sword against Danik.

The flush from the wine left Danik feeling silly. He snickered as he dodged a tap and lunged for his own sword. "Aha!" His weapon lifted, wobbling in his unsteady grip.

"Careful there," Magnus said, leaning away from the wild blade.

"Don't worry," Danik said. "I'm in complete control."

He waved the weapon over his head, swinging in a wide arc, punctuating the motion with a laugh before holding his weapon in front of him with a tight, two-handed grip.

The smirk on Nicolar's face evaporated. His eyes widened and his jaw dropped. Magnus gripped the armrests on his chair and sat up straight. Geneva's hand covered her mouth. Several servants gasped. Everyone stared at him.

Danik relaxed his shoulders and loosened his grip. "What's wrong?"

Discolored steel at the tip of his sword caught his eye. He angled the blade until the light picked up a red stain.

Nicolar's line of sight ran to the side and over his shoulder.

They're not staring at me. Danik turned. The sight behind him felt like a kick in the gut.

Lisette staggered at the edge of the barge. A hand pressed against her neck. Blood dripped down her arm and fell on the blue fabric of her dress.

"Lisette!" Danik shouted. The buzz in his head vanished as a wave of devion rushed through his system.

Her desperate, begging eyes held his. A gurgle at her mouth formed a bubble of blood. It popped, staining her chin.

"I—I—" He could find no words to say.

Lisette's foot caught on the pile of chains sitting on the deck. Her arms flailed, but her balance shifted toward the edge. With a gurgling scream, her body tumbled over the unprotected edge of the boat, the chain still wrapped around her ankle.

Danik stood, too stunned to do anything as the rattling chains followed Lisette into the water.

Landing on her back, Lisette floated just under the surface, churning the water with her flailing arms. The blood gushing from the gash in her neck stained the river, which blended in with red hair billowing around her.

When the coil of chain had disappeared from the deck, the anchor jerked after it. The heavy metal object popped over the side and landed in the middle of Lisette's chest.

Her eyes widened. A burst of bubbles exploded from her mouth, stirring the red water. Her body sank. The blue dress and pale skin faded into the darkness of the river until it consumed her.

Danik's jaw hung loose. He remained frozen, watching the water. "It was an accident," he whispered.

"Of course it was," Quentin replied.

"Yes," Nicolar sniffed, "most unfortunate."

"I will make sure her family is notified," Quentin said. "They will hear that despite His Majesty's attempts to coax her away from the edge, their daughter fell in and was unable to be rescued before the current pulled her under."

Danik continued to stare. His chest felt empty. *I killed her. It was my sword and my carelessness.*

"Are you all right with that, sir?"

Danik turned. The others watched him with their heads inclined forward. "All right with . . . ?"

"With telling her parents of her . . . unfortunate accident—because of her carelessness."

Danik swallowed. The lie sat heavy on his heart, but he pushed away the guilt. "Do it."

29

A FEAST OF DISCONTENT

"I can't believe I'm doing this," Danik muttered. His steps echoed in the cavernous hallway, bouncing off the walls and high ceiling. Though Lisette's death was still fresh in his mind, the scowl on his face was from a new frustration.

Nicolar kept pace beside him. "I believe being a leader requires participation in some tasks that you might prefer to avoid. That sometimes includes celebrating pretentious rich kids."

"They probably all grew up eating with golden utensils and had servants who dressed them. I bet not one of them knows how to work a day of hard labor or what a grumbling stomach feels like. And to reward them . . . we tell them how great they are and feed them enough food to stuff a bear."

They drew near the entrance to the ballroom. The stone of the rebuilt supports looked lighter than the rest of the walls. With a twist of his lip, he recalled when Raiyn and Lia destroyed them and made off with the stolen book only a few weeks before.

Nicolar walked next to him but paused, extending an arm when they reached the entrance. "After you."

Workers had only just finished rebuilding the entrance to the ballroom the day before. The smell of new mortar and fresh paint filled the air. Danik stepped between the columns and stopped at the top of the short flight of steps that led to the ballroom floor.

A long table decorated with flowers, plates, and covered dishes filled the center of the oversized room. Dozens of mostly empty chairs surrounded the table. Ten young men and women mixed through the crowd, the top graduates from the most recent class at King's Academy. The young men were dressed in sharp white collars and pressed suits while the women wore dresses. They stood straight, talking with loud voices and animated expressions.

Deans, city leaders, and dignitaries schmoozed the next generation of talent. Familiar faces of the city's high lords stood out to him. Bilton spoke with Hillegass and Miligan. Hampton gathered with Stokes and Windridge. A cadre of royal guards stood on watch, spaced around the perimeter of the room. At Danik's arrival, conversations faded, and heads turned his direction.

A royal attendant dressed in black-and-purple velvet stepped away from the wall and stood next to the steps. He projected in a clear voice, "Welcome, His Majesty, Danik Bannister, King of Feldor."

Applause filled the room. Danik gritted his teeth but forced a smile.

The attendant continued, "Please, would you all find a seat?"

Danik waited for Nicolar to join him, then descended the steps, muttering to himself.

Quentin approached. "Your Majesty," the advisor greeted. "Thank you for coming. Allow me to introduce Dean Oliver Shelton."

A plump man with thinning hair and a wrinkled face pressed forward and offered a bow. "Your Majesty, it's an honor to meet you." His words spilled out as if reciting a well-rehearsed speech. "Thank you for joining our students as we celebrate their achievements. You are making their day."

Danik grumbled a recognition and nodded before turning his attention to the table. The young faces settling into chairs looked like children, although they were only a few years younger than himself.

As the Dean left, High Lord Bilton took his place. "Your Majesty," Bilton said, "I heard about Lisette. I'm so sorry."

Danik's back stiffened. His desire to ignore the subject and move past it warred with appreciation of the high lord acknowledging it. "Thank you. It was tragic."

"If you need to . . . talk or anything after the feast, please let me know."

The offer impressed Danik with its kindness—a trait he rarely saw. "Thank you, Geoffrey." He nodded. "For now, I should . . ." He gestured to the empty high-backed chair at the end of the table.

"Of course." Bilton gave a slight bow before stepping back. "Enjoy."

Danik took his seat. Nicolar occupied the chair to one side, while Dean Shelton took the opposite with an oversized grin.

Servants showed as the king sat. They lifted covers from dishes sitting on the table, filling the room with the aroma of beef and potatoes. Some bowls contained piles of rolls while others held leafy greens. Plates held cheese and fruit. Roasted peppers and verquash sat next to sizable dishes of roast beef, already sliced and still simmering.

Carried on multiple serving trays, dozens of drinks arrived. The wine steward served one to each guest, placing the glasses with red liquid before each of them.

The last drink was for Danik. His glass stood taller than the others, with a rim of gold around the lip. Holding the stem with a white-gloved hand, the steward extended the glass to him. "For you, Your Majesty."

The sight of the dark liquid reminded him of what happened to Lisette earlier in the day. His stomach turned. Catching himself in a scowl, he forced what he could of a smile and accepted the drink.

The people sitting around the table looked at Danik. They waited, silent and patient. The young men snuck glances at the dishes, nearly drooling, but still restrained themselves.

Danik motioned to the uncovered dishes. "Please, begin."

The young graduates moved first, grabbing at the beef, potatoes, and bread while the adults took portions of the greens and roasted vegetables. It wasn't long before conversation had picked back up, a welcome return from the staring.

Quentin arrived at Danik's side. "Your Majesty," he began. "It's customary for the king to say a few words of recognition and encouragement to the graduates."

Danik bristled.

"It doesn't have to be much," the advisor added. "They just want to hear something from you."

"Oh, do they?" Danik retorted. The plans of the Shadow Knights, the death of Lisette, and Cedric's lack of discipline all fought in his mind. *This is the last thing I want to be doing.*

"Perhaps I could say a few words?" The dean raised his eyebrows and gestured toward the table.

Danik exhaled, then nodded, his nerves settling.

Dean Shelton stood, picking up his glass as he did. "Graduates of King's Academy, I'm sure you're tired of hearing my voice over the last few years." He allowed the polite laughs to settle. The crowd continued to eat but kept their attention on the dean. "But I'd like to say a few words to honor you this evening. We graduated forty-nine students this year, but you ten are the exceptional ones."

The students' faces turned up in beaming smiles.

The dean pointed at one of the young men. "Adam, your paper last year on non-linear mathematics baffled even Professor Grumpkin. He still talks with me about how impressed he was." He walked as he spoke, carrying his drink with him. He tapped the back of a chair where a blonde woman sat. "Nina, I don't think there was an exam you weren't top of your class in." He pointed across the table to a curly-haired young man with a face full of freckles. "And I can't forget Jonathan. The experiments you conducted in the lab . . . I think Professor Soole is still trying to replicate them."

Polite applause again filled the room.

"You all are the future of Feldor. The greatest minds from the greatest families." The dean raised his glass. "It has been an honor for me to have you in our school, and I wish you all the best of success."

Calls of "here, here," dotted the room, followed by a drink to commemorate the dean's words.

Danik took a large swallow, letting the blend of sweet and bitter wash over his tongue. As he lowered his glass, he spied the guests along the table glancing in his direction. They waited, keeping their glasses hovering in midair.

He groaned. *I guess I'm not getting out of it so easily.* He pushed back his chair and then stood.

He felt their eyes boring into him. They all waited as he stood. One young man had frozen with a fork full of food halfway to his mouth.

"You graduated," Danik said. "Congratulations. Now you can go on to . . . solve math problems and take tests." His chuckle was the only sound. "We can't all be warriors. Not everyone has physical ability, so it's nice that people like you can exercise your brains."

The guests shifted in their chairs and glanced at each other around the table.

"Take Quentin here, for example."

The advisor stiffened and lifted his eyebrows.

"He will never lead an army or have the strength to defeat another warrior. But he knows stuff. That's why he's been an advisor to the king for—I don't know how long. A long time. His advice is mostly good, with periodic exceptions for making me speak at events I don't want to."

Danik lifted his glass higher and shifted his gaze to the graduates. "Maybe you can do great things. And, who knows, if you find yourself in a battle someday . . . if an enemy attacks you, you can always slap him with some philosophy."

He burst into laughter. A few men joined him, albeit more subdued.

A sharp feeling registered in Danik's stomach, making him wince. *I need to get some food in me,* he thought. *I've had nothing but alcohol for hours.*

He stepped closer to the table, then leaned between High Lord

Bilton and one of the young graduates. He grabbed a roll from a basket on the table.

"Don't let me discourage you, though." Danik tore the roll. "Our kingdom needs people of all kinds. In academics, I hear you ten show great promise."

A fresh pain twisted in his side. He held his palm against the spot and pressed inward.

"Are you all right, Your Majesty?" Bilton asked.

"Of course," he replied. "I just—Gah!"

The pain intensified. A flush crept up his neck, and sweat beads prickled his forehead. He bent over, dropped the broken bread, and rested a hand on his knee.

Chairs pushed back as guests stood. Bilton jumped to his feet. Nicolar ran around the table. A murmur of commotion rose as people crowded around him.

"Stay back!" Danik shouted through gritted teeth. The pain grew more intense every second. His gut felt like he was being stabbed.

What is going on?

His vision blurred. The room swayed. He held out his empty arm to keep balanced when he caught sight of his wine glass. It swayed along with the room.

The wine.

An acrid aftertaste remained on his tongue—stale berries mixed with burnt wood. While unfamiliar in wine, the taste lit a memory.

He recalled sitting with Lia in the common room of the Shadow Knights' center. Liquids and powders lined the table in protected jars —jars filled with poisons. They took turns tasting a minuscule amount of each, to aid in detection. He remembered the bottle of clear liquid, a poison so strong they couldn't even touch a drop. *Night-drop.* The smell of it lingered in his nostrils, an acrid scent of charred wood with a hint of stale berries.

"Nightdrop," he muttered. "What is . . ." His words slurred, fading to nothing. He set the glass on the edge of the table a moment before a fresh agony racked his gut.

Danik fell to his knees and pressed his eyes together. A groan grew into a yell, tearing from his throat.

No! I can do this. Keeping his eyes closed, Danik pulled the power of the devion into his body. He willed it to heal what the nightdrop threatened to destroy.

Power rushed through him. His limbs shuddered. He clenched both fists and flexed his muscles. The pain in his gut flickered, then subsided to a dull ache. Soon, it faded to nothing.

Danik inhaled deeply. After holding for a long moment, he blew the air out in a slow breath. The pain was gone. His heart pounded, and his breath felt short, but he no longer sensed any trace of the poison.

He flicked open his eyes. The staring crowd flinched backward. Danik set his jaw and stood.

"What happened?" Bilton asked.

Nicolar seemed to understand. "Was it poison?"

Danik turned to the glass sitting on the table. His fingers grasped the stem. He lifted it into the air, watching the liquid slosh inside. He held it under his nose and inhaled. The tainted aroma from the nightdrop was faint. He would never have recognized it if it weren't for Lia having studied it.

"Bring the wine steward here," he said to no one in particular.

Royal guards snapped to attention and rushed toward the kitchen.

"It was poison, right?" Nicolar repeated.

Danik's blood boiled. Fury simmered inside at the attempt on his life. He didn't bother answering the question. He let the silence grow the mounting tension.

When footsteps arrived, he turned. The wine steward stood in the middle of four guards. The man's eyes shifted around the room. "You called for me, Your Majesty?"

Through much effort, Danik replaced the vengeful expression of fury with a forced smile. His chest still gave away his shortness of breath, but his hands were steady.

"What is your name, steward?"

"My name? Armando, named for my father."

"Armando." Danik widened his smile. "You know your wines, do you?"

"Um . . . I like to think so."

"Good, because I have a problem with mine."

Armando's eyes grew wide. "I'm so sorry. A bug? A smudge on the glass? It hasn't turned to vinegar, has it?"

"None of those things."

The steward's forehead remained pinched. He held out a hand for the drink. "I'll get you a new one straight away. Was it the vintage you didn't care for?"

Danik held onto the glass. "I would like you to taste my drink, Armando."

Gasps sounded from around the table.

"See if you can tell me what is wrong with it."

The steward pulled his arm back. His eyes flitted around the room, and a sheen of sweat glistened on his brow. "Your Majesty, I-I cannot. I—"

"I insist. As your king, it is my right to do what I choose, and I order you to taste this wine. If you are so good at your job, you will recognize the issue."

Armando's jaw quivered. He glanced at the guards on either side, who kept him pinned in place. There was nowhere for him to run. "Y-Y-Your Majesty, I am devastated that the wine wasn't to your liking. I will make it right, but—" His eyes flitted again through the room. "When a king drinks from a cup, that vessel becomes sacred. As much as I want to please you in your request, I cannot do this. It breaks the basic tenets of my profession."

Danik chuckled slowly, but no one joined him. As the laugh dwindled, he let his smile fade. "Very well. I understand where you're coming from."

The tension in Armando's shoulders faded. The worry lines on his face relaxed until the king spoke again.

"And with that insistence, you have also confirmed your guilt."

Armando tensed again. "What do you mean?"

"Had you been willing to drink, it would have proved you had no knowledge of this."

"Knowledge of . . . what, sir?"

"Drink it!" Danik shouted, causing the steward to flinch. "Now!"

Nicolar stepped forward. "Sir, we can question him. Perhaps find out who put him up to it and why."

"I want him dealt with *here* and *now*." He waved his arm to take in the room. "I want *all of you* to see what happens when someone turns on me."

"I don't know what you're talking about," Armando argued. "I didn't do anything. I—"

"Are you going to drink it or not?"

The steward closed his lips tight and shook his head.

"Very well," Danik passed the glass to a guard. "Pour it down his throat."

Another guard appeared through the doorway to the kitchen. He paused and lifted a funnel, raising his eyebrows in question.

Danik nodded. "Do it."

30

TESTING NEW IDEAS

L ia chipped at the wall with more vigor than she'd felt since arriving in the mines. Chunks of rock tumbled onto the cave floor. She had to take breaks and shovel debris herself because the shovel team for the Garronts couldn't keep up. The well-conditioned team worked tirelessly, pounding at the rock. Thurman and Manne had already found a crystal each, and barely an hour had passed since they began.

She strained her ears with each swing of the axe, hoping to catch the telltale sound of an uncovered crystal. Her heart thudded. Sweaty hands made the handle of the tool slick. Her water flask leaned against the cave wall, blocking the square-shaped object concealed behind it. She worked at the far end of the line, away from the workers and far from the nearest lantern. Long shadows splashed against the wall.

Thunk.

Her axe hesitated while she scanned the clumps of stone tumbling in the pile at her feet. A flutter made her heart leap.

There it is!

She fought the urge to yell. Rather than race for the team's box, she crouched to where her shovel lay on the ground, worried that the other workers would notice. "I'm getting too much debris here," she mumbled. "Need to move some of this out."

At her left, Waylon kept working without a glance in her direction.

She moved the water flask and opened the latch on the wooden box she had rescued from the abandoned cart. While trying to not look suspicious, she grabbed the chunk of dull crystal and dropped it in the box. She snapped the lid closed and tightened the latch again.

Her pulse pounded in her head. Her hand shook. She moved the water flask back in front of the box and stood with the shovel. She strained her senses, listening for growls, smelling for odors, and checking either direction for dimming lights.

Nothing changed.

She slid the spade under the rocky debris, then dumped it in a nearby cart. She listened again.

Nothing.

Another shovel of debris.

Her hearing turned muffled, and her breath came quickly. She glanced in each direction, but nothing seemed awry. Waiting felt interminable, but gradually, her pulse settled.

"Everything all right?" Waylon asked.

Lia jumped. "Oh, sorry. You surprised me. Yeah, I'm, uh . . . fine. Thought I heard something, but I guess—" She paused again to listen, and a faint smile grew on her face. "I guess it was nothing."

She traded the shovel for her pickaxe. Cautious swings didn't do as much damage against the cave's wall. The pauses to listen between swings became shorter as her confidence grew. Before long, Lia was humming along with powerful arms and punishing blows like before. A tingling sensation ran through her body, not from nerves, but from something she'd not felt for a long while.

Hope.

NORMALLY EXHAUSTED and ready to retire after team training, Lia's heart pounded as she entered the barracks. She had rehearsed what she would say in her head for most of the day, but everything she came up with felt wrong.

The small wooden box hid at the edge of her bed, tucked under straw. No one had seen it, and better yet, no fiends had attacked it. To attempt what she wanted, she'd need the entire team on board, but— Her eyes flicked to Anton. She wasn't sure if she could trust the new guy to not be a spy.

"Chris," she pulled their leader to the side of the room. "Can you do something for me?"

"Sure."

"I need you to trust me."

He nodded, his brows creased. "What do you need?"

"I need you to get rid of Anton for about ten minutes, and he can't be suspicious."

His head stopped moving, and his eyes jumped across the room. "Do I get to know why?"

"You will. I just need some time with the rest of the team. It's important."

The team leader paused. Lia wasn't sure if he debated the request or if he was deciding whether or not she'd lost it.

"Anton!" Chris called. The new guy perked up, and Chris waved him to follow out the door.

While she waited for Chris to return, Lia walked to her bed and checked under the straw. Her box waited, just where she'd left it. The wood grain traced under her fingers. Excitement surged in her.

She tucked it back in, then watched the men of Team Garront. They laughed and joked with each other, wearing smiles and exuding energy—a marked difference from when she'd arrived weeks before.

Chris ducked back into the barracks. He crossed the room and nodded to her. "You should have around ten minutes."

"Where'd he go?"

He grinned. "I sent him back to the mine site to pick up the team's tally sheet that I left."

She frowned. "What's a tally sheet?"

"Pfff! You've got me. But it should take him at least ten minutes to look."

She chuckled. "Perfect."

"So, what's this important thing that needs to be done?"

Lia turned to the rest of the barracks and cleared her throat. "Uh . . . Garronts. I have something I need to discuss."

"Before you do . . ." Waylon raised a hand and stepped past the edge of his bunk. "I have something I wanted to say."

Lia glanced at Chris. "Um, all right."

"My wife, Cecilia, died a year before the Marked Ones caught me. She was the light of my life, and I've never been the same since. My oldest, Tommy, is married with a two-year-old. I'm sure he took over the sheep farm in Karthun when I left. My daughter, Malon, was engaged to a bright young man in our village. He wanted to move to Bromhill to find a job in banking. I hope they made it."

He nodded toward Lia. "I appreciate you sharing what you did. I was hesitant because it's difficult to think about them. The memories hurt, and it's easier to block them out. But hearing you share yesterday made me realize I miss the joy of their memory. I've decided they're the reason I mine. I dig for crystals because I hope to one day make it out and see them again."

Lia smiled at the insight into Waylon's life. "Thanks for sharing. Now, what I wanted—"

"For me, it's my wife," Thurman interrupted. "We live in Cairn, two houses down from Bridgebain and his wife."

Chris smiled and nodded.

"Lallymede and I have been married for twenty wonderful years. We could never have children, which is why we love Chris' son so much. She made clothes for the women in the village and had quite a knack for it. Even though I don't talk about her, I think of her every day. She's my motivation. I want to get back to her one day."

"That's awesome, Thurman," Lia began.

"My motivation is my son," Doyle blurted.

Lia paused with her mouth open. While the conversation was great, she needed to move on.

"He'll be sixteen now and probably taller than me. I don't want the marked ones to find him and bring him here, so that's why I keep going."

"My village has forty other capable men," Harold added, "and some women who could sling a pickaxe as well. I don't want the marked ones to find them."

Lia held up a hand. "That's great, guys—"

"I haven't seen my wife and four kids in almost two years," Manne said. "The thought of holding them again keeps me going."

"I just want sausage," Stewart added, earning a round of laughter. "I'm serious. My family passed years ago. I'm just an old man waiting out his life. I have one thing to keep me motivated, and it's the thought of earning those morning sausages."

Lia stepped forward when the sharing ended. "I love knowing more about you all, but I need to change the subject for a bit. I have something serious to discuss, and we don't have much time."

"Time before what?" Waylon asked.

"Before Anton returns."

He frowned. "I don't understand."

Lia took a deep breath, then blew it out. All eyes were on her. "I'm not just a girl from Felting who is learning her parents' business. I am, kind of, but their business happens to be . . . what they do is—" No words sounded right. "My parents run the Shadow Knights."

A silent pause fell over the room. The men gaped, glancing at each other.

"Wait—" Waylon began. "Does that mean . . . ?"

"That's right. I'm a shadow knight, too."

Shocked exclamations came from each corner of the barracks. Even Vekko and Jarno stood and stepped closer.

"You can breathe fire?" Waylon asked.

She laughed. "No fire breathing, sorry." She rushed through a brief explanation of her recent journey to rescue the other knights and how the Marked Ones planted Marcus as a spy. The men in the barracks listened with rapt attention.

"And you think Anton is a spy like Marcus was?" Chris asked when she came to a pause.

"It's possible," she replied. "I prefer we keep him out of the loop until we know for sure."

"What was it you needed to discuss?" Thurman asked.

A nervous grin pulled at her face. "I have an idea. I'm not sure it will work, but I'd like to try."

"For getting out of here?" Chris asked.

She nodded. "Shadow knights have incredible abilities, even better than breathing fire. I don't have time to go into them all, but trust me when I say I could get all of us out of here if I had my full capability."

"Um . . ." Waylon stepped closer. "That sounds great. What's the catch?"

"Two things hold me back. One—" She extended a foot. "These metal anklets impede my ability."

"What do you mean?" Chris asked.

"Basically, they're like a damper that holds my powers back."

"Rasmill has the keys, right?" Waylon said. "We could attack him together. I'm sure we could get them."

"That's only part of the issue," Lia said. "The glowing red crystals are the other thing. They also stop the abilities, but there's a way to disable them. My father did it at this Core crystal they have when we broke out the other knights."

"Is that what Rasmill spoke about when you first arrived?" Vekko asked. "What you did that caused our quotas to rise?"

"Um . . . yes, that was it."

"Why would we want that?"

Lia's stomach clenched. "It's a chance to be free! If I can disable the crystals and get these metal cuffs removed, I can get out of here and get help!"

"*You* can get out of here?" Vekko repeated.

"Yeah." Lia glanced around the room, noting the loss of enthusiasm in the men. "But I'd get out of here, then get help . . . for everyone."

Mutters ran through the room.

"That's a lot of risk," Stewart said. "If it doesn't work, that just leaves more work for us."

"But if it *does* work . . ." Harold started.

"We have to try something!" Lia pleaded.

"How would you disable the crystals?" Chris asked.

She turned to him.

"*If* we wanted to try, how do you propose it?"

"One way would be to get to the Core, somehow. I've considered trying to sneak out of the mines and get there, but without my shadow knight powers, there's no way I'd make it."

"What's the other way?"

She paused, scanning the crowd. "I suggest we build our own."

Waylon squinted. "Our own . . . Core?"

She nodded. "You know how I've talked about wanting to save up the crystals? We need to get ten. That's how many you need to create a miniature version."

"You've done this before?"

She shrugged. "Not exactly. It's a theory."

"A theory?" Jarno exclaimed. "You want us to risk our lives and support you in some crazy prison escape for *you* all because of a theory?"

"Would you rather sit here and keep mining every day?"

"Maybe!"

Chris held up his hands. "How would you even get ten raw crystals? The chances of finding that many simultaneously is impossible."

She shook her head, her smile returning. The men watched as she turned toward her bed and extracted the box from the straw. They watched in silence as she held it up.

"What's that?" Chris asked.

"This . . ." Lia rattled the contents of the box. "is two crystals."

Gasps filled the room. The men fidgeted and looked toward the door.

"I found two today and put them in this box."

"Are you crazy?" Vekko asked.

Chris stepped closer. "Lia, that was not wise. You could endanger us all."

"It's safe! I've had these all day. The box blocks the scent as if they remained buried in the cave walls. The fiends have no idea. There should be space in here for ten."

The men continued to grumble.

"We can't keep doing what we're doing—mining every day until we die. We need to *try* something! These crystals are our way out!"

Jarno leaned forward. "So, just by touching those things, you can have incredible power?"

"Yes!" Lia said, her exasperation coming through. "Assuming I can get these anklets off, too."

"I don't know, Lia," Chris said. "There's a lot of chance in that plan, with plenty of room for things to go wrong."

"Sometimes it's worth taking a chance," Waylon said.

"I'm up for it if everyone else is," Harold added.

"Not me," Vekko said. "Sounds like a good way for all of us to either die or have our lives made miserable."

"Are you not miserable now?" She glanced around the room. Waylon and Harold looked intrigued, but the rest wouldn't meet her eyes. "We've been working toward hope, but what's it all for if we never try?"

"I'm sorry, Lia," Chris said, shaking his head. "We're a team. If everyone else were on board, I'd be with you, too. But . . ."

"It's too great of a risk," Thurman said.

Chris nodded.

"Gah!" she yelled, then slammed the box back on her bed. "I can't believe you!" She stormed across the room.

Anton appeared at the door, looking lost and confused.

"Move," Lia growled, pushing past him to leave the barracks.

She stumbled outside, the larger cavern feeling less stuffy than the Garronts' barracks. A handful of men sat around a table, playing cards and talking. Lia walked toward the lake in a huff.

This is a real shot at getting out of here. Why won't they try?

"Argh!" Her frustrated cry echoed off the cave wall on the far side of the lake.

She'd come to appreciate her team during her few weeks with them. The way they opened up about their personal lives gave her that much more fondness, so the unwillingness to attempt her idea left an even greater hurt.

What do I do now? She stared across the lake, watching the red glowing reflections off the surface. *Maybe they'll come around. Or . . .* She considered an alternative. *Maybe I'll do it on my own. I can mine the crystals. I can get the keys. It might take a few weeks, but—* She smiled. *I can do this.*

31

GUEST IN THE BARRACKS

Lia rolled to her opposite side for what felt like the hundredth time. The rustling of her straw mattress filled the room. The poor excuse for a pillow barely kept her head supported. In the barracks, snores emanated from multiple directions, but the sounds had long faded into background noise. Despite her fatigue from the hard day of work, her mind raced through escape plan scenarios, keeping her awake.

Rasmill kept the keys on him. If she had help from the others, they could strike during the day, but on her own, her best shot was at night. A guard would always be awake, but she could figure something out.

The piece of the plan that left her most uncertain was the fusing of the crystals. Gathering ten raw crystals would take another few weeks on her own. *But what do I do with them? How do they fuse?* Talioth's explanation left plenty of holes, but she would cross that bridge when she got there. *And after I create a mini Core, what do I do to drain the power?* Veron didn't have time to go into details before they all had to battle for their lives.

She breathed in, then blew out the air while an image of Raiyn popped into her mind, his shaggy black hair and smile. The thought of seeing him again bolstered her.

I can do this.

She felt at her side and touched the wooden box tucked under the straw.

All of this is assuming the box works. Hopefully, it will do its job, and—

Lia stopped. The box shifted but the rattle inside was not what she expected. She lifted the wooden container, her fingers sensing an object sliding inside—a *lone* object.

Her breath caught. She raised to her elbows and touched the clasp of the box. She angled it toward the nearest light. Leaning in close, she lifted the hinge. A red glow splashed into the container, illuminating a single crystal.

She snapped the lid shut. Turning the box over, she searched for a hole but found nothing.

What happened? She thought back to when she spoke with the group. Two objects had rattled around.

She turned toward the room.

I must find it. We can't have a loose—

The red light coming from the crystals in the wall dimmed—slight but noticeable.

Lia swallowed. She tucked the box back into her mattress, then stood. No one in the barracks stirred. The snoring continued unabated.

Maybe it's nothing.

The light proceded to grow dimmer and dimmer until it was nearly gone. She glanced at the unlit lantern on the wall as a guttural sound rumbled into the barracks. It reverberated around the bunks, low and choppy as it meandered through the room. Lia's insides shook.

Before the light disappeared, she crossed the room to the lantern. The handle creaked as she lifted it off the wall. She kept an eye on the door while striking the flint starter with one hand. With the red light of the room nearly gone, a blue glow approached the doorway.

"Come on, lantern, light," she muttered.

"Lia?" Chris said in a bleary voice from the closest bed. "What's wrong?"

She ignored him and kept working on the flint. It scraped and sparked, but she only saw it from the corner of her eyes. She trained her sight on the door.

An odor hit her—rotten, like an animal carcass. Her eyes watered. The room seemed to shake. She looked down. It was her legs quivering.

The room was nearly pitch black, lit only by the approaching blue glow and the sparks from the flint.

"Come on!" Lia grumbled, turning her attention to the lantern. Seeing where the flint struck allowed her to light the wick in two quick attempts. A flame roared to life, cutting through the darkness of the barracks.

Men moaned at the sudden light.

"What's that?"

"What are you doing?"

Lia held the lantern up, extending the light source toward the door until her arm froze. Her stomach lurched. Her mouth opened to shout, but nothing came out. A fiend stood just inside the doorway.

On all four limbs, the monster grazed the roof of the barracks. Oversized horns in a tight curl protruded from its forehead, scraping dust from the ceiling. A tight row of jagged teeth showed in its loosely hanging mouth. A rolling tongue pushed saliva from the lower jaw, making a faint *splat* as it hit the floor.

The legs rippled with muscles that flexed and spun as the beast scanned the room. What kept Lia's attention most was the forearms. Extending from either side of its chest, its arms ended with clacking pincers that looked like they could skewer a rydannor.

In the center of its chest, a pulsing blue object throbbed. The skin over it looked transparent, letting the blue light fill the room with an unfamiliar glow.

The fiend stopped looking around and Lia gulped. Two eyes, black as night, stared at her. Her arm trembled, causing shadows to dance where the lantern threw light around the scattered bunks.

A rumble sounded fresh from the beast's mouth, amplified in the small barracks. It lifted its head and appeared to sniff.

"Lia," Chris breathed to her side. "Is that—"

His words cut off when a roaring bellow shattered the silence. Lia tucked her head into her shoulder and covered the other ear with her free hand.

The men in the barracks leaped from their beds, shouting and scrambling away from the monster. They pushed each other, fighting to put bodies and beds between them and the beast.

The fiend stepped farther into the room, its paws silent. It swung its head in an arc, sniffing until it froze, locked on the man plastered against the wall.

Jarno's entire body trembled, his legs knocking against the wall. His hands clenched together in front of his chest, holding something in a firm grip. The fiend moved closer to him. A rough snort rippled his clothes and blew the sheet from the closest bed. He lowered his snout close to Jarno's hands and breathed in. More drool fell from his ragged mouth. The pincers clicked and clacked, pinching the air on alternate sides.

With nowhere to go, Jarno whimpered. His shaking head turned away from the monster.

The fiend prodded his hands with its pincers.

"Ahh!" he shouted. Red spots appeared on his hands, but his grip remained firm. His eyes found Lia's. His jaw quivered as he struggled to speak. "I-I'm s-s-sorry."

A roar from the fiend shook the room.

Jarno closed his eyes for a moment until he looked back at Lia. "I w-wanted the power." His hands loosened and opened up.

Lia knew what was there before she even saw it. The missing crystal. It rested in his opened hands, reflecting blue from the object glowing in the monster's chest.

After one last roar, the fiend lowered its head and charged. Although it had little room to build up momentum, the horns slammed into Jarno, crushing him against the wall. His shout was short-lived and desperate. The beast stepped back and charged again.

Time after time, it crashed into the unfortunate man, stabbing with its lightning-quick appendages. The walls shook. Debris fell from the ceiling. The other Garronts cried out and hid.

A light tinkling sound drew Lia's gaze to the floor where the crystal had fallen. The fiend adjusted its head and rammed it against the ground, crushing the crystal.

What was left of Jarno's body collapsed to the ground, a dark stain marring the wall behind him. Muffled cries filled the room from the other men.

The fiend sniffed the ground where it had crushed the jewel. Appearing content with its work, it turned toward the next closest person and brandished its pincers at Vekko.

It's going to go for each of us, Lia thought with a flash of terror. She glanced around the room and spotted a half-dozen heads and arms poking out from behind columns and beds. *If only I had access to the origine. Then, I could—* She stopped her thought. A faint tingle in her gut seemed too good to be something she could trust. *Is that it?*

She glanced at the closest red crystal in the wall and noted how it was dim. A nervous laugh bubbled up. She extended the lantern to Chris. "Take this," she commanded.

He did it without hesitation.

The beast surged toward Vekko with its head down. The man raised his arms in a futile attempt to stop the inevitable.

Lia pulled from the origine, the power flowing through her. It felt stifled and distant, but there, nonetheless. She moved in a flash, crossing the barracks in a split second. The fiend had its horns lowered, hurtling forward, ready to crush Vekko. She slid between them, so fast the rest of the room appeared frozen. She grabbed onto its horns, used the origine to power her arms, and wrenched the creature as hard as she could. The horns turned, then the neck and body came with it.

Instead of crashing into Vekko, the fiend flipped, its momentum sending it careening into the rock wall of the barracks. It collided with a massive crash, shaking another round of dust from the ceiling.

"W-w-what?" Vekko stuttered, patting himself as if checking that he was still whole.

"Get out of here," Lia shouted, motioning to the others. "All of you."

Vekko and the other Garronts stared at her.

A roar from the beast turned her around just in time. Snapping jaws lunged at her face. She spun unnaturally fast to avoid a face full of teeth. She blocked striking pincers with her origine-infused arms, dodging killing blows. An uppercut struck the monster under its jaw, clacking its teeth together and knocking its head back.

"Go!" Lia tried again. "I've got this!"

Raging through the room, the fiend pulverized empty beds and slammed into walls. Wood and rock splintered in every direction. A ferocious roar bellowed toward Lia, but the beast stayed back.

The men ran one at a time, giving the monster a wide berth as they sneaked past.

It saw them leaving. Waylon cried out when the fiend lowered its head and ran at his fleeing form.

"I don't think so." Lia grabbed the horns again and jerked it toward her. It rolled, crashing to the floor. She had to leap back to keep her legs from getting crushed.

On its back, the pincers came fast and furious, snapping at the air around Lia. With a jerk of its body, it righted its massive form and turned toward her. The blue glowing object pulsed brighter than ever as the creature rose to its full height. The horns again scraped the ceiling, and its arms extended forward, trapping Lia in a corner of the room.

"Hey!" Chris yelled. He waved the lantern, flinging the shadows around the room.

"Chris! Get out of here," Lia urged. "I'm fine."

"Come and get me," the team leader yelled.

"I'm serious Chris. I can—"

A flash of the fiend's arm sprang to the side. Chris' body jerked as the double-edged pincer retracted from his abdomen.

"No!" Lia yelled.

Chris fell to the floor, his knees popping against the stone. Red spread over his tunic. He held Lia's eyes as his body tumbled like a fallen tree.

"Lia, get out of there!" Waylon yelled from the doorway.

An image of the fiend tearing through the rest of the barracks came to her mind. She shook her head. *No.*

The beast roared, sending putrid breath washing over her. The jaws hung open, spraying spittle. Its black eyes narrowed. It snorted and stamped at the ground, and finally, it charged.

Lia pulled at the origine. The effort grew more and more difficult, causing her forehead to pinch. She twirled to the side as the monster crashed its horns into the wall. It spun toward her. The teeth gnashed together but kept their distance as if afraid of what she might do. The razor arms stabbed at her. She dodged and stayed ahead of the beast, but only enough to keep alive. Her energy grew faint.

The animal drew closer. She stared down its gullet, a blue glow emanating from deep within. Lia strained to hold on to the origine as she knocked its deadly arms away.

Rip!

A searing pain tore into her arm. She screamed in agony as the bladed appendage retracted from her flesh. She stumbled backward against the corner of a broken bunk. The other limb came at her, missing her neck and striking the cave wall behind.

She drew in short breaths, refusing to look at or think about the wound.

The pincer came at her again, striking for the center of her chest. Lia had nowhere to go. The bunk blocked her escape, and there was no time to duck. She gulped as the razor-sharp claw lashed at her. Straining to find any energy, she brought both arms together in a powerful cross block. One arm pressed against the side of the fiend's pincer while the other buckled it just behind. She flexed her arms and yelled. A crunch filled the air, followed by a hideous roar.

The sharp skewer never made it to her chest. The monster reared back, howling with its teeth thrashing the air. Lia glanced at the end of its arm and found the pincer cracked through, dangling on a thread of fiend flesh. Blue liquid spurted from the broken appendage, spraying onto her clothes.

Without pause, she grasped the broken object and yanked. The pincer jerked free, sending the fiend into a fresh wave of howls and roars. Its horns hit the roof as it leaned its head back and flailed its mangled limbs. Lia turned the double-bladed sharp claw around and lunged at the beast, stabbing into its body with all the strength she could manage.

After penetrating the rough outer hide, the sharp pincers slid into the fiend's chest. She pushed deeper until the object pierced the glowing blue core of the monster. The shriek that filled the room split her head. The animal dropped to the floor, pulling out from the sharp object that had skewered it. It writhed all four legs and tossed its head, knocking against the debris in the room. Blue glowing light poured onto the barracks floor from the gaping wound. The twitching slowed. The moans quieted. After a few more jerks, the fiend fell still.

Lia stumbled forward, watching its eyes. The two orbs held an unseeing stare. She winced at the sudden pain that lanced through her arm. She paused, closed her eyes, and pushed healing toward the injury. Her body resisted. The power was faint and hard to find. She groaned until the tingling arrived, prickling her arm with fresh healing power.

Healed and spent, she collapsed to her knees, panting and heaving. Her heart pounded, and her body longed for relief from the exhaustion. She stared at the fiend's body while she took breath after breath. The blue light in its chest faded. Even the glowing blood on the ground lost its luminescence. As soon as it died, the red glow of the barracks returned.

"Lia?" Waylon called from the door.

"I'm fine. It—" She paused to breathe. "It's dead."

Waylon crept into the room, followed by Thurman, then Harold.

Lia rose to her feet. She stumbled toward her bed and tossed the creature's claw down.

"Chris?" Thurman jogged across the room, staying clear of the fallen fiend. He stopped where their team leader's body lay still.

The rest of the Garronts shuffled into the room, their jaws hanging loose.

"He's gone," Thurman breathed.

"I'm sorry." Lia hung her head against her rising and falling chest. "It was my crystals that drew it here."

Waylon stepped forward. "Did it crush both crystals?"

Lia paused, then reached for the box in her bed. It shook with a faint *clink*. "No, just the one Jarno took. Had I never saved them—"

"Stop. This happened because Jarno was selfish."

"I saw you fight it," Harold said with wide eyes. "How did you do that? Was that . . . shadow knight stuff?"

She nodded. "A bit. My ability came back when the red crystals dimmed." She glanced down at the metal anklets on both legs and cocked her head. *Even through those. Interesting.* "But it was short lived. The power is gone again."

"So, we tame one of them and get it to walk around with you," Waylon suggested. "How's that for an idea?"

"Probably not a brilliant plan."

"I think I was wrong," Thurman said. "We should have listened to you, Lia. We risk no matter what we do. Why not hope for something more? If the others are in, then I am, too."

"I'm in," Waylon said.

"Me, too," Harold added. "I want to get back to my village."

The other men nodded with eager eyes.

Waylon leaned forward. "We've seen what you can do, and it's incredible."

"Lead us, Lia," Harold said.

A pained smile crept over her face. "Chris was a good man and a great leader. He will be missed." She turned to the other crumpled body against the wall and swallowed back the anger that tried to bubble to the surface. "As will Jarno."

A few grumbles muttered through the room.

"Although his actions led him astray, he worked hard every day. For that, I respect him."

None of the men replied, but a couple nodded.

"We *will* get out of here. It will be my sole focus. With all of us working together, we can make it." She paused as an idea came to her. "Although what happened here was tragic, at least one positive thing came out of it."

Waylon's forehead scrunched up. "What?"

Lia lifted the claw of the fiend. Blue blood stained the sharp tip, dripping down its length.

A smile tugged at her lips. "Now, we have a weapon."

Smug grins reflected across the Garronts' faces.

Lia scanned the room, nodding. She paused when she arrived at the new guy. A bundle of nerves caught in her throat. Anton stared back, his face mimicking the others. She swallowed, forcing herself to keep calm.

I hope I haven't made a big mistake.

32

PERFECT TIMING

Veron blinked against the bright morning sun that had just risen over the castle walls. He raised his bound hands to shade his eyes, trying to get a view of the courtyard.

"Move!" a guard shouted, prodding his back with a spear.

Veron tottered down the steps until his feet reached the stone floor of the open area in the center of the castle grounds. A tower blocked the sun, giving him a better view.

A small crowd already gathered in the courtyard, but the number of people looked much less than Veron had expected. Men, women, and children craned their necks to see around each other. The gathered people stared in their direction. They pointed and jeered. Some spat.

The air was thick and still, already warm from the first rays of the sun. No breeze found its way past the tall walls of the castle. Where they had entered the day before, the castle gate stood open with its portcullis raised. The bridge that led to the city contained more men and women walking toward them, but not in the numbers they'd hoped for.

Chelci leaned between Veron and Raiyn. "We need more people if

Raiyn's announcement is going to have the effect we want. There aren't even a hundred here."

"I wonder if we're only drawing the Bale sympathizers," Brixton said. "Maybe the people who would support what we did are staying away."

Veron's stomach turned. "That doesn't bode well for our plan."

Separated from the crowd by a rope, four large wooden blocks spread out in a straight line. Uniformed guards with swords at their hips stood by each block, and the man who had sharpened the axe the night before stood at attention with the same weapon held at his side.

Standing in the courtyard stirred up memories for Veron. His eyes drifted up to where a bridge ran from the main keep to a tower. He recalled being trapped and pushed off the side. A cracked flagstone on the ground drew his eye under the bridge. He blew a faint laugh through his nose. *That's where I landed using the origine.* On his other side, his stomach turned at the sight of the wide raised balcony—where he had watched as his father passed from life.

"It's weird, isn't it?" Chelci asked, walking next to him. "It seems so long ago, but here we are . . . about to die again . . . in the same courtyard."

"Don't give up," Veron said, speaking to himself as much as the others. "We survived last time, and I believe we will today."

King Darian sat on a raised platform with a wooden railing lining the front. His son sat beside him, while Desmond and Ryker stood on his opposite.

Rough hands pushed Veron and the others in front of the wooden blocks. They spun them to face the king.

"Should he say something now?" Brixton asked.

Veron glanced at Raiyn, but the young man had craned his neck around. His eyes darted over the crowd while a frown pulled at his mouth.

"I'm not sure this crowd will be sympathetic," Veron said. "But we have to try."

"Not yet," Raiyn said, his eyes still searching. "People are still coming."

"Ryker!" Chelci called. "Did you think about what we said?"

Standing beside the king, the general stiffened. He averted his eyes, looking at the crowd.

Darian turned toward his military leader, piercing him with a stare. Neither man replied.

"I'm not sure I made the right call about Ryker," Raiyn muttered. "Winning over this crowd doesn't sound like much of a better prospect than the shot we had with him."

Footsteps turned Veron's head as the guard, Beldrick, approached.

"Not so powerful now, huh?" he taunted, punctuating his words with a laugh.

A fist in Raiyn's side doubled him over. He grabbed his ribs while a grimace covered his face.

Beldrick laughed again. He feigned a fist to the face, causing Raiyn to duck back. The guard shuffled away to stand near the king.

"You all right?" Veron asked.

Raiyn puffed and wheezed. His nose wrinkled, and he sucked air through his teeth. "I'm fine. It just caught me by surprise." When he lifted his head, his eyes surveyed the crowd again.

"There's still time," Veron said. "People are still coming."

Raiyn nodded. When he straightened, he stepped closer to the man with the axe. "Hey." He waved his shackled hands, attracting the man's attention. "What'd you decide?"

The axeman's face remained stoic. His head stayed forward toward the wooden blocks, but his eyes looked toward Raiyn. A faint nod broke his frozen position.

A glimmer of hope trickled through Veron.

"You went?" Raiyn asked, shuffling a step closer. "She was there?"

The guard checked on either of his sides as if making sure no one drew near. He opened his mouth to speak.

"Welcome, people of Daratill!" Desmond boomed from the king's dais.

The guard's mouth shut. His eyes lingered before turning toward the king.

Veron's stomach clenched as the murmur in the crowd faded.

"Your king brings you a gift this fine suether morning. I present King Darian."

The crowd applauded. Darian grimaced as his bulky form rose, but flashed a smile once he regained stability. He held up a hand as if accepting their cheers, then rested it on the railing.

"Terrenor has not been kind to Norshewa," Darian said. "We've been cast aside and looked down upon. The other kingdoms think they can impose their will on us. Only yesterday, representatives from Feldor arrived, asking us to give them our greatest military advantage."

Boos peppered the crowd.

"Thankfully . . ." the king paused, allowing a smile. "We discovered who these representatives are—the same people who assassinated our beloved Norshewan leader, Edmund Bale."

A roar erupted from the spectators. Veron braced himself to be hit by rocks or debris, but nothing came. He chanced a look at the crowd and found only a third of the people responded to what the king said. The others stood with unreadable expressions.

"The audacity they show in returning to the scene of their crime is foolish. We will not tolerate their brazen demands, and we will not forget their acts. Today, we will put these criminals to death, and you will bear witness."

The crowd cheered as the king took his seat. Chelci met Veron's gaze. Her eyes held an intense determination. "I think it's time," she said.

Veron nodded and turned. "Raiyn." The young man craned his neck again, peering into the crowd. His eyes jumped back and forth while rows of creases marked his forehead. "Do it."

"I don't see her though," he protested.

The guards positioned at each wooden block moved toward the prisoners.

"We can't wait." Veron's heart beat faster as the guard closest to him drew near. "Tell them who you are!"

Raiyn nodded, then lifted his eyes to the crowd. His chest puffed out, and he opened his mouth.

Beldrick appeared at Raiyn's back before Veron could warn him. A black gag wrapped around Raiyn's head and pulled tight. The young man's eyes bulged. A moan muffled behind the fabric, and he shook his head from side to side.

"No!" Veron shouted. "He needs to—" A gag passed over his head and jammed across his mouth. He strained to speak, but the fabric blocked his efforts.

A guard at his back pushed him forward while a man in front guided him to a wooden block.

No! Veron thought. *Not yet! Raiyn needs to speak.*

Veron's legs caught the edge of the wooden block. The guard yanked at his restraints while the man behind him pressed against his upper back. Unable to resist the force, his chest pressed against the block. The guard ran a rope around the chains holding his hands, then pulled against a hook near the ground. The force stretched Veron's arms down until they couldn't move any more. His chest scratched against the surface. His face turned to the side with his cheek pressed against the rough wood. He tried to turn his head to see Chelci, but the pull on his arms pinned him so tight that he couldn't move. The mumbles coming from his other side brought a tear to his eye.

I'm sorry, Chelci.

Raiyn thrashed on his block. He rubbed his face against the surface, but the gag wasn't budging. He mumbled again, louder than before.

"Quiet, you!" Beldrick punched Raiyn in the side, causing him to squirm and groan.

The executioner walked forward with his oversized axe held out.

Raiyn continued to rub against the gag. The bare skin of his neck stood in stark contrast to the black stone walls of the castle in the background.

The man with the axe stopped next to Raiyn.

Veron took a deep breath, then blew it out. He relaxed his muscles. He searched inside for the origine and found it as distant and difficult to use as he expected.

I'm not sure what I plan to do, but . . .

Veron strained to access his power. The impeded ability fought against his efforts, but a faint tingle responded. He pulled. Between the restraints and the rope pulling him down, the pressure was more than he expected.

"Whoa," a guard said. "Help me out here."

A solid thud resonated through Veron's head. His vision flashed bright white before searing pain jolted his body.

"Hold still," a guard barked.

The restraints around his wrists dug tighter into his skin. Veron slumped, unable to fight while the agony tore through him. His chest and head settled against the wood.

No.

The weak thought couldn't rouse him from his stupor. He blinked to bring the hopeless scene into focus once more.

Raiyn's gag angled sideways over his chin. The young man wriggled his jaw, fighting to free his words.

The executioner looked down at Raiyn. Holding the axe with two hands, he lifted the weapon above his head.

Veron held his breath. The tightness in his chest clenched along with all his body. With a final jerk of his chin, Raiyn's gag fell away from his mouth.

"Khardol dyn Justiri!" Raiyn's desperate voice ripped through the air. "I claim Khardol dyn Justiri!"

The axe halted in midair. A hush fell over the crowd, and the pull against Veron's restraints lessened. His mind reeled as it tried to make sense of the words. The pinched faces of the crowd looked equally confused.

"What's that?" Desmond's voice wavered.

"It is my right!" Raiyn shouted. "Norshewan law states that anyone facing death with no proof of their crime has a right to trial by combat . . . Khardol dyn Justiri—Justice of the Truth. I claim it for my group, and I cannot be denied."

"Raiyn," Veron projected in a whisper. "What are you—"

"No proof," Desmond scoffed. "Ha! You're a shadow knight. Do you deny it?"

"No, but since when is that a crime?" Raiyn struggled to look toward the dais, pulling against his bonds. "You say we're being put to death for killing your last king? I was four years old at that time."

"The Justiri act hasn't been invoked in—" the king devolved into mumbling.

"Over one hundred years," Desmond finished.

"Thank you," Darian said. "You can't come in here and claim a dead law."

"Was it ever written out of law?" Raiyn asked. "Did someone nullify it?"

"It doesn't matter," the king said. "It's a Norshewan law. It's not for—"

"And I am Norshewan," Raiyn called out so all could hear.

The crowd grew quiet. Veron held his breath.

"I was born here, then moved away with my mother when I was four."

"That's not proof that you're a Norshewan," the king said.

"How else would I know about it?" Raiyn asked.

"Who was your father?" the king asked.

Raiyn's lips trembled. His eyes darted through the crowd.

"Say it, Raiyn," Veron whispered.

"My father?" his weak voice barely passed his lips. All heads turned toward him.

"Your Majesty," Ryker interjected. "The law, while archaic, is still active, and the question of where he's from would not be relevant. Khardol does not exclude outsiders."

The king's face screwed up in a sour expression. "So be it," he muttered. "If you want to fight on behalf of your group, then we'll all enjoy the show." He addressed the guards. "Free his chains but leave the shackles on. Shadow knights are not to be trusted. Then run and fetch Brutar. I want this done, now."

The pressure pulling against Veron's arms lessened. He made it to his feet along with the others. A guard untied his gag.

"Raiyn," Chelci said, "what are you doing? Why don't you tell them?"

"Not yet," he replied. "She's still not here."

"She may *never* be here. We're out of time, and we need to try something else. Tell them."

"I *am* trying something else."

"Will you fight for yourself?" Desmond asked from the dais. "Or do you choose a second to stand in your place?"

"Raiyn," Veron held his hands against his chest. "Nominate me." He shook one of his hands, letting the chains rattle. Lowering his voice, he whispered, "The metal. I can . . . You know."

Raiyn nodded. "I know, but that's not what we need to do." He turned toward the stage. "I will fight."

"Raiyn," Veron rebuked, his jaw hanging loose.

"Trust me." Raiyn winked. "I have a plan."

33

KHARDOL DYN JUSTIRI

Raiyn rubbed his wrists, feeling the metal press against his skin. He paced between the king's platform and the crowd. Guards with spears kept the curious spectators from coming too close.

The beating sun grew warmer as he waited. Sweat beaded on his forehead and soaked through his tunic—only partially caused by the temperature.

When he turned back toward the crowd, he scanned the heads again, unsure of exactly what he sought. He locked eyes with the executioner.

The man with the axe glanced at the crowd then shook his head. "I'm sorry," he mouthed.

Raiyn's heart beat fast. His lips fought against his desire to blurt out his lineage. *Not yet. The risk of getting killed is too great.*

Ryker arrived, his hand stabilizing the sword at his hip. "Norshewa's champion will be here in a moment. The rules are that you fight to the death. The king alone can choose to stop the fight if he wills it."

"Why would he stop it?" Raiyn asked.

"If you're beating his champion, he might stop it to save his life. He won't stop it for you, though."

Raiyn swallowed a thick lump in his throat.

Veron stepped forward. "What will they fight with?"

"The king's champion gets to choose." Ryker nodded toward two men who lugged a stand with a variety of weapons out from the gatehouse.

Pairs of various weapons leaned against the supports: short swords, longswords, poleaxes, spears, and staffs. Two chain maces draped over the rack with their heavy, spiked balls bouncing against each other.

"And we fight with whatever he selects?" Raiyn asked.

Ryker nodded. "There's no winning though. Brutar is . . . well . . . he's good at everything. You'll see."

Veron's voice hushed. "It's not too late, Ryker. You can stop this."

The general shook his head. "Not after he invoked the ancient ritual, I can't. It doesn't matter how sympathetic I may be. Sorry, Raiyn, you're committed."

"It's all right." Raiyn took in a deep breath and raised his chin. "I'm ready."

"General, you don't realize everything." Veron's voice grew strained. "There are *things* about Raiyn—things that will change everything."

"Veron." Raiyn shook his head. "Not yet."

"Then, when?" Veron's raised voice turned the heads of many spectators.

Raiyn held up his palms. "Trust me."

Ryker's face held a suspicious glare. After a long moment, he shrugged. "Say your goodbyes, young man." After the ominous words, the general headed back to his platform.

A rumble grew in the crowd. Raiyn looked toward the noise, then followed the turned heads toward the entrance to the courtyard. With guards on either side, a massive beast of a man strode forward.

Two heads taller than Raiyn, the man towered over everyone in the vicinity. His mostly shaved head contained narrow strips of black hair, braided tight and running around the side of his head. His shirtless chest puffed forward with a thick covering of dark hair. Silver bracers covered each arm, restraining the bulges of muscles that tried to burst from his skin. A twisted smile left Raiyn unnerved, but it was the wild look in the man's eyes that created a watery feeling in his stomach.

Brixton leaned in. "Maybe that's not him."

"Brutar!" a man called from the crowd.

"Brutar the Brutal!" another shouted.

Claps and cheers filled the courtyard. The hairy man lifted an oversized arm in recognition and nodded toward the applause.

"Okay," Brixton said, "never mind."

Brutar's wild eyes intensified. He took two lumbering steps forward and bent at the oversized wooden block where Raiyn had been a few minutes before. His arms wrapped about the object, flexing into arms of steel. With a roar, he stood. The block lifted off the ground, and the man flung it to the side with a shout. A deep thump filled the air when the heavy object collided with the ground.

After a glance at Raiyn, his eyes drifted to the weapons display. The side of his mouth pulled up higher, and a throaty chuckle bounced past his lips. He approached the weapons, inspecting them as an art collector would view a rare painting. He pulled a poleax out of the stack and bounced it in his hands.

"What do you hope he chooses?" Veron stood next to Raiyn while watching the other fighter.

Raiyn raised his eyebrows and took a deep breath. "The axe or the longsword would be my best weapons. At least I sort of know what I'm doing with those, but—"

With a grunt, Brutar swung the poleax down with both arms. A whoosh filled the air until the blade bit into the end of the wooden display. The sharp edge cut into the wood, slicing a thick chunk off the end.

"—but, uh . . . those may not be great options."

"How are you hoping to win?" Veron asked.

"I don't need to win. I just need to survive." He scanned the crowd once again, but no fresh faces had arrived.

"Spectators of Daratill." Ryker's voice cut through the noise and brought the simmering chatter of the crowd to an end. "You are here to bear witness to Khardol dyn Justiri, the ancient right granted to Norshewans—and those within its border—to protest a sentence of death through combat." He gestured to Raiyn. "This foreigner has invoked the right, and your own Brutar champions the king's interests."

The crowd cheered at the mention of their warrior.

"The fight is to be to the death or until royal intervention."

Raiyn nodded, the tightness in his chest growing more pronounced.

"Brutar, as the king's champion, you choose the weapons."

The wild man stared at Raiyn. He opened his mouth then exaggerated chomping his teeth with three sharp clacks. Finally, he threw his head back and cackled.

A shudder ran through Raiyn.

"I choose . . ." Brutar's deep voice drew out his words as he turned back to the weapons. He ran his hand over the hilts of the weapons as if appraising each one. Spinning on his heels, he faced Raiyn and crossed his bulging arms. "I choose fists."

Raiyn felt the blood drain from his face.

Beldrick walked to Raiyn with a smirk. The guard raised his hand and jingled a set of keys. "Give me your hands."

Raiyn monitored the pacing fighter while the guard worked at his chains. After a minute, both his hands were loose, but metal clasps still covered his wrists.

"Have fun," Beldrick chuckled as he walked away.

Veron stepped up. "If you won't say something, I will."

Raiyn shook his head. "Not yet. I have a plan."

Veron paused, then nodded. "He's big, so he'll be slow. Stay just out of reach and tire him out. Then get in close when you're ready to attack. Focus on one place: the stomach, side, or groin. His head may be tough to reach."

"Good luck." Chelci's doleful smile told him how she felt about his chances.

"Begin!" Ryker shouted.

Veron and Chelci backed away as Brutar barreled forward.

Raiyn sucked in a breath. His pulse shot up. He searched for the origine on instinct, but the well of power was inaccessible.

The man continued toward him, clapping the silver bracers on his arms against each other. The ground shook with each of his pounding footsteps. Raiyn's eyes grew wider. At the last moment, he dashed to the side, avoiding a massive blow from a flying fist. The other fighter grunted when the swing of his arm found nothing but air.

Raiyn backed away, but Brutar turned toward him with fists raised. He ducked under a blow at his head. He sidestepped another to the body. A raised arm deflected a punch to his shoulder, leaving the glistening skin of the man's rippled stomach exposed. Raiyn seized the opening. He tightened his hand into a ball, locked his wrist, and punched as hard as he could. The wall of abdominal muscles felt like stone. His fist bounced off. He shook his hand while Brutar grinned.

"Ha! Is that all you have?" the fighter taunted.

Raiyn stepped away, moving in a circle to keep out of reach. Brutar followed step for step. He threw teasing punches that kept Raiyn moving and ducking.

After turning to his right, Raiyn glimpsed a woman beyond the fighter who had just passed through the gate. Attired in a humble brown dress, she approached the crowd, her eyes on the fight. Long hair fell past her shoulders, gray with hints of black. A faint limp marred her smooth walk until she melted into the back of the crowd and Raiyn lost sight of her.

Raiyn turned to the axeman with raised eyebrows. With a firm line across his mouth, the executioner nodded in a slow, deliberate motion.

It's her!

Raiyn's pulse thumped. Veron, Chelci, and Brixton huddled together, watching from the sideline. Fear covered their faces as they watched. Raiyn turned back to Brutar. The beast stood with his arm cocked against his chest. He stepped forward, his grin wild and full of malice. Raiyn's instincts told him to sidestep. The fist flew toward him, hurtling toward his face. He could move. He could duck. Instead, he stood firm and clenched his teeth.

The blow crunched into his jaw. Searing pain shot through his body while his sight flashed white. He spun, dropping his hands against his knees to keep from falling. Several rapid breaths did nothing to ease the pain or subdue his swirling vision. A coppery taste bloomed in his mouth.

Brutar stood gloating. A faint laugh bubbled into the air. When he stepped forward with the next fist cocked, Raiyn held up a hand.

"Stop!" he shouted.

Brutar paused, his forehead wrinkled. A murmur ran through the crowd.

The king stood on his dais. "What is this? You fight to the death. Brutar, don't stop!"

The champion's face hardened again. His shoulders moved as if about to deliver a blow.

"You cannot!" Raiyn yelled, pausing the man once more. He sucked in a breath. "It is treason to strike royalty! This cannot continue."

Brutar took a step back, his face again twisted in confusion. The spectators muttered between themselves, filling the courtyard with a rumble of conversation.

A laugh turned Raiyn's head toward the king. "That's preposterous. Brutar isn't royalty. Finish him, champion!"

"No!" Raiyn shouted. "I don't mean him."

The words silenced the courtyard. Veron stared at him with shackled arms and a grim smile. Brutar stood erect, relaxing his arms and cocking his head.

Raiyn's heart pounded in his chest. In each direction, the crowd watched him, waiting for what he would say. When he opened his mouth, his words felt stuck. Eyes bored into him. Chelci leaned toward him, nodding.

"You're saying that you're royalty?" General Ryker said. "From where?"

Raiyn spun to take in the courtyard. He glanced up at the castle walls, then back to the spectators. His mouth pulled up at the sides. "With its proud tradition of kingly succession . . . from here."

Gasps filled the air.

Raiyn's nerves had settled, and his tongue felt loosened. "I was born in this castle to my mother, Catina, and my father, Edmund. My name is Raiyn Bale, and by birthright, I am the rightful King of Norshewa."

Chaos erupted. Five guards with spears pressed in on Raiyn, holding sharp metal tips to his body. The spectators shouted, creating a blasting roar of noise. King Darian stumbled backward, knocking into his chair and nearly tumbling.

Raiyn's breath came quickly. His head jerked side to side.

"Treason!" Desmond shouted. "His dangerous lies mean to unsettle our kingdom. Guards, execute him, now!"

An icy fear washed through Raiyn. The men with spears tightened their grips. They readied their arms to thrust the weapons.

"Wait," a faint shout raised over the crowd. "Wait!"

The roar of the crowd dimmed. Bodies parted in the throng of spectators, and the black-and-gray-haired woman stepped forward. One hand held against her chest, and her lips pursed as if struggling to speak. She leaned forward, squinting. "Raiyn?" Her voice barely reached his ears.

Raiyn nodded.

Her eyes widened, forming rings of white. A hand raised and pointed at his side. "Lift your shirt."

"Kill him!" Desmond yelled.

"No!" the woman shouted. "Bale's son had a birthmark on his left side—a star. We need to see!"

"Who are you?"

The woman stood taller. "I am Esserie. I once lived in this castle and attended Catina Bale. I helped raise her son . . . Raiyn."

A tense silence filled the air until Ryker's order split it. "Show us."

The guards hesitated. After a long pause, one took a half step back. The others followed suit but kept their spears raised. Brutar remained gawking a few steps away with his fists held loosely.

Raiyn kept an eye on the guards as he pulled the hem of his tunic. Sidling closer to the woman, under the close attention of the guards, he lifted the coarse fabric.

Cries of shock peppered the crowd.

Raiyn looked down and stared at the dark mark on his side—the one with five points. A star. "Mother always said I was mar—"

"Marked . . ." Esserie spoke over him, ". . . destined for greatness."

Raiyn smiled. "That's right."

"It is you," she breathed. "How's Catina?"

His smile faltered, and he shook his head. "She passed."

"I'm sorry." Esserie raised his chin toward the king. "Your Majesty, I can confirm this is indeed the lost son of Edmund Bale."

Raiyn exhaled, loosening the tension that had built in him.

"And the rightful ruler of Norshewa," Veron added.

King Darian's mouth formed a thin line. He glanced at his son, then tottered forward to the edge of the dais. His corpulent body swayed as he balanced on weak legs.

No one in the courtyard spoke. A faint whistling breeze and the flutter of a flag were all that could be heard. The guards kept their spears raised.

"Bale's son, returned home after all these years." The king's mouth tweaked up at the corner. "You have his look."

"Guards, lower your weapons!" Veron shouted.

Desmond stepped forward. "Only the king can order that."

Everyone looked at Darian. The king watched Raiyn. He shifted. "Guards . . ."

Raiyn held his breath.

"This man is clearly an imposter."

A sinking feeling tore through Raiyn's gut.

"Kill him!" Darian shouted.

34

FINAL EFFORT

For a moment, no one moved. The crowd remained silent. The king's words rang in Raiyn's ear for only as long as the guards hesitated. When they snapped into action, so did he.

Grabbing the closest spear behind the head, Raiyn wrenched the weapon away from the unsuspecting man. He spun the shaft in a circle, striking the helmeted heads of the other nearby guards.

Veron, Chelci, and Brixton were already sprinting toward the weapons stand. "Raiyn!" Veron shouted. "The axe!"

Raiyn joined in the race. He tossed the spear to the ground and yanked an axe from the stand. Veron had already spread his hands across a wooden end post, stretching the chain that held his wrists close. A glance at the disoriented guards confirmed they had a few moments before they would arrive.

"Go, go, go!" Brixton shouted.

Raiyn raised the axe with both hands. His muscles contracted as he brought the blade down.

Veron turned his face away. His arms clenched, the chain between them strained.

Raiyn's strike was true and strong. A spark accompanied a

metallic clang. The blade bit through the chain links, embedding in the wooden post below.

To the side, the guards closed fast, yelling with spears raised. Raiyn tried to yank the axe free, but the wooden post gripped it tight. A burst of fear rushed cold through him.

The restraints remained on his wrists, but the chain connecting them was broken. Veron snatched a sword from the stand. He flung himself toward the guards, moving with incredible speed that could only be achieved through the use of origine. His weapon severed the ends of the spears before he knocked them to the side. His blade moved as fast as lightning, catching a man in the chest, another in the gut, and a third across the side.

The injured guards fell, clutching their injuries and crying out in pain.

Veron's frantic movement slowed. He kept his sword up, facing off with two remaining guards, blocking them from Raiyn. "Free them!" he shouted over his slumped shoulder.

His words were forceful, but Raiyn caught the underlying exhaustion. Straining against the end of its handle, he pried the axe free.

Chelci stretched her chain across the same post. Two swift hacks later and all four of them wore wrist cuffs with no chains binding them together. Chelci and Brixton both grabbed swords from the display, and Raiyn held onto his axe.

The two standing guards had been supplanted by a dozen more. Beldrick stood in their center, wielding a massive two-handed broadsword that leaned against his shoulder. The champion, Brutar, paced behind them, swinging the spiked metal ball of a chain mace. Even the executioner had traded in his axe for a crossbow, although the droop in his face indicated he was less than thrilled to be fighting. To the side, General Ryker had descended from the dais. He rested a hand on the sword at his hip, but his brow furrowed. He kept his distance.

The crowd of spectators had scattered. Some ran in all directions through the courtyard, but most rushed toward the gatehouse, where an open passage yawned toward the city.

"Let's go!" Brixton shouted, pulling Raiyn's shoulder toward the gate.

Veron and Chelci kept their eyes on the guards as they stepped backward, following Brixton. The guards moved with them.

"No." Raiyn shook his head. "We can't leave. We need the Fire."

"We can't get it if we're dead!" Brixton argued.

Raiyn risked a glance at Veron. "How's your energy?"

"Not great." His chest rose and fell with rapid breaths. "It takes a lot to do the simplest thing. I can't use it to fight them all."

"They know we want the Fire. If we run, they're bound to guard it, hide it, or be ready to use it on *us* when we return. I'm telling you, this is our best chance!"

Chelci stopped backpedaling. "He's right. We've got to act now."

Brixton exhaled. "All right." He stepped to Raiyn's side. "We do this now, then."

Veron and Chelci fanned to their left, and the four of them stared down the threatening guards.

"We don't want to hurt you," Veron called out. "We're not here to overthrow your rule. We just need the weapon."

"You heard your king," Desmond said. "Kill them all!"

"Take their lives if you must," Veron spoke to their group. "Spare them if you can."

Raiyn lunged forward, swinging his axe with a roar. The nearest guard's eyes flared wide as he raised his sword to block the weapon. The heavy head of the axe pushed the weak swing to the guard's side. With his arms low, Raiyn found himself in prime position for a thrust. The toe point pierced the man's uniform below the shoulder of his dominant arm. He yelled and dropped his weapon. Raiyn pivoted the axe handle and crashed it against the side of the guard's head with a solid blow, knocking him to the ground.

Chelci and Brixton paired off with a guard each while Veron battled three at once. The Shadow Master's movements were fast but only barely more than usual. A guard in the back leveled a crossbow at Brixton. As his finger moved over the trigger, Veron blurred toward the man. His crossbow knocked to the side, shooting its bolt into the side of the weapon display.

"Thanks," Brixton said without taking his attention off the man he fought. "I owe you."

Raiyn's attention snapped to a sword swinging toward his head. He jerked his axe in time to block the descending blade, catching it against the head of the weapon. With the sword tied up, he pushed his axe up and away. The guard's hands rose as his sword lifted. Raiyn grabbed under the hilt and pushed higher. With his weapon out of play and hands out of position, the man's eyes widened. Keeping one hand under the hilt, Raiyn brought the axe back, then jammed the butt into the man's forehead. His wide eyes rolled back in his head as his legs gave out.

Two down. He managed a smile until his eyes locked on a spiked metal ball about to slam into his torso. Rising on his toes, he threw his hips back and stretched his arms forward. The metal ball wooshed as it swung in the cavity of air his body formed.

Holding the flail at the end of the chain, Brutar bared his teeth. His massive hands wrapped around the handle while his eyes conveyed a sadistic delight. After missing the blow, he delivered a downward attack, aimed at Raiyn's head.

Worried it would get caught in the chain or pulverized by the weight, Raiyn opted against blocking with his axe. He lunged to the side and dropped to the ground as the spiked ball crashed into the flagstone where he had stood.

Brutar's unprotected leg was close. Raiyn extended his arms and swiped with the axe.

The king's champion didn't let the blade reach him. He stepped in and caught the axe against the shaft. His weight continued forward, pinning the weapon to the ground.

With his hand caught behind the handle and pressed into the stone, Raiyn yelled. He jerked his arm back, scraping the skin of his hand against the rock. He was free . . . but unarmed.

Straddling him, Brutar wasted no time in swinging the ball again. Raiyn blanched. He had nowhere to roll and nothing to block it with.

As the man lifted his arms, preparing for a death blow, Raiyn responded in the only way he could—kicking as hard as he could.

His shin caught the man in the crotch. The tension in Brutar's raised arms deflated like a limp sail that lost the breeze. The ball dropped harmlessly. His chest curled forward as a groan erupted from his throat.

Raiyn scurried like a crab, hustling backward, out of the way. He scrambled to his feet by the weapons stand, grabbing the spear he had dropped on the ground earlier. Spinning toward Brutar, he paused.

The larger man took stumbling steps. Bent over, he braced one hand against his knee while the other held onto the flail. The spiked ball rested against the ground. His mouth made a circular shape as he sucked air in and blew it out.

Raiyn raised the spear, his muscles clenched.

Brutar's eyes flicked toward him. The groan stopped. His lip curled and his eyes turned wild.

Raiyn lunged and thrust his weapon toward the man's bare chest. The tip grew closer. He extended his arms, pushing from the end of the spear. When the metal end drew near the man's skin, the metal ball circled the shaft, wrapping it in a length of chain. The spear's forward progress stopped. A yank from Brutar's arm ripped the wooden shaft from Raiyn's grip. The spear flew into the air then clattered to the ground.

Raiyn tottered backward until his legs hit the weapons stand. Brutar walked forward. With his wild eyes, he swung the spiked ball in a wide arc. With nothing to block it, Raiyn leaped to the side. Splinters of wood exploded into the air as the ball crashed into the wooden stand. Raiyn turned his head away. Wooden pieces collided into his side, and weapons clanged across the courtyard.

He pulled at the shackle around his wrist. *This would be a lot easier if I could get this off.* He spared a glance toward the others.

Brixton traded sword blows with a heavyset guard. Chelci pulled her blade out of a man's stomach as he fell to the ground. Veron and the familiar guard, Beldrick, faced off against each other, circling in a pile of unmoving enemies who littered the ground. Veron remained upright, but his body slumped and his chest heaved through heavy breaths.

A guard with a crossbow aimed at Brixton again.

"Brixton, watch ou—" Raiyn stopped as Veron pivoted. The Shadow Master's sword arrived in time to knock the weapon away again. The errant crossbow bolt flew close to Raiyn, whistling as it passed.

Brixton nodded toward an exhausted Veron before returning his attention to the man he fought.

A growl brought Raiyn's attention back to Brutar. The champion advanced. Raiyn picked up the axe he'd lost earlier without taking his eyes off the man. He kept the head pointed forward, the sharp spike at the top facing the other man's face. His left hand gripped near the heel while his right rested along the haft. He gritted his teeth and crouched, ready.

Brutar stopped his advance. Out of attack range, he twirled the ball at the end of the chain while a grin returned to his face. "Trying to take the throne, huh?"

"I'm not," Raiyn said, "although it would be my right."

"Kill him!" Desmond's voice called from his unseen location behind the railing. Neither the king nor his son were visible, either.

Ryker remained on the ground, pacing, remaining at a distance.

"You don't have to kill me to defend your kingdom," Raiyn said to Brutar. "I'm not here to overthrow it."

The man chuckled. "That's not why I do it."

"Then why?"

He leaned his head forward. "I kill . . . because it's fun."

A sinking feeling ran through Raiyn's stomach. His body felt cold, and his muscles clenched.

Brutar moved in. He swung the flail in a powerful motion, just out of reach of Raiyn's chest. At the end of the arc, he stepped forward and continued the momentum with another swing.

Raiyn moved backward, stepping quick enough to stay out of range. The attacks continued, step after step, swing after swing. The spiked ball wooshed as it flew through the air. Raiyn gulped, imagining the damage it would do if it hit him.

During a step back, his heel hit something solid. A wave of fear rushed through him. *I reached the wall.*

Brutar's eyes flared as he stepped in and swung with renewed vigor. His arms bulged. A roar grew in his chest.

In a desperate motion, Raiyn ducked, his body nearly on the ground. The spikes dug into the wall above his head. Stinging prickles covered his head and neck. He couldn't tell if it was from the ball or shards of stone chipped off the wall.

A jingling sound drew his attention. The slack from the ball caused the chain to sag. It only lasted a moment, but it was enough. Raiyn hooked the heel of his axe around the chain and yanked as hard as he could. The axe head tugged on the chain, which pulled the ball and flail from both the wall and the fighter's hand.

Brutar's eyes widened a moment after the handle was ripped away.

With the chain mace hooked around the axe head, Raiyn slid to the side and pivoted the handle, flinging the mace in a wide arc.

The wild look on Brutar's face had turned into one of terror. He raised his arms above his head, turned his face away, and closed his eyes. Most of the weight of the spiked ball collided with his arms, just above the bracers, but a portion of the impact crashed against the side of his head.

His cry filled the air. He bent over, clutching his head and arms while bright red blossomed from the impact sites.

The hit knocked the chain loose, freeing Raiyn's axe head. The heavy ball fell to the ground with a thud and a rattle of chains. Raiyn grabbed the handle of the axe and stepped in again. He drove his hips forward and swung the head. The blade bit deep into the man's chest made a sickening crunch, the sound of breaking bones.

Brutar released his hold on his head wound and tried to straighten. His unfocused eyes stared ahead. Blood dripped down the side of his face and both arms. When Raiyn pulled the axe head out of his chest, the king's champion fell. First, he hit his knees, then he toppled to his side where he lay still.

Raiyn puffed out a relieved breath. Taking a second to revel in the victory, he turned to the others.

Brixton raked his sword across the upper arm of a guard. Chelci kicked an extended hand of another, sending a weapon flying. The man turned and ran after it while she advanced.

When Raiyn looked at Veron, his heart dropped. The man was pressed against a wall with Beldrick wailing on him. Strike after strike descended, with Veron barely parrying them away. His shoulder slumped. His arms strained to keep his sword up. A strong hit knocked the hilt from his hand. Veron cried out, then slumped forward, panting.

"Finish him," a guard with a crossbow yelled as he turned the crank to reload his weapon. "That one's trouble."

Beldrick sneered as he pulled his arm back, pointing the tip of his sword at Veron's chest.

"No!" Raiyn yelled. With both hands on the hilt of his axe, he flung it forward. The weapon tumbled end over end.

Drawn by the yell, Beldrick inclined his head toward him.

The rest of the world stood still as Raiyn watched the flipping axe. It twirled until the blade sank into the guard's temple. Without even a cry, his body collapsed in a heap.

Raiyn gasped, a laugh dribbling out after the lucky throw.

"Veron, are you all right?" Chelci shouted, deflecting the blade of a guard.

No, he's not. Raiyn could see it. The man could barely stand. Straining to use the origine through the metal cuffs drained him too quickly. A click from the crossbow drew his attention to the guard who wielded it.

The man had finished turning the crank and loading a bolt. He leveled the weapon, pointing it at Veron. "He won't be trouble anymore," the guard muttered.

"Veron!" Chelci's strangled cry filled the courtyard. She abandoned the man she fought and ran toward her husband.

Raiyn was too far away. Chelci was too far away. Raiyn's muscles clenched out of desperation, but he had nothing left to throw. He could only gawk as the guard with the crossbow took aim.

Veron lifted his head. Weariness showed on his face. His body tried to respond, but only an arm twitched.

The guard's arm ran along the stock and his finger pulled at the trigger.

Raiyn held his breath.

As the bolt loosed, a body flew in from Raiyn's peripheral. With an arm extended and legs trailing him, Brixton leaped into the air to pass through the line of fire. His dirty blond hair flapped behind him. Raiyn thought he smiled when the projectile entered his body, just under his collarbone. Brixton hit the ground with a hard slap and a groan.

"Brixton!" Chelci stormed at the guard, but the man with the spent crossbow melted into a line of other fighters who raised spears and swords.

Raiyn made it to Brixton first. Having rolled onto his back, a dark spot bloomed on his tunic where the end of a bolt stuck out of his upper chest.

"Brixton," Veron wheezed from against the wall. "You shouldn't have."

"Of course, I should have." Brixton winced, pressing his eyes together. "Gah! It stings!"

Chelci made it to Veron and put an arm around his back. They stumbled forward and knelt next to their old friend.

Raiyn set his hand on Brixton's shaking shoulder.

Chelci inspected his injury. "No vital organs. Looks clean. We should be able to fix this. No trouble."

The clink of metal drew Raiyn's attention back to the circle of guards. A half-dozen surrounded them. The men stepped closer, eyes hungry for vengeance. Raiyn stood, taking a half step back with nothing in his hands.

A pang of regret flowed through his mind. *Maybe we should have run.* The closest guard flexed his muscles as he stepped forward, his two-handed broadsword ready to strike.

"Stop!" The commanding voice rang through the courtyard, stilling the guards and causing Raiyn to hold his breath. Any remaining spectators huddled amongst themselves, pressed against the far side of the courtyard. General Ryker stepped forward, holding his hands out. "This is enough."

Raiyn glanced around him for a nearby weapon. The axe embedded in Beldrick's skull was the closest option, but the guard with the sword could strike him down before he got there. The soft look in Ryker's eyes also made him hesitate.

"This is wrong," Ryker said. "I remember you, Raiyn." He held his hand below his hip. "When you were about this high. You would run around the castle, interrupting meetings. He had a lot of children, but Edmund was fond of you. I remember."

A lump formed in Raiyn's throat.

"We should not turn away his son—his direct descendant." Ryker turned and approached the dais. "Your Majesty, I know you don't want to hear this, but—" He stopped at the railing. His eyes grew. "Darian!"

Raiyn's jaw tensed. *What happened?* He jogged forward, then slowed and leaned over the wooden barrier.

Desmond sat on the ground, looking at Ryker with a loose jaw and terror written across his face. Alvin cowered behind a chair, his head peeking out. Splayed across the ground, King Darian's body lay motionless. His head stared at the sky. Raiyn tensed when he saw it— an errant crossbow bolt embedded in the man's neck. His chest didn't move. His eyes didn't blink.

"Is he—?" Raiyn couldn't finish the question.

Desmond nodded. "He's dead."

Raiyn's eyes flicked to the guards carrying crossbows. The sympathetic executioner caught his eyes for a second before the man shrank back into the huddle of other guards. *Accident or not . . .* The weight of it hit Raiyn like a bucket of water. *The throne of Norshewa is empty.*

Alvin stood. His wide-eyed expression jumped between Raiyn and the general. "I-I-I—"

"I don't want it," Raiyn blurted. "I'm sorry about your father. We didn't come here to take the crown. You can continue the tradition of passing it through your lineage."

Alvin's eyes held his. His body shook until he finally nodded.

"There is one thing we need, though."

"Bravian Fire," Ryker said.

Raiyn nodded.

Alvin straightened. No tears pooled in his eyes. He brushed down the front of his clothes and glanced around. Desmond and the guards looked at him, waiting in silence. Finally, the king's son nodded. "You can have it."

35

SECRETS LAID BARE

"**M**ove your feet!" Danik yelled.

The closest pair of sparring knights turned to him. The taller one nodded and wiped the sweat off his brow. He shuffled his feet, then lifted his sword to his opponent. After a beat, their weapons clashed again.

"Lazy and undisciplined," Danik muttered.

His hands gripped the edge of the stone wall at the first row of seats in the Feldan Arena. A cool morning breeze filtered into the bowl. The fresh air lightened his spirits, which were down after the attempted poisoning from the evening before.

In the open space below, dozens of men paired off, trading blows. The Knights of Power had grown too large for the old Shadow Knights facility. The arena gave them room to train, spar, and even use the devion more fully.

As if on cue, two sparring men blurred. A flurry of blows ended with one flying into the air. He hit the arena wall so hard it cracked the stone.

Danik chuckled.

The man who hit the wall took a moment to get up. He held the back of his head until he paused and closed his eyes. A deep breath filled his chest, and when he blew it out, his body was alert again. He lifted his sword and rushed at his opponent once more.

Nicolar and High Lord Bilton walked across the arena floor, dodging the fighting men and heading toward Danik. The training knights gave them a wide berth. At the wall, they took the steps to join Danik in the first row of the stands.

"Anything new?" Danik asked.

"We questioned the rest of the staff all morning," Nicolar said. "No one seems to know anything else."

"Are you even sure it was the steward?" Bilton asked. "He never admitted it."

"He must have been involved," Nicolar said. "Wine stewards care for their drink as if it's their own children. No one could have tampered with it without his knowledge."

Danik formed fists and pressed down on the stone. He spoke barely louder than a breath. "I have all the power in the world, but I can't make them respect me."

"They do respect you," Nicolar said. "But that doesn't mean they're happy about everything."

"Trouble from the counterfeiting . . . and the Shadow Knights."

"You killed almost all of them," Nicolar added.

"I know, but . . . it still feels like I'm losing. The crystals. The caverns' pull. The black marks." He lifted his head and unleashed a groan into the air. "It was supposed to be different."

"You're still king," Bilton said. "That's something."

A knight caught his eye. A tall man he hadn't seen before.

"Who's that?"

Nicolar turned. "Who's who?"

"The tall one. Long hair. Tattoo down his neck."

A pause. "I'm not sure," Nicolar said.

"What do you mean? How did he get here?"

Nicolar moved to the steps, and Danik descended quickly on his heels. Taking long strides, the king passed Nicolar, pushing another man out of the way.

"You!" Danik called.

The tall man lowered his sword from where he squared off against Kauno. He snapped to attention. "Your Majesty." He bowed his head.

"Who are you?"

"This is Samu," Kauno said. "He's a friend of mine. I've been training him."

"You've been . . . what?"

Kauno blanched. "Um . . . teaching him about what we do."

"About the devion?"

His throat contracted as he swallowed hard. "Yes, Your Majesty. I thought we needed good fighters. I've known Samu for years. He's already well trained with the sword."

Danik clenched his fists. "You can't—" The breath through his nose puffed.

Nicolar's tap on his arm kept him from lashing out. "Sir, perhaps we can speak about this."

Danik's arms shook with a bottled-up rage. "Gah!" he shouted into the air. He spun on his heels and stomped back to the stands.

Nicolar and Bilton kept with him. "Do you want me to take care of them?" Nicolar asked when they were out of earshot.

Danik clenched his teeth and continued to huff.

"They both know about the devion, so if we let them go . . ."

"We can't just kill everyone," Danik said, arriving at his previous place in the stands. "We have to stop this from spreading. The men can't just teach whoever they want!"

Nicolar raised an eyebrow. "You don't *own* the devion. You realize that, don't you?"

The words hit Danik hard. A tight feeling grew in his chest. *He's right.*

"As loyal as we can hope these men are, the power we control is separate from us. When we invited these men in and trained them, we gave them the same access we have."

"It's gone too far," Danik whispered. His palms were sweating and his heart beat faster. "We need a better process."

Nicolar leaned in. "For . . . ?"

"Vetting potential knights. Only people with loyalty, who can follow rules. And we should have some sort of swearing-in ceremony."

"I'm sure we could do all of that."

Danik cleared his throat and straightened. "For now . . . no more men. We don't have the crystals, and we'll lose influence the more powerful they get. If anyone else trains a new person without authorization, kill them both. Make sure they know."

Nicolar kept his jaw tight. "Will do."

Bilton leaned in. "Would you like me to have the army provide a guard, Your Majesty? Perhaps set a curfew to keep the men in line?"

A quick burst of laughter escaped from Nicolar.

"No, Geoffrey," Danik said. The humorous comment only made him more depressed. "These men could kill any of your guards in the snap of a finger."

Danik watched the action in the arena. The men continued pounding at each other, slipping in and out of using the devion. In awe of the raw power on display, a faint tremble rumbled inside his body. "I still feel the pull," he said to Nicolar. "How about you?"

The man nodded.

"It's getting stronger again."

"A bit. Maybe. Cedric should be back soon with more necklaces. Hopefully, that will help."

Danik's pulse thudded in his ears. "We might need to leave all of this."

"Sir?"

"If the crystals don't work. If the pull continues to grow. How long can we stand it? The caves may be our destiny."

Nicolar frowned, then gestured with open hands toward the city. "This is what we worked for. We're not just going to give this up." He grabbed the crystal around his neck. "It's working fine for now. Plus, we're bringing more. Don't look too far ahead and worry about things you can't predict."

Danik blew out his breath, then nodded. "We'll see." He flipped his hand toward Nicolar and Bilton. "Leave me."

After a glance at each other, Bilton and Nicolar bowed and turned to walk away.

BILTON'S HEART POUNDED. Surrounded by the raw power in the arena, everything he said and did had potential life-threatening consequences. A step behind Danik's right-hand man, he cleared his throat. "Nicolar, do you have a moment to speak?"

The other man looked over his shoulder, his black goatee sticking forward from his chin. "Of course, Geoffrey."

Bilton gestured up a flight of steps, hoping the sweat on his forehead wasn't conspicuous. "Up here, perhaps?" He turned up the steps, his ears straining to catch the sound of the other man following. He did.

At the top of the arena, a stone deck opened up with a sweeping view of the city. The castle towered above them, but the rest of the city sprawled within the walls, bordered by the two rivers on either side.

"What is this about?" Nicolar asked, his thick Norshewan accent cutting through the cool wind that blew over the arena wall.

Bilton gazed across the city. He felt the gaze of the knight of power boring into the back of his head. His mouth trembled as he readied his words. He spun. "I saw you."

Nicolar stared back.

"Yesterday afternoon, in the kitchen, before the feast. I had just finished speaking with the chef and was leaving."

"What did you see?"

"The wine steward didn't poison the wine," Bilton said. "It was already in the cup, wasn't it?

Nicolar's eyes narrowed.

"I saw you put something in the king's goblet, looking over your shoulder to see if anyone was watching. I thought it odd but not enough to be suspicious.

The knight of power's hand crept to his hip, where his sword rested in a sheath.

Bilton sucked in a breath. He took a step back, then held up his hands. "I didn't tell Danik what I saw."

Nicolar paused with his fingers on the hilt of his weapon. "Why not?"

"I wanted to know why."

"Why?" His goatee flicked as the corner of his mouth lifted. "You want him dead, too."

Bilton swallowed hard.

"You think our goals align, and you want to know my motivation."

"No, that's—" He shook his head. "I don't want him dead." The lie sounded hollow.

Nicolar stepped closer. "Then tell me why *you* assisted the Shadow Knights with that attempt to wipe out the Knights of Power with gas?"

Bilton's throat swelled.

"Our goals *do* align, Geoffrey. We should work together."

"Who told you?" Bilton asked. "Hampton?"

The other man's eyes twinkled. "Yes."

He took a long breath. "Danik is dangerous," he blurted. "The Shadow Knights were the best chance to stop him. They came to me for—"

Nicolar's smirk had grown into a grin that took over his face, and Bilton clamped his mouth shut.

"Did Hampton really tell you?" the high lord asked.

"No," Nicolar said. "You did. Just now."

Bilton's stomach lurched.

"I had a hunch, but . . . Thank you for confirming it. A high lord turning on his king, hmm. I wonder what Danik will think of that?"

"I wonder what he'll think of his right-hand man trying to poison him?"

Nicolar took another step. The smile was gone, replaced by a grim, flat line. He wrapped a hand around his sword's grip, but his eyes focused on Bilton.

The high lord's eyes flicked to each side. He crept backward. "We both want the same thing, Nicolar, that's why I didn't tell him. You don't have to kill me." The back of his feet stopped at a wall.

"We don't want the same thing. You want *all* of us gone and yourself on the throne. All I want is Danik."

"I'm fine with that." Sweat prickled on Bilton's forehead. "Let's work together."

Nicolar continued forward.

Bilton's breath grew rapid, and his mind raced. "How would it look if you killed me, huh?"

The knight of power paused.

"Wouldn't that draw attention? Why would you kill a high lord? Danik will ask questions and get suspicious. Do you want that?" He held a hand to his chest. "I'm no threat to you. I can't say anything because of what you know."

Nicolar extended his chin but didn't draw his weapon.

Bilton imagined the scenarios playing through the man's head: *kill me, let me go, or stand here staring at each other.*

"Nicolar!" someone called from the arena. Broderick stood in the middle of a huddle of trainees, beckoning to the man. "We need you for a demonstration!"

Nicolar turned back to Bilton. The two men stared without moving for a long moment. "If you say anything"—Nicolar tapped the end of his sword—"this blade will be the least of your worries." Leaving the high lord, he turned to take the steps down to the arena floor.

Bilton's chest deflated as he exhaled. His pulse thumped in his head. He stretched his clammy fingers, trying to work feeling back into them. Danik caught his eye, standing as he had against the railing of the stands.

Now what do I do?

36

BETRAYER IN THE LIGHT

Bilton hurried up the hall of the castle. Winded from the stairs and the rush to get there, his curiosity for the meeting kept his mind occupied. Darcius had never called last-minute Advisor Council meetings, but Danik seemed to make a habit of it.

Royal guards at the chamber entrance pushed the double doors open when the high lord approached.

Bilton stepped into the council chamber and froze. The oval table was empty, with a ring of chairs tucked in. At the head of the table, King Danik leaned on a chair. The rest of the room was practically deserted, with a handful of flickering torches and a royal attendant against the wall. Bilton's throat turned dry. "Am I early? Or too late?"

The king flashed an enigmatic smile. "Not at all. Your timing is perfect."

His stomach turned. "I thought this was a council meeting?"

Danik swatted the air, dismissing the idea. "No, not tonight. I was hoping to speak with just you. I told the messenger that to avoid suspicion."

"Suspicion of . . . what? What's going on?"

Danik waved him forward, heading toward the balcony.

The sun had set, and only a lingering shade of orange hung in the west. The edge of the balcony faded into black where the platform disappeared with a lack of railing.

"Since I took the throne, I've tried to surround myself with people I could trust. A king can only do so much, so we must have a team to help: advisors, guards, armies . . ." He turned. "High lords."

Bilton swallowed, but a lump in his throat wouldn't settle.

Danik stopped at an outdoor table that held several glasses and a bottle. He pulled the cork out of the top of the bottle and poured a dark wine into two glasses. "I learned something disturbing. One of my team—someone I trusted—betrayed me."

He knows! Bilton's heart beat faster. His eyes shifted, gauging the options of escape. *Going over the edge of the balcony would mean death. Running back into the chamber, I would be caught.*

Danik handed him a glass, an enigmatic smile taunting him. "Can you believe it? I gave him everything he could want—power, money, a seat at the table. He pretended he was on board, then he plotted to stab me in the back."

Bilton held his drink out, his trembling hand creating ripples on the surface.

"Loyalty." Danik shook his head. "It's so difficult to come by." He nodded toward Bilton's cup, then lifted his own glass. "Drink up. I think you'll enjoy this vintage."

Bilton's voice cracked as he spoke. "Who are you referring to?"

The king tilted his head. "I'm sorry. I thought it was clear." Danik raised his glass to his lips and took a long drink, finishing with a swallow. "It was Nicolar. He turned on me."

Bilton huffed a short laugh. "Nicolar?" *He found out.* "I can't believe it. He seemed . . ." *He seemed like he would turn in a heartbeat.* ". . . loyal." Bilton raised his cup and drank. The earthy wine trickled down his throat.

The king's eyes hardened. "You can't believe it? Like you could never imagine it?" His voice had turned crisp, with a biting edge.

Bilton's pulse raced. He swallowed a lump of fear, his mind spinning. He took a half step back and opened his mouth, not knowing what words to use.

A strip of fabric dropped past his vision and pressed against his mouth. It pulled taut and tied against the base of his skull. He strained to protest. His intended objection turned into a mumble. He jerked his head to the side and paled as Nicolar and Broderick stepped into view.

Danik crossed his arms and sneered.

The gag left no room for words. All Bilton could do was strain to form sounds. Broderick's firm hand on his shoulder kept him from moving.

"Nicolar," Danik said. "Ha!"

The goateed man stood next to the king, his grin telling Bilton everything he needed to know.

"Nicolar told me what he discovered. The poisonous paste you used to line my cup at the banquet. How he and Broderick found the bottle hidden in your house."

No! It wasn't me. It was Nicolar! Bilton's desired words escaped only as a smothered mess. *I didn't do it!* He jerked his head, trying to escape the gag.

"They also found out how you conspired with the Shadow Knights before that."

Bilton's thrashing eased.

"How you tried to kill not just me but *all* the Knights of Power."

The high lord sensed his defeat. There was no way to escape and nowhere to go.

"You know how I feel about traitors, Geoffrey," Danik growled, pulling his sword. "I gave you a chance to serve with me, but you threw it in my face." He nodded to his men.

Nicolar joined Broderick and grabbed Bilton's other shoulder. Their grips were like stone. He tried to shake loose, but the effort was useless.

The king drew his blade along Bilton's arm where his jerkin's protection ended. The slow motion bit into his skin, drawing a bright red line of blood across the flesh. Bilton clenched his teeth together. He wouldn't let the man hear him cry out.

When the cut was complete, Bilton's feet moved forward, propelled by the inexorable grip of the two knights of power. His stomach turned when the destination became clear. The edge of the balcony drew close. He pushed back with his legs, trying to stop his momentum. He struggled against the holds on his shoulders, but his strength waned. No matter how hard he tried to shake, he couldn't break free. Three steps away. Two steps.

"Wait." Danik's command stopped their progress. "If army leaders give us trouble, we could lean on him to persuade them. He may be more useful alive. Guards!"

Bilton's captors pulled him away from the edge and turned him. Two royal guards appeared.

"Take him to the darkest cell in the dungeons."

The royal guards grabbed Bilton by the arms and pulled him away.

"Goodbye," Danik said without pity.

Bilton's feet followed where they led him. A heavy weight sat in his gut. He had dared to hope, but any chance of optimism had been shattered.

"Good riddance," Nicolar said as the high lord walked away.

Conflicting emotions swirled in Danik. He stared at where the High Lord of Defense had disappeared. *He was a good leader. It's a shame he couldn't have been on board.*

His attendant appeared, gesturing toward his weapon with his eyebrows raised. "Shall I clean it, Your Majesty?"

Danik passed his sword to the man, wincing as another drop of red fell to the balcony.

"Bilton sure doesn't look happy," a voice called from inside the chamber.

Danik turned as Cedric, Alton, and Rankin stepped onto the balcony. Rankin stared wide-eyed, taking in the surroundings. Cedric held an armful of necklaces with red crystals hanging from the ends of the blue leather straps.

"You're back," Danik said. "Excellent."

"High Lord Bilton turned against the king," Nicolar said. "Now he will receive his punishment."

Danik nodded toward the necklaces. "I see your visit to the caverns was a success. No issues?"

"I wouldn't say no issues." Cedric chuckled. "But we got what we needed—thirty new necklaces, primed and ready."

"Good. Maybe this is a sign that our fortune is turning around. Now, we'll need to find a new high lord—someone who can command the will of the army but will be more loyal than Bilton."

"Let's encourage competition within the army," Nicolar said. "We can train the captains to use the devion, then have them face off and see who wins."

Danik's jaw dropped. "Absolutely not." He gestured to the crystals. "These are a rare commodity. We need to ration their use. No more training of new recruits unless I give the order."

No one responded.

"You all hear that?" Danik turned to look at each of the men. None of them returned his gaze. An unsettled feeling grew in his gut. *Why aren't they answering?* "Nicolar? Do you understand?"

The man with the goatee lifted his chin. Mischief filled his eyes. After holding Danik's gaze, he turned to Cedric. "Gather the captains. Tomorrow, let's meet with them in the arena at noon."

"Excuse me?" Danik kept his voice quiet, but the simmering anger bled through. "I said we *don't* involve the captains."

Nicolar sniffed. "And I couldn't care less *what* you said." He pulled his sword from the sheath at his hip and held it toward the king.

Danik's voice caught in his throat. His jaw dropped. He glanced at the other men, who stood tense and alert. The unsettled feeling grew into terror when all four of the others pulled their weapons in unison. They fanned out across the balcony, blocking the arched entryways into the castle.

Danik felt at his hip and blanched when he found nothing in his sheath. His eyes flicked toward the indoor chamber, but there was no sign of the attendant with his weapon. "What is this?" he muttered. He hoped for them to laugh as if it was an inappropriate joke. "Nicolar, what are you doing?"

The knight of power stepped forward. "What I should have done a while ago."

Danik backed up. His red crystal flared to life even though he knew the effort would be wasted. "We're a team. We did this together. We rule together. We—"

"We're not a team," Nicolar scoffed. "You live in the palace with servants that wait on you. You don't care about us. You only want us as lackeys to do what you want."

"That's not true," Danik said.

"You needed *us* to get where you are, but *we* no longer need *you*." Nicolar smirked. "Did you never wonder how you made friends with all of us so quickly in Tienn?"

Danik blinked several times. The question left his mind reeling.

"You were so drunk, half the tavern knew who and what you were. Our crew was the only one smart enough to do something about it. We latched onto you—riding you to power and fame, and you pulled us along every step of the way. It's too bad the poison didn't do its job last night. That would have made this easier."

Danik's eyes grew.

"No, it wasn't Bilton." He laughed. "You're quick to believe any lie I tell you."

Rankin was the least experienced. The miner's grip on his sword looked unpracticed and loose. Danik considered his options. *If I charge him, I should be able to get past before the other knights—*

"Go ahead." Cedric's body flashed, then appeared next to the greener fighter. "Make a move and see if your skills outclass the four of us."

Danik gulped. *I can't beat them.* "What do you want?"

"I want you . . . gone," Nicolar said. "We've all agreed that I should take the throne. We're going to elevate the Knights of Power to a new level of authority. Our number one goal will be wiping out the rest of the Shadow Knights. After that, anything we want will be ours."

"That's my goal, too!" After another step away, the stone wall of the castle hit his back. Desperation bled through his words. "None of you know Lia and Veron like I do. You'll need me!"

"We'll need you? Because you've been so useful in finding them thus far?" He scoffed. "I think not. You're weak, Danik. You don't have the stomach to stand behind the Purification Act. Well, I do. We'll enact it tomorrow. Within weeks, cities across Feldor will be stronger and wealthier when we rid them of their trash. But we'll start with the trash on this balcony." Nicolar glanced at the other three men. "Kill him."

Danik tensed. He could use the devion, but so could the others. His lack of weapon was a great disadvantage. The wall stopped him from retreating, and swords stopped any advance. The yawning darkness at the edge of the balcony was his only option.

Cedric lunged forward. Danik matched his enhanced speed, twirling away from the blade. Its steel tip hit the wall, chipping stone into the air. Danik aimed a devion-powered punch toward the man's side. He strained his muscles, trying to crack the man's ribs with a blow. Before his fist landed, the hairy knight knocked his arm away. Danik whirled to try again, but a stony blow met his jaw, filling the air with a loud *pop*.

The king's sight flashed white. Pain filled his mind as he stumbled closer to the edge. He held his arms out to keep balance and blinked. The four men were all closer. He locked eyes with Nicolar. The thief stared until he rushed in.

Danik had nowhere else to go. Rather than receive a death blow, he lunged for the brink. A sharp pain lanced the back of his arm. Although it missed his vital areas, Nicolar's blade still left a sting. The bite of the weapon was far from his mind. His body sailed over the edge of the balcony and dropped like a stone.

Wind buffeted his clothes and hair. His arms flailed. He squinted, trying to discern what waited for him below. A slanted roof approached. With no holds to grasp, Danik landed in a crouch, angling his feet with the slant of the roof. He didn't try to stop, only control his fall. The roof cracked beneath the immense pressure. Before he could tumble farther down the castle, he kicked out. The jump sent him flying sideways instead of down. An opposing wall loomed. He sighted a window sill and flung his hand over the lip when his body crashed into the vertical stone.

"Gah!"

Searing pain rippled down his injured arm, forcing his fingers to release their desperate grip. He fell again. His feet collided with a gutter. He stretched his good arm to grab the lip, but it remained out of reach.

Twisting, his back hit another slanted roof. The impact sent him tumbling end-over-end down slate tile. His legs, knees, elbows, and head crashed into the hard roof in an endless circle. He slapped his hand against the surface, but there was nothing to grip. The edge of the roof arrived, and he sighted below. A long drop to the ground waited for him.

Past the edge, a downspout jutted from the roof. The stone protrusion looked within reach. He stretched as far as his arm would allow. His falling body whipped by, but his fingers curled over the top. His arm held. With the devion to strengthen his muscles, he gripped with the ends of two digits. His legs swung in the air, dangling far above the ground.

Blood dripped down his opposite arm, creating macabre streaks of red. He angled his shoulder forward and apprised the wound. *Clean. Tight.* He sighed with relief. A wave of devion washed through his body, directing healing power to the wound. The sting and steady throb faded as the cut healed before his eyes.

His vision blurred as the effect of the energy use hit him. *Whoa!* He held on with his fingers, straining to keep his muscles engaged. After several blinks, his vision returned to focus and the weak feeling faded.

He spun to the castle wall and grinned at the sight of a drain pipe that ran from the downspout to the ground. He wrapped his two good arms around the metal, then shimmied his way down. Hand over hand, the ground grew closer. When he finally touched down, he slumped over, letting his arms hang loose. Several deep breaths settled his breathing.

The thought of Nicolar and the others rushing down through the castle to find out if he survived prompted him to action. He glanced toward the city but paused. *I'm the king, but . . . where do I go? The high lords, the army, they're useless. No one else can stop Nicolar.* The sobering thought struck him at his core. *No one will have my back.*

Staying in the castle was out. The Shadow Knights' old facility wouldn't work. The people of Felting would have no love for the deposed king who brought them little more than trouble.

A crash sounded around the corner. Shouting voices pierced the air.

They're coming.

Danik turned away from the noise and ran toward the city wall. Devion powered his bounding steps as the barrier drew closer. With a massive push, he leaped. His clothes rippled in the wind as he flew over the barrier, disappearing into the darkness.

37

A PLAN TO FUSE

I t took the entire team of Garronts to drag the fiend from the barracks. A trail of blue leaked behind as they pulled and heaved the creature's limp carcass, dropping it at the side of the boneyard. Chris' body was easier, and Jarno's, which had torn in two, was no trouble. They spent the remaining hours of the night cleaning out the busted beds, depositing the wooden pieces next to the beast's body.

Wakened from the raucous encounter with the monster, the other teams watched for a while, keeping their distance. When the danger was done, they lost interest and returned to their own barracks. None helped clean up. The guards didn't even come out of their office.

"We'll see what response they get if they ever get in trouble," Stewart muttered as he tossed a board onto the pile.

"They're still people," Lia said. "Like you and me."

"I'd help," Thurman said. "If *they* needed it."

"I would, too," Lia confirmed. She set her hands on her hips and took a deep breath. "That's most of it, isn't it?"

Waylon nodded, approaching with a small chunk of broken wood. "Yeah, except for the blood stains and what's left of Jarno's insides. There are still four good bunks that weren't obliterated, but they all have a funky smell from the splattered fiend blood. Should be interesting trying to sleep tonight."

"Maybe the other teams have some spare beds."

Shuffling feet drew her attention to where Vekko approached. He fidgeted with his hands while looking at the ground. "Lia?" He cleared his throat. "Do you, uh, have a moment?" The man's eyes flitted anywhere but at her.

"Sure." She turned back to Waylon. "Check the guard's office. See if they have any way to clean up the blood and—" She cut herself off.

"And the bits of Jarno?" Waylon finished.

Lia grimaced. "Yeah."

He nodded, then glanced at Vekko before jogging off.

"Come on." Lia waved Vekko to follow toward the lake, giving them space from the other teammates. "What's on your mind?"

"I, uh . . ." He continued to avoid eye contact. "I—" He stared at Lia, mouth frozen.

She inclined her head, waiting.

His eyes glistened and his jaw trembled. "I just needed—" He sniffed. The pooling moisture beaded and dribbled down his cheek. He wiped it away, then met her eyes. "I'm sorry," he whispered.

Lia's shoulders relaxed. A faint smile pulled at her lips.

"I've been rude to you since you arrived. At first, to be honest, I didn't want you."

She raised an eyebrow.

Vekko held up a hand. "But as soon as you started working, I could tell you were more than I expected. I guess I never let my guard down, though. I should have, and I regret it. The thing is . . ." He kicked at the ground. "Death terrifies me. It threatens us every week, and we can't escape it. But I'm not ready for it. I thought if I . . . if I pointed out what a poor job you were doing, you would be chosen before me." He chuckled. "But then it was clear you were putting us all to shame. I agree with the others. You're a good leader, and if someone is going to lead us out of this place, I'd put my money on you. I'm sorry for how I treated you."

"Thanks, Vekko." She set her hand on his shoulder. "That means a lot."

"Today, when the team trains, do you, uh . . . mind if I join you?"

She smiled. "Not at all." She shook his shoulder. "I'll warn you, though. It's gonna hurt."

Approaching feet announced the arrival of the thick-necked mine boss.

"I hear you're the new captain?" Rasmill's inflection turned up as if stating a question.

"Yeah, I guess so."

"What happened last night?"

"One of those fiends attacked our barracks."

"I gathered that." Rasmill paused and glanced between her and Vekko. "Is that it?"

"What do you mean?"

"Why was it there?"

Lia shrugged. "You think we know?"

His eyes narrowed. "We've never had one in the barracks before."

"What changed?"

"Why are you asking me?"

"I thought we were supposed to be safe outside the mines. Chris and Jarno died last night. Do we need to start posting guards? Wouldn't that be *your* job? How did you let it get past *you*?"

Rasmill huffed. "We'll do our work the way we want to. If you don't like it, post your own guards." He pointed at her. "Crystals due today, team leader."

Lia stared as the man walked away, not at the smug side of his grin, but at the ring of keys affixed to his belt.

"Get them now?" Vekko said when the guard and his keys were out of earshot.

"Not yet. We need all the crystals first. Then, we'll attack." A smile came to her face. "And I know where he keeps them at night."

Breakfast consisted of looking up to chase away stares from other tables. The teams whispered among themselves while the Garronts yawned and shook off the events of the night before. Broken sleep and moments of terror left them exhausted.

Lia felt a strange anticipation, as if she were about to begin a new mission. Her nerves rattled as her mind raced through options of how to get out. Most of the scenarios involved attacking the devion-filled guards, a prospect she shuddered at. She spooned down gruel, hoping the food would settle her stomach. It didn't help.

When the Garronts arrived at the main cavern, the team looked to Lia. She swallowed the nerves down, recognizing that she was the one to decide for them all. "Down there." She pointed to one of the side tunnels. "We need to be out of sight from the other teams."

She stopped in a wide section of the cave. There was space to work but would also be free from prying eyes. "Manne and Stewart, you two take the first shift of shovel duty. Everyone else, chip away as much as you can." She raised her voice. "As of this morning, we are five crystals ahead of the Valcors. I want to beat them, but . . . I also want to save crystals back. The longer we hold on to them, the more likely it is the guards or the fiends will notice them. But if we save too many today, we could end up losing the golden pickaxe reward."

The men's faces reflected mixed feelings about the dilemma.

"Do you have a preference?" she asked.

They perked up, eyebrows lifting.

"Which do we focus on: rewards or crystals?"

"You know how I feel about the reward," Stewart said, earning faint laughter. "But at the same time, I'd like to see what we can do with the crystals. I'm good with whichever."

"I say we save them," Thurman said. "Who cares about a nicer breakfast if we won't be here to eat it?"

Mumbled affirmation ran through the crowd.

"We need nine before we can do anything with them," Lia said.

"Let's save them up," Waylon said. "Blast the Valcors and blast the Marked Ones!"

The consensus was clear. The unified team turned to the cave walls and went to work.

Lia worked as hard as she had any day, slamming her axe into the wall and repeatedly knocking rocks to the ground. Part of her wished a fiend would arrive, so she could use the origine to knock out some quick work with a burst of energy.

"Got one!" Doyle shouted thirty minutes into the day.

The Garronts froze while he rushed to Lia's box. She opened the lid and immediately shut it after he dropped the object in.

Silence filled the passage. The team held their breaths, glancing in every direction. Lia strained her ears and tested her nose. No signs of fiends arrived.

"Good work," she said. "Everyone, take a quick break. Harold, can you pass around the water?"

Lia set her axe down and took several deep breaths. *One crystal down. Eight more to go.* She took a heavy swig of water when the flask arrived to her. She tensed when she noticed Anton standing next to her.

"The Shadow Knights, huh?" he said.

She nodded.

"I've heard about your abilities and stuff. What you did last night with that fiend was amazing."

"Thanks."

"Do you really think we can get out of here?"

She weighed her words before speaking. "I do."

"What do you think you'll do? How will you get the keys?"

Her eyes narrowed. "Why do you want to know?" It came out sharper than she intended.

He held up his hands. "I'm sorry. I was just curious . . . I want to be ready."

"I'm still working it out, but I'll let you know."

"Do you think you'll—"

"Break's over!" Lia called, interrupting him. "Sorry Anton, but we need to get back to work."

He backed off. "Of course."

The men picked up their axes and turned back to the mine walls. Lia's gaze lingered on Anton as he resumed work.

"You think he's one of them?" Vekko whispered over her shoulder, making her jump. "Sorry. Didn't mean to scare you."

"It's all right," she whispered back. Lia kept an eye on the newcomer. "I'm not sure. If he is, it could spell trouble."

"You want me to, um . . . *do* something about it? There are plenty of accidents in the mines."

Lia spun to him, eyes wide. "What? No!" She shook her head as if reinforcing it to herself. "No, we can't do that."

"You're the boss." He shrugged and then returned to his position on the line.

The team returned to work. Chipping. Shoveling. Sweating. They labored with full wind in their sails and drive in their limbs. Crystals came quickly, dropping one after another into the box. Lia's excitement increased with each addition.

Late in the day, the ninth shout of discovery echoed through the passage. Waylon found the last one. He scrambled to Lia, then dropped the crystal into the box.

The lid barely shut. Lia had to press it together to get the latch to close. She looked up with a quirk of a smile and rapid breath. "We did it," she breathed.

The rest of the team looked on, a cloud of anticipation hovering over them.

"What do you do now?" Waylon asked. "How do you fuse them?"

She set her hand on top of the box, reaching out with her senses to see if anything registered. No tingle, hum, or rumble answered her back. "I'm not sure."

"Wait?" Stewart stepped forward. "I thought you knew how to do it."

"Not yet. Be patient." She projected confidence, but inside, her nerves rattled.

Waylon held his hand out. "Let me see."

She passed the box. Waylon walked to the nearest glowing red crystal in the wall and held the box up to touch it. Lia trailed behind. "Anything?"

He shook his head. "I don't think so. Maybe if I . . ." The latch popped.

"Waylon . . ." she warned.

"Just for a second." He lifted the lid, then tilted the box so the dull crystals pressed up against the other. "I-I don't feel anything."

"Close it!"

Waylon listened.

Her heart pounded as she held out her hand. "Here." Waylon passed the closed box back to her.

The other Garronts continued to watch, leaning forward against their pickaxes.

"Look at the bright side. If it doesn't work, nothing will hold us back from beating the Valcors this week." She forced a chuckle while her insides turned. *If it doesn't work, I'm not sure how we'll ever get out of here.*

The glowing object set into the wall at chest height. She raised her hands and pressed the wood of the box against it. Like Waylon's attempt, nothing changed. She tried to summon the origine, knowing the effort would be futile. She was right.

Last effort.

She rested her fingers on top of the box and adjusted her stance. A glance at her team revealed all of them watching in silence.

"Do it, Lia," Waylon whispered.

She pressed the box against the wall and took a deep breath. Her pulse pounded. Her fingers trembled as they gripped the edge. With a flick of her fingers, the lid opened, and she pressed the opening against the cave wall, covering the glowing crystal. A round of gasps sounded behind her. Vibrations through the wood told her the box contents shifted, clattering against the wall in direct contact with the infused crystal.

Lia held her breath and listened for any change. She searched for the faintest dimming of light, but nothing happened. A sinking feeling filled her gut.

"It's not working," Waylon said. "What do we—"

"Close it!" Thurman stepped forward, his voice shaking. "We don't want those fiends to catch wind of it."

Murmurs ran through the group.

"Hold on." Lia took a deep breath, then blew it out. An image of the monster's dripping jaws from the previous night flashed into her mind. She pushed it away, focusing on the box before her. She flexed her muscles, straining to find any connection to a greater power. The box shook along with her hand. The crystals clinked together as they scraped against the stone wall.

"Lia!" Thurman shouted.

"I said, wait!"

Her face scrunched together, clenching her teeth. She moved her other hand to bolster the first, but the shaking continued.

Why is it not working? Maybe I—

A faint glow lined the edge of the box where it met the cave wall, and a rumble grew. The box shook, not from her hand but from the objects inside.

A puff of air expelled as her mouth turned up. "It's working!"

"Lia . . ." Waylon's voice over her shoulder sounded eerie. Distant.

"Almost there. This is working!"

"Lia!" His insistence jerked her from her trance. Waylon stared down the cavern passage.

That's when Lia noticed the change in the light. Their team's lantern glowed where it hung on the wall, but the crystals lining the passage dimmed. A tremor shook the ground, repetitive like massive feet pounding in rhythm.

"Stop, Lia. It's coming!"

"I'm so close!" The smell hit her next—rancid decay mixed with the rot of death. She glanced over her shoulder and froze. The other eight miners backed away, their faces filled with terror. They feared the monster—the beast she lured to them. Chris' and Jarno's deaths came to her mind. She didn't cause that tragedy, but there was no one else to blame if the situation turned deadly.

The box snapped shut with a clap. Lia shrank against the wall, rolling the wooden container up in her shirt. The footsteps continued. The smell grew worse. She attempted to stifle her short, ragged breaths, but her pulse wouldn't slow.

After a moment, the footsteps stopped. Lia strained her ears to pick up any sign of the fiend, but it seemed to have vanished. The glowing crystals in the wall stabilized and then brightened, returning the familiar red light to the passage.

Sighs filled the passage from the other workers. Waylon hurried to her. "Did it work?"

She pulled the box out of her shirt. After a glance down the passage to confirm no fiend lurked a few feet away, she peeked through a slit in the box. Her body slumped. "No."

"It was working, though, right?"

"I think so," Lia said. "It needed more time."

"More time and that beast would be on you," Thurman said.

She nodded. "Let me think. I'll figure it out."

The men went back to work. They had the ten crystals they needed, but another goal was still at stake. They still wanted to beat the Valcors.

Lia paced the tunnel with the box in hand. The dull crystals shook inside. She acted as if she were deep in thought, but it was unnecessary. She didn't need to plan. Lia knew what to do. The only downside was everyone around could die if she attempted it. That meant there was one way to do it.

Tonight, when the only person at risk is me.

38

A WEEK TO REMEMBER

The Garronts dropped four additional crystals into the team box before the day was over. That made thirteen for the day —a team record. Spirits were high on the walk back through the caverns.

"Bronson! How many did you get?" Harold called to where the Valcors picked up their supplies in the main room.

The dominant team captain glared back but didn't reply as the Garronts dropped off their carts and continued through the cavern.

"I can't tell if that's good or bad," Harold said.

"They don't look happy," Thurman said. "We may still win."

"I hear the Bears are on the brink of quota this week. Even if we don't win, at least we don't have to worry."

"Lia." Waylon waved Lia to him. She dropped back, Thurman sticking with her. "What'd you decide about the crystals?"

"I, uh—" The question caught her off guard. "I don't know."

His eyes narrowed. "Liar."

She blinked, stunned. "What?"

"You know exactly what you're going to do, and I won't let you."

"What is she doing?" Thurman asked.

Waylon raised an eyebrow. He paused, but Lia refused to fill the gap. "She's coming back tonight to do it on her own."

"On her own? But she'll—" The pieces seemed to fit together for Thurman. "You'll die!"

"I won't," she insisted. "But if I fuse the crystals when you're all around, there's a good chance you will."

"I'm coming with you," Waylon said.

"No, you're not."

"I can protect you."

"With what? A pickaxe? You saw what they can do."

"I can help."

"Me, too," Thurman added.

Lia blew out her breath. After a moment, she chuckled and shook her head. "Fine. If you want to help that badly. I guess it couldn't hurt to have a few more hands. Keep the rest of them out of it though. It does no good for everyone to become martyrs."

Waylon and Thurman both nodded. "What about the keys for your anklets?" Waylon asked.

"I have a plan for that." Her grin grew. "I'll tell Rasmill we need another cart for training. There's one where I got the first from, and the path to get it walks right by where they keep the keys."

"Won't he stop you with whatever special power he has?"

"If he sees me lunge for the keys, sure. But if he's got a fiend's pincer stuck through his neck before then, he won't raise an alarm."

Waylon's eyes grew wide.

"So you fuse the crystals first, then you steal the keys and unlock yourself," Thurman said.

"That's right," Lia confirmed. "We'll go during training. Keep the rest of the team occupied, avert suspicion, and it will give us an excuse to visit the mine office."

"Then, what?"

"Then . . ." Her grin grew larger. "Wait and see what I can do."

Their team dropped off their tools and then crossed the cavern to the barracks. Lia kept the wooden box tucked against her side, under her shirt. She walked tense and alert, her eyes shifting. Waylon and

Thurman traveled next to her to obscure anyone else's view. She relaxed when they entered the barracks.

"What'd you decide, Lia?" Stewart asked. "Plan ready?"

She stopped in front of her bed, nodding. She tucked the box into the straw of the mattress and patted to make sure the claw was still there. "Yeah, it's ready."

"All right, then. What do we do?"

She glanced at Waylon before turning to the rest of the team. "Be patient for now. After the reaping, we'll go through a training session, just like normal. Then we'll gather and discuss."

"They're back," Manne called from the door, waving the others ahead. "Time to see if we won."

Lia's heart skipped. *If we could collect ten extra crystals and still get enough to win, that would be something.* She followed the Garronts to sit at their team table.

Across the room, her eyes found Bronson. He and his Valcors settled into their seats. Her hopes rose. They looked anything but confident.

Rasmill and the other three guards shuffled up. The teams' chatter wound down as heads turned to the front.

"Another week down. Another reaping to celebrate." Rasmill's sneer accented the groans that ran through the crowd. "The top team for this week—"

Lia held her breath, hoping they found enough.

"—with a team record of forty-four crystals, the Garronts take the golden pickaxe for the first time."

Lia's team erupted into cheers. Stewart pumped his fist in the air, and the others hit each other on the backs. *And that was without our other ten*, she thought.

"Congratulations to the new team captain, Lia."

Her shoulders wobbled from the men shaking her in appreciation.

"Two crystals behind, the Valcors took second place."

Lia found Bronson. The captain stared forward, his mouth forming a thin line.

"Nice job Mountain Wolves. You jumped up to thirty-four—the best you've seen in a while. Blood Panzils came in fourth at thirty-two. And bringing up the rear were the Bears."

The unfortunate team looked at Rasmill with ashen faces.

"Your goal was twenty-six, and you got . . . twenty-six."

A chorus of sighs filled the Bears' table.

"Nice work."

"Everyone made it," Waylon whispered. "I can't remember the last time that happened."

"Nice work, teams. You deserve to celebrate, but there is some bad news."

A knot formed in Lia's stomach.

"While the crystal output was strong, the Marked Ones still need people for the reaping, now more than ever. By special order from Talioth himself, one of you has been selected."

Her knot tightened. Mutterings of unrest filled the large room.

"That's not fair!" one of the Panzils yelled. "We all did our part!"

"Yeah!"

Rasmill held up a hand. "This week's sacrifice . . ." He scanned the room.

Men fidgeted when his gaze passed. Lia held her breath when the mine boss glanced in her direction. She continued to hold it. His eyes didn't move on.

". . . is Lia."

Her mouth hinged open, stuck in a gaping display.

"No!" Waylon's yell shattered the silence. "We need her!"

"Choose a new captain," Rasmill droned while the three guards approached.

Lia's limbs wouldn't move. She wanted to explode from the table in an origine-fueled frenzy. Rather, her body rose from the seat, lifted by a guard.

Thurman rose. "Leave her alone!" His arm cocked, ready to strike the guard, when another swooped in and pinned him against the table. A muffled groan replaced the defiant shout.

Waylon jumped up next but had his arms pulled behind his back in an instant. A knife appeared at his throat from the fast-moving guard.

"Do you want to die, too?" Rasmill turned to the rest of the crowd. "Any of you? Do you want to test us? We'd be happy to take more than just her today."

"Stop," Lia breathed, her weak voice barely reaching her ears. She looked across at her team. Thurman strained against the body holding him to the table, and Waylon winced at a blade against his neck. "Stop this, everyone. It will do no good."

"She gets it," Rasmill said. "Garronts, good job this week. Sorry, you still lost someone."

Lia stumbled forward, pulled by the guard's stony grip. Her mind reeled. *The crystals. The plan. My team. We were almost there.* The mess area faded behind her. She trudged along, her feet heavy, like stone blocks.

Two guards held either shoulder. Lia waited while they unlocked the main gate. The metal clink caused her to flinch, and soon the gate rolled open. Pulled along in the men's unbreakable grip, she exited the mines for what she knew would be the last time.

She didn't remember telling her legs to move, but they plodded along. The cave walls passed by. Her eyes watched without seeing. The guards didn't speak. There was no point; she was about to die. Everyone knew it.

Lia slowed her gait when they entered the Hub. The empty scaffolding looked forgotten where it climbed against the wall. The statue of Talioth behind it seemed incomplete—waiting for a finishing touch that may never come. She gazed up at the light shining through the hole in the ceiling. It fell at a heavy angle, dim, as if the sun prepared to set. The glimpse of a world outside the caves reminded her of what she was about to lose.

Raiyn, where are you? Father, Mother, do you know I love you?

A firm hand pushed her. "Keep moving," the guard said.

Lia stumbled forward, her head craned back toward the outside world as they passed into another tunnel. The world—her world—disappearing forever.

Two dozen men and women filled the Siphon Room when she arrived. Talioth stood next to the pit, his mouth forming a thin line. Her old sword, Farrathan, showed its hilt over his shoulder, tucked into its sheath. Gralow, the broad-shouldered one who had tortured her, sneered when she arrived, his stringy gray hair pulled behind his head. Meliand waited beside them. Her hands folded in front, as if they waited for their time to act.

"I told you that your turn would come soon," Talioth said.

Lia wanted to shoot back a snarky comment, but nothing came to mind.

He motioned to the spot before the central pit. "Position her."

"This is pointless," Lia's voice shook. "I've told you, I won't talk."

Talioth chuckled. "And I believe you. But we are not here to talk." He nodded to Meliand.

A guard pushed Lia to her knees. The metal clamps around her ankles clanked against the ground, digging into her skin. The older woman left Talioth's side to position behind Lia.

Her pulse raced. Her mind scrambled to find anything to grasp onto. "Why? Why now? You just did it to Dayna. Wasn't that enough?"

Talioth's mouth curled down. He paused for a moment, then looked at the Core. Its glowing light pulsed. "In the past, it was enough. Siphoning a shadow knight could sustain us for an entire season. But now, the power is spread too thin. And after whatever your group did a few weeks ago, it's even worse."

"It sounds like you're only delaying the inevitable, Talioth. Killing me will buy you a bit of time, but it won't last. The other men don't provide the same power, right? You can't kill all your workers. You need them to mine."

He glanced at Meliand, exchanging a look she couldn't decipher.

"Let it fade," Lia pleaded. "It's going to go out, eventually. You can't keep it up. Let me go back to the mines. I can—"

His chuckle silenced her. "Let it go out? Your knights would be in for quite the surprise."

Lia frowned, then glanced between him and Meliand. "What do you mean?"

"Plus," he continued, ignoring her, "what use do we have for you in the mines if we let this go out? Once we kill the rest of the Shadow Knights and the Knights of Power, we'll be fine." He straightened and rolled his shoulders. "Enough of this. Proceed!"

Lia's head clamped in place, nails digging into her scalp. She pulled against them but the claws dug further. Another hand rested on her shoulder, keeping her still like a stone. "No!" she shouted. "This can't—This can't be it!" Tears sprang from her eyes, blurring her vision and affecting her words. "Please, don't do this!"

"Do it!" Talioth growled. "Now!"

Lia jerked forward with all her strength, but her body didn't budge. The force holding her was beyond anything she could resist. She strained to find the origine. Her muscles flexed; she pulled with all her might, but no hidden power came to her aid.

The light from the Core intensified, and a deep hum filled the room.

I can't die like this! I was about to break out. She had planned it all. She would flee the mountains and find the rest of the knights. With a fused crystal, they could exploit the weakness in the devion's ability. They could take on the Knights of Power before they grew to a size impossible to defeat. Then, they could return to the caves with the full strength of the Shadow Knights and the armies of Terrenor behind them. They would rescue the miners, destroy the Core crystal, and be done with the Marked Ones for good.

Chanting filled the air, men and women unifying in a pulsing rhythm. Lia's head shook. She felt a tingle inside as power drained from her.

No! I'm not ready!

The light from the crystal grew. She closed her eyes to block it out. A tremble ran through her, horrible and empty. She pictured her parents training her while she grew up in the Shadow Knights facility. An image of Raiyn flashed in her mind but faded as her life seemed to drain. Her mind grew sluggish. Her straining muscles relaxed. Her will to resist faded.

I guess this is it.

The chanting faltered. The fingernails biting into her head twitched. A new roar filled the room, covering the thrum. *What is that?* She risked opening her eyes.

The marked ones in her vision no longer regarded her or the Core. They looked to the wall behind her. Meliand let go. The hand on Lia's shoulder disappeared. She could move again. Lia spun. She blinked to ensure her eyes weren't a trick of wishful thinking.

Men poured into the room, eight in all. Waylon and Thurman barreled into marked ones, knocking them off their feet. Harold, Manne, and Stewart waved pickaxes through the air, spinning toward anyone in their way. Doyle and Anton wielded shovels. They swung into crowds of gray-clothed onlookers. Even with the devion at their disposal, not everyone could dodge at once.

As the Garront crew spread out, attacking any marked ones in their way, a man pushed through, coming toward Lia. *Vekko.* His eyes held hers as he ran. His hand raised, and an object tossed through the air. She traced the item as it flipped until she grasped it. It jangled and fell against the back of her hand—a metal ring with four keys.

A female marked one rushed toward Vekko in a flash of movement. The pulling of her sword filled the air with a loud scrape.

Vekko stared at Lia, his face carrying an intensity she'd not seen in him. His lips seemed to move in slow motion. "Run!"

Lia gaped back, processing the words as the marked one ran her sword through Vekko's chest. He didn't even cry out. He nodded to her as he fell to his side.

Lia held her breath. She pressed her fingers against the key ring and sensed the metal cuff digging into her ankle. Clarity flooded into her hazy mind.

Her team came for her, to save her life, to help her escape.

I can escape.

I can do this.

39

TEAM SUPPORT

The Garronts sowed chaos with their arrival. Although the marked ones' abilities could easily put down a crew of eight poorly armed, underfed miners, the surprise of the attack and the ferocity with which they fought created a striking impact.

Talioth pulled Farrathan from its sheath and faced the new threat. Meliand had let go of Lia and brandished a dagger. The marked one Waylon collided into flailed his arms as he fell into the pit yawning beneath the Core. His desperate hand caught the hole's edge, and Gralow lunged to grab onto it. A devion-strengthened pull brought the man out.

A cacophony filled the chamber. Although the hum from the Core wound down, it remained a piercing intensity. The shouts of arriving Garronts added to the yells of the marked ones, building into a disorienting mess of sound. In all the chaos, one thing was forgotten about. The marked ones overlooked the pivotal danger—Lia.

She fit the slender key into the lock on her ankle cuff and twisted with a wild desperation. A click rewarded her rapid flick of the wrist. The metal cuff loosened, and her heart jumped. The next cuff clicked as smoothly as the first. Her pulse raced as she flicked the metal from each restraint, and the bonds clinked to the cavern floor.

Somehow, despite the loud hum and deafening yells, the marked ones heard the faint metallic noise. Time seemed to stand still as Talioth, Meliand, and Gralow turned as one to face her. Their eyes grew impossibly large. Lia smirked. Before they could lunge for her, she reached out and pressed her palm against the Core.

"No!" Talioth sprang in her direction with stretched-out hands.

Lia pulled from inside. The intense glowing of the crystal seemed to infuse itself into her. Light exploded out of her pores, dancing through the room and throwing shadows in all directions. A pulsing energy rushed through her body, vibrating and humming. She couldn't tell if the metallic sound came from inside her or from the crystal.

The Core dimmed. The glowing, pulsing surface faded to a dull purple color. Smaller crystals set in the walls and hanging from the necks of the marked ones paled as well. Lia's glowing form became the principal source of light for the entire chamber.

The marked ones recoiled, stopping their brutal attack on Lia's teammates. Talioth froze in place, cringing. His arms were tucked into his chest. He squatted, bringing his knees to his body. His face contorted, eyes closed.

Lia gritted her teeth. Her body shook, rumbling with power. Her muscles strained, as if they might snap. When she couldn't take it anymore, she yanked her hand off the hard surface of the crystal.

The light in the room had dimmed. Her glowing pores faded while the luminescence from the crystals climbed. The hum in the air waned, and Lia's shaking limbs calmed.

Talioth's head lifted. "What did you do?" He remained contorted in a mass of twisted limbs.

I have no idea, Lia thought. But what happened was exactly what she had hoped. While the momentary infusing of the Core's energy was gone, the tingling power of the origine lay in its wake, brimming and ready to be used.

Her first move was to fly at Talioth. He held Farrathan up, ready to strike, but Lia's rapid, origine-powered move caught him by surprise. She jerked the weapon from his unsuspecting hand and spun away, slicing at his body. A gash tore across his arm, ripping a yell from his throat. He stumbled away. Lia rushed to finish him until Gralow and another marked one appeared in between them, holding swords of their own.

"Lia!" Waylon yelled. "Get out!"

The sight of him pressed against the wall gave her pause. He strained against men who held a knife against his chest. Several miners of Team Garront lay bleeding on the ground. The others struggled against impossible forces.

Her breath faltered. *They're dying for me.* The ultimate sacrifice, saving her despite impossible odds.

She lunged at Gralow, letting the origine speed up her movement and strength. Her familiar sword cut through the air, raining blow after blow on the man. To her dismay, the equally enhanced marked one parried away her heavy strikes.

"Go!" Waylon called again. "This is why we came!"

Lia paused, thinking over his words. All the other Garronts were captured or killed. The rest of the marked ones gathered to her, moving cautiously. She feigned an attack, sending them dodging backward. Talioth's head came into view over Gralow's shoulder, his face holding a simmering rage as he rolled the shoulder of his freshly healed arm.

I can't take them all.

A last glance at Waylon showed him nodding his head and flashing a weak smile. "Run," he mouthed. She pulled power into her limbs and sprinted to the nearest tunnel.

It felt like breathing after emerging from underwater. Life after death. Her body tingled from head to toe, fueled by the power she'd missed for weeks.

The passage was darker than ever. She bumped into walls while trying to navigate the unfamiliar tunnel. Her hands splayed in front and to the sides, keeping her from slamming into rocky walls. They gained scrapes and bumps, but she continued. Corners led to more corridors. Side passages seemed to lead in circles. Footsteps and shouts echoed over her shoulder. Lia continued forward, her legs pumping and her life depending on it.

Light from ahead teased her. She ran faster until she exploded into the Hub. The light through the ceiling had morphed into a subdued gray, but it felt like a burst of sun compared to the dim passages. She paused to check her bearings.

Her breath came in heaving gulps. The red crystals in the walls remained dim but looked to be growing in intensity. The sight formed a catch in her throat. *I need to get out of here.* The statue and scaffolding rose to her right. She spotted a dark tunnel exiting the far side of the room. *There!*

Lia ran forward, sword pumping in her arm. She gasped as she crossed through the overhead beam of light. Her feet skidded to a halt. Spread out between the stately columns, a dozen marked ones waited. Swords rested in their hands, and crystals hung from their necks, struggling to reach their former glow.

Her grip tightened on her weapon. Men in gray blocked her path with more streaming behind them. Thundering steps spun her around. Marked ones crashed into the room from the passage she had entered through.

Her head turned on a swivel. A few more passages exited the room, but men and women in gray blocked any hope of reaching them. Her breath magnified in her ears. She turned, hoping a plan would present itself.

"Get her!" someone yelled. The surrounding force moved as one, weapons flailing through the air as they ran at her.

Lia pulled from the origine and sprinted to the nearby scaffolding —the only object that could provide any cover. Her feet ascended the ramp without pause. When she shifted her weight to change directions at the first switchback, the structure shuddered. Thankfully, it held.

Marked ones were only steps behind. They roared after her, climbing the ramp with frightening speed. Lia spun at the next turn and found a knife hurtling toward her head. A deft dodge left the dagger clattering into the cave wall and shattering into pieces. The female attacker followed behind the thrown blade with a short sword. Lia lifted Farrathan and parried a frenzy of attacks. Sparks lit up the dim room. She backed up the ramp. A line of marked ones piled behind the woman, eager to get to Lia but unable to on the narrow path.

Lia ducked, a furious strike slicing through a vertical support. Wooden planks fell, hitting men who climbed below. Her kick sent the attacker flying back, knocking over several bodies who clambered up the scaffolding to get to her.

With a momentary space, she ran higher, turning the corner, winding up and up until she stopped. A railing blocked her path. There were no more levels to ascend. The unfinished carving of Talioth projected from the wall, staring down in judgment. She scanned the room.

The exit tunnel was far away—too far. She could leap off the scaffolding in its direction, but three marked ones remained, blocking it. More gray-clad foes entered the room with each second. The structure beneath her wobbled as a line of attackers closed in.

She allowed the origine to simmer through her body, heightening her senses and powering her muscles. But the ability felt like it snagged against an unseen object. Something fought against her, preventing its use. The glowing red crystals drew her attention. Their strength increased.

Just like when Father weakened it before.

In a matter of moments, the block against the origine would return to full power. She would be surrounded, with no hope of fighting.

And I will be dead.

The realization settled in her gut, turning her stomach with a sharp twinge.

I can't die like this. Father, Mother, and Raiyn—I want to see them again.

Talioth stepped into the center of the room below. His long gray hair waved against either side of his face. The black mark on his neck seemed to glow in the slanted, dusty rays of the sun coming through the ceiling. A smirk tugged at his face. He didn't run to her but waited for the inevitable.

The scaffolding shook, drawing her attention back to the approaching enemies. They would be on her in seconds. She readied her sword and faced the onslaught. Her grip tightened, slick with sweat.

If I can't escape, at least I can put up a good fight.

Her gaze flicked to Talioth again. His blue eyes stared back, squinting against the sun.

The sun!

She spun to check the oculus in the center of the cavern. The rim hovered over the center of the room, a carved circle etched into the rock. No path led to it. No holds formed a ledge. Its height was well beyond anyone's ability to jump to it.

From the floor, at least.

With the approaching marked ones only steps away, Lia tucked Farrathan into her cracked leather belt. Her legs pumped, racing her down the few steps that remained of the scaffolding. At the end of the line, she raised a leg, bracing it against the wooden rail at full speed.

A whooshing sound told her a swinging blade barely missed her from behind. The wall of marked ones was upon her. There was nowhere else to go. She was committed. It was either escape or die.

The origine strained against her as she pulled it into her limbs. Her momentum brought her atop the rail. Nothing but air remained past her. Air and a long fall.

And a hole in the ceiling.

Her leg exploded with force. Muscles contracted, blasting off the final surface she would find. Her body sailed into the air, hair whipping behind. With her focus locked on the illuminated eye in the ceiling, the rest of the room faded. She didn't hear anything. She saw nothing other than her target.

Closer.

The lip of the opening drew nearer. She searched for a ledge or a hold of any kind. She extended her arm, clawing through the air.

Open air yawned below, stretching to swallow her. Men and women in gray waited for her to fall.

Almost there.

Her eyes watered from the rush of wind. Her body angled sideways, unable to reposition in midair. Weight shifted as gravity worked to redirect her course. Her breath felt like someone pulled it from her lungs. She pictured her body falling to the stone floor, breaking as the marked ones pounced on her.

No.

No!

Her hand touched the rock. Fingers scrabbled, flailing to find purchase. Gravity pulled her down. Fingertips dragged down the smooth rock, and her stomach jumped into her throat.

There!

A finger caught. She stopped. Origine flooded into her arm, her hand, her finger. It strained, grasping to a minuscule crimp.

"Gah!" she yelled, her legs swinging side to side, hanging above the chamber.

Toned muscles rippled along her arm, the strain on her finger bolstered by the power rushing through her. Origine leaked like water in a sieve. She kicked at the air but found nothing to push off of. Another finger found purchase, then another. Her other hand dusted the vertical wall until it found traction of its own. With two hands secure, she chanced a glance below.

The red crystals below looked almost at full power. Pulsing and glowing brightly, their presence sucked against the origine, rendering Lia's efforts to hold on to it a struggle. Marked ones clustered below and craned their necks toward her. The ones looking toward the sun shaded their eyes. All of them sported drooping jaws. All except Talioth. His vicious glare brought a chuckle to Lia's lips.

An arrow pinged against the rock, the harmless shaft knocking against her head. The shock almost made her lose her grip. With her legs kicking through the air, she pulled up. Minuscule holds led to others. Her body ascended the aperture in the opening of the ceiling. Soon, her feet reached the rock, giving her a place to press them against. Progress came quicker. Another arrow from below whistled toward her. With the trickle of remaining origine rushing through her, she swung, dodging as the projectile missed. A few more moves up the rocky face brought her over the lip and out of the cave.

She rolled onto a snow-covered rock, back against the cold stone and face toward the waning sun. Her breath fogged in the air, mixing with the clouds in the blue sky. She took deep breaths, pushing air through her lungs, trying to slow her pulse.

Her limbs were free, without restraints. Nothing held her back. No one guarded her. And the origine—although faint and nearly used up—simmered in her. The barrier she had felt around the crystals was gone.

An angry voice shouted from somewhere below, "Stormbridge!"

Lia's mouth curled up at both ends, her broad grin so wide it hurt.

PART III

LAST STAND

40

BRAVIAN FIRE

A brisk wind blasted Raiyn when his horse topped the incline. The temperature had dropped steadily during the journey, despite the sun sitting high in the sky. They had left Daratill early in the morning, heading south, toward the foothills of the Korob Mountains where the Bravian Fire waited in hiding.

"There it is," Ryker called over his shoulder.

Raiyn craned his neck around Veron and Chelci and glimpsed stony ruins coming into view. Four square-shaped structures spread out in a semi-circle atop the rocky bald they climbed. Trees were scarce. Behind the buildings, the mountains rose sharply, turning to snow after what would only be a few more hours of travel.

Ryker stopped his horse and motioned for them all to dismount.

A groan turned Raiyn around. Brixton grimaced as he swung his leg over.

"Need a hand?" Raiyn jogged to him.

Brixton closed his eyes, shook his head, and lowered himself to the ground. "Argh!"

"How is it?"

Brixton pulled his cloak off his shoulder and looked at the site of his wound from the day before. A small dark spot marked his shirt.

"Not great. Should change the bandage soon." He flashed a pained smile and walked toward the others.

"What was this place?" Veron asked.

"It used to be an outpost," Ryker replied. "We'd bring squadrons to train in the mountains. We could house up to forty."

"Sure doesn't look like it anymore." Raiyn rested a hand against a partially standing stone wall.

Three of the buildings were destroyed. The roofs were gone, and rubble littered the ground. Black marks raked both the inside and outside of what remained of the walls. He slid his hand across the stone, noting a gritty residue that covered the surface.

"What did this?" he asked.

Ryker chuckled. "What do you think?" He waved the party toward the only building still standing. "Come and see."

Two guards in red-and-black uniforms were posted on either side of the entrance. They stood straighter the closer Ryker drew.

"At ease, men," the general said.

The guards' shoulders relaxed, but they remained in place.

"Is Niles here?"

A guard nodded. "In the shop, sir."

The hinges of the wooden door protested with a loud creak as Ryker opened it. The inside room was spacious. Five sets of bunks lined the far wall. A table and ten chairs filled the close half of the room, along with a countertop. Ryker crossed the wooden floorboards to where a large section of flooring pivoted up, revealing a hidden staircase that led underground.

"Down here."

A musty, acrid odor drifted up the stairs as Raiyn descended. The room below was dark. Two narrow windows centered on opposite walls, but the sunlight coming in struggled to light up the space.

"General," an aged voice greeted from the dark. "I wasn't expecting you."

"We had a recent development," Ryker said. "Niles, this is Veron, Chelci, Brixton, and Raiyn. This is Niles Fallreng, head chemist."

A wiry man stepped forward, catching the light from the window.

A wild mane of white hair bushed above his prominent forehead that protruded over wide-set eyes.

"It's good to meet you, Niles," Veron said with a nod.

An eager smile filled the chemist's face. "Are you here to see what it can do?"

"That," Ryker said, "and . . . they're here to take some."

Niles' eyebrows lifted.

"They represent the Shadow Knights from Feldor." Ryker pointed to Raiyn. "And this is Edmund Bale's heir."

The eyebrows moved even higher as a gasp escaped the white-haired man. "Bale's heir," he breathed.

A nervous flutter filled Raiyn's stomach. "I'm not here for the throne, but we do need the Fire."

"Terrenor is in danger," Veron said. "We need it to put down a threat that will soon reach your borders."

"King Darian is dead," Ryker said, "and his son Alvin has agreed to give it to them."

Niles paused as if mulling over the news. After a moment, he nodded, waved the group forward, and headed toward the wall. "We discovered it by accident, trying to create an elixir to extend life. The potassium sulfate and terrelium were stable, but when we added korron . . ." He chuckled. "My eyebrows have only just filled back in." He shook his left hand in the air. "This wasn't so lucky."

Seeing the limb for the first time, Raiyn winced. The man's smallest two fingers were missing, and the other three curled inward. The rest of the flesh looked black and crusty to just past his wrist.

"We named it Bravian Fire after the legend."

"Fire from stone," Veron breathed. "Is it true?"

"It's more like . . . fire *through* stone," Ryker said.

Three chests rested against the far wall. Niles stopped at the closest one. The clasp on the front fell. Setting his good arm and the mangled one against either side of the lid, he lifted. The top opened soundlessly.

Raiyn craned his neck over the man's shoulder but couldn't see anything inside the dark box. A sharp odor grew stronger.

"Do you have any light?" Brixton asked.

"No torches," Niles said. "No lanterns."

Ryker nodded. "It's too much of a risk. We learned the hard way. You know the husk of a building we passed a moment ago? We lost three good men that day."

A wave of nerves rushed through Raiyn.

Niles continued, "The insulated metal in these chests keep it protected when closed. But when it's open . . ." The chemist dipped a spoon into the box. His hand remained steady as he lifted it again. A rounded substance filled the spoon, too dark to see clearly. He brought a small bowl closer. With a slow tipping motion and a tight shake, some of the spoon's contents fell into the bowl.

"Here." The chemist extended the bowl toward Raiyn.

His hands shook as he lifted them. The bowl was cold and heavy. His fingers strained as they cupped the curved shape. "What is this? Iron?"

Niles nodded. "The only substance we've found that the powder doesn't stick to. Take it outside and we'll show you what it does."

Raiyn swallowed and pivoted toward the stairs. Ryker ascended first while the others gave Raiyn a wide berth.

"You want me to carry it?" Veron asked.

Raiyn shook his head without taking his eyes off the bowl. "I've got it." The narrow climb felt agonizingly long. The grit under his boots scraped with each step. Dots of sweat prickled on his forehead.

The light felt blinding when he arrived upstairs. The guards outside the front door leaned away when he passed. He followed Ryker to the farthest set of stone ruins and stepped through the crumbled doorway. Four stone walls remained partially standing, but much of the original structure had crumbled, burned, or simply disappeared.

With the sun shining, he got a better look at the contents of the bowl. The width of a thimble, the powdery substance was black and gray with speckles of red mixed in. The red sparkled as it caught the light. He shook it gently, causing the powder to shift inside the container.

"What causes the sparkle?" Raiyn asked.

"That would be the korron." Niles placed a wooden stool on the floor and pushed it against the ruins of a wall. "It dances in the sun and incinerates under flame. Beautiful but deadly."

"What does it do?" Veron asked.

"I'll show you." Niles pointed to a section of wall above the stool that remained intact. "Spread it on there."

Raiyn's eyebrows lifted. "Spread it?"

The chemist nodded. "Toss the powder on the wall."

"Is that safe?" Chelci asked.

"It needs fire to activate. Shaking won't ignite it."

Raiyn stepped closer to the wall and flung the contents. The powder leaped from the bowl. He expected it to bounce off the stone and fall to the ground, but the material clung to the rock like a lizard to a tree. A small portion landed on the stool. He looked in the bowl. *Empty.*

"Like I said, it doesn't stick to iron," Niles said.

Footsteps crunched, and Ryker approached with a lit candle. Raiyn's pulse spiked. He jumped back from the wall along with Veron and the others.

"It's all right," Ryker said. He extended the candle to Raiyn. "Light it. But once it catches, back up."

Raiyn took the candle. He stared at the flame but didn't move any closer. "Light it?"

"Yes. Hold the flame to the powder. When it flares, scoot back past the walls." Ryker motioned for the others to step outside of the structure.

Raiyn gulped and looked at the others.

"You want me to do it?" Veron extended his hand.

"No." Raiyn shook his head. "I can do it."

He padded closer, as if sneaking up on an animal in the woods. The black-and-gray powder continued to stick to the wall and the stool, with red specks shimmering. He extended the lone flame that danced in the light breeze. It hovered next to the powder. He angled his feet to run.

"Go ahead," Ryker encouraged.

He leaned closer. The flame licked the edge of the stone, touching the powder. He flinched, pulling the candle away. It hadn't caught yet. He stretched again, bringing the candle closer. Raiyn held his breath. His muscles flexed, taut and ready to spring.

Not yet.

Closer.

The flame surged, hissing as it leaped to the powder on the wall.

Raiyn jumped away. The candle extinguished in the flutter of movement. He backpedaled through the doorway until Chelci caught him.

The sizzling grew as the flame spread across the section of powder and then jumped to the top of the stool. Raiyn squinted, but the light wasn't as bright as he had expected.

"Is that it?" Brixton stepped forward until Ryker's arm stopped his progress. "I thought it would be . . . bigger."

"Just wait," the general said. "This is phase one."

Raiyn leaned his head in, squinting. The light simmered, sparking when it burned the red specks.

"It's getting louder," Chelci said.

She's right, Raiyn thought. The hiss intensified.

"Step back a bit more." Ryker placed his fingers in his ears. "And cover your ears."

Without taking his eyes off the fire, Raiyn took another step away. "Our ears? What should we expect—"

The hiss of flame exploded into a deafening roar. The fire surged to life, shooting into the room's open space. Raiyn stepped farther away. He covered his ears and closed his eyes. He expected heat to gush through the crumbled doorway, but the temperature didn't change. Shading his face with his arm, he forced himself to look.

Blue flames blasted in each direction, burning bright and fierce. He squinted to keep from blinding his eyes. A glance around the side of the wall showed a blaze tearing through the stones to burst out the opposite side.

"How long does it last?" His shouted words didn't even reach his own ears.

The sapphire flames continued, roaring their thunderous racket. The noise was unbearable. He ducked again and took another step backward. As suddenly as it had erupted, the tumult subsided. The fire receded, turning the flickering flames into a blueish plume of smoke that puffed through the ruins.

Raiyn removed his protecting hands and straightened. His ears rang. His vision spun from the disorienting assault to his senses.

"Incredible," Veron breathed.

"And that was phase two," Ryker said.

Raiyn turned to Niles. "Is it safe?"

Sporting the proud smile of a father showing off their child, the chemist nodded. "Go ahead."

Raiyn's hand fanned the smoke. He peered into the blue haze, curious about the aftermath of the fire. The breeze picked up wisps of the smoke, curling it and dragging it away as it rose above the crumbled walls. He stared at the site where he had lit the powder, and his jaw fell.

In a wide circle around the focal point, the stone was gone. Incinerated. At the edges, crumbled black debris was all that remained of the wall. Above the burned spot, an arch of blackened stone held, but only for a moment. When it collapsed, the charred remains disintegrated, falling to the ground and tumbling into chunks. The wooden stool splintered under falling lumps of stone.

Raiyn cocked his head. *Interesting.* The light-brown wood of the three-legged seat had kept its color rather than turning into a blackened lump.

"It burned *through* the stone, but not the wood?" Brixton asked.

"The flames are unique," Niles said. "They will *travel* through wood but won't burn it."

Raiyn frowned. "But I didn't feel any heat."

"That's right. It doesn't consume fuel like regular fire. The powder itself *is* the fuel, and there's no heat to ignite wood."

"So the flames don't spread," Veron said.

"Correct. It's not really a flame, but that's the best word we have to describe it. It will break down most substances, but steel and wood are impervious to its chemical makeup. Stone clearly is not, as well as"—He wiggled his blackened mess of a hand—"flesh. Iron is the only material we've found that can shield the flames."

"That's why you keep it in an iron chest," Veron stated.

"That and we don't want it leaving a powder residue on the surface." The man pointed to the new hole in the wall. "We've tested the burn with walls up to eight times that thick."

Veron raised an eyebrow. "And it still burns through?"

The chemist nodded.

"A thicker coating helps," Ryker said, "but the result is the same. Utter desolation."

Chelci turned to Veron. "Do you think this will work?"

Lines dug into his forehead. "It depends on how we use it."

"We could blast a hole in the city walls or even the castle," Brixton said.

"That won't stop Danik's men, though," Veron said.

"Have you experimented with projectiles?" Chelci asked.

"Yes," Ryker answered. "We pack clay around a small amount of powder and run a wick to the center. It can be quite effective."

"Attacking in an open space will do nothing. They can run or leap away." All heads turned to Raiyn. "We need to trap them."

"King Bale's son, huh?" Niles said.

Raiyn's jaw formed a grim line. He swallowed, then nodded.

"Bravian Fire is dangerous and is nothing to be taken lightly. I trust you to be its guardian, Raiyn Bale." The chemist lowered his head and lifted a leather necklace from around his neck. A metal sphere dangled at the end, connected to the necklace. "This contains the same amount of powder as you just used on that wall. I keep it with me always to remind me of the substance's peril."

Raiyn accepted the necklace as the man extended it toward him. "Is it safe to wear?"

The man nodded. "It's iron. It's shielded."

Raiyn chuckled.

Niles didn't break his serious expression. "Never forget what you're dealing with."

"I won't." He looped the strand over his neck and tucked the sphere under his tunic.

Veron interrupted the silence. "We need to leave soon."

"Where do we head?" Brixton asked. "Felting?"

"If we're going to set a trap, we need to bring them to us, and we need someone we can trust." Raiyn turned to Veron. "Let's go to Karondir."

41

UNKNOWN RECEPTION

The massive walls of Karondir towered over the surrounding plain. Veron had approached the city many times before, but never with the nerves he felt at the moment. Baron Devenish had always supported the Knights and owed Veron in particular for multiple occasions where he had helped their city. But loyalty often followed opportunity. Allegiance could be swayed.

"And you're sure Bilton said Devenish was against Danik?" Chelci asked, giving voice to the same doubt rolling through Veron's head. Her horse walked next to his, hooves clopping on the road.

"That's what he said," Veron replied. "But it's the type of thing he wouldn't know for sure."

"It would stink if he turned Karondir's army on us."

"I've known Rodrick for seventeen years, and I feel pretty confident in his support. Plus, we don't have any other good options."

Veron pushed on his saddle horn to turn his body. Raiyn and Brixton followed behind on their horses. "How's that necklace?"

Raiyn's eyes flicked up from staring at the horse's mane. His hand moved to his chest and pressed against his shirt where the sphere would be. "It's fine. I try not to make any sudden movements."

Brixton spoke up, "If it takes fire to set it off, it should be safe."

A nervous laugh bubbled up from Raiyn. "Say that when you're the one wearing it."

"You don't *have* to wear the necklace," Veron said. "We could put it in the chest."

The metal chest strapped behind his saddle caught his eye. Bronze clasps held the container shut tight, keeping the incendiary contents safe. Even so, the potential power and destruction of the box filled him with terror.

"I know," Raiyn said. "I appreciate the reminder, though."

The road grew crowded the closer they got to the gates. Men, women, and children headed in the same direction, mostly on foot, but some riding in wagons. Each person who turned in Veron's direction gave him pause, as if they were about to call out who the travelers were and raise an alarm.

Keeping their heads down, they dismounted and entered the city gates without incident.

"Sure is crowded." Brixton held onto his horse's reins.

"It's Marketday," Chelci said. "It's always busy the day after the shops are closed."

Veron's eyes roamed the main street. "I've never been here when it was *this* bustling, though."

They passed by shops and stalls. Vendors hawked food and wares, calling out to get their attention. Veron continued forward. A crowd gathered in the square before the central keep. A man stood at the base of the main steps, speaking to the people. At the top of the steps, guards at attention flanked the closed metal doors to the keep.

"This is more than Marketday masses," Chelci said. "I wonder who this is." They stepped closer to the crowd.

". . . and that's what they do," the man on the steps projected. "They protect you. Not just Felting, but all of Feldor. King Danik and his knights have your best interest at the heart of everything they do."

The man wore a pressed blue-and-gray army uniform with a sword hanging on his hip.

Chelci leaned toward the group. "Do you know him?"

"He has a captain's insignia," Veron said, "but I don't recognize him."

"In fact . . ." The captain motioned to a half-dozen people at the side of the crowd. They stood at the rear of a wagon, unloading stacks of baskets and burlap sacks. "Danik sent me to bring you gifts: bread, cheese, and smoked meat."

The crowd burst into a murmur of excitement. They surged as one toward the wagon.

Veron motioned the others forward. "Come on. We can walk around this guy and talk with the guards at the doors." They resumed walking across the square.

The captain raised his hands toward the crowd and called out. "There is plenty to go around. Please, no pushing."

From the outskirts of the square, more people abandoned the other vendors and filtered toward the wagon.

Veron tied his horse to the post. "Raiyn, can you watch our gear—especially the box?"

Raiyn looped his reins around the wooden railing. "Sure. I'll stay here."

"Should we bring these?" Chelci rested her hand on the sword tucked in her saddlebags.

Veron looked toward the keep, then panned across the crowd. After a pause, he shook his head. "Best to avoid the attention." He lifted his hood to shade his face. "Let's go." With Chelci and Brixton following, he climbed the edge of the steps, giving a wide berth to the captain and his crowd.

"Did King Darcius pass out food in the square?" the captain called.

A pensive pause filled the people.

"Did the *Shadow Knights* bring you meat?"

Veron's feet stopped. Although angled toward the doors, his eyes flicked to the edge of his hood.

The speaker kept his attention on the people. Mutters rumbled through the gathering.

"No! Of course, they didn't," the captain said. "They were too busy looking after themselves."

Chelci touched Veron on the arm. "Easy," she whispered.

Veron looked at where her fingers rested. His arm and fist clenched, straining his muscles.

"Ignore him and keep going," she added.

He forced his feet onward. The guards at the doors angled toward them.

"They were found to be traitors. They colluded with foreign powers to put Edmund Bale's son on the throne! Corrupted by their power, the knights thought they were above the law. They forgot what matters is the people. Today, the Knights of Power are more powerful than the Shadow Knights ever were. And they know what it means to care for the people of Feldor."

Veron's blood boiled.

"State your business," a guard at the doors to the central keep ordered.

"Uh . . ." Veron faced the guards, but his mind was on the man at the bottom of the steps.

"I was there," the captain shouted. "I *saw* Bale's heir in Felting."

Veron spun, his breath held. Raiyn rested a hand on his horse, but his body stood rigid.

"I saw the rogue shadow knights who tried to put him in power. They betrayed us."

"He's seen you," Chelci whispered.

"What business do you have at the keep?" the guard restated.

"We should get out of here," Veron whispered to Chelci and Brixton, ignoring the guard and feeling suddenly exposed on the steps. "All of us should get out of sight."

Raiyn seemed to have the same idea. He moved around the horse, where its body would shield him from view.

"The Knights of Power will not betray you. King Danik will not —" The captain paused, staring at Raiyn, who had not yet made it around his horse. "He, uh . . ."

The crowd stared.

"That's him." The captain's accusation was barely audible.

Veron's stomach dropped.

"That's-that's the Norshewan. It's Bale's heir."

A rumble grew.

The captain pointed. "Get him! Guards, seize that man!"

Raiyn gave up any pretense of secrecy. He checked in both directions, then ran toward an open part of the square. Guards came from nowhere and caused him to halt.

"No!" Veron shouted. He stood on the last steps and held up his hands to the captain. "Stop this!"

Raiyn stopped moving. The guards held their ground. The crowd grew quiet, and the captain turned his way.

"Who are you?"

"Should we run?" Chelci asked at his back. "We can clear the way for Brixton and flee the city."

Veron swallowed a heavy lump in his throat. "No. We don't run." He gripped the edges of his hood and paused. His heart pounded. The captain and the people in the square all stared at him. Exhaling a slow breath, he lowered his hood. Chelci and Brixton followed suit.

The captain gasped. His eyes seemed to grow larger. "You!"

"Yes, me." Veron turned to the crowd. "I am Veron Stormbridge." His firm words echoed across the square.

The captain took a half step backward. His hand moved to the hilt of his sword, but he resisted pulling it.

"He's right." Veron gestured toward Raiyn. "This is Edmund Bale's last surviving heir."

Gasps filled the crowd.

"But that is where the truth in this man's words ends."

"Guards . . ." The captain's command never completed its thought.

"The Shadow Knights did not kill King Darcius. Your new king, Danik, spread that lie. In truth . . . Danik was the one who killed Darcius. I was there when it happened. I saw him slit the king's throat."

The people in the audience looked at each other and muttered.

"And we have *not* been trying to put Raiyn Bale on the throne. Raiyn himself is actually a shadow knight."

Raiyn stood taller, with a hint of a proud smile.

"He trained alongside me and even Danik Bannister before we kicked Danik out for not living up to the standards of the group. Raiyn has no interest in ruling and even declined the throne of Norshewa which his blood gives him the right to. We are not the people you should be worried about. Danik and his men killed most of the shadow knights in an act of selfish aggression. They took the throne of Feldor in a bloody coup, and now they intend to march on our neighbors to take over the other kingdoms of Terrenor."

"You're lying!" The captain shook a wavering hand at him. "There's no proof of anything you say."

"There was no proof of anything Danik said, yet you believed him."

A fresh voice rose above the others. "I never thought I would again see the day that Veron Stormbridge showed up at my door."

Veron spun toward the doors of the keep. Baron Devenish stood near the top of the steps, his back bowed and wispy white hair combed. Next to him, men in uniform with crossbows and swords spread out in a line.

"Baron," Veron greeted. His muscles were tense, ready to respond to whatever came next.

Devenish stepped forward, descending a step at a time, looking strong despite his age. He pointed a finger and wagged it. "When this condemned 'Traitor of Feldor' speaks . . . we all must be careful."

Veron's gut twisted until he caught a quick wink from the baron that no one else would be able to see.

Devenish's face remained stoic, but a playful look danced in his eyes. "You must come with us," he ordered. "We will question you inside the keep."

"We have horses and cargo," Veron said. "It's important they remain with us."

"We will bring them." Devenish pointed to a group of men who jumped into action.

Veron nodded to Chelci and Brixton, then headed toward the metal doors of the central keep.

"Sir," the captain stepped closer to the baron. "Would you permit me to join you? It would be helpful to hear what they say firsthand."

"That won't be necessary, captain," Devenish said. "We will handle it from here."

The captain stepped again. "In that case, we will inform Felting of this discovery at once."

The baron's eyes flicked to Veron's for a split second. He shook his head. "There's no need, captain. I will send a bird to the capital once we find out the purpose behind their arrival here. Thank you for the food you've brought our people and for your presence. You may go."

The captain frowned but stepped back and nodded.

Inside the keep, Devenish continued on. He passed tables filled with gawking men and women, guards, and servants. Ascending a flight of stairs, he didn't stop until he arrived at a large meeting room. A long, rectangular table filled the space while oversized windows let in light and gave the room a cheery feeling.

The baron looked at the five guards. "You all can leave us."

The men's faces paled. "Sir," one said. "You can't possibly—"

"Leave us!" he repeated.

The guards jumped and then scurried out the door, closing it behind them.

A broad grin grew on the baron's face. He closed in on Veron and wrapped him in his aging arms.

Veron relaxed. He returned the gesture, embracing the baron.

"The word spread that you all were killed," Devenish said. "I never believed it for a second."

When Veron pulled away, sorrow filtered through him at the memory of the others. "Most of us were. Chelci, Raiyn, and I are the only knights left. There aren't many places we can go. Thank you for taking us in."

The baron's warm smile put him at ease. "You're always welcome here. Now, how can I help you?"

42

A NEW TRAP

The room was silent as the servants entered. They carried platters of roasted meat, vegetables, and baskets with warm bread. After several days on the road, Veron's stomach growled. Raiyn seemed to have the same idea and grabbed a skewer of beef before they had even set the platter down. Veron started with a roll.

Lord Boyd had arrived just before the servants. He leaned on the table with his jaw hanging loose.

"That will be all." The baron shooed the servants toward the door. "Thank you."

When the door clicked, Boyd snapped to life. "Bravian Fire? Are you serious?"

Veron nodded. "We came from Daratill." He turned toward the end table that sat against the wall. The metal chest with brass clasps and heavy hinges rested atop it.

The Lord of Defense shook his head. "I can't believe it." Wrinkles formed on his brow. "Should we, uh, have it in here with us?"

Brixton blew a soft laugh from his nose. "Probably not."

"We need to keep an eye on it, though," Veron said. "We can't leave it in the stables."

"It should be safe when the chest is closed," Raiyn added. "Still, don't let any flames near it."

"Let me get this straight." Baron Devenish leaned back in his chair. "Danik murdered the king to take the throne . . ."

"We've always assumed that," Boyd added.

The baron continued, "The Knights of Power have abilities more powerful than the Shadow Knights and can even take away what you *can* do with their special necklaces. And now they want to kill the rest of you and conquer Terrenor."

"That's about it," Chelci confirmed.

The baron's lips formed a grim line. "No matter what I insisted, that captain outside has probably already sent word to Felting. How quickly could they get here?"

Veron looked at Chelci with a pinched brow. "If they change out their horses and ride them into the ground . . . possibly by tomorrow evening."

"How many do you think will come?" Raiyn asked.

"Knowing we're all here . . . I'd guess all of them."

"You need to flee," Devenish said. "As much as I welcome you here and am glad to see you, we cannot protect you."

"We can't run," Veron said. "We must face them at some point, and now we have a weapon they're not prepared for. What we need is to draw them to us and be ready."

"You want them to come to you?"

"Yes."

"And you want to use Karondir?"

Veron nodded. His stomach turned. "I know it puts your city in great danger, and I'm sorry for that. But this is our only chance."

The baron looked at his lord of defense. Both men's faces held solemn gazes. "Of course. What do you need from us?"

Veron exhaled and allowed a weak smile. "Thank you. What we need is a place to set a trap."

"What sort of place?"

Veron turned his palms up and looked at Chelci. "What do we think?"

"Anything too open would allow them to rush out of danger before phase two ignites," Chelci said. "I think our best bet is a pit. Trap them, then rain down flaming debris."

"Arrows could work," Brixton said. "Coat the tips with powder and light before we shoot. Or maybe those projectiles Ryker mentioned."

"They could have over twenty men," Veron said. "A pit would be great, but I'm not sure we could get them all inside."

"How about a ravine," Raiyn suggested. "Lead them through until they have nowhere to go. Then block the ends." He turned to the baron. "Can you think of one?"

"Would an alley in the city work?" Devenish asked.

"Maybe," Veron answered, "but it'd need to be tall so they couldn't jump out."

"How tall?"

Veron glanced out the window and took in the buildings around the keep. "Five or six stories, at least. But there couldn't be windows either. With their reflexes, they'd be able to burst through them and escape."

"Hmm," the baron turned to Boyd.

"That would be tough to find," the lord said.

"Also," Veron frowned. "I'm not sure about raining projectiles down on them. They'd be able to knock them away or even throw them back at us unless we got the timing perfect."

"I didn't think about that," Chelci said.

"What if we lined the ground with the powder?" Brixton asked. "Funnel them to stand where we want, then light the powder they're standing on?"

"No." Chelci shook her head. "Phase one would give it away. As soon as it simmers, they would use the devion to blast out of there."

The group grew quiet. Veron racked his brain, but no other ideas came to mind.

"What about a meeting room?" Raiyn asked.

The baron motioned to the chamber. "You mean like this?"

Raiyn shook his head. "The room's good, but the upper levels would collapse on it when the walls burn out. What's on the top floor?"

"The top of the keep? It's—" The crease in the baron's forehead smoothed out. "There's a room large enough for fifty people."

"And it's a ten-story drop, so they wouldn't jump out of the windows. That could work. If we could get them all in the room—" Raiyn frowned. "They could still see the primer light, though. They'd have time to back out the way they came in. Even if we tried to barricade it, the devion could—"

An idea came to Veron. A grin formed on his face, stopping the younger knight mid-sentence. "They don't have to see it." He pointed up.

Raiyn lifted his chin. The floorboards of the next level formed a ceiling. "I don't get it. We hide in the ceiling and drop it on them?"

"No, we light the floor underneath them."

Raiyn's mouth curled up at the corners. "Yes, that could work."

The baron raised a hand. "And that won't . . . burn down the keep?"

Veron shook his head. "The fire doesn't spread and wood doesn't burn at all. You will lose the walls and probably the roof, though."

The baron nodded. "We can deal with that." His chair scraped as he pushed it back. "Another thing that could help . . . I didn't want to bring this into the mix, but it may be necessary." He walked around the table toward the door.

"What is it?" Veron asked.

"Information." The baron poked his head out the door and spoke to someone in the hall.

Brixton leaned toward Veron. "Maybe he's got one of those huge glowing crystal things that you can suck the juice out of."

Veron chuckled.

"How do we get them into the room?" Chelci asked.

"Ask nicely?" Brixton replied. "Invite them to a party?"

"We use bait," Raiyn said with a grave finality. "Me."

Veron's stomach twisted. "No. Absolutely not."

"Why not? We don't need all of us. I lead them into the room, then you set off the trap."

"How do you get out?" Chelci asked.

"We'll figure something out."

Veron shook his head. "It's too dangerous."

"All of this is dangerous," Raiyn said. "We can't avoid that."

"If anything, it should be me."

"Why? You have a wife. We know they want me."

A tense pause filled the room. The baron clearing his throat at the door interrupted it. "Um, I hope this can be useful." Devenish's hands fidgeted, folded in front of his body. "I, uh . . . Have someone who might give insight." He glanced over his shoulder, then pushed the door open farther.

Escorted by two guards, a young man stepped through the doorway with his head bowed. He wore a sharp-looking blue doublet with silver accents down the front. His leggings ended at leather boots that would appear expensive except for the scuffs marking them. Smudges and rips decorated the rest of his clothing. His head of dirty-blond hair lifted.

Veron's heart stopped. He felt like someone had kicked the wind out of him.

Blue eyes stared back, and a black stain marked the young man's neck.

"Danik!" Veron growled. He jumped to his feet, fueled by a rush of origine. He grasped at his hip for the weapon that had been left with the horses. Raiyn and Chelci followed with the same motions.

Danik held up his hands and took a step backward. "Whoa! Hold on."

If Veron had worn his sword, he would have already attempted to thrust it through his chest. A wave of terror gripped him. He spun, searching for any sign of the rest of the Knights of Power.

"Hear him out," Baron Devenish said.

"What?" Veron's pulse thudded in his ears. "You're working with him?"

"Veron," Chelci's calm voice gave him pause. "Look." She pointed at his hand.

Peeking out the end of Danik's sleeve, a metal band circled his wrist. *What in the*—? The leather necklace caught his eye. A red crystal dangled from the end—a *dull* red crystal.

"What is this?"

"He came to me this morning," the baron said. "Alone and unarmed. You should listen to him."

Danik's eyes held a sorrow Veron did not expect. His forehead creased and his arms lowered. "Veron . . ."

"No! I won't listen." His hands clenched, nails digging into his palms. "You killed them! Gavin, Bridgette, the others."

"I'm sorry," Danik said. "Honestly, I didn't mean to kill them. That was all Nicolar. Still, I've done so much. I messed up in every way." Tears brimmed in the young man's eyes. "I can't believe—" He held his finger under his nose and quieted.

"You get no sympathy from us." Veron scanned the room again. "Why are you here?"

"I want to help."

"Liar!" Chelci shouted.

"I swear! Nicolar and the others turned on me. They're out of control. I didn't have anywhere to go. You all were the only home I ever knew. I know I betrayed you, but I don't know what else to do. We'd heard you were headed to Norshewa. I wagered you'd come back this way."

No one replied. Danik looked from person to person, his breaths quick.

The baron said, "We received a messenger bird two days ago confirming Danik was out and Nicolar had taken the crown. Most people don't know it yet. Not even the army, as you heard a moment ago."

"I want to help," Danik said. "I messed up, and I want to help bring Nicolar and the others down. They want to kill you."

"Nothing we're not used to," Veron said.

"Nicolar's initiating a new law called the Purification Act."

Veron frowned. He looked at Chelci who seemed equally confused.

"It targets people who are a drain on others: the poor, the sick, the old—anyone who can't contribute to society. Nicolar's been pushing for it for a while, but I held him off." He glanced between Veron and Chelci. "He's going to kill them."

Chelci inhaled a sharp breath.

"I know it's impossible to trust me after what all I've done to you, but . . . I have nothing left, and I'm here to help. I let Devenish put this on me"—he shook his wrist with the metal band—"and I'm unarmed."

"You're not unarmed." Veron pointed at the necklace. "You wear that and you pretend we should trust you."

"Here." Danik lifted the necklace over his head and held it out. "Take it. Destroy it. Whatever you like."

Veron lifted his chin and narrowed his eyes. After a pause, he stepped forward. With tense muscles, he grasped the leather and lifted it off Danik's hand. Conflicting emotions swirled in him. He stepped back and stared into the dull red facets of the crystal.

"What do we do with it?" Raiyn asked.

Veron clenched his teeth and twirled the necklace. The crystal spun in a loop, then hurtled toward the ground. When it hit the floor, it thunked against the wood, but the gem remained intact.

Is this a trap? Veron wondered. *It has to be.*

Brixton cleared his throat. "Veron. I can never thank you enough for the grace you showed me after I messed up. If he really wants to help, I imagine we could use whatever information he could give."

Chelci bit her lip and stared at Veron. "What do you think?"

Anger, hurt, and hope warred inside. *Use him? Ignore him? Kill him?*

"What do you want me to do with him?" Devenish asked. The guards on either side of Danik pressed closer.

Veron stepped toward Danik, narrowing his eyes. As much as it pained him, he did the only thing he could stomach. "Take this traitor away. Do whatever you want with him. We can't trust anything he has to say."

43

RUSHED PREPARATIONS

Raiyn braced his hand against the wall while he balanced on the ladder. His bowl of powder rested precariously on the top rung. He dipped the brush. Red particles shimmered as he worked the bristles through. When he pulled it out, the powder stuck to the brush.

Craning his neck, he stretched his arm as far as it would reach and swept against the ceiling. Black-and-gray powder stuck to the wooden boards, thicker than the test he observed in Norshewa. He worked the brush, dabbing to spread the volatile substance across the area he could reach, careful to keep from getting any on him or his clothes. They had put out any lanterns in the area, but the sun through the window was enough to light the room.

"That looks good." Brixton guarded the metal chest at the base of the ladder. "I think you've covered it all."

Raiyn glanced across the ceiling. A shimmer of red speckled through the dark powder that coated it. "Good, because my muscles are killing me." He stretched his arm, groaning at the soreness. Balancing the brush on the bowl, he stepped down the ladder.

"Should we check on the others?" Raiyn asked.

Brixton nodded.

Raiyn grabbed one handle on the metal chest, and Brixton held the other. Stepping together in short, measured strides, they left the room. Raiyn led toward the main staircase. He nodded at the posted pair of guards before heading up. His steps slowed, giving Brixton the chance to match his pace on the stairs. They moved slowly, rounding the landing and heading up to the next floor, where they passed another two guards.

Veron and Chelci stood in the hallway, painting powder against the wall on their right. The opposite wall held a tapestry and a bookshelf. Veron turned his head. "You finished?"

"All done," Raiyn replied.

"And it stuck to the ceiling?"

"Just like paint."

"We're about finished here." Veron nodded toward the corner. "Chelci already finished up her area and is helping me."

After setting the chest down, Raiyn went to inspect. The wall around the corner was shorter and contained a layer of black-and-gray powder with red speckles. He returned to the group. "Looks good."

Veron backed up from the wall and wiped his sleeve across his glistening forehead. "That's about it." He and Chelci left the brushes leaning against the wall and returned the bowls to the iron chest.

"Nice timing, too," Raiyn said. "It's been a day and a half. Do you think Nicolar will get here this quickly?"

"Tomorrow would be more likely, but it's possible, depending on how motivated they are to kill us."

"I hope your box is ready," Chelci said.

Raiyn's stomach twisted. *Me too.*

Veron called to the guards at the top of the stairs, "Could you see if the baron is free?"

The men snapped to attention. One spun and hurried down the steps, his boots thumping against the stone.

Veron turned back to Raiyn, Chelci, and Brixton. "We should check in with him and see where we are."

While waiting for the baron, Raiyn walked to the nearest window. The sun hung low in the sky, spreading an orange light over the roofs of the city. From the top of the keep, he had a clear view of the trees and fields outside the city wall. The hard-packed dirt road ran south, disappearing around a bend.

The Straith Mountains loomed to his left. Snow-capped peaks rose like towers from the river valley Karondir occupied. His heart ached. *Lia.* The image of her crushed by falling stones filled him with sorrow. *I wonder what we could have had if she had lived?*

Veron stepped beside him. "What's on your mind?" His face contained a concerned pinch of skin between his brows. His eyes held a genuine interest.

"Just thinking about Lia." Saying her name aloud tugged harder at Raiyn's heart. "She wasn't like anyone I'd ever met. You and Chelci did a good job raising her."

Shimmers formed at the corner of Veron's eyes. "Thank you." His voice cracked. "It wasn't always easy, but I'm proud of her. I'm especially thankful for these last few weeks. Even though the circumstances have been difficult, the time with her meant a lot. It's like she was a different person." He wiped at his eyes and sniffed. "It sure would have been nice to have her help here."

Footsteps on the stairs turned their attention as Baron Devenish arrived. Two guards with him carried three unlit lanterns.

"Any word?" Veron asked.

Devenish shook his head. "Nothing yet."

"How are the preparations?"

"Is the box ready?" Raiyn asked, a sudden jolt of nerves flaring.

Half a smile pulled at the baron's face. "They're finishing it now. I instructed them to bring it up as soon as it's ready."

"Let's hope we get it before they show," Veron said.

"We will." Raiyn's words sounded more confident than he felt. "Do you mind if we talk through the plan again?"

The others nodded.

Raiyn pointed toward the stairs and looked at the baron. "You'll be at the entrance to the keep."

Devenish nodded.

"The Knights of Power will be looking for us."

"I'll tell them we're keeping you up here and will bring them up myself," the baron said. "I'll let them in this room—"

"Where I'll be waiting," Raiyn interrupted.

He crossed the hall and pushed open the double doors. His throat tightened upon entry. He imagined the Bravian Fire lining the backside of the walls and the floor, out of sight but able to be ignited at any moment. Two lanterns lit the room, the flames turned low as a precaution despite the walls of stone separating them from the Fire waiting to ignite.

"We'll set the box by that end, where we left a blank area without powder on the ceiling.

"I'll make sure they all enter, then I'll tell them to wait while I bring you others." Devenish pointed at Veron, Chelci, and Brixton.

"When the baron leaves and the doors are closed, I'll signal with a shout. Brixton, you be ready down below. Chelci and Veron, you both take your walls. Everyone light on a three count after the signal."

Veron pointed at Raiyn. "Then you close the lid and pull it tight. The rest of us run for the stairwell. We'll return as soon as the flames are out."

Raiyn's heart pounded. The plan made sense but contained holes.

"What if they kill you?" Chelci asked.

The question jarred Raiyn. "In the room?"

"Yeah. What if they don't wait for the rest of us?"

"I'll look tied up. They won't think I'm a threat. And if they start to get suspicious—if something goes wrong, I'll go ahead and give the call."

"Are you—" The baron paused with his mouth pursed. "—interested in asking Danik if he has any ideas?"

"No," Veron said. "Absolutely not."

The silence that followed sat heavily in the room. Chelci's eyes flicked toward Raiyn, then to Brixton.

Raiyn shrugged in slow motion. "If he's restrained . . . ?"

"I don't want him around." Veron walked to the window, showing his back.

Chelci's forehead pinched as she followed her husband. Her whispered words carried across the room. "Veron . . . it might benefit us to speak with him."

His shoulder flinched.

"If he really got kicked out, and if he wants to make amends—"

"I don't want him to make amends." Veron's words strained with emotion. "I don't want him feeling better about his mistakes."

"I don't either, but . . . we could use any advantage we could get."

Veron's shoulders rose and fell with his breaths.

Raiyn swallowed his nerves. "I'm with Chelci on this one. It wouldn't hurt to talk."

Veron nodded.

Raiyn turned to the baron. "Can you have him brought up?"

Devenish called out orders to his guards, who hurried down the stairs in response.

Veron left the window to rejoin the others. "We should be careful what we share, though. I'm still not convinced that this isn't a trick—getting information to turn against us."

"It seems possible," Raiyn said, "but . . . if he had wanted to kill us, I don't think he would have turned himself in or handed over his crystal."

"Good tactics for earning our trust."

"But he could have blocked the origine with the crystal, then killed us all in a matter of seconds, right?"

"Right," Chelci confirmed after a drawn-out pause.

"Still," Veron said, "we should be careful."

Laboring steps and grunts sounded from outside the door. The baron stepped toward the doorway. "I expect that should be . . . ah, yes. In here!"

Six men entered through the open double doors carrying a large metal box. Sweat dripped from their red faces. The muscles in their forearms strained. The rectangular object looked like a coffin. The gray sides contained hammered dents, as if they'd constructed the box in a hurry. Raiyn's stomach twisted at the sight.

He pointed toward the far wall. "Over in that corner."

The men crossed the room, panting and grunting. A deep *clunk* filled the room, shaking the floor as they set it down.

"It's all steel?" Raiyn asked.

The largest of the men stepped forward. A thick brown beard covered his mouth, falling well past his chin. His sleeveless tunic showed off the sweat and grime covering his bulging arms. "Yes. I'm not happy with the finish though. I'd love a couple more days to smooth it out, but—"

"But we don't have that time," the baron finished.

Raiyn ran his hand along the lid. The surface slid beneath his fingers. "It's perfect," he said. "Thank you for rushing it."

With Veron's help, he lifted the lid. The hinges were silent as the heavy top pivoted open. The harsh, steel interior sent a wave of anxiety through him. *I'm going to trap myself inside this while the room explodes in flames? What am I thinking?*

A metal handle caught his eye. He bent forward to wrap his hand around it.

"As requested," the bearded man said. "When the lid is closed, if you turn that handle, it will lock it so tight a rydannor couldn't bust it open."

Raiyn stepped inside the box, then crouched, estimating the width and height. "This should work."

More footsteps arrived up the stairs. Through the door, Danik's shaggy blond hair came into view. Raiyn swallowed a lump in his throat.

"Thank you," the baron said to the bearded man and the others who brought up the iron box. "We appreciate the fast work."

The men stretched their necks and arms as they exited the room, trading places with Danik and his two guards.

Danik stopped in front of Veron. His eyebrows lifted while his face contained a glimmer of hope. "How can I help?"

Veron flinched. His hand balled into a fist at his side. His clenched jaw grew sharper as his hand reddened. He looked ready to explode. "I can't do it," he said, snapping the tension in the room. He threw up his hands and turned away.

Danik's face fell.

Raiyn cleared his throat and stepped forward. "We were hoping for, uh—" He glanced at Chelci, who gave an encouraging nod. "For any information you may have about your crew."

"What do you want to know?"

The readied willingness to help jarred him. He steadied his nerves with a breath, then met Danik's eyes. "We need to know everything. What are their goals? Who is in charge? How are they organized? And most importantly . . . what are their weaknesses?"

"It's difficult to say," Danik replied. "I'm not there."

"You say you want to help," Raiyn challenged. "This is your chance. Tell us anything."

Danik dropped his gaze to the floor, then nodded.

Veron turned back. He made no move to speak, but his head angled forward as if he didn't want to miss anything.

"Nicolar will be in charge," Danik said. "The others were loyal to him before I met them. He's shrewd and ruthless, and his grasp of the devion is strong. The rest of the recent recruits are questionable and newer in their skills. If you take out Nicolar, Cedric, Broderick, and Alton, the others could give up."

"That's good to know," Chelci said.

"Their weaknesses . . . " Danik tilted his head as if thinking. "Metal, of course. If you can get something around them, you'll be set. Without the devion, they're nothing—undisciplined and lazy. Maybe you could attack with metal bolos?" He raised his eyebrows. No one responded.

"What else?" Impatience laced Veron's question.

"Their necklaces." Danik moved to grab the one that used to hang around his own neck and startled when he realized it wasn't there. "That will be their primary attack plan. They'll come in with these blazing, trusting on the power of the devion to overpower you. If you want to have a chance, you need to take these out—all of them."

"Anything else?" Chelci prompted.

Danik frowned then shook his head after a moment.

"What about their goal?" Veron asked.

Danik shrank back. "You're their only threat. Once you're gone, there will be nothing to stop them. Their goal is to kill you."

"That was *your* goal," Veron growled.

Danik took a step back and raised his palms. "It *was*, and I'm sorry. I—I don't want it anymore."

"After you lost your fighters. Convenient."

"It's not convenient, but it helped me see what a fool I'd been. The devion is a death sentence."

Raiyn jerked to attention. "What do you mean?"

"The power is driven by selfish ambition, and once you let it in, it takes over your life. I want to give it up. I want to go back to the origine, but—" He sighed. "You can't separate yourself from the devion without sacrificing your body. I feel it already. Every day I grow weaker, and before long, without giving in to its pull, I'll die."

"I'm tired of listening to this," Veron called to the guards, "Take him away."

"Wait," Raiyn held up a hand. He stepped toward Danik. "Is there anything else? Anything you can think of that could help us?"

Danik's brows pinched together as if deep in thought. He shook his head again. "Nothing I can think of." His eyes flickered with fresh interest. "Do you have a plan? Are you hoping to trap them here?"

No one answered.

"If you tell me what you're doing, I could help you think about what might work. Or . . . if they arrive, I can help fight them."

"No," Veron said. "Absolutely not."

Rapid footsteps echoing in the hall stopped him. Everyone spun as Lord Boyd burst into the room, panting and wheezing.

"What is it?" the baron asked.

Boyd held a hand against the wall as he bent over, sucking in air. "The gates. They're here."

"Who's here?"

Raiyn's stomach churned. He held his breath while the lord took another deep breath.

"Nicolar," Boyd managed. "The Knights of Power."

Danik stepped toward him. "How many?"

Boyd straightened, his breathing still painful. "We counted twenty-three."

"That's all of them," Danik breathed.

"And they're heading for the keep."

44

FACING THE ENEMY

Aweight settled in Raiyn's gut. "This is our chance."

"Is everyone ready?" Veron asked.

"Ready or not," Raiyn said, "we won't get another chance like this. Baron, get your men downstairs. All of you, run!" Raiyn turned to Veron and Chelci. "Light the lanterns. Get in place. Brixton, hurry downstairs and be ready for my call."

People scurried in each direction. The baron, lord, and guards hurried down the stairs. Veron and Brixton rushed to get the lanterns. Chelci grabbed the prepared length of rope and ran behind Raiyn.

"Are you sure about this?" she asked.

Raiyn brought his wrists together. "Just keep it loose. They only need to *think* I'm bound."

Strands of rope looped around his arms. "No, I mean, you being in the room?" she clarified. "The baron could just let them in without you being inside."

His arms jerked as a knot slid home, tightening his arms and a knot around his stomach. "We need them to stay in the room. If I'm not there, they might be suspicious. Plus, we don't have time for anything else at this point."

"You won't be able to use the origine."

"I wouldn't either way. I'm sure they'll have their necklaces going."

"All set," Veron called from the doorway. He held two lit lanterns, standing well away from the powder-covered walls. Brixton and his own source of fire hurried down the steps behind him. A somber expression marked Veron's face. "Come on, Chelci. Raiyn . . . good luck."

Raiyn set his jaw and nodded. A lump in his throat wouldn't dislodge, no matter how many times he tried to swallow.

"What can I do?" Danik's words turned the three shadow knights toward where the ex-king stood by the wall.

"Danik!" Veron shouted. "What are you—?"

The man shrugged. "They left me. I can help, though."

"Gah!" Veron looked at Chelci. "Grab him. We can't have him in there."

Danik flinched when Chelci grabbed his shoulders. She pushed him forward until they passed through the doorway and joined Veron.

Raiyn returned to his box and stepped inside. He sat, facing the door with his fake bonded hands sitting on his knees. His thumping pulse blocked out all other sounds. A slight tug against the ropes proved there was enough slack for him to wriggle free.

Chelci pushed one door closed, then grabbed the other. She looked at him. Her mouth formed a grim line. "We can do this."

He nodded, hoping his response would convince the rest of him. It didn't help.

The second door closed, sending a reverberating *boom* through the space. Raiyn winced, thinking of the volatile powder waiting to ignite. He held up his chin, but his body felt flimsy. A chill ran through him from his legs to his neck. *What have I gotten myself into?*

VERON LOOKED OVER THE RAILING. Multiple flights of stairs circled down, ending at a hard floor far below. Brixton exited the stairs at the floor under them while the descending hands on the railing showed the baron and his crew approaching the bottom.

"We can't take him down. There's no time," Veron muttered. He turned to Danik. "Stay with me. If you make a sound or move in a way that displeases me—" Using the origine, he pulled a dagger from a sheath at his hip so fast that Danik jumped at the sudden arrival of the blade. "I won't hesitate to plunge this into your neck."

Danik shrank back, then nodded.

Veron pulled on his shoulder, dragging the young man around the corner. Chelci pulled a knife of her own and slung Danik against the back wall. The tip of her blade held him in place. Veron folded the shades against the glass panes of the lanterns. They only let out a faint bit of light—nothing that would give them away with the setting sun still allowing light through the hallway windows.

Out of sight from anyone who walked up to the top floor, Veron teased his eyes around the corner to watch the top of the stairs. Next to the wall, the chest caught his eye. His stomach dropped. "We left the Fire."

Chelci leaned around the corner. "Leave it. Getting caught is not worth it. It's just a chest. They won't think anything of it."

Tension filled his limbs. He wanted to rush for it but remained in place.

"How long do you think they'll take?" Chelci whispered.

"The baron should be down by now," Veron replied. "If the knights came straight to the keep, they should be talking now."

"I'm sure they will," Danik said.

"Hush." Veron spun, scolding the young man with his eyes. "What did I tell you?"

Danik swallowed hard, then rested his head against the wall.

"They'll insist on coming straight here," Veron said, "so . . . maybe a minute?"

Chelci blew out a breath. "My heart's pounding."

"Mine, too."

"Do you think this will work?"

He considered the question and the odds that everything would go according to plan. A sinking feeling grew in the pit of his stomach. He kept his eyes forward. "I do."

They waited in silence. Veron rested a hand on the hilt of his sword, making sure it didn't scratch against the back wall. His breath sounded louder than normal.

Before long, the sound of boots and distant voices drifted up the stairwell. It grew louder and clearer the longer they waited.

"They're coming," he whispered over his shoulder. He glanced at the floor, making sure the lanterns hadn't moved.

"One more floor," the baron's voice echoed down the hall.

Veron took in a deep breath and held it. The acrid odor of the dusted walls tickled his nostrils. His nose wriggled.

Oh no. Don't sneeze.

The steps grew louder. Multiple pairs of feet drew closer—dozens of them.

Exhaling only sharpened Veron's tickle in his nose. Air surged in when his lungs flexed. He held it off. The sensation lessened, and he breathed out. After a fresh tingle, another rush of air puffed his chest. It went away again.

Peering one eye around the corner, Veron spotted the baron's head mounting the stairs. A grungy head of black hair followed him. *Nicolar.*

The urge to sneeze redoubled. Veron couldn't hold it off. He leaned away from the corner and pinched his nose. His body shook as the violent reflex shuddered through him. It was done. His nose held and his mouth stayed shut. The arriving men continued their climb up the stairs, oblivious to his disturbance.

A click of the door sounded down the hall. "One is through here," the baron said.

Nicolar barked a laugh then said in his Norshewan accent, "Raiyn, it's so nice to see you again."

"Go on in," Devenish said, his voice wavering. "There's plenty of room for you all."

Laughter, muttered conversations, and stomping boots echoed down the hall.

Veron passed a lantern to Chelci then picked up the other. A flame flickered behind the shade. Oil sloshed in its well. His muscles tensed. He tested his connection to the origine, but it was nowhere to be found—as they had expected. "Be ready," he whispered.

RAIYN'S STOMACH dropped as the men filed into the room. He felt the blood draining from his face.

Nicolar smirked. The black stain on his neck looked as dark as night, matching his shaggy hair and goatee. "Where are the others?" Two crystals around his neck filled the room with a red glow—one hanging from a brown leather cord and the other from a blue one. "Veron? Chelci? Your list of friends grows lean."

As planned, Raiyn said nothing. He lowered his head and slumped his shoulders. His heart pounded. *Close the door. Cue the shout. Close the box. Three seconds.*

"I will bring the others," the baron said. "You all wait a moment. They're just down the hall."

The door creaked.

Raiyn took in a breath. His lungs were ready to shout.

"Wait."

Raiyn looked up. Nicolar held up a hand toward the door. It had stopped moving. A crack showed the baron's wide-eyed face.

"Stay with us, please."

"I need to get the others," the baron said. "I'll only be a moment."

"No." Nicolar's firm command echoed in the following silence.

A hollow pit formed in Raiyn's gut. *Close the door. Close the door.*

"I am your king, and I have questions for you. Send your men to bring the others. Cedric, Rankin, go with them."

The crack widened.

No!

Cedric and another knight pushed the door open. A stunned baron blinked several times, then turned to his guards and muttered something. Leaving them, he stumbled through the doorway, his eyes flicking to Raiyn's.

What do we do now? The baron is here. Two knights are outside of the room. His mind raced, but no good options presented themselves.

"Baron Devenish." Nicolar motioned for the older man to join him. "I received a message that Veron and his remaining knights arrived here. The captain who sent it mentioned a doubt that you were going to relay the information."

The baron's mouth hung loose.

"As you know, these traitors are the most wanted people in Feldor, so we came as soon as possible."

"I-I sent word," Devenish said. "I wanted to question them myself, but we dispatched a bird first thing this morning."

Nicolar lifted his nose. "Did you?"

Raiyn looked past them through the doorway. The guards and the accompanying knights of power had disappeared. *We should light it. I need to make the call.*

Nicolar turned his attention to Raiyn. "And you. What is this box for?" His eye twitched.

Raiyn didn't reply.

A quick turn to Devenish made the baron flinch.

"Is it the metal?" Nicolar asked. "Surrounding him to take his powers?"

The baron managed a nod. "Yes, that was my intent."

Nicolar chuckled. "Hardly the most effective solution, but I guess it works."

The baron met Raiyn's gaze. Raiyn jerked his chin down, hoping the older man would understand his intent. *Jump in the box. Come on! We can both fit.*

Devenish's brows pinched together, deepening the lines on his forehead.

He doesn't get it.

Nicolar's gaze drifted between the two. His eyes narrowed.

The baron nodded, slow and deliberate. "Do it," he mouthed.

He's willing to die, but he's close enough for me to pull him in.

"Do what?" After a pause, Nicolar tensed. His nostrils flared.

Raiyn sucked in a breath, preparing to give the call, jump up, and pull the baron toward him.

Nicolar blurred, stopping only when a sword tip pressed against Raiyn's neck.

Pulled roughly to his feet, Raiyn's prepared shout got trapped in his throat.

"What are you doing?" Nicolar craned his neck to glance around the room before turning back to Raiyn. He pressed the sword harder. "Something's going on. Check the halls!"

The sharp tip of the blade bit into Raiyn's neck, dripping something wet.

Several men rushed into the hall.

It's all falling apart, Raiyn thought. *He took a deep breath, preparing his lungs.*

The baron lifted his hands, helpless.

"Nicolar!" someone called from the hall. "You have to see this!"

The knight's head turned—distracted.

Raiyn leaned his head back and smacked the flat side of the sword away. "Now!" he shouted, bellowing the cue for any who could hear. He grabbed the baron's wrist and yanked him forward. The older man managed two stumbling steps before he fell headfirst toward the iron box.

One, he counted in his head.

Nicolar cocked his head, appraising the action from a step away.

Raiyn dropped into the box. An elbow landed on the baron's side, earning a groan.

Two.

Stuck on his side with his legs crammed in, he reached up and grabbed the handle on the inside of the lid. His arm strained, pulling from an awkward angle. The heavy metal top pivoted until gravity took over. The opening grew smaller and smaller.

When it was nearly closed, the entire box shook with an ear-splitting *bang.* The lid flew back open, kicked by Nicolar's boot. The force with which it flew open ripped the back hinges and sent the lid tumbling to the floor. Raiyn's heart plummeted.

Three.

. . .

"WHAT'S HE DOING?" Chelci whispered.

Veron frowned. His lantern swung from its handle while his head leaned along with Chelci's around the corner. The baron paused. "He's just standing there. Come on. Close it."

The door opened wider and Cedric emerged with another knight.

Veron ducked back, his heart pounding. "They're not going for it." He glanced down the short hallway behind them, knowing what was already there—dead end.

Cedric's voice sounded down the hall. "Where are they?"

Veron peeked an eye around the corner again. The baron's men stood frozen, looking at each other. "Um . . . the next floor down." It sounded more like a question than a statement.

"I thought they were 'just down the hall'?"

The guards didn't appear to have a response.

"Something's up," the second knight said. "Let's search the floor."

Cedric's eyes flicked down the hall, and Veron jumped back.

"They're coming," Veron whispered to Chelci.

"Let me fight," Danik whispered. "Take off this bracelet. I can help."

Veron's blood ran hot. "No." Despite his adamant rejection, the idea had merit.

Footsteps moved in their direction. Chelci grabbed his arm. "They're going to find us," she whispered. "Should we . . . ?" She lifted her lantern, leaving the question unasked.

He shook his head. "Raiyn won't be ready—or the baron—and Brixton needs the cue."

Veron set his lantern down and pulled his sword. The footsteps grew closer.

"What's this?" someone asked.

Veron frowned. *What's what?*

The footsteps moved in the opposite direction, away from their corner.

A metal clasp fell. "It's heavy."

"Here, let me."

Veron peeked around the corner and gasped. The two men leaned over the metal chest, staring at the remaining powder of Bravian Fire. "We can't let them have it," he whispered to no one. He tightened his grip on his weapon and stepped out from around the corner.

"Veron," Chelci hissed. Her arm flailed after his, but he was too far out of reach.

Veron slunk low to the ground, keeping to the darker side of the hallway. The men faced away as he padded closer. Their crystals glowed, so he couldn't use the origine, but the element of surprise was a formidable weapon.

Four more men spilled into the hall. Veron froze. He crouched in the shadows to the side of a bookshelf.

"What is it?" one of them asked the two men huddled around the chest. The newcomers joined in, staring into the box.

Veron's hand twisted as he clenched his sweaty grip. *Still distracted. I can take them.* If he killed those outside of the room, he could stop the rest by springing the trap. *I have to.* He stepped out of the shadows.

"Nicolar!" Cedric shouted. "You have to see this!"

Veron's feet stuttered, brushing against the wooden floor. His heart dropped as the knights turned, crystals glowing and swords at the ready.

Cedric's eyes widened. "Get him!"

In a rush of devion-powered movement, the men split—two surrounding Veron and the rest passing him to rush around the corner.

"Now!" Raiyn's voice reverberated through the wall and bounced down the passage.

Veron's lantern waited impossibly out of reach. *Come on, Chelci!*

His heart stopped as Chelci and Danik walked around the corner with hands up in surrender. Knights of power flanked them on each side. No lanterns were seen.

Maybe Brixton was able to— He spun toward the stairs and froze. Brixton mounted the last steps with his hands on his head and a man holding a sword at his back.

No! This can't be happening!

The knights surrounding him prodded him toward the double doors. His legs stumbled forward, lifeless and hopeless, joining Chelci and Danik. They met Brixton at the entrance and stepped through the doorway.

RAIYN CONTINUED to clench long after the three count. Nothing simmered or fizzled. No flames erupted. He kept his head down, even though the missing lid meant he would not be protected.

"Is it lit?" the baron asked, their bodies crammed next to each other.

Raiyn lifted his head. He squinted, bracing himself for an explosion of fire. Nothing happened. Then, they walked through the doorway: Veron, Chelci, Danik, and Brixton. He felt like someone had kicked him in the gut. "No, it's not."

"Drag them out," Nicolar ordered.

One of the other men lifted with an iron hand, ripping him from the box that was his modicum of safety. The baron followed.

"You thought you could, what . . . trap us?" Nicolar turned to Danik. "Well, this is a surprise. It's good to see you again, Danik. Were these people foolish enough to take you back? Ha! It's no wonder the Shadow Knights fell. Too forgiving and trusting."

Jerking his head forward, Danik spit in Nicolar's face.

Nicolar tensed then wiped it away.

"Should we restrain them?" Cedric asked.

"Leave them alive longer?" Nicolar chuckled. "Let them come up with another plan while I prattle on about what we're going to do? No. Kill them, now. Slit their throats."

A twisted grin covered Cedric's face. He and several other men stepped forward, pulling out daggers.

"Any ideas?" Raiyn attempted to step backward, but a man held him still.

The others pulled against their captors with the same results. Veron jerked harder, causing a second man to grab his shoulders.

Cedric stepped closer, dangling a long knife in front of Raiyn's face. "With pleasure," he drawled.

Raiyn closed his eyes and clenched his teeth. *This is it. We tried our best, but—*

A fresh tension drifted through the room. The expected blade didn't reach his neck. His jaw trembled. After an agonizing wait, he opened his eyes and gasped.

Dressed in their usual gray robes, Talioth stood centered inside the double doors, and a dozen marked ones fanned out on either of his sides. Their hands contained swords, and their faces held a casual confidence.

Great, Raiyn thought. *Just what we need.*

"Talioth?" Nicolar said. "What are you doing here?"

"You took something of ours," the leader of the Marked Ones said.

Nicolar touched the crystal on the blue necklace that rested against his chest. "We have a right to them as much as you do."

A wicked grin split Talioth's face. His shrug showed an indifference to the knight of power's words. "We didn't mind you taking them. In fact . . ." His hand wrapped around his own crystal. The other marked ones followed suit. Talioth's smile twisted into a sneer of loathing. "We counted on it."

A powerful light grew inside his clenched hand. Tendrils escaped between his fingers, shooting into the room. The rest of the marked ones had similar experiences until dazzling rays of light filled the entire room.

The knights of power glanced between each other. A growing hum soon drowned their mutters. The crystals around their necks increased in brightness and pulsed.

Raiyn shaded his eyes. Watching between his fingers, he made a curious observation. It wasn't all the crystals that thrummed with intense light. It was only the ones with the blue leather.

"What is this?" Nicolar shouted. He looked at his chest, seemingly noticing the different behavior between the necklaces. "What did you put in these?" He grabbed the pulsing crystal and yanked against his neck. The blue cord broke, leaving the gem in his hand and the leather dangling.

The noise grew deafening. Raiyn felt as if his ears would burst. When he could no longer stand it, the light of the crystals intensified. A cracking noise filled the air, prompting the ear-splitting hum to fade. A burning odor filled the room.

Is that the Fire? Raiyn thought with a rush of fear.

He removed his hand from his eyes and looked around the room. While he didn't see any signs of the powder having caught, his jaw dropped. The crystals suspended by blue necklaces had shattered, leaving gaping holes in the chests of the knights of power. The holes were black and smelled of singed flesh and burnt fabric. Bodies tumbled, hitting the wooden boards with heavy thuds.

Nicolar fell to his knees. He held up his arm, which ended with a stump at his wrist where his hand had been. He cried out a generic muttering of pain and shock.

Talioth stepped forward and thrust his sword into the man's chest.

The knights of power were dead—every one of them. Their bodies lay crumpled on the ground, twisted in macabre shapes. Nicolar was the only one who still made a sound and even his groanings faded after a moment.

I can't believe it!

Raiyn's heart leaped. The enemies who had threatened their lives were dead. The Bravian Fire plan had been a long shot. Facing impossible odds, he had barely hoped to believe they could do it. He longed to celebrate and sigh with relief, letting the stress and fear drip away, but the rest of his body wouldn't allow it. The moment of elation was quashed by the grim reality around them. Talioth and his men had taken the knights' places.

Freed momentarily, Raiyn, Veron, Chelci, Danik, and Brixton backpedaled. Raiyn grabbed the battle-axe that was tucked behind the steel chest, then joined the others at the far end of the room where the stone wall halted their progress. He tested the connection to the origine. *Still blocked.*

"A brilliant gamble on the necklaces," a marked one said, looking at Talioth.

"Cedric said he *took* those," Danik said. "How did you . . . ?"

Talioth's eyebrows raised. "It seems your allegiance has shifted since we last met, Danik. Interesting."

"He's not with us," Veron said. "Just to be clear."

Talioth ignored the outburst. "Yes, Cedric took them, but only because we wanted him to. The essence of infused Gharator Nilden led us here, and the incendiary resonance built into them proved to be as helpful as we expected. They were foolish in their approach. You"—he pointed at Danik—"were reckless and irresponsible. Like the origine, the devion is powerful, but it's not without constraints. We welcomed you with open arms and warned against spreading the power too wide. You didn't listen. They didn't listen."

Talioth turned to Veron. "We knew they'd be looking for you, so we waited until we felt the pull of their travel. They were a challenge to keep up with as they tore north to you here, but thankfully, we were already down the mountain. Now, we have you all right where we want you." He pointed over his shoulder to the doorway. "Did I detect Bravian Fire on the walls of this room?"

The comment barely phased Raiyn after what they'd experienced.

"It's been hundreds of years since I've seen that. Did *they* put you in here?" Talioth cocked his head. His eyes grew as if a revelation had come to him. "No. *You* did it. This was a trap, wasn't it? You wanted them to come so you could kill them." He chuckled. "It appears we've done your work for you. We decided we needed to rid Terrenor of any remaining devion users outside of our group—which we've now done. Our next step is to siphon *all* who use the origine." He turned to another marked one. "Now that we have them captured, we'll only need to recover the girl."

The word sat heavily in the room. Raiyn stiffened. *The girl?*

"What girl?" Veron's voice cracked. His eyebrows quirked in an arch.

Talioth stared for a long moment. His grin grew. "You thought she was dead, didn't you?"

"Thought *who* was dead?" Raiyn asked with more conviction.

"She's been working in our mines since you left. She got out this week. Tracking her will be first on our list after bringing you in."

"Who?" Veron repeated.

"Your daughter, of course."

"Lia," Raiyn gasped. His lungs refused to work, like a weight pressed against his chest.

"She's young and impetuous. It shouldn't take too long to find her. I'd guess one week."

Footsteps sounded through the door. Blocked by Talioth, a female voice said, "Should be *much* less than that."

A black puff of powder flung into the air, shimmering with red specs. Coughing and sputtering filled the room as the marked ones waved their hands against the cloud of dust. A sliver of light pushed through the cloud. The shades of a lantern lowered, and the fiery light illuminated a young woman. A ponytail pulled back her straight brown hair. Grime and dirt darkened her torn clothes. A sword with a ruby in the hilt tucked into her belt. She held the lantern with an outstretched arm as she rushed past Talioth to stand between the marked ones and the others.

Raiyn opened his mouth, but his voice wouldn't work. *Lia!*

45

FIERY ESCAPE

Raiyn's heart pounded. He blinked, making sure his eyes weren't lying to him. Chelci gasped. A choked cry sounded from Veron.

As the powder settled, the marked ones' gray clothes contained a black tint. Talioth's face turned a shade of red. "What did you—"

His exclamation cut off as Lia extended her hand with the burning lantern. The marked ones shrank back. Two of them raised bows with arrows nocked, but they didn't fire.

"Lia," Veron gasped. "You're alive."

She half-looked over her shoulder with a grin. "Yeah, I found that 'pure connection' you always talked about. Sorry it took me so long to escape. How does this Fire stuff work?"

"You're doing great," Veron said. "They'll all die if they catch flame."

"So will you!" Talioth shouted, his words laced with desperation. "If any of this powder catches, what's plastered to the walls will too. You all will burn up just like us." He brushed a hand down his robe, but the powder clung to the fabric.

"At least you'll be gone." Lia's arm wavered, but she kept the lantern extended.

"How did you get here?" Talioth asked.

"You tracked them. I followed you. It was easy."

"Push them back," Raiyn said.

Lia looked over her shoulder and flashed him a smile. "What do you mean?"

"We need a way out of here. Use the lantern. Push them out of the room."

Nodding, she faced the marked ones again and stepped forward. "Out!"

Each of the marked ones stepped back in response to her movement.

"Through the door! Don't make me throw this."

Backpedaling, they exited through the doors, swords at the ready and arrows prepared to fly.

"Keep going. Farther."

Powder coated the hallway, growing fainter as it approached the stairs, where the marked ones stopped their retreat.

Raiyn's stomach turned as he looked closer at Lia. The grime that covered her clothes and face wasn't all dirt. Bravian Fire powder covered her as much as the marked ones. "Here." He extended his arm, beckoning for the lantern. "Why don't you give me that?"

Lia passed the handle to him and stepped back from the fiery source of light.

"What do we do now?" Chelci asked. "Can we push them all the way down the stairs?"

"We need to separate ourselves from them." Veron turned to the baron. "Is that old passage still there?"

Devenish's eyebrows lifted. "Behind the bookshelf out in the hall?" He nodded.

"If we can escape down it without the marked ones following, we might get free."

"We won't be free." Lia's words turned all heads to her.

"What do you mean?" Veron asked.

Her shoulders slumped. "They'll never stop. Talioth vowed he was going to track you. Using the origine sucks away some of their power. It all comes from that Core crystal in the caverns."

"She's right," Danik said. "They need you all to return the power to them."

Lia's eyes narrowed. "What is *he* doing here?"

Veron waved a hand toward Danik. "Ignore him."

Raiyn kept the lantern extended and watched through the doorway where Talioth paced back and forth in the hallway.

Chelci chimed in, "If we run away today, they will keep looking for us. We need to eliminate them."

"So I toss the lantern?" Raiyn suggested, his nerves rattling as he thought of the amount of powder attached to the floor they stood on.

"Actually . . ." Lia's voice was light, as if an idea had struck her. "We don't have to eliminate them. We just need to take away their power."

Raiyn frowned. "You . . . know how to do that?"

Danik gasped. "The Core."

"Yes, the Core, but again . . . why is he here?"

"What about the Core?" Veron asked. "Drain its power?"

Lia shook her head. "No. We destroy it."

In the hallway, Talioth paused his pacing as his chest expanded.

"I think they heard that," Raiyn whispered.

"But the Core . . ." Danik began. "It doesn't just power the devion."

Lia looked at him and blew out a heavy breath. "He's right. If we do this, we wouldn't just kill the devion. We'd kill the origine, too."

Raiyn's gut twisted. The origine made him special. It's what gave him strength and speed. It's what brought him to Lia. *Without the origine, what am I?*

"Then we kill it," Veron said.

Raiyn nodded. No other ideas came to his mind. He swallowed around the lump in his throat. "I'll push them back." His words cracked as he spoke them. "I may not get them all with a lantern toss, but I should be able to move them back down the stairs. While I drive them down, you all sneak out the passage."

Lia frowned. "But how will you—?" She cut off with a look at his face. "You aren't coming."

"Get to the cavern. Destroy the crystal."

"No!" The corners of her eyes glistened. "I didn't escape from their mines to find you just to see you throw your life away."

"Someone has to do it," Raiyn said. "You three are a family."

The baron raised a hand. "I'd do it, but . . . I'm not sure I'm spry enough to threaten them."

"Raiyn, no." Lia wiped at her face.

Raiyn's heart twisted in a knot. An ache seemed to tear him limb from limb. He opened his mouth to speak but then stopped. Where Lia's palm had brushed across her face, the black-and-gray powder sticking there dusted away. It fell through the air, settling to the floor.

Lia looked down. Her hair bounced, dropping more of the volatile substance. She brushed her hand against her hair and across her face again. A fresh quantity of powder fell.

"It's not sticking," Raiyn breathed. He looked through the doorway and caught Talioth staring with rapt attention.

The leader of the marked ones ran a hand through his hair, knocking off the dust.

"It sticks to clothing but not to the body. That would mean—"

As if they all understood the implications, the marked ones rushed to wipe the Fire from their skin and hair.

"We need to go!" Raiyn stepped forward, holding the lantern before him. "Come on!"

He gulped as he stepped through the doors. Powder flecked with speckles of red covered the floor. It created a path that led to the open steel chest.

The marked ones furiously worked at cleaning themselves. Their faces and hair were mostly clear. Some had unbuttoned their stained outer garments.

"Down the stairs!" Raiyn shouted, lunging forward. His lantern swung from its handle, threatening the marked ones with its contained flame.

Talioth held his ground, but the others shrank back.

"One toss and you'll go up in flames," Raiyn warned. He waved his hand to the side, motioning the others to head to the bookcase. "Lia, go!"

"You won't do it," Talioth sneered. He pointed at Raiyn's feet. "You'll incinerate yourself, too."

Raiyn clenched his jaw and took a deep breath. *I can do this.*

He gasped as the handle of the lantern jerked from his hand. In a rush of motion, Brixton lunged past him. "He may not, but I will!"

Talioth backpedaled. Every marked one scampered down the steps, only slowing halfway to the next landing as they continued to take off their clothing that contained the Fire powder.

Brixton turned. "Go! All of you. I lived my life. I had my shot."

"Brixton." Veron shook his head. Heavy lines marked his forehead, but a hint of pride pulled at the edge of his mouth. "You don't have to do this."

Brixton blew a laugh through his nose. "I know I don't have to. But I *get* to. I should have died several times over for my poor decisions. Now . . . I get to die for a good one. Go!"

Raiyn joined Chelci and Lia in running toward the bookcase while Brixton kept the marked ones pinned on the stairs.

"Pull on the side," Devenish called as he arrived at the bookcase, already panting.

Raiyn and Lia pulled. The bookshelf pivoted, sliding open to reveal a dark, musty passage into the wall.

"Go!" Raiyn shouted.

The baron led the way, with Chelci and Lia behind. Raiyn turned down the hall as Danik arrived. "What do you think you're doing?" Raiyn shouted.

"Will you leave me here to die?" Danik pleaded.

Over his shoulder, Veron paused, standing in the trail of Bravian Fire between the bookshelf and Brixton.

Gritting his teeth, Raiyn nodded toward the passage. "Go."

Danik hurried past, not waiting for him to change his mind.

"Veron!" Raiyn shouted down the hall. "Come on!"

Veron wavered.

Brixton looked over his shoulder. "Go, you fool! Don't make my—Gah!"

An arrow pierced his chest, the tip poking out his back. A second struck him on the other side. He tried to fling the lantern forward, but his arm collapsed under the effort. He fell to his knees, landing in a trail of black-and-gray powder.

"No!" Veron shouted.

The marked ones—free of residual powder—surged up the steps but halted at the crash of glass.

The lantern lay on its side. Oil leaking from the base spilled across the floor, darkening the powder. A lone flame continued to burn from the wick, flickering close to the spilled oil.

"Don't . . . come . . . closer," Brixton wheezed, followed by a groan of agony. He looked over his shoulder, locking eyes with Veron. "Thank you for everything, friend. Now, go."

Veron nodded and stepped back. He moved slowly at first, then turned and ran. Raiyn moved out of the way to usher Veron inside the passage.

The marked ones pressed close to Brixton, eyeing Raiyn and their hidden passage. As Talioth's foot touched the top step, the flame of the lantern jumped to the oil. A roaring *whoosh* filled the hall as the powder ignited. It rushed along the floor and jumped to the wall. It climbed up the opened steel chest and lit the contents inside. Although it was only the phase one burn, the flames filled the hall with an ear-splitting sizzle and a blinding light. Raiyn ducked inside the passage and pulled the bookshelf back.

"Go! Go! Go!" he shouted.

The others were already sprinting down the dark and winding staircase. A lone window against the far wall brought in a faint amount of light from the setting sun. The wooden steps creaked under his pounding descent. Above him, the flames continued to roar, muffled by the wall and the bookcase.

Faster. Faster.

He urged his feet to move quicker, circling down the rotten boards, ignoring the danger of a potential misstep. Panting breath filled his ears. Sweat, fear, and the musk of the forgotten passage pervaded his nose.

A rumble began, filling the secret passage with a deep reverberation. The walls shook. Dust and small rocks fell, pinging off the ancient stairs.

"I hear it," Veron shouted into the darkness. "It's—"

A deafening roar smothered his words as a blast of light illuminated the space above them. Raiyn ducked and covered his ears. A glance up showed a ceiling made of fire, the flames twisting and weaving their way around the top of the tall, circular passage. A rush of wind carrying a blast of pressure flew down the stairs. The force pushed Raiyn forward, knocking him off his feet to fall headfirst into Veron's back.

Bodies tumbled, cracking into stone walls and wooden boards. Glimpses of fire rushed past his vision as he tumbled end over end. He shouted, but the yell didn't even reach his own ears because of the overhead tumult. Far enough away from the marked ones and their crystals, the origine rushed into his body. His muscles absorbed the blows. Sighting the next step for his foot, he pulled against a rail and jerked to a halt.

Veron stopped below him.

The blinding light still reached them. The roar of the flames thundered overhead. Under control once more, Raiyn dropped to the next step. His stomach leaped into his chest as the rotten board collapsed under his weight. With nothing to stand on, he dropped like a stone.

His mind raced. His arms flailed to find anything to grab. Everything he touched disintegrated under his frantic grasp. Like dominoes falling in a line, the subsequent steps crumbled as well. Veron was the next to fall, then Chelci's and Lia's shouts filled the air.

Raiyn flapped his arms to no avail. He slammed through another circle of rotten steps, but the impact did nothing to arrest his momentum. An interminable amount of time later, he crashed into the ground. The origine flooded his legs with strength, letting his muscles and bones absorb the impact far past what should have been possible.

Other bodies landed moments after him. Veron and Chelci panted, checking each other to ensure they remained in one piece. Danik also landed on his feet, crouched, holding Lia in his arms.

How did he—

His wrist was bare. The metal band that had surrounded it lay broken on the ground.

"It broke in the fall," Danik said. "Which is good because I could catch Lia."

"Put me down!" she yelled, struggling in his arms.

"Are you all right?" Raiyn asked as Lia's feet returned to the ground.

She brushed against her clothes and appeared to inspect her limbs. A quick nod helped his worry to ease.

Veron stepped toward a body at the bottom of the stairwell—a broken and lifeless baron. His stomach dropped. "He's dead," he declared after a quick inspection.

"Without our powers, I think we all would have been," Chelci said.

A chunk of stone hitting the ground next to Raiyn caused him to jump. Broken wood and rubble rained down. Raiyn covered his head with his arms and spun. *Need shelter.* A metal gate caught his eye. He rushed to it, lifted a latch, and pulled at the rusted barrier. It creaked heavily but swung open. "Through here!" he shouted.

Chelci and Lia ducked through the opening first. Veron grabbed the gate and motioned for Raiyn to proceed. Raiyn ducked and dropped off a steep step into a pool of stagnant water. A revolting odor hit his nose as he sank to his knees.

Before Danik made it to the gate, Veron passed through and pulled it closed. It shut with a heavy clang, reverberating across the water.

"What are you doing?" Danik asked. "Let me through."

"No," Veron growled. "After what you did—"

A chunk of wood hit Danik on the shoulder, causing him to wince and groan. He kept his hands on the bars of the gate, but Veron held the latch on the other side. "I'm sorry. I truly am!"

"You don't get to be sorry. You had your chance, and you blew it." Veron picked up a metal rod that rested against the wall and dropped it in the cutout slot that appeared to be made for the brace.

Danik's shoulders drooped. He nodded then lowered his head. "I know. I did." A chunk of stone crashed against the ground next to him. He flinched but didn't move. "Please, don't leave me here."

Veron's chest raised and lowered. After a long moment, he turned to the rest of the group. His eyebrows raised as if asking for the others' input.

A softness washed over Lia's face, but her jaw remained clamped tight. Chelci averted her eyes from the scene.

Raiyn's stomach twisted. *I don't want him around. I don't trust him. But he seems to be repentant.* Although his thoughts warred inside, he didn't open his mouth to speak.

Veron spun toward the gate.

"Please," Danik repeated.

After a tense moment, Veron sighed. He lifted the metal bar and tossed it against the wall. A creak filled the passage as Danik opened the barrier. He stepped through just as a pile of debris collided with the ground where he had stood.

"Thank you," he said.

"You don't deserve gratitude." Veron pointed a finger and shook his head. "And I *still* don't trust you."

Both men dropped into the stagnant water, Danik keeping his distance from the others.

"Where to now?" Lia asked. "Back to the caverns?"

Ignoring the question, Chelci wrapped her daughter up in her arms. Veron joined after he sloshed his way to them. The family of three pulled against each other, sniffing and choking back tears of joy.

"No more of you almost dying," Veron said, his words laced with emotion. "My heart can't take it anymore."

Lia laughed. "Deal."

Veron pulled back from the embrace. "Dayna?"

She shook her head. "She didn't make it."

He nodded. "We figured. So . . . 'pure connection', huh?"

Lia extricated herself from her parents embrace. "That's how I survived. It's about sacrifice."

"What do you mean?"

"I was willing to die to save you. I gave up caring about what happened to me, and that's when it happened."

Veron gasped. "Just like I did in Norshewa. What was it like? Unlimited energy filling all of your body?"

She nodded.

"You felt like you could do anything and the power would last forever?"

Another nod.

"Incredible."

"Until their crystal drew close."

Veron stopped smiling. "That's unfortunate."

Lia's eyes fell on Raiyn. She stepped toward him.

Butterflies flitted in his stomach and his hands grew clammy. "Hey." His greeting was little more than a whisper.

A tender smile grew on her face. "Hey."

Veron and Chelci stepped away, giving them privacy.

When Lia touched Raiyn's arms, a tingle radiated through him. His hands found their way around her waist as hers draped over his shoulders. They pulled each other close. The touch of her body against his sent a shudder of warmth through him. Her head nestled into the crease of his neck. Blowing out her breath, her body relaxed, melting into his.

"I'm so glad you're safe," he said.

Her muffled laugh tickled his neck. "I'm not sure any of us are safe, but . . ." She pulled back, smiling at him. "I *am* alive."

Chelci cleared her throat. "Speaking of which . . . I think you're right. Back to the caverns it is."

Lia nodded, separating from Raiyn. "We've got to take out the Core. It's our only hope."

"Do you think there's a chance the Fire took the Marked Ones out?" Raiyn asked.

The others shook their heads. "Their clothes and skin looked clean," Veron said. "Using the devion, it should have been easy to rush down the stairs during phase one of the burn."

"Talioth heard us talking," Raiyn said. "He knows we'll be coming for the Core. Do you think we can beat them back?"

"We can try," Veron said. "But if they get there first, it's going to be tough for us to get through those tunnels."

A smile grew on Lia's face. "I know a better way to get in."

Danik raised a hand. "They gave me a tour of the caverns. I should be able to help us navigate when we're inside."

Raiyn tensed.

"You're not coming." Veron pulled at Lia's shoulder and led away from the gate. "Come on, the rest of you."

Water sloshed as Danik took two lunging steps. "Where am I supposed to go?"

"I don't care. You're lucky I haven't killed you. Go anywhere but with us."

We can't let him go, Raiyn thought. *He could train up his own army again.*

Veron paused, his forehead creased as if the same thoughts ran through his head. "We can't let him go."

"Veron," Chelci said. "I was there for weeks, but I know next to nothing about how to get around."

Veron held her gaze for a long moment but didn't reply. He turned to his daughter. "What do you think?"

Lia's mouth formed a flat line as she looked at Danik. "I trusted him once. I vowed never to make that mistake again."

Veron nodded.

"However," Lia continued, "we share a common enemy. Talioth

wants him dead, too. There are only four of us. Five could be helpful."

Veron blew out a long breath. He turned to Raiyn and raised an eyebrow.

"I'm fine with whatever you all decide," Raiyn admitted.

"Fine." Veron turned to Danik and pointed a finger. "You can come . . . but I still don't trust you."

46

INFILTRATION

Bitter wind blasted a wave of icy precipitation into Lia's exposed face. Her thick gloves and wool hat helped, but the frigid air still cut through her clothes, chilling her to the core. The heavy clouds hid most of the moon, leaving only a faint glow that bounced off the white blanket of snow covering the ground. Her boots crunched as she continued, calves burning from the never-ending climb.

A rocky overhang emerged in the high-altitude gloom. Lia stopped underneath it and sighed in relief at the drop in the wind. "Take a break?"

The rest of their party nodded as they trudged into the sheltered alcove, panting.

"That other entrance was easier to get to." Raiyn's ruddy nose glowed in the frigid night.

"I agree," Lia said. "But if they beat us here, it will be heavily guarded, even at this hour."

"They could still be searching the roads," Raiyn suggested.

Veron shook his head. "The Core is too important to them. They won't risk it. Even though we rushed, keeping to the woods slowed us down. I'm guessing at least some of them will have hurried straight back to warn the others."

"The devion gives them incredible stamina, too," Danik added. "They could have moved quickly."

Lia tensed. Although she appreciated the information, whenever he spoke, it heated her blood.

"How much farther do you think it is?" Chelci asked.

Lia leaned past the overhang and raked her eyes across the craggy surface ahead. "Should be soon."

Raiyn tipped back a water flask to his lips. He frowned, then lifted the spout from his mouth. Only drips fell from the opening.

"Are you out?" Lia asked.

He shook the container. "Not out . . . it's frozen."

Lia grimaced, then pulled her bottle out from inside her cloak. "Here, take some of mine."

"How confident are you about your plan?" Veron asked.

"Assuming Danik can lead us to their laundry like he says . . ." She pierced her ex-friend with a withering gaze.

"I can get there," he insisted.

Lia continued, "I feel . . . *pretty* good about it."

Veron chuckled. "I'll take that. It sounds like much better odds than our last infiltration attempt."

"I'm sure I'll be able to get what I need. Whether I can make it back to the Core or not will depend on your ability to get to it and deplete it like you did before."

Her father nodded, then looked at Chelci. "We'll get it done."

Chelci shivered. "Whew. It cools down when you stop moving."

"Yeah, it does," Veron agreed.

Lia tucked her water flask back into her cloak. "Let's move then."

When she left the shelter of the overhang, the wind picked up again, forcing her to lean forward as she plodded on.

After walking another thirty minutes, the site she'd been looking for came into view. "We're there," she called, fighting to be heard over the wind.

She stopped at the edge. The snowy lip of the mountain ended at a round hole as wide across as two grown men. She leaned forward.

The gaping blackness turned an eerie red as her view caught more of the chamber below, including the bottoms of two columns.

Raiyn's hand pulled back against her shoulder. "Careful."

Veron sloughed a coil of rope off his shoulder and tossed it on the ground.

"I don't see anyone down there," Lia said.

Chelci added, "At this hour, hopefully, the only ones awake are at the cavern entrance or the archway on the mountain."

"Raiyn," Veron said. "Would you hold this end?"

Raiyn held the coil of the rope while Veron tied the end around a nearby boulder and knotted the end.

"How's that?"

Raiyn tugged against it. "Feel's solid."

Veron turned to the rest. "You all ready?"

Solemn nods answered.

"Ready," Danik said last. "If we run into someone and they activate their crystal, I can still use the devion, so don't worry."

Veron turned to the young man. "You insist you want to help?"

Danik nodded.

"If this breaks down into a battle, you're ready to fight with us?"

Another nod.

Lia's stomach clenched. *We must take chances, but trusting him may be the worst idea we've had.*

Veron pressed a sheathed dagger against Danik's chest. The young man wrapped his hands around it. "Don't make me regret this, Danik," Veron said.

"I won't." Barely audible over the wind, his words inspired little confidence.

Lia exhaled, her nerves still tingling. "I'll go first."

Veron stepped to the edge of the hole with the rope coiled in his arms. He leaned as far as he could over the drop.

"Do it," Lia said.

The coil flung through the air, unraveling as it dropped into the darkness. A faint tap sounded as it touched down, but no cries of alarm rang out.

Lia grabbed the rope. With her sword tucked into her belt, she moved to the edge.

"I'll be right behind you," her father said.

She nodded. Gripping tight, she leaned back and dropped a foot over the edge.

Hand over hand, she lowered herself. At first, her feet walked down the walls, but soon they disappeared when she dropped farther.

The sight of the glowing red room caused her to shudder. *I can't believe I willingly came back.*

As she dropped lower—closer to the glowing crystals set in the walls—her connection to the origine faded. Her arms felt heavier. She wrapped her legs around the rope and continued to drop herself, slowly, so she didn't burn her hands.

When her feet touched the ground, she ripped Farrathan from her belt and spun to take in the room. The columns remained as she remembered. Passages led in several directions. Scaffolding surrounded the unfinished statue of Talioth, standing where she had last seen it.

Empty.

She exhaled but didn't relax.

Another form came down the rope moments later. When Veron hit the ground, he pulled his sword just like she had. "Anything?" he whispered.

She shook her head.

"Which way to the mines?"

She pointed to the left of the scaffolding. "Should be through there." Turning to the opposite side of the room, her finger wavered between two similar-looking passages. "And . . . one of those should lead to the Siphon Room."

"The one on the left." Danik's feet hit the ground, and he pointed to emphasize the corridor he meant.

Lia ground her teeth but didn't reply.

"First, we'll need to go . . ." Danik spun and pointed to another passage that ran by a fountain that gurgled water from a hole in the wall into a stone basin. "Down there. The laundry."

After Chelci and Raiyn touched down, the group followed Danik toward the fountain.

"Lia," Veron whispered. He pulled her arm to let Raiyn and Chelci get ahead. "Did you ever travel down here?"

"Not this passage," she answered.

"Stay alert. I've got a bad feeling that I can't shake."

She nodded. The pit in her stomach seemed to grow larger.

Passing the basin of water, Danik disappeared into a darker passage that cut into the wall.

Lia listened for any noise or sign of danger. She gripped her sword, taking care to keep the steel from clanging into the narrow walls of the passage. The dim red crystals in the wall gave enough light to see, but the lack of access to the origine troubled her.

A terrifying realization hit her. *Danik has full access to the devion, but we're blocked from the origine. He could kill us at any time.* Her pulse quickened.

At the front of the line, Danik stopped and spun.

Lia gasped and brought her other hand to the hilt of her weapon. Her muscles flexed. Her eyes prepared to track his devion-powered speed, but he didn't move.

His whisper carried down the passage to her. "We're here."

Lia blinked. Letting herself relax, she pushed forward. Danik had stopped at an opening to a larger chamber. She followed her father, her sword tip relaxing as she entered the room.

A lazy trough of water flowed against the far wall, entering and exiting the room through small slits in the rock. Next to the water, a flat area of stone created working surfaces. One side of the room contained dozens of lines strung from wall to wall. Sheets draped from some lines. Others contained various cloaks, pants, undergarments, and tunics.

Veron approached a row of shelves against the wall. "Here we go."

Piles of gray clothing stacked on top of each other, filling each shelf. Veron thumbed through the stacks until he pulled down a garment. The folds unfurled, revealing a long gray cloak.

"Perfect," Lia said.

Veron passed the garment to her.

She pushed her arms through the sleeves and buttoned it up the front. It fell to her knees, covering any of her clothing that would stand out.

"Try the hood," Raiyn said, working on his buttons.

Lia lifted the hood and let it sit low on her head. It blocked her peripheral vision but would do a great job of hiding her face. Her mouth pulled up at the corners. "This should work."

She turned to Danik, who slid his arms into a cloak. Her words felt stuck behind her lips, but she forced them out. "Thank you." Her stomach turned as she spoke.

He looked at her with lifted eyebrows. A smile grew on his face. "You're welcome."

Veron pulled his hood over his head. "This is where we split," he said. "Lia, how long will it take you and Raiyn to get to the mines from here?"

She tossed her head to the side as her eyes drifted up in thought. "Five minutes?"

"And once you're there, how long to do what you need?"

"Probably another five."

Veron nodded. "We'll be ready. They'll probably have a guard at the Siphon Room, but between our disguises and—" He paused, flicking his eyes to Danik. "—Danik's ability, we'll disable the crystal's power for as long as it gives us."

Lia rested her hands on her father's and mother's arms. "We can do this." She squeezed, then turned to Raiyn. "Let's go."

LIA KEPT her head deep in her hood. Her eyes tracked the floor, lifted high enough to determine the correct passages to travel through. At each turn of the corridor, her nerves spiked with worry that they'd run into a marked one. Thankfully, the path remained clear. Despite her pounding heart, she kept her stride at a walk, to not draw attention.

At the end of a long slope, the entrance to the mines opened up before them. The familiar metal gate blocked their way with two guards sitting on stools. A male guard leaned against the wall with closed eyes and a drooping head. A female one looked like she had been fighting to stay awake.

The woman straightened at their arrival, then stood. Her hand made no move toward the sword at her hip. The crystal around her neck remained dim, but that wouldn't matter with the other crystals already dotting the walls.

"Need to see Rasmill," Lia said, forcing her voice to be deep and gruff.

The sleeping male guard jerked awake and jumped to his feet. "What? Who?" He blinked and swayed.

Lia pointed to the gate. "We need to see Rasmill in the mines. Open it."

The awakened guard turned toward the gate. He extended his arms to grab a chain that dangled near his stool.

"Stop." The woman lifted her palm toward the other guard but faced Lia. She leaned her head forward and squinted. "Who are you?"

Lia's pulse quickened. "Talioth sent us," she said, stepping toward the woman. She patted the front of her cloak. "He gave us a note. I have it right . . ."

She whipped the dagger from the sheath inside her cloak and stabbed it through the woman's neck before she reacted. The guard's eyes bugged. She made a gurgling sound before falling over.

Lia spun. *One more.* She halted.

Raiyn stood over the male guard's body as it hit the ground. He wiped his knife on the man's tunic, then tucked the weapon back in his sleeve. His mouth formed a grim line as his eyes found hers.

Lia nodded. "Open it."

Raiyn pulled at the chain. A grinding sound rumbled as the gate slid open.

She winced.

When the gap was wide enough to fit through, Raiyn released the chain. "Where to, now?"

Lia stepped through first. The sight of the mess tables and the barracks beyond turned her stomach. *It took me weeks to get out of this place. Now, I'm just walking back in.* The dark passage to her left led to the mines where she had worked for long hours every day. Her feet remained frozen in place.

"Where should we go?" Raiyn whispered.

Lia snapped out of her trance and pointed to the last barracks door. "Back there. Let's go."

The lanterns that were lit during the day were dark. Only the red glow from the walls illuminated the empty chamber. Lia dodged empty tables and stopped at the entrance to the Garronts barracks.

"Let's hope it's still here," she whispered. After blowing out a breath, she ducked through the entrance.

In the dim light, the remaining four bunks looked as she had left them. With the other beds smashed and removed after the fiend attack, the room felt empty. Despite the few beds, several bunks lay empty. She counted only four bodies snoring in their beds.

"Where is it?" Raiyn whispered.

Lia spied her old bed on the far side of the room. She tiptoed across the space, holding her breath as she approached the empty bed. Crouching next to it, she rummaged through the mattress. Her heart sank when her hand found nothing.

No, it can't be gone!

She moved lower down the mattress, tearing into the straw but still returning nothing.

"Is it not there?" Raiyn asked.

"It's not where I left it." She stood, then spun to face the rest of the room.

A white pair of eyes looked her way from the bed across the aisle, but they blinked out as soon as she saw them.

"Anton?"

The eyes popped open again, but wider. "Who are—" The man on the bed sat up, his mattress crinkling.

Lia lowered her hood.

"Lia?" He tossed off his cover and moved to the edge of the bed. "Is that you?"

Another voice chimed in from a bed by the wall, "What? Lia?"

The remaining two bodies rustled awake, rising to their feet in quick succession. Anton, Waylon, Thurman, and Harold gaped as they shuffled closer.

"What are you doing here?" Waylon asked. "We thought you escaped."

"I did," she said. "And now I'm back. We're hoping to stop the Marked Ones for good and free you all at the same time."

The eyes of the four men lit up.

"Are you all that's left?"

Thurman nodded. "They beat us nearly to death after the escape. But I guess they decided they'd rather have us alive."

"Thanks for what you did. I *did* make it out, and I would have been dead if it weren't for you."

The eyes of the four men drifted over her shoulder.

"This is Raiyn," Lia blurted. "He came with me."

Waylon's eyes grew. "Raiyn! He's the 'humble and sweet' one who likes you too, right?"

A blazing heat washed across her face.

Raiyn averted his eyes and stared at the floor with a blush of his own.

"How can we help?" Thurman asked.

Ignoring the warmth that radiated from her, Lia pointed to her old bed. "I need the box. Please tell me you still have it."

Waylon's face pulled up into a broad grin. He turned back to his bed and rummaged through the straw near the wall. "You mean *this* box?"

He held the wooden object up with a proud grin.

Lia snatched it from his hands. "Yes!" She shook it. The tight rustling indicated the box was as full as when she had left.

"We were too afraid to do anything with it, but I moved it to my bed in case someone new came."

Lia moved toward the door. "I wish I could stay and talk, but we need to go. If all goes well, in a few minutes, all of you should be able to walk out of here."

"Are you trying to fuse them again?" Waylon asked.

"No." She stopped in the doorway. "Trying something different this time. You all wait here."

Breaking into a jog, Lia and Raiyn left the barracks and rushed past the tables. *Step one complete*, she thought. *Now the dangerous part.*

At the end of the chamber, Lia stopped where the gate, the guards' quarters, and the tunnel to the mines all met.

"The crystals look to be at full power," Raiyn said.

The red objects embedded in the walls remained glowing with their usual intensity. Lia tested her connection to the origine, but as expected, it didn't exist. She looked at the box. *Come on, Father. Bring them down.* Her chest rose and fell rapidly with her breath.

"How long can we wait?" Raiyn asked.

"Not long. The longer we wait, the higher the chance of us getting caught. If the guards come out of those barracks . . ." She didn't want to finish the thought.

"Can we do it without the Core getting depleted?"

She shook her head. "I don't know, but I'd rather not find out."

47

FINAL PLAN

Back in the Hub, Veron padded behind Danik. He kept a hand on the hilt of his sword while his eyes darted around each corner. His worry of Danik betraying them again overshadowed his fear of running into marked ones.

"This way," Danik whispered, waving his hand down a passage that veered left.

Chelci walked next to Veron with a row of worry lines marking her forehead. Veron reached for her hand and squeezed. Her face jerked toward his, then softened.

"It's going to be okay," he said.

She flashed a nervous smile, then squeezed his hand back. "I hope Lia's safe. I hate letting her go on her own."

"Me, too, but we don't have much choice. As long as we can bring the power down, she should be fine."

"What if we can't do it?"

Her question triggered a fear that he had tried to ignore. "We'll do it," he breathed. "We have to."

Voices traveled down the passage from somewhere ahead.

"Here we are," Danik breathed.

Veron's muscles tensed. "I'll go for the crystal. You two distract if needed." They turned a corner and his heart dropped.

The Siphon Chamber opened up before them, but it was far from the empty sight he experienced the last time he was there. Ringing the Core crystal, six marked ones stood equidistant from each other, facing out with drawn swords. Although they were in place to guard Veron's target, they looked anything but prepared. Some looked ready to fall asleep on their feet. Others chatted between themselves. On the far side of the room, Talioth huddled in conversation with another marked one, making eight in total.

Danik pivoted upon entering the chamber, turning his back to the Core and facing an alcove. Veron and Chelci followed him, keeping their heads deep in their hoods. Muttering voices continued behind them, either oblivious or uncaring of their arrival.

"What do we do?" Chelci whispered.

"I could run at them with the devion," Danik said. "I could surprise a couple of them, but eight is too many."

Veron's head spun. He had expected one or two guards. *We can't handle this, but Lia is counting on us!*

"You, there."

Talioth's voice sent a chill through Veron's bones. "What are you doing here? It's not time for the guard to change yet."

There was nowhere to hide. If they ran for the exit, they'd be tracked down before they entered the hall. If they turned and fought, they'd be killed in seconds. Veron kept his face to the wall. The rock wall of the cave provided no help.

Boots padded across the cavern floor. "Hey! I'm speaking to you."

Metal rings with dangling chains caught Veron's eye in the alcove. A desperate idea came to his mind as a hand landed on his shoulder.

"When I speak, you pay attention!"

The hand pulled him around. While Veron spun, he grabbed the shackle that dangled at the end of the nearest chain. Flinging it to his shoulder, he snapped the restraint over the thick wrist clamped on him.

"Wha—"

Veron turned to see the whites of the marked one's eyes flare. Talioth jerked his arm back, but Veron had clicked the restraint in place. Without the use of the devion, the old man's strength waned. Veron spun their leader to face the Core crystal.

Suddenly alert, the guards positioned around the pit rushed at him.

"Stop there!" Veron shouted. One arm wrapped around Talioth's neck while the other pinned the tip of a dagger to the underside of his chin. "One step closer and your precious leader dies!"

The marked ones stopped.

Danik and Chelci stood by Veron's side, swords extended.

Talioth wrestled against Veron's grip, stilling as the knife point pressed harder against his flesh.

"Back away from the Core," Veron ordered.

The guards didn't move.

"I know you're fast, but not fast enough to stop me from driving this blade into your leader's neck. Back away!"

They flinched at the shout and glanced between each other.

An eerie laugh filled the room, coming from Talioth. "Veron, you are desperately outmatched. While I applaud your bravery, your actions are foolish and your hope is misplaced."

"We'll see about that," Veron replied. "Tell your men to move."

"Why would I do that?" Talioth said. "You want to siphon the Core, don't you? You think that will somehow give you the ability to destroy it. Again . . . misplaced hope. You cannot break it."

"If it's not possible, then why don't you tell your men to leave, *Talon Shadow*?"

The marked one's body tensed.

"That's right. Lia told us about you. How far you've fallen."

Talioth's shoulders shrugged as he looked at his men. "Go ahead. Step aside."

Wrinkled brows washed across the faces of the marked ones guarding the Core. One by one, they moved aside.

"Go on. Approach it. It won't do you any good."

Veron's stomach turned at their leader's confident taunting. Still . .

. the Core waited, open and unguarded. "Chelci, can you do it?" he asked.

"Try all you like," Talioth said. "But you'll find your plan falls short. You have your secrets, and we have ours."

"We don't have secrets," Veron said.

"Ha!" Talioth blurted. "No secrets. This is coming from the alloshifter."

Veron's breath caught. *Ignore him.* He tightened his grip on the dagger and nodded to Chelci.

She stepped forward, angling away from the marked ones who stood on the far side of the room.

"You don't think the ability to use the origine through metal counts as a secret?" Talioth asked.

Veron kept his eyes on Chelci. "Something I don't understand myself can hardly be considered a secret."

"Would you like to understand it? Do you want to know how it works?"

The question teased his mind, but he pushed it away.

Chelci stepped closer to the Core. She lifted a tentative hand as she crept closer.

"Your blood is special, Veron. Exposed to the Core many years ago, it imbued you with a special ability that resists the effects of metal."

"I was never 'exposed to the Core,'" he muttered.

"Not only does it manifest itself in you, but it passes along to your offspring."

Chelci spun at the marked one's words. A gasp escaped her.

"That's right," Talioth said. "She may not realize it, but your daughter should have the same ability—not that it would do *her* any good in these caverns."

"I don't believe you," Veron said. "My father—"

"William, right? Bled out, nearly to death, when he was young, yes?"

Veron's mouth snapped shut.

"He likely lost the ability from that injury, but he would have had it before then—whether or not he realized it."

"You can't possibly know that."

Talioth's deep chuckle filled the room. "Yes, I can. That's what threw me at first. I never realized William had a child, so your ability had me confused. But it makes perfect sense now."

Veron looked at Chelci and lifted his chin. "Do it!"

"It has remained consistent, following the bloodline for ten generations—all the way back to when I first stumbled across this place three hundred years ago."

The implication hit Veron like a battering ram. "But that means—"

The tip of his dagger flicked away, breaking the grip he had on the handle. His arm that wrapped around the marked one's neck gave out, his flexed muscles unable to counter the raw burst of power. Metal links shattered as the marked one blurred. Veron blinked to find Talioth standing before him with his own dagger held toward his face.

"Tell your wife to back away," Talioth growled. The loose end of a broken chain dangled from the shackle that remained around his wrist.

Veron's eyes flicked over the man's shoulder where his wife had already backed away from the Core. "Chelci, no! Do it!"

The other marked ones surrounded Chelci in a flash, pushing her toward Veron with outstretched swords that gave her no room to escape.

Veron's stomach felt like someone had tied a knot in it. *This can't be happening! Lia needs us to come through!*

With a wicked grin, Talioth placed the dagger between his teeth. With his free hand, he gripped the restraint around his arm and wrenched it. Metal groaned and snapped until the mangled band fell to the stone floor with a thud.

· · ·

LIA LOOKED past the rows of tables filling the cavern and spotted the men from Team Garront poking their heads out of the entrance. Not only did she want to stop the marked ones, but she longed to set the miners free. Every second she waited for the crystals' glow to fade raised her doubts about achieving either.

Across the cavern, another head poked out from the Valcor barracks. Even from a distance, Lia knew who it was from the slicked-back black hair.

She cringed. "I hope he doesn't wander down here."

Raiyn glanced down the chamber and narrowed his eyes. "Who's that?"

"Bronson, the leader of Team Valcor. He's the worst."

The middle-aged miner emerged from his doorway and sauntered in their direction.

"I think we might need to do it," Raiyn said. "The box."

Lia nodded, her stomach turning circles. "I think you're right. We can't wait forever." She turned to face the mine tunnel. With a trembling hand, she flicked the latch that kept the box closed. Blowing out a steady breath, she opened the lid.

The compartment dazzled with dim crystals that reflected the existing glow of the room. Packed tight in the box, she didn't have to count to know there were ten of them.

Raiyn's voice wavered. "How long will it take?"

"Normally, only a few seconds, but we *are* outside of the mines. Shouldn't be long."

Her mind drifted down the shaft. She pictured the glowing passages and their excavated rooms. Somewhere in the darkness, the fiends waited. She shook the box, causing the contents to rattle.

"What are you doing?" Bronson's loud question shattered the silence of the chamber. "I thought you ran away."

Lia flinched and lowered the box to her side opposite him.

"You know, they'll kill you if they see you in their clothing. What, are you impersonating them?"

Lia's eyes turned back to the mine tunnel. *Come on. Where are you?*

"What are you hiding there? What's in the box?"

"Bronson," Lia said. "Go back to your barracks. You can't be here."

His piercing laugh made her cringe.

Raiyn touched her arm and pulled the hilt of his sword. "Do you want me to deal with him?" he asked.

Bronson's eyes widened. "Who's this, and how do you have swords?" With a gasp, he took a step backward. "The gate? It's . . . open."

The concern on his face told Lia he realized there was more going on than he bargained for.

"Bronson, I'm telling you . . . you shouldn't—"

"Well, what do we have here?"

The taunting voice chilled Lia to her core as the mine boss, Rasmill, emerged from the office.

"Should we run?" Raiyn breathed.

She felt the blood draining from her face. "No. We wouldn't even make it to the gate."

The massive bald guard smiled, showing off the gap in his graying teeth. "Lia Stormbridge. I thought we might not have seen the last of you. And you've brought a friend."

Three guards exited the office, following Rasmill.

On the far side of her body, Lia dumped the crystals from the box into her pocket while the marked one inspected Raiyn.

"And you brought weapons," the mine boss said. Moving with the power of the devion, he snatched the sword from Lia's sheath and turned the tip toward her. Another guard did the same with Raiyn.

Lia held her breath.

"Shackle them both," Rasmill ordered. He stared at her while the other guards went to work with metal restraints. "What are you doing here, Lia?"

She swallowed around a lump in her throat. "I wanted to free the miners."

Rasmill's eyes flicked to where Bronson stood a few paces away. "Like this guy? Ha! I don't think so. You're here to destroy the Core, aren't you?"

She didn't answer.

"That's what Talioth said you'd do." His eyes narrowed. "But why come to the mines?"

Lia didn't answer.

"Fine," Rasmill huffed. "I'll let someone else deal with you." He turned to the other guards. "You two, make sure that one makes it back to his barracks. We'll take these two to Talioth."

Freshly bound, Lia and Raiyn moved toward the opened gate, prodded forward by the tips of their own swords. Keeping her eyes up, she dropped a crystal from her pocket. Shuffling her foot on the rocky ground covered the faint *tink* of the object falling.

They passed through the gate. The marked ones didn't even pause at the sight of the dead guards. "Up the ramp," Rasmill growled. "And don't even think about trying to run. You'll be dead before you realize you've been caught."

Lia leaned forward as she climbed up the incline. Near the top, she let another crystal fall from her pocket. When they left the large room and entered the narrow corridor, a sound reached Lia's ears. Somewhere deep in the caverns, a low rumble began.

A BROAD GRIN covered Talioth's face. "That's right, Veron. You're not the only special one. You and I are related. Why else do you think the power is so strong in your family?"

Veron's mind reeled. "How is that possible?"

"I had children before I ended up here. Most descendants lived in obscurity, but a few wound up as shadow knights. I kept tabs on them over the years." Waving the topic away, he motioned toward the remaining shackles and chains hanging from the wall. "Bind them!"

The other guards made a move to pen Danik next to Veron and Chelci, but the young man evaded their attempt. Using speed the devion provided, he snuck around them and backed to the far side of the pit, keeping his sword raised.

Talioth laughed. "That's right. This one won't be cornered so easily." The newly freed leader left Veron and Chelci and circled the room. "It's not too late for you, you know."

The concern on Danik's face flickered.

"Danik," Veron called. "Drain the Core! You're our last hope."

The ex-shadow knight turned to the massive Core that hung over the pit. He raised a hand. The red glow intensified as his skin drew near its surface.

Talioth extended open palms on either of his sides. "We are marked ones, united by our embrace of the devion. More powerful than anyone in Terrenor, we live in harmony with each other. The Core amplifies the length of our lives. Your drive led you to this same power. Your problem was you over-extended your group, and now they're dead."

Danik relaxed. He snuffed a laugh while keeping his eyes on the Core. "Good riddance."

Veron's voice strained, "Do it, Danik!"

"Join us," Talioth said. "We forgive and forget past differences. The rest of your group was disorderly, rough, and unpolished. You are different, brought up to a higher standard. If you swear to follow our rules, we will accept you with open arms."

Danik's arm shook, hovering next to the Core. His eyes found Veron's. Furrowed lines marked his forehead with a sheen of sweat.

"Danik," Veron said, barely above a whisper. His voice cracked. "Think of Lia. Think of us. Please."

Talioth stepped closer.

A glisten shone on Danik's cheek. He averted his eyes and wiped his face with the back of his hand. His hand stopped shaking.

Do it! Veron thought.

The hand lowered. Danik took a step back.

Veron felt as if he'd been kicked in the gut. "No! Danik!"

A broad grin formed on Talioth's face. "Excellent!"

Keeping his head down, Danik trudged across the room with his sword lowered.

Anger simmered in Veron.

"We should have killed him when we had the chance," Chelci said.

Talioth propped a hand on Danik's shoulder, waiting until he looked up. "We welcome you to the Marked Ones."

A rustling sound turned Veron's head to the entrance. His aching heart broke again as Lia and Raiyn entered with swords at their backs and their wrists in chains.

"Well, isn't this nice timing?" Talioth said. "Lia, it's nice to have you back."

Her raised chin amplified the effect of her piercing glare. She scowled at Danik, who looked away as if it would help him avoid the shame of his betrayal.

"We found her in the mines," the marked one with her said. "Trying to free the others, I'm guessing."

"It matters not," Talioth said. "We're going to wrap up what we should have done long ago." He pointed toward the central Core. "Bring them here. We siphon them, now, all of them. No more delays."

The words sounded hollow in Veron's head, bouncing around without meaning. They had lost. It had been a gamble to begin with, and now their cards had been played.

A marked one pushed Lia down in front of the pit. Her knees hit the ground with a *thud*.

Veron strained against the chain holding onto his wrist. "Lia, no!" His breaths came quickly, sucking in air faster than his body could absorb it.

She looked at him.

He expected to see sorrow or failure in her eyes, but they held something else. Readiness. Tension. His breathing slowed. *She's luring them.*

"Are they coming?" he mouthed.

Her mouth formed a grim line as her shoulders lifted, neither confirming nor denying the question.

Talioth stood behind her and rested his hand on her head. His fingers dug through her hair, and a jerk pulled her face forward toward the Core.

The light of the large crystal brightened. It pulsed, filling the room with a humming noise that grew louder.

Lia's head shook. A mutter of, "No, not yet!" escaped her lips. A tremble ran down her arms.

A low, guttural rumble filled through the room, bouncing off the walls.

Veron's forehead tightened. *What is that?*

The marked ones didn't seem concerned until the intensifying crystal dimmed. Talioth's rigid arm relaxed, and he stood to his full height, staring at the Core.

The other marked ones stepped forward. "Why is it dimming?" one asked.

Talioth redoubled his effort, clamping tighter on Lia's head. A yell tore from her mouth.

"Lia!" Veron shouted. "Let her go!"

A putrid stench wafted across his nose, like a rotting animal lay in the sun nearby. His face puckered, but there was no way to escape the assault on his senses.

The marked ones noticed, too, turning their attention from the Core toward each other. Their feet shifted and shoulders tensed as their hands rested on the swords at their hips.

Talioth even abandoned his focus. He kept his hand on Lia's head, but his neck craned around the room as if searching for the source of the odor.

The crystals in the wall dimmed along with the Core. The room grew darker.

"Light that!" Talioth ordered, ditching his hold on Lia to point at a lifeless lantern on the wall. "Ready your swords!"

The marked ones and Danik formed a line facing the main entrance.

It must be them, Veron thought.

Lia lay forgotten. Her head lolled as she roused. Raiyn moved to her side and crouched.

Veron pulled against his chains again, but escaping was useless.

A low growl rumbled through the chamber. The deep resonating sound made the hair on his neck stand on end. The smell grew worse, turning his stomach. Only a trace of the red glow remained. The Core crystal had been reduced to nothing more than a glimmer of color, and the walls were nearly dark.

A new light arrived. Through the main passage, a blue glow oozed into the chamber. Deep thuds reverberated in a steady rhythm, adding to the ominous presence of a low growl.

Rounding a corner, a throbbing blue object came into view. It seemed to float as it crossed the threshold of the chamber.

After a scrape of flint, the lantern on the far wall flickered to life. The fresh light illuminated the chamber, and Veron's jaw fell. A monster blocked the entrance to the room. The curled horns on its head nearly scraped the ceiling, but it was the jagged teeth that made his stomach drop. A clacking sound drew his attention to the pincers held out on each side of its body.

It's okay, he reassured himself. *This is what we wanted.*

The monster leaned forward and unhinged its jaw, showing off teeth that dripped with saliva. A deafening roar filled the room, shaking the walls and forcing Veron to cringe.

"Stand fast," Talioth shouted over the sound of the beast. The row of marked ones held out swords with shaking arms.

Between the blue glow coming from the monster's chest and the single lantern, shadows filled the room, cascading at various angles—shadows that hid him and Chelci. *They're not watching us.*

A sharp *clink* turned his eyes toward the central Core. With a swath of lantern light splashed across her body, Lia's extended arms had freshly broken chains dangling from each end. She flashed a hopeful grin as her eyes flicked in his direction.

The crystals are dim, Veron thought. *She broke them. Talioth was right. She is an alloshifter.*

With a twinkle in her eye, her body blurred as she rushed toward the closest marked one. Rather than attack him, her hand darted to his pocket.

Veron focused his energy and strained against the chain that held him to the wall. A weak rumble of power grew in his chest. He pushed the strength into his arms, straining through the barrier that resisted against him. With a shudder, a link in the chain broke, releasing his arm.

"Here!" Lia called. Her restraints had fallen to the ground, and she made a tossing motion.

Veron caught the small object that sailed across the room: a metal key. He went to work on the clamp around his wrist.

Lia rummaged in her pocket and pulled out what looked like a clear rock. She held it up for Veron to see. The facets caught the light of the lantern and refracted it toward the wall. "Last one," she mouthed.

A flare of hope germinated in Veron's chest. A surge of emotion caused his eyes to well up at the sight of his daughter. Grime and dried sweat covered her face. Her hair pulled back in a tangled mess of brown locks. The oversized, borrowed gray robes swallowed her form in their long sleeves and billowing folds. Despite the chaos in the room, she took a moment to smile. The twinkle in her eyes filled him with renewed strength.

A fresh roar bellowed from the beast, filling the room with hot air and a rotten stench. It angled its head, locking in on Lia.

Without losing her grin, Lia shouted, "Here! Come and get it!"

The monster knocked marked ones to the ground like dry stalks of wheat. Pincers stabbed into flesh. A jerk of a head ripped a set of horns through a guard's gut. With its path clear, it lunged in Lia's direction.

Lia backed up, circling the edge of the pit. She held the crystal out. "This is what you want. Crush it!"

She stepped to the edge of the shaft and leaned toward the Core. Veron gasped. She fell toward the gaping nothingness but caught herself with an arm against the massive crystal. Her hand smacked against its dim surface, echoing a *clink* across the room. Splaying between her fingers, the final crystal rested, dangling over the pit.

With clacking pincers and a snapping jaw, the fiend rushed forward. Frothing in a display of rage, it charged toward her at a frightening speed.

"Lia, move!" Veron shouted.

The creature's snarls and roars were deafening. Its feet pawed the ground, closing the distance in a heartbeat. Lia hung over the pit while the fiend drew closer. It lowered its head, turning the curved horns toward her body.

Veron held his breath as he watched.

Just before the beast crashed into her, she pushed off. Her body flew to safety away from the pit, but the monster's horns continued forward, colliding with the central crystal.

The room shook and a thunderous explosion of crystal split the air. Piercing fractals of light filled the room. The massive fiend roared as its body fell. Scrabbling claws and stabbing pincers thrashed at the brink, but the glowing blue light inside its body disappeared into the depths. The roars turned to howls, quieting, then fading to nothing.

"No!" Talioth yelled.

Veron couldn't tear his eyes from the Core. Shards of the crystal fell, raining pieces into the pit and around the chamber. It dissolved, chunks breaking off in succession as if each sloughed layer loosened the one behind. The grin on his face grew with each fallen chunk.

When about half the Core had crumbled, the falling pieces stopped. The room grew quiet. A dropped pin would have reverberated in the silence.

"What have you done?" Talioth gasped.

Veron held his breath, staring at the object. *Was that enough?* He scanned the room. The marked ones still standing contained looks of horror on their faces. The fiend was gone. Three of the marked ones sprawled across the ground with bloody wounds on their bodies, but the others stood, waiting.

A low drone returned. Like a flame consuming a dry stick, a red glow built. The walls emanated from it. The remnants of the fractured Core illuminated, returning to its previous strength.

Veron's stomach clenched. He sought the power of the origine, pulling desperately from any part of him that would respond. It was gone again, blocked by the glow of the damaged but still operable crystal.

"No!" Lia hacked at the object with the hilt of her blade, delivering blow after blow. Nothing happened. No more chunks flew off. Nothing crumbled. The glow retained its intensity.

"Lia." Veron's call captured her attention.

"That was a valiant effort," Talioth taunted. His confidence returned as he spoke. "Foolish and desperate, but bold nonetheless."

Keeping his eyes on Lia, Veron nodded toward the Core and mouthed, "Drain it."

She inhaled then slapped her hand against the surface of the crystal.

Talioth's face twitched. His eyes shot open wide. "No!"

The marked one rushed forward. His cocked sword and swinging arms blurred. Thankfully, Veron was closer. He stepped between Lia and the marked one and extended his blade. The sheer force from the crash of steel nearly tore his weapon from his grip. The sharp blade that would have taken off his daughter's head, glanced up, missing her.

A metallic hum intensified as light shot into Lia. Her arm shook. Radiant beams escaped her pores. The light in the room dimmed to nothing more than the single lantern on the wall. When Lia released her hand, the glow of the Core crystal grew again but stopped at half-power.

Veron stood by his daughter with a grin. The origine burned in him, eager to be used. Near the wall, his wife's shackles fell, unlocked by the key he had passed to her. She flew to Raiyn's side to assist, and in a moment, his manacles dropped as well.

The stunned marked ones stared with dropped jaws as the shadow knights joined together. Standing side by side and back to back, they held up their weapons. Despite the marked ones' necklaces glowing with fierce desperation, the origine was ready, bolstering their skill and increasing their strength.

48

EQUAL FIGHT

Lia panted, trembling from the influx of power. The light that had filled her from the Core still left a tingling residue in her nerve endings.

Standing a few paces away, Talioth's eyes held a fear she had yet to see in him. Four other marked ones slid to his side, with Danik joining at the end.

Lia glared at the two-time betrayer. Danik held up his sword but wouldn't meet her eye level.

Veron attempted to ram the hilt of his sword into the Core.

"It won't work," Lia said over her shoulder. "I tried. You'll break the sword before you break it."

The pounding stopped. "We need to kill them," her father said.

His words sat in her gut. She knew they were true, but accomplishing the feat was more difficult than it sounded. They were outnumbered. The origine was outmatched. And their secret weapon had fallen into the pit without giving the win she'd hoped for.

"I've got this one," Raiyn said, stepping toward Danik with his battle-axe held at the ready. The hard line of his jaw could have cut stone. "Don't even think about pretending to switch sides again."

Stepping away from the others, Danik raised his sword and sighed. "Are we going to do this again, Raiyn?"

Raiyn answered with a savage yell. He lunged, swinging his axe with a fierce blow she would have missed had she blinked. Danik stepped to the side, parrying the axe blade away from his head by the slimmest of margins. He managed a smirk until the heel of the axe slammed into his gut. Danik bent over, clutching his stomach and avoiding the butt of the axe head that almost collided with his skull.

The other marked ones charged at Veron and Chelci with swords flying. Her parents spun and twirled, matching the men's speed with a dazzling display of skill. Despite their incredible ability, four on two was unfortunate odds. Lia wanted to help, but her feet remained rooted in place. Her eyes stayed locked on the gray-haired man with the black beard.

Talioth's lip turned up at the edge. Leather creaked as his hands tightened around his sword's grip. "We've been here for hundreds of years. You think you can come here and put an end to everything we've built?" He snuffed a laugh, then lunged with lightning-fast speed.

Lia parried the attack. The point of his sword caught on her cloak and ripped a gash in the side. She risked a glance down and blew out a breath. It didn't reach her body. *Too close.*

The sword came at her again and again. Enhanced by the origine, she spun and ducked, knocking away strike after strike. Speed was her friend and the only way to avoid the stronger and faster opponent. Their blades clashed, and Lia took a step back. She gasped when her back pressed against the cavern wall.

"Where will you go?" Talioth asked, pressing forward.

Lia's arms strained as she pushed against the marked one's bulk. His bared teeth gritted while his face turned red. The edge of his blade turned toward her, creeping closer to her neck. His arms surged with pressure, pulsing, then resting. Each swell of effort nearly did her in.

I can't keep him off!

When his push lightened, Lia released her defense and ducked.

His sharp steel crashed into the wall, raining sparks on her head. She leaped away and somersaulted to the other side of the room.

Raiyn and Danik remained locked in fierce combat. Sweating and red faced, Raiyn had moved to a defensive strategy. The haft and head of his axe alternated blocking Danik's attacks. A raised leg pushed the ex-king back. He followed up with a jab from the toe point, but Danik was too fast, jumping away to stay out of reach.

A wave of anger ran through her. "Finish him, Raiyn!"

He kept his eyes on his opponent. "I'm trying!"

Chelci and Veron stood back to back, trading blows with the four marked ones engaged with them. A fast slice from her father caught one of their arms. The man groaned and backed away. He grabbed the wound, red dripping down his sleeve.

A flash of steel turned her attention back, nearly too late. Farrathan lifted in time to deflect the attack. A frustrated scowl covered Talioth's face. He barreled forward, swinging for her shoulder, then her side.

Lia's well of power held, keeping her moving as quickly as necessary and strengthening her arms to deal with his punishing blows. But with each near miss, she could sense it growing thinner. Escaping Talioth's attacks moved her next to Raiyn.

When the Marked One's leader drew beside Danik, they exchanged a glance and a nod.

"I can't keep this up," Raiyn whispered.

Although she already knew it, Lia's heart fell at hearing his words. "None of us can."

She glanced at her parents. The marked one who had been injured was already back in the fight, raining blows against her father's defense.

"I wish the Core would have fallen," she said. The red glow of the room was brighter than it was a few moments ago. Her stomach turned as she felt for the power of the origine. "The origine is fading."

"I feel it," Raiyn said. "We don't have much longer. Can you get more of those fiends?"

She shook her head. "No more crystals to draw them."

He sighed. "I wish we had *something*."

A cry drew her attention across the room. Veron fell to the ground, clutching his side.

"Father! No!"

Veron's face twisted in pain. He pressed against his side, where red bloomed across his gray clothing. Chelci put her body between him and the four men they fought. She held out her sword and bared her teeth, but fear and exhaustion reflected in her eyes.

All Lia wanted was for their family to be safe. Seeing the vulnerability of her parents nearly broke her heart. Sucking in a breath, she formed a resolve that pushed through her fatigue. *No! We will not die like this!*

She clenched her teeth and turned back to Talioth. "You do not get to write the ending of our story," she said.

His head cocked. The smirk on his face made her blood boil.

"Though you abandoned them years ago, shadow knights today are more than you ever were. We stand for others. We make a difference in the lives of those who need it. I refuse to believe your desperate attempt to grasp power will take us down." She lifted Farrathan and pointed the tip toward their leader. "And I, for one—"

A searing pain jolted her mind while a blade ripped her shoulder. Her scream sounded vague and distant. Talioth faded from her sight as everything turned white, blinded by the pain of her wound. Her two hands that wrapped the grip of her sword released out of reflex, and her weapon fell against the stone in a clatter that spoke volumes.

Lia dropped to her knees. She blinked several times to clear her sight. When she could see it, she reached with her good arm for her weapon, but the blade scooted away, knocked by a solid kick.

Danik's kick.

"Give it up," her ex-friend said. He held his sword forward. A sheen of red coated its tip. Red with blood . . . her blood.

"You . . . stabbed me," she breathed. Each word she spoke felt like another knife in her flesh.

Danik stepped closer. "I'm sorry, Lia," his voice cracked, "but you should have joined me."

A roar filled the room. A blurry form flashed before her eyes, followed by a deep thud.

Danik stumbled backward, his eyes opened wide. A wooden handle stuck out of his chest. The metal butt of an axe head was barely visible where the bulk had dug through his clothes and lay embedded in his flesh. A gurgling sound bubbled from his mouth. A red stain crept down the gray fabric of his stomach.

Raiyn panted. His legs wobbled after the burst of origine. "Heal that," he spat.

Danik touched the end of the handle. His face screwed up, as if he couldn't understand what had happened. Wobbling, he swayed side-to-side. "Lia," he gasped, eyes rolling back. His legs suddenly gave out, and he collapsed to the ground in a heap.

Lia's conflicted heart clenched. Despite it being what they needed to do, he had been her friend for years. At one time, he had truly cared about her. That history didn't change who he had become though. *Good riddance*, she thought.

"Enough!" Talioth roared. He lifted his sword toward the unarmed Raiyn. "On your knees!"

The marked ones on the other side of the room knocked away Chelci's blade and held her by the arms.

Raiyn lowered himself until his knees hit the floor. He continued to gasp for breaths, leaning forward.

In the silence that followed, the hum coming from the Core felt louder than ever. Lia turned her head and her stomach sank. The red glow looked back to full power. She reached inside herself, scouring to find any trace of the origine, but nothing was there.

"We tried," Raiyn said.

Footsteps sounded at the entrance to the chamber. Lia paled as another ten marked ones filed in.

"Are you all right?" one of them asked.

"They damaged the Core, but it's still intact. We're okay now," Talioth replied. He looked at the men holding Chelci and the injured Veron. "Bring them over."

Veron groaned as marked ones pulled him to his feet. He and

Chelci stumbled forward until they pushed them down next to Raiyn. "I'm sorry," Veron said. "I didn't think it would end this way."

Lia opened her mouth to tell him it was all right, but no words came out. *It's not all right*, she thought. *Why do they get to win?* The injustice of it burned her up. They had tried and tried, but everything they'd done led them there . . . to failure.

A spasm of pain rushed through her body. She pressed harder against the gash in her shoulder and shook her head. *I can't accept it. There must be another—*

Her thoughts jolted to a stop as she looked at Raiyn. Still on his knees, he bent over, sucking in air. Sweat tinged his shaggy black hair. What held her attention was the strip of leather hanging from his neck. At the end dangled a small metal sphere.

A metal sphere filled with Bravian Fire.

Her heart sped. "Raiyn." Muttering voices and shuffling feet covered her whisper. "Hey."

He lifted his head. His eyes contained a distant gaze.

Lia nodded down.

He tracked her motion and stopped when he focused on the necklace. His body tensed.

She looked in the other direction and found the sole lantern resting on a hook a mere body length from her. A flame flickered behind the glass.

"Start with Veron," Talioth called.

Marked ones surrounded her father and one placed a hand on his head.

Lia got Raiyn's attention again. "Use it," she mouthed, then pointed to the Core.

Raiyn's hand wrapped around the sphere. With his mouth in a grim line, he nodded.

The Core crystal brightened. The humming sound grew louder as Veron's body shook.

Lia's heart pounded. Her shoulder screamed in pain, but she did her best to ignore it. She returned a slow nod to Raiyn, then mouthed a single word. "Go."

Using both hands, Raiyn wrenched the connector that attached to the top of the sphere. A light *click* filled the room as the sphere separated from the leather strap. With the marked ones distracted by the siphoning of Veron, he lunged closer.

While Raiyn moved, Lia sprang from the ground toward the wall. With nowhere for her to go, the closest marked one only stared.

The hand of her good arm wrapped around the handle of the lantern and pulled it off the wall. When she turned, she caught sight of Raiyn flinging his arm forward. Backlit by the pulsing red object, a spray of powder spread through the air until it stuck to the glowing surface.

Lia flung the lantern forward. The closest marked one reached his arm out, but the object had already passed. Talioth's eyes grew wide, but it was too late.

The lantern struck true. Glass shattered as it hit. The reservoir of oil ignited and sprayed onto the crystal, lighting the powder of the Bravian Fire. Flames erupted across the close half of the Core.

Phase one.

The marked ones jumped back. The shock of the crash and the flames caught them off guard.

Talioth glanced at Lia with a wrinkled brow. "What did you do?" His question was curious, not fearful.

Lia allowed a smirk to cover her face while the back of her mind counted the seconds.

It took a moment for Talioth to understand. After a long beat, his eyes grew so wide Lia thought they might pop from their sockets. "No!" he yelled. He pushed other marked ones aside to get closer to the Core. After dropping his weapon, he ripped his cloak from his back and rushed toward the central crystal.

Veron, Chelci, and Raiyn didn't need instruction. As chaos erupted amongst the marked ones, they joined Lia in sprinting toward the door. Lia flinched as an arm wrapped around her back. Prepared to fight, she relaxed when she realized it was Raiyn. Her shoulder screamed at her, but Raiyn's yell for her to move was louder.

At the entrance to the chamber, Lia glanced back. Talioth stood before the Core with his cloak cocked. As his arms extended to swat at the Fire, phase two ignited.

The blast knocked Lia off her feet. She flew into the tunnel. Her hurt shoulder collided with her mother's back, spinning her around. A heavy thunk of her head hitting something was the last thing she remembered before she blacked out.

A TWINGE of pain registered somewhere deep in Lia's subconscious. Everything was dark. Her shoulder throbbed. Her head ached. She blinked, but the darkness remained. She blinked again, her heart rate increasing.

Something's wrong.

She sensed other bodies nearby. "Who's there?" she croaked.

Small rocks crunched underfoot of turning bodies. A gasp echoed in the darkness.

"Raiyn! Bring the light."

She'd know that voice anywhere. "Father?"

A faint orange glow grew on the walls as footsteps jogged closer. The light grew stronger until a young man with black hair rounded the corner.

Lia smiled. "Raiyn." It took effort to say his name, and it sounded more like a sigh.

Raiyn crouched with a torch in one hand. A broad smile covered his face. "Lia, are you all right? You were out for a while."

The light of the torch illuminated her father and mother, who were already crouched next to her. Deep furrows in their foreheads lightened when she made eye contact. Her back rested against a hard wall. She sat forward, clenching her teeth with a groan as she moved.

"Take it easy," Raiyn said.

Lia glanced at her shoulder. Her cloak was a mangled mess of rips and dried blood.

"The bleeding stopped," Chelci said. "I'm sure it hurts, though. How's your head?"

Lia touched her head where the pounding emanated from. It was tender and stung with prickles of pain from where she'd hit the wall. "It's been better. Nothing I can't handle, though." She turned to her father. "How about you?"

Ripped cloth wrapped around Veron's chest. He winced as he looked down. "It's been better." He chuckled and managed a smile as he mimicked her. "Nothing I can't handle."

Chelci touched Veron's hand. "We'll stitch you both up and get some barkleaf potion as soon as we leave here. That should fix you right up."

Lia glanced down the inky passage where Raiyn had come from. "What happened?"

Raiyn lifted an eyebrow. "You able to walk?"

Lia took in a deep breath, then nodded. Letting him lift under her good arm, she worked her way to her feet. A pressing pain throbbed in her head at the rush of blood. She held his hand for balance and took a moment to let the sensation pass. The hopeful smile on his face brought warmth to her body. His fingers squeezed, gentle, reminding her he was there. She nodded.

Keeping a hold on her hand, Raiyn led the way. They rounded the corner and entered a room that felt familiar, yet foreign. Scorch marks covered every surface. The rock walls looked like they had melted. Charred objects littered the floor. Raiyn held up the lantern, giving light to a gaping pit in the center of the room.

"This is the Siphon Chamber," Lia said.

Raiyn nodded.

Lia gasped. The crystal that had hung above the pit was gone.

"The Core is destroyed," her father said. "Burned by the Fire."

She turned to the wall. It took her a moment to place what was different. "The red glow is gone."

Veron touched an object that was embedded in the wall. A clear mineral with sharp facets, but not a trace of red. "After the Core burned, the rest faded. Not just here—throughout the caverns."

Her eyes widened. "What about—"

She reached inside herself, seeking the familiar power she'd known most of her life. As she struggled, her father's shaking head stopped her.

"The origine is gone," he said. "The devion, too. We found marked ones. They had survived the Fire, but—" He winced as if disturbed by his thoughts.

"Their ancient bodies couldn't survive losing what sustained them," Chelci added.

"They're dead?" Lia asked. "All of them?"

Her mother nodded. "All of them. We found some back in the room with the columns. Dead."

Lia's gaze drifted to the ground. Letting loose of Raiyn's hand, she stepped forward. A blackened, disfigured lump caught her eye. The human-shaped form contained an axe head still buried in what would have been the chest.

Danik.

The body was nothing more than a charred shell. She swallowed around a lump in her throat.

Past her old friend's body, another form leaned against the wall. The legs were black, but the upper body mostly avoided the flames. The singed clothing could have indicated anyone, but the long, gray hair and black beard identified Talioth. His familiar black stain remained on his neck, but the rest of his skin was unrecognizable. Brittle and wrinkled, it looked as if something had sucked all the moisture from his face. Bits of skin had flaked off, revealing the white bones of his skull underneath. His jaw lay open, showing his teeth in what looked like an agonizing pose of death.

"We did it," Lia breathed. A chuckle escaped her lips as the edge of her mouth pulled up. "I can't believe it."

"You did it," Veron said. "You two with those fiends. You brought the Bravian Fire. That was incredible."

Lia beamed. "Thanks."

Chelci spoke up, "If you're up to it, we should head down the mountain. The trip back will take a while, especially in our condition."

"Before we go, there's something we need to do. A group of miners nearby will want their freedom. And they're probably unnerved at the sudden darkness now that these crystals are out."

Raiyn smiled. "Sounds like a plan. Then . . . we head home."

49

WHAT THE FUTURE HOLDS

"There's a branch to your right," Raiyn said from below.

Lia glanced up and sighted the branch. She took a deep breath, letting the air fill her lungs while her shoulder rested.

"The one next to the rock. It's not far."

"I see it." Lia didn't move. "I'm just taking a second."

"Is it your shoulder?"

The concerned tone of his question warmed her heart.

"I'm so sorry. I knew I shouldn't have led you up here."

"It's all right, Raiyn. This was my idea. I'm just being cautious."

The absence of origine left a hole she'd found difficult to fill during the days when they traveled back from the mountains. She'd reach for the power, having forgotten that it disappeared when they destroyed the Core crystal.

Pulling against a rock with her weak arm, she grasped the waiting branch and pushed up with her foot. Three more cautious footholds and tender pulls with her arm brought her over the lip of the cliff.

Raiyn's supportive hand rested against the small of her back as it had done much of the climb up the cliff. Lia wanted to grumble about not needing his help, but the sweet way he looked after her convinced her to hold off.

"I know you can do it on your own," Raiyn said as if reading her thoughts. "I just don't want you to strain your shoulder."

After dusting the dirt from her clothes, Lia stood and took in the scene. The top of the cliff created a flat area that formed a wide circle around the Glade. A step away from the edge, she cautiously leaned forward. Her house with its hammock in the trees rested below. A rocky path led from it to the main hall with its cleared courtyard. Looking down from such a high vantage, her vision became dizzy.

"Careful," Raiyn said as his tender hand touched her arm.

Lia shuffled a step back and chuckled. "That's a long way to fall."

She turned away from the Glade and lifted her eyes. "Oh!"

The forests of Feldor spread before them. The limbs of a few trees reached the height where they stood, but most topped out well below. Yellow and red leaves speckled through the dominant green blanket, a sign that cooler weather was coming soon. In the distance, a break in the trees indicated where the Benevorre River flowed from the north.

To the south, the walls of Felting rose from the landscape. The distance made them look small, but the castle connected to them still towered above the rest of the city. To the west, the falling sun painted the low clouds a rich shade of orange that fell across the landscape.

"It's beautiful," she breathed.

"Yeah, beautiful." Raiyn was looking at her rather than the landscape.

Lia felt her neck reddening. "I, uh—" She cleared her throat then craned her head to peer into the woods. "I don't see my father yet."

"Don't worry. I'm sure he'll be fine. I think most everyone who wished him ill are dead now."

The reminder of all the people who had been against them made Lia shudder. "Have you decided yet?" she asked, to change the subject.

"About where to go? I have some ideas, but I'm not committed.

I'm, um, curious about"—his gaze shifted—"what everyone else is going to do."

A warm tingle worked its way through Lia's body. "'Everyone else,' huh?"

Raiyn shrugged. He glanced at the sky, then out to the city. "Yeah, like do you, uh, know what you're planning?"

Lia fought not to smile at his coy response. "Move back into Felting, probably."

"And be a shadow knight again?"

She shook her head. "I'll miss it, but I think those days are finished. I guess I'll need to find a regular job."

"A miner?"

"Ha!" Lia's burst of laughter echoed off the far side of the Glade. "No, thanks. I've had enough of mining."

A faint smile curled Raiyn's lips. "I thought it might be nice to start a lumber company."

"I was curious if you'd changed your mind about Norshewa's throne."

It was his turn to burst into a short laugh. "No, thank you. I think lumber is much more my speed. There's only one mill around Felting, but people pack the city. Thought I could set up just outside the northern gate." He pointed toward the west, where the forest ran thick next to the road and the river.

"There are plenty of trees," Lia said.

"I'd need some supplies and a few workers."

She adopted her best suggestive grin. "You taking applications?"

Raiyn's oblivious brow wrinkled. "Applications? No, I haven't done anything yet. I'll need to check with the commerce department first. Then, I'll have to find a plot. Once I—" When he looked at her face, he blushed and chuckled. "Oh, you mean . . . you." A broad grin covered his face. "I'd *love* it if you'd join me."

"I'll warn you," she said. "I don't know a lot about lumber."

"That's all right," he said before she'd even finished her sentence. "I can teach you."

"And without the origine, I may not be the best worker."

He shook his head and beamed from ear to ear. "There's no one in Terrenor I'd rather have beside me."

LIA'S FEET crunched the gravel as she walked hand in hand with Raiyn. Their fingers intertwined, holding firm enough to where they wouldn't let go but not so tight as to be uncomfortable. Raiyn held open the door to the main hall when they arrived. Lia entered first. Her heart leaped moments later when his hand found hers again.

Veron and Chelci looked up from the bench where they sat next to the hearth. Wood burned in the stone fireplace, pushing the chill out of the building. Chelci regarded Lia's and Raiyn's held hands and managed a smile.

"Father, you're back!" Lia said. "What'd you find out?"

Veron took a long drink and then set a cup on the table next to him. "All things considered, Felting's in decent shape. Word reached them days ago about the fall of the Knights of Power, and the city sighed a collective breath. Bilton had been rotting in the dungeon, but he's released now and is nearly back to full strength."

"What will they do about a king?"

"The high lords are discussing options. It's back to Bilton, Hillegass, and Culbert, but it sounds like Bilton will get the nod." He exchanged a knowing look with Chelci. "They asked if we'd come back."

"Come back?" Lia asked. "As shadow knights?"

Veron nodded.

"Do they know about the origine?"

"They know. I told them we were no different from anyone else now." He smiled and looked down at the surface of the table. "Bilton said it wasn't the origine that made us so important. It was our character. They want us to continue doing what we did: stand up for those who needed it and make Terrenor a better place."

Lia raised an eyebrow. "Are you going to do it?"

Her parents turned to each other. Chelci's hand found Veron's, and they both smiled. "No," Veron said. "We're not. Your mother and I have been talking about settling down. After twenty years of fighting and danger—"

"And stress," Chelci added.

Veron nodded toward her before continuing, "We're looking forward to a quieter life. We decided we're going to stay right here in the Glade."

"On your own?"

He shrugged. "There's no one else I'd rather be with." He squeezed his wife's hand.

"We plan to reach out to some friends as well," Chelci said. "Morgan and Jeanette. Matthew and Emma. Some others. Not sure if they'll want to come, but it could make for a fun village."

"And the city is close by for supplies." Veron shifted his attention to Lia and Raiyn. "Do you two have any thoughts about what's next?"

"We were just talking about it," Raiyn said. "I'm thinking about starting a lumber mill."

"Both of us are," Lia added. "Raiyn knows what to do, and I—" She blushed and looked at him. "I can learn."

"No interest in Bilton's suggestion? Either of you?"

Lia turned back to her father. "Bilton?" She thought back through the conversation, then gasped. "You mean the Shadow Knights?"

Veron's eyes held a twinkle of sincerity. "Of course. Who else do you think wields that sword over there?"

Lia followed where his finger pointed until she spotted her sword, Farrathan, leaning against the wall in its sheath. "But surely Bilton was talking about you."

"He was talking about *us*. Our team. Working together to help others. We don't center on one person. And although the origine assisted us until now, it's not what defines us."

Nervous excitement swirled in her gut, making her pulse race. "But . . . I wouldn't know what to do. I haven't—" She stopped herself. She'd trained for years. Her body was a finely tuned machine. She had stood up to the Knights of Power and the Marked Ones. She could lead people. And her time in Tienn proved something very important—she cared.

Veron nodded. "You'd know what to do. You couldn't do it alone, though."

Lia spun toward Raiyn. "What do you think?" she asked. He opened his mouth, but she cut him off. "But your lumber company?"

"Pfff," he sputtered, then laughed. "If you think I want to be doing that while you're out there putting yourself in danger, then you don't know me at all."

Butterflies flitted in her stomach. She looked at her parents, searching for signs of uncertainty or fear. All she found on their faces were smiles and confidence.

They think I can do it.

She thought back to the mission she had led to Searis. She learned a lot from that experience and had grown exponentially since then.

I can do it.

Taking in a deep breath, her chest lifted. She stood to her full height, using her physical presence to make up for the apprehension that filled her. She turned to Raiyn. "If I did this. If I started a new chapter of the Knights, are you sure you'd be on board?"

Raiyn answered with a sparkle in his eyes. "Where you go, I go."

A smile pulled at her face, lifting the side of her mouth into a smirk. "That settles it then."

"THE SHADOW KNIGHTS' story is done???? This is RUFF! What am I supposed to do now, just sit around and chew on tennis balls? I left a review online to let all my puppy pals know what I thought. 5 out of 5 dog bones from me!" - Charlie

PLEASE LEAVE an honest review on Amazon or wherever you got the book from. Do it for Charlie.

Get a FREE prequel novella to the Shadow Knights series - Shadow Knights: Origine - by signing up for my mailing list at www. subscribepage.com/michaelwebbnovels or scan this QR code

ACKNOWLEDGMENTS

After five years of writing, the Shadow Knights series comes to close. I cannot express how thankful I am to all of you for giving my stories a chance. What began as a crazy idea to write a book turned into a passion, and none of it would have continued if it weren't for you.

I want to thank my dedicated beta readers, Eli, Tara, David, Manton, Aden, Johnny, Andreas, and Don. You all were critical to the writing process. Thank you for taking the time to help me with my story. I couldn't create what I did without you.

Thank you to my editor, Sarah. You catch what I miss and smooth everything out to make it professional. Thank you for your diligence and care with my work.

Julia, thank you for always loving and encouraging me. You give me the freedom to pursue my passions, and none of it would mean anything without you being with me.

Made in the USA
Columbia, SC
23 February 2025

48c84347-58ff-4f0f-ae90-827f7ac5d57fR01